Praise for *B*

**Midwest Independent Publishers' Association
2012 Best Mystery of the Year**

**Named Best Mystery of 2012 by
Reader Views & *Rebecca's Reads***

". . . *Bone Shadows* is guaranteed to hold reader's attention until the last page . . . Valen's highly moral Santana character is golden . . ."

—*Library Journal*

". . .With a compelling and believable hero and a colorful cast of supporting characters, this turned out to be another superbly written tale of convoluted motives and surprising twists and turns. I would highly recommend Christopher Valen's *Bone Shadows* to anybody who enjoys a well-written, contemporary story . . ."

—*Reader Views*

". . . *Bone Shadows* has a well thought out plot that is up to date with today's society and current social issues. Valen writes with an easy to follow style, and he is adept at keeping his tale interesting, intriguing and exciting. I appreciated the many convoluted twists and turns of the story . . . I am also certain that this book will elicit at least one or two gasps of shock/surprise . . . *Bone Shadows* was a great read . . ."

—*Rebecca's Reads*

Praise for *Bad Weeds Never Die*

Named Best Mystery of 2011 by
Reader Views & *Rebecca's Reads*

"... *Bad Weeds Never Die* ... delivered on all fronts. Once again I enjoyed Mr. Valen's well-plotted and intriguing mystery for all the obvious reasons: flowing and well paced storyline, great dialogue, multi-layered and vivid characters, a great sense of place and time, relevant issues and believable events ..."

—*Reader Views*

"... This is the first of Valen's books that I have read in the John Santana series and surely will not be the last ... Valen's novel is gripping, fast-paced and will have you guessing until the end. The characters are intriguing and there are many plot twists and turns. It is a true page turner in every sense of the word ..."

—*Rebecca's Reads*

"... The latest John Santana police procedural is an excellent investigative thriller ..."

—*Midwest Book Review*

"Christopher Valen's third novel, *Bad Weeds Never Die*, continues the story of John Santana, a homicide detective in St. Paul, Minn., who was introduced in *White Tombs*, and whose story was continued in *The Black Minute*. The three novels are all great police procedural stories ... I have thoroughly enjoyed reading Valen's novels ..."

—*Bismarck Tribune*

Praise for *The Black Minute*

Named Best Mystery of 2009 by *Reader Views*
Midwest Book Award Finalist

". . . *The Black Minute* grabbed me from the first page on, and pulled me into a complex world of evil, violence, deceit, bravery and a search for justice . . . While the plot is complex and anything but predictable, his storyline stays comprehensible and easy to follow. The characters are well developed, very believable and constantly evolving. The setting of the story is vivid, detailed and engaging . . ."

— *Reader Views*

". . . There is not one reason why this book isn't a winner! Everything about it screams success. The book is masterfully written with a tightly woven plot, visually detailed settings and well-developed characters . . ."

— *Rebecca's Reads*

"Santana—an appealing series lead, strong and intelligent . . . Readers who enjoyed *White Tombs* will settle easily into this one; on the other hand, it works fine as a stand-alone, and fans of well-plotted mysteries with a regional flair . . . should be encouraged to give this one a look."

— *Booklist*

". . . as in *White Tombs*, Valen writes well about St. Paul and surrounding areas. He gives just enough sense of place to make you feel like you're there, but he never loses track of his story's fast pacing. And he does a super job of keeping the suspense going as the action reaches a crescendo . . ."

— *St. Paul Pioneer Press*

". . . John Santana was introduced in Christopher Valen's first book, *White Tombs*. This second book is just as exciting as the first and one that keeps the reader guessing right up to the final page. Either book can be read as a stand-alone, but I hope Valen brings us more stories involving Detective Santana."

—*Buried Under Books*

"The second John Santana St. Paul police procedural is a terrific thriller . . . Christopher Valen provides the audience with his second straight winning whodunit."

—*Midwest Book Review*

Praise for *White Tombs*

Named Best Mystery of 2008 by *Reader Views*

". . . Christopher Valen addresses a very wide range of extremely relevant social issues in *White Tombs*, and this book goes well beyond being just a detective story. The characters are fantastically well developed . . . the writing is solid and elegant without unnecessary detours. Any lover of solid writing should enjoy it greatly. *White Tombs* also screams out for a sequel—or better yet, sequels."

—*Reader Views*

". . . Valen's debut police procedural provides enough plot twists to keep readers engrossed and paints a clear picture of the Hispanic community in St. Paul."

—*Library Journal*

"John Santana of the St. Paul Police Department is a man you will not forget . . . The book is a great read, and Santana is destined to become one of my favorite detectives. Truly a five-star read from this author."

—*Armchair Interviews*

Also By Christopher Valen

White Tombs

The Black Minute

Bad Weeds Never Die

Bone Shadows

To Dave & Anne

DEATH'S WAY

A John Santana Novel

Thanks for your friendship & support!

Christopher Valen

Christopher Valen

Conquill Press

St. Paul, MN

This book is a work of fiction. Names, characters, places and incidents either are products of the author's imagination or are used fictitiously. Certain liberties have been taken in portraying St. Paul and its institutions. This is wholly intentional. Any resemblance to actual events, or to actual persons living or dead, is entirely coincidental. For information about special discounts for bulk purchases contact conquillpress@comcast.net

DEATH'S WAY

Cover Design: Linda Boulanger

Library of Congress Control Number: 2013952538

Valen, Christopher

Death's Way: a novel / by Christopher Valen – 1st edition

ISBN: 978-0-9800017-7-8

Conquill Press/March 2014

Printed in the United States of America

10 9 8 7 6 5 4 3 2 1

For my cousin and true friend

Dave Knudson

Thanks for always being there

Our birth is but a sleep and a forgetting:
The Soul that rises with us, our life's Star,
      Hath had elsewhere its setting,
      And cometh from afar.

                    William Wordsworth
            "Ode: Intimations of Immortality"

Chapter 1

In the moment before dawn breaks along the horizon and the veil of night is lifted, there is a stillness, a darkness in the world when it seems as if nothing moves, nothing lives. St. Paul Homicide Detective John Santana was reminded of that darkness now as he looked into the dead woman's wide, sightless eyes.

She lay naked on her side across a queen-sized bed, a clear plastic bag wrapped tightly over her head. Her mouth was open in a desperate search for oxygen, her face the purplish color of a bruise. A long cherry charmeuse scarf was tied around her waist. The hooks of a red bungee cord bound around her waist were attached to the hooks of a second strap that stretched up her back, around her neck, and down to the waist strap again. A dildo protruded from her vagina. Her bladder and sphincter had released, and the room smelled strongly of urine and feces.

Santana was breathing through his mouth as he stood on the opposite side of the bed from Reiko Tanabe, the Ramsey County medical examiner. He watched as she leaned over and peered at the woman's eyes through a magnifying glass. Behind Tanabe a pair of large windows offered a view of the High Bridge and the Mississippi River, lit by the rising sun, that the dead woman would never see again.

"There's petechial hemorrhaging," Tanabe said, referring to the tiny capillaries that had ruptured from increased pressure

1

on the veins in the head when the airway was obstructed, causing blood to leak into the eyes.

She straightened up, adjusted her wire-rimmed glasses, and looked at Santana. "The lower elastic strap served as a stabilizer for the upper strap. The controlled flexion of the head and the body caused pressure on the neck. In most of the cases I've seen, the mechanical device used to induce hypoxia normally has protective padding between the neck and the ligature."

"To prevent visible abrasions or bruises on the neck?"

Tanabe nodded. "Abrasions might arouse the suspicion of friends and family members. There's no padding present here. Still, I can't say that the lack of padding indicates a homicide."

"Pulling off the bag was the self-rescue device."

She nodded again. "The decrease in blood and oxygen supply to the brain supposedly enhances the experience. She assumed she could pull off the bag to control the degree of hypoxia. But she lost control the moment she lost consciousness. The ligature continued to compress and obstruct the carotid arteries."

"So she unintentionally killed herself twice," Santana said. "Once by suffocation from the plastic bag over her head and second by strangulation with the neck ligature."

"Looks like it. When death occurs from autoerotic asphyxia, it's almost always due to the failure of a fail-safe strategy. I'll know more this afternoon when I cut her."

Considering the lack of a suicide note in the room, the victim's position on the bed facing the television, the pornographic movies that had been playing when she was found, the dildo, and the locked room that provided isolation, the woman's death appeared accidental. Still, Santana always considered strangulation homicide until proven otherwise.

"Any estimate as to time of death, Reiko?"

Tanabe thought about it. "The room was only fifty-five degrees when we got here, John, so her body temperature was very low. The air-conditioner cooled the body and slowed the rigor. It's difficult to estimate TOD. I'll check the stomach and small intestines."

If the dead woman had been murdered, Santana wondered if the perp had deliberately turned down the room temperature to confuse the ME. The room was a spacious, private suite with a king-sized bed, two couches and a coffee table, a wet bar and desk, and two armoires with large flat-screen televisions. Dark, gray-black images of latent fingerprints dotted the surfaces.

Tony Novak, the head of the SPPD's forensic lab, was kneeling beside the desk, the round bald spot on the crown of his head shining brightly under the ceiling lights. A painter's mask covered his gray mustache and guarded against the odor and intake of black carbon powder on the fiberglass duster in his hand. Large white letters written across the chest of his maroon-colored T-shirt read: LET'S ASSUME I'M RIGHT, IT'LL SAVE TIME.

Santana gloved up and searched the black purse on the bar. A driver's license identified the dead woman as Catalina Díaz. She was twenty-two years old and had a St. Paul address. He found no keys and no cell phone in her purse, which immediately piqued his curiosity. Everyone carries keys to his or her house and car. And nearly everyone has a cell phone.

He felt certain that whoever had been with Díaz had taken her phone and had probably destroyed it. He wanted to know whom she'd been in contact with and where she might have been in the last few days. Real time cell tracking, e-mail, or text messages sent within the last six months, and the physical search and seizure of a phone, required a warrant and probable cause. But he had no idea what cell phone service Díaz had used.

He did find a small envelope inside the purse. The envelope contained five one hundred dollar bills and a business card for a Dr. Philip Campbell. A Minneapolis address was listed under his name. A phone number was written in ink on the back of the card. Santana suspected it was either Campbell's cell or home number.

Inside a small suitcase on a luggage rack near a closet he found a black lace bra, garter belt, and chemise. A black lace tank dress hung on a hanger in the closet over a pair of black high heels. Santana knew what Díaz had been doing in the hotel room now, and he figured she hadn't been doing it alone.

"John."

He turned toward the exterior door and saw his partner, Kacie Hawkins, in the hallway outside the room. Standing beside Hawkins was a stocky, big-shouldered, balding man in a blue suit and tie. Santana peeled off his latex gloves and tossed them in a container brought to the scene by the forensic techs. As he headed toward the stocky man, Santana noted the nameplate identifying him as Dwayne Stryker, hotel security.

"Haven't seen a body in more than five years," Stryker said with a lazy grin. He spoke slowly, the lids of his brown eyes narrowed, his forehead wrinkled with a cop air of habitual disbelief.

"Where'd you work?"

"Chicago," he said. "Homicide. Did my twenty and took a job with the hotel chain. Thought I'd be done with this." He gestured toward the body on the bed. "We've interviewed the guests on this floor. No one heard or saw anything."

"Anyone staying in the connecting room?"

He shook his head. "No one across the hall either."

"Anything going on at the hotel yesterday?"

"A conference for the Twin Cities Medical Society."

"We'll need the names of everyone who stayed here last night and anyone who attended the conference, including a man named Philip Campbell."

Stryker nodded. "My staff is working on it."

4

Hawkins gave Santana a questioning look. He shook his head, indicating he wanted her to wait for an answer. Then he turned his attention to Stryker again. "How long was Ms. Díaz staying?"

"One night."

"Had she stayed here before?"

"I'll see."

"I'd appreciate it." Santana's gaze was momentarily drawn to the exterior door leading into the hallway. It had a push-button lock and another lock operated by a key card. He'd already checked the dead bolt leading to the adjoining room, which had been locked.

He looked at Stryker again. "Who would have access to the room besides Ms. Díaz?"

"Housekeeping."

"What about maintenance?"

"Of course."

"The housekeeper who discovered the body is waiting in another room, John," Hawkins said. She shifted her eyes to Stryker. "We need to contact whoever was working in maintenance last night."

"I'll find out."

"And check your central computer as well," Santana said. "Let Detective Hawkins know when Díaz used her key card to enter the room."

Santana knew that all hotel locks had a memory that recorded the time, date, and key code for every entry. In the event of a problem, the security staff could read and print the log to see who had entered the room at what time.

"What about security cameras?" he asked.

"Only in the main lobby and pool area."

Santana handed Stryker a business card. "We'll need those security tapes. If you remember anything else you think might be helpful, please give me a call. Detective Hawkins will follow up with you regarding the maintenance man, the tapes, and Philip Campbell in a minute."

"All right," Stryker said. His gaze drifted to the body in the room before settling on the business card in his hand. He looked at the card a moment longer and then at Santana, as if he were about to say something. Then he appeared to change his mind. He turned and headed toward a set of elevators at the far end of the hallway, still holding the card in his big hand.

Leaving Homicide was like leaving a woman you loved, Santana thought. You never truly forget her.

When Stryker was out of earshot, Santana said to Hawkins, "I found Dr. Philip Campbell's business card in Díaz's purse."

"Boyfriend?"

"I think he was her client."

Hawkins cocked her head. "Díaz was a hooker?"

"Or escort."

"One and the same."

Santana was surprised by the hard edge in her voice.

"Appears that Díaz—or someone she was with—was into BDSM," Hawkins said, referring to bondage, discipline and sadomasochism. "Campbell could've gotten carried away."

"Possibly."

"Maybe this wasn't the first time he'd seen her."

"Probably not. But if he accidentally killed her or deliberately murdered her, Kacie, why leave his business card in her purse?"

"Maybe he gave it to her on a previous occasion."

"True. But if I'd killed her, I would've checked her purse before leaving the room."

"That's why you're the detective," she said with a smile. "And why you'd probably make a good murderer."

"I'll keep that in mind. But I didn't find any keys or a cell phone in Díaz's purse. An escort whose livelihood depended on keeping appointments would have a cell. And who doesn't have a set of keys? Someone checked her purse."

"But if it was Campbell, he would've taken his business card."

"Unless he was incredibly careless."

"Why take her keys?"

"Maybe to gain access to her residence. Check with the manager regarding the conference and Campbell. And check Díaz's hotel registration. See if she drove a car and left it in the ramp. If so, have it towed to the impound lot."

"What about the bungee cords and silk scarf?"

"I'll run a check on them. The cords are probably sold all over town. But I might get a lead on who purchased the silk scarf. Where's the housekeeper?"

"She's in the second room on your left."

A short, dark-skinned woman with large frightened eyes and small hands clasped tightly together in her lap was hunched in a cushioned desk chair in the room Hawkins had indicated. She was looking around like a little bird checking for predators.

The plastic nametag clipped to her coffee-colored house-keeping uniform identified her as Lorena Gonzales. Santana pulled up a small rectangular hassock and sat down across from her. He wanted to establish a connection and ease her anxiety. Figuring she was fluent in Spanish, like so many of the housekeeping staff in the hotels around the city, he spoke in her native language.

"No te preocupes. No estas en problemas."

She drew herself up in the chair, her brown eyes shining with light. Though she bobbed her head as if she understood that she was in no trouble, her lips remained a thin, tight thread.

"Where are you from?" he asked, continuing to speak in Spanish.

"Guatemala."

"I am from Colombia."

A hesitant smile brightened her face.

Santana took out his notebook and pen. "How long have you worked at the hotel?"

"Three years."

"Have you always worked the morning shift?"

"Yes."

"Please tell me what you saw when you entered the room and found the dead woman this morning."

Her voice grew stronger the longer she spoke in her native language. Nothing she'd observed upon entering Díaz's room contradicted Santana's initial observation. The housekeeper had seen no one entering or leaving the room. He wrote a short summary of the interview in his notebook. But he had one more question before he was finished. He wanted to know if the housekeeper had ever seen Díaz in the hotel before discovering her body this morning.

She looked down at her hands the second he asked the question. When she failed to respond, Santana figured he was on the right track.

"You have seen her here before."

She lifted her head slowly and nodded.

"Did you know her name?"

"No."

"It was Catalina Díaz."

Her eyes looked up and to the right for a second, as if she were recalling something. "She would speak to me in Spanish."

"What would she say?"

"Just a greeting or a wish that I would have a good day. She was nice."

"Did you hesitate when I asked if you had seen her before because of what went on in the room?"

Gonzales nodded again.

"How did you know?"

She averted her eyes. "There are many young women who use the hotel for this business. Sometimes I see different men entering the same room."

Not wanting to embarrass the housekeeper further, Santana asked for no more details. "Do you think you could identify any of these men if you were shown a photograph?"

"Perhaps."

"Did Ms. Díaz usually stay one night?"

She nodded. "Many of the young women only stay one night or two. No more."

Santana finished writing in his notebook and gave her a business card. "Please call me, Ms. Gonzales, if you remember anything else."

She nodded again, stood up quickly, and hurried out of the room. Santana had seen the same reaction with many he interviewed. He'd gotten used to it. Usually it wasn't personal. Most drivers had the same reaction when they saw a patrol car behind or beside them. Cops called it black-and-white fever.

As Santana walked into the hallway, two attendants from the ME's office were wheeling a gurney and black plastic body bag containing Catalina Díaz out of her hotel room. Exiting the room directly behind the gurney was Pete Romano, the homicide commander. Santana was surprised to see him. The previous commander, Rita Gamboni, had rarely come to a crime scene unless it was a very high-profile case. Gamboni had recently accepted a job as commander of the department's Safe Streets Initiative and its liaison to the FBI. Romano, the SPPD's most senior homicide detective, had been promoted to fill her position.

"Detective," Romano said with a nod.

"What brings you here, Pete?" Santana asked. He'd known Romano long enough that he felt comfortable using Romano's first name rather than the more formal "Commander."

"I like to see the actual crime scene. It helps me fill in the blanks when I read through the reports. It might help expedite the whole case."

Santana wasn't sure what the rush was. In his experience, the more brass present at a crime scene, the more likely boundaries would be crossed, conflicting orders would be given, and something important would be overlooked. For those reasons, he preferred to work his own crime scenes with Hawkins. Although she was younger and less experienced, he trusted her judgment and respected her skills. They'd been together long enough to understand their roles and responsibilities—and who was in charge of the crime scene.

"We don't know if it's a homicide yet, Pete."

"Hopefully, it isn't." His olive skin wrinkled in the corners of his dark eyes as he smiled.

Santana noted that Romano had cut his jet black-hair shorter since becoming commander, but he hadn't lost any of his burgeoning belly. Detectives in the department had called him "Cheese" when he was one of them. Santana was unsure if the name would stick now that Romano had assumed an administrative role. It probably would depend on how Romano conducted himself and how effective he was—at least that was how Santana saw it.

He'd never partnered with Romano. But he'd heard from those who had that Romano operated strictly by the book. His unwillingness to bend or break the rules had served him well when the time came for the big promotion. Under Gamboni's leadership, the department had maintained an extremely high clearance rate. Santana suspected that Romano was here to make certain the rate remained high while he waited for his next promotion.

Seconds of uncomfortable silence lingered before Romano attempted to engage Santana in conversation again. "Looks like an accidental death."

Santana had already drawn an initial conclusion, but he had no intention of sharing it with Romano until he had evidence to support it. But he was well aware that no other type of case generated the amount of public interest and media scrutiny as murder, particularly if it involved sex.

At that moment, Hawkins returned. She gave Romano a nod before turning her gaze on Santana. "Catalina Díaz used the hotel two weeks ago, probably for the same purpose. I'm having her car towed to the impound lot. According to the key card log, she entered her room at nine thirty-two last night and never left. Philip Campbell checked out at six this morning."

"Why Campbell?" Romano asked, looking at Santana. "Are you suggesting the woman was murdered?"

"It's too early to tell."

After some thought, Romano said, "Budgets are tight."

"Meaning?"

"Let's clear this up as quickly as possible, Detective. I don't have money for overtime. Oh, and I'll handle the media." Not waiting for Santana's reply, Romano headed for the exit sign.

"What's Cheese doing here, John?" Hawkins asked when Romano was out of earshot.

"You heard him. Budgets are tight. He wants this wrapped up soon."

"That explanation sucks."

"It does," Santana said. "And I'm not buying it."

* * *

Catalina Díaz lived in downtown St. Paul. Hawkins rode with Santana through raindrops that slid like heavy tears down the windshield. Another cold front had rolled in from the north, killing any promise of spring.

A security guard gave Santana a key to the condo where Díaz lived. It had gleaming maple floors, abstract art, and a wall of floor-to-ceiling windows that overlooked the city ten stories below. Copies of *Vanity Fair* and *Vanidades* magazines were neatly arranged on the coffee table. There was a small bar, kitchen, and dining area. A set of stairs led to an open bedroom with a railing that overlooked the living area. A hallway off the kitchen led to what Santana assumed was a second bedroom and bathroom.

"Hooking must've been paying off," Hawkins said as she stood just inside the door next to Santana, surveying the condo. "Maybe I should look at a career change."

Before joining Homicide, Hawkins had made a name for herself working sex crimes, where she'd acquired the nickname "Designer" because of her shapely backside. She worked out regularly and kept her lean ebony frame in excellent shape. Santana wondered if she was angling for a compliment, but he kept his feelings to himself.

"You ever come across Catalina Díaz when you were working vice?"

Hawkins shook her head. "She doesn't strike me as someone who worked the streets or for a pimp. Still, how was she able to afford something like this?"

"Check with the neighbors. Maybe we'll find out."

Santana set down his briefcase. He was looking for information on Diaz's family or friends. Someone he could contact regarding her death. He inspected the living room and then the first floor bedroom, where he found more abstract art, a coffered ceiling and fan, and a door to a private bathroom. A four-poster, queen-sized canopy bed was against one wall. On a second wall was a raised brick fireplace with a cast iron stove insert.

A framed sketch of a female skeleton wearing an extravagantly plumed hat and elegant early 20ᵗʰ century attire sat on a nightstand beside the bed. Santana recognized the sketch immediately as the figure of Catrina Calavera, known throughout Mexico as *la Catrina*, an image of death commonly seen at Day of the Dead celebrations. But it was the small statue of *Santa Muerte*, or Saint Death, on a matching nightstand on the far side of the bed, and the four unlit votive candles surrounding it—red, gold, purple and black—that drew his attention.

Sometimes called *Señora de las sombras*, Lady of the Shadows, or *Señora de la noche*, Lady of the Night, the twelve-inch skeletal statue was clad in a red hooded robe and carried a long-handled scythe across her body. Santana recalled that the long handle symbolized her ability to reach anyone, anywhere, at any time. Upon death, those who worshipped *Santa Muerte* believed the scythe cut the silver cord that attached the soul to the physical body.

The statue reminded him of *los sicarios* from Colombia, the teenage assassins from the slums of Medellin hired to kill anyone who challenged the cartel's authority. They had killed from the backs of motorbikes during the time of Pablo Escobar. Like those who prayed to *Santa Muerte*, *los sicarios* prayed to *la virgen de los sicarios* for the successful completion of the murder and for protection from the police or jail.

Santana checked the bathroom next and found nothing unusual. Then he checked the clothes on hangers in the walk-in closet that smelled of expensive perfume and those folded neatly in bureau drawers. Inside a bottom drawer Santana found an envelope containing a letter written in Spanish to a woman named Nina Rivera. According to the date, the letter had been written five years ago from Heredia, Costa Rica. The wording left no doubt that Rivera's mother loved her and wanted her to come home. No mention was made of a father or siblings, and no return address was written on the envelope, which wasn't surprising since Costa Rica had a poorly developed address system. Locations were usually given using known landmarks and distances from them. From what Santana knew about the country, many residents had an *apartado*, or mailbox at the local post office.

13

Santana figured that the beautiful young brunette-haired woman standing with her arm around Catalina Díaz in the framed color photo on the dresser was probably Nina Rivera. Beside it was a framed black and white photo of an old, gray-haired woman in a simple cotton dress. She was standing in front of a small adobe house that was nearly surrounded by dense tropical vegetation and tall *ceiba* trees. The trees reminded Santana of those near his parents' farm in La Victoria, Valle, in Colombia. They grew very rapidly and were good for reforestation. Though the wood wasn't durable enough for construction, he remembered that it was often used for canoes—and coffins.

As he stepped closer to the photo, he could tell by the old woman's bone structure and the shape of her face that she'd been very pretty at one time. But deep lines were etched in her brow now, and her hands were those of a person who had worked hard all her life. Still, there was no mistaking the face. Santana guessed that the woman in the photo was Nina Rivera's grandmother. If Rivera was Catalina Díaz's roommate, why were there no photos of Rivera's parents or her brothers and sisters, if she had any? He wrote Heredia, Costa Rica next to Nina Rivera's name in his notebook.

Leaving the bedroom, he went upstairs to inspect the second level bathroom and bedroom. The bathroom had a Jacuzzi tub, an assortment of hygiene products, a hair dryer and electric curler, and an array of perfumes, make-up, lotions, face creams, and nail polish. The bedroom had a round bed and more fake plants than books on the built-in shelves. A 13" Apple MacBook Air computer and a small Hewlett-Packard printer sat on a shelf beside a flat screen TV.

Next to one of the plants was the same photo of Díaz and Rivera that Santana had seen in the other bedroom. Figuring he might need a photo to show to neighbors, Santana removed it from the frame and placed it in his briefcase. He could return

14

it to Diaz's next of kin once they had been contacted. A second photo showed a younger Díaz with what Santana assumed was her mother, father, two older brothers, and three sisters. She was smiling shyly at the camera, and her face looked gentle and unmarked by any ugliness.

In the nightstand drawer were a box of condoms, a tube of vaginal lubricant, and a Costa Rican passport. He paged quickly through the passport and placed it back in the drawer. As he pushed in the drawer, he noticed that it felt slightly loose when it rolled back in the rails. He pulled it out and dumped its contents on the bed. Then he turned the drawer over and examined its underside. Nothing appeared out of the ordinary.

He removed the mini-Maglite from his pocket, squatted down, and shined the beam inside the empty slot where the drawer had been. Immediately, he saw what he'd been looking for. Reaching inside, he pulled out a wooden key that was inlayed into the case bottom. The back of the nightstand dropped down, revealing a drawer at the top. Inside the drawer was a sheet of paper folded in half. When he unfolded it, he saw that there were three names listed: Philip Campbell, Matthew Singer, and Nathaniel Burdette. He was curious as to why Catalina Díaz would have this particular list of men in a hidden drawer unless it was important. Maybe one of the men could help him locate Díaz's family? Santana put the list in his briefcase.

Then he took the Apple computer off the shelf and sat down on the corner of the bed with the computer in his lap. He was surprised to see that it was on and relieved to find that he could access the desktop without the need of a password. He was hoping that Catalina Díaz had been as careless with her data as she had been with her life.

He scanned the standard list of icons in the dock along the bottom of the blue screen. Oddly, there were no files or folders on the desktop. Before searching the hard drive, he clicked on the Safari browser, which opened to an Xfinity homepage. Santana typed "Catalina Díaz" in the Google search bar and found a link for her website.

A paragraph warned that if you were under the age of eighteen it was illegal to view adult material. Santana was certain seventeen-year-old males would be dissuaded by the warning. Further down the page a sentence assured readers that this was not a site for prostitution and that money exchanged was for companionship only. To the right side of the paragraph was a photo of Catalina Díaz in a red dress facing away from the camera. Her long black hair hung halfway down her back as she looked out one of the floor-to ceiling windows of the condo.

Santana clicked on the ENTER button and was immediately taken to a page featuring a professionally-shot black and white photo of Catalina Díaz sitting naked on a bedspread. Her right ankle was tucked under her left thigh, her left arm raised and bent at the elbow so that her arm rested on the top of her head. Her right hand was placed strategically on her right calf to cover her vulva. Her eyes were dark, her breasts large and heavy, and her lips full and slightly pursed as she looked seductively at the lens.

A WELCOME page described her as an upscale, highly rated escort/companion who took great pride in what she did. She had a spiritual approach to life and was extremely non-judgmental and caring. She listed her hours and stated that non-smokers were a must. There was a page with colored photos and a page with her e-mail address and a statement that she required verifiable references.

Santana clicked out of the web browser and clicked on the Macintosh HD icon, then on the Documents folder on the left side of the screen. Inside it he found folders titled Microsoft User Data and Digital Editions, but there was nothing in either folder. It was as if the computer had never been used.

As Santana shut down the computer, he saw Hawkins coming up the stairs. "Anything?"

She shook her head. "Her neighbors are either working or out somewhere. I'll see if I can contact them later. What about you?"

"There's no evidence of ligature marks on the ceiling beams and no video recorder, camera, or tape recorder she could use to replay autoerotic activity at a later date in order to become sexually stimulated."

"You find any charmeuse scarves?"

Santana shook his head.

Hawkins picked up Díaz's passport and flipped through it. "She spent quite a bit of time traveling back and forth from Costa Rica."

"I think that's where she was originally from," he said.

"How 'bout her computer?"

"She had a website advertising her escort services. But the computer was on, and there are no files or folders on the desktop."

"What's this?" Hawkins asked, pointing at the hidden drawer.

"Where a list of names was kept."

"How'd you find it?"

"When I was kid in Colombia, most homes didn't have safes, so woodworkers often designed furniture with hidden compartments and drawers."

"She must've had this nightstand custom made in the States."

Santana nodded and gestured toward his briefcase. "Take a look at the list of names."

Hawkins removed the list from Santana's briefcase. She stared at it and then at him. "Well, if it's a list of clients, it's an awfully short list."

"Maybe the important ones," Santana said.

Hawkins looked at the list a moment longer. "They all have the first names of apostles. But why did Díaz hide this in a secret drawer?"

A key turned the entrance lock to the condo. Santana put a finger to his lips, then placed his hand on the butt of his holstered Glock and moved to the top of the stairs.

Chapter 2

The condo door swung open, and a tall brunette in high heels and a short red dress stepped into the living room and closed the door behind her. Santana recognized her from the photo he'd seen in the first floor bedroom. She was Nina Rivera, Catalina Díaz's roommate. Rivera started toward the sofa and then stopped, as if sensing something. When her gaze found Santana and Hawkins standing at the top of the stairs, she inhaled a quick breath and dropped the shopping bag and small suitcase from her hands.

"We're police officers," Santana said.

A hand reached into the purse slung over her shoulder.

Santana drew his Glock and yelled, "Freeze!"

The loud command startled Rivera. She fixed her eyes on the barrel of Santana's gun as he came down the stairs with Hawkins following close behind him. Hawkins held her gun on Rivera as she removed a compact Glock 19 from Rivera's purse.

"You could've gotten yourself killed," Santana said, sliding his Glock into his holster again.

"How do I know you are police?" she said, speaking with a Spanish accent.

He held out his badge wallet.

She peered at it for a long moment. Then her eyes shifted back to Santana. "What are you doing here?"

"Looking for information on Catalina Díaz."

Her gaze darted toward the upstairs bedroom and then settled on him again. "Why?"

Santana wanted to break the news to her gently, but she'd left him little choice. "We're homicide detectives."

She canted her head and processed what he'd just said. Then the color drained from her complexion and she stepped back, as if buffeted by a strong gust of wind. "Homicide?"

"That's right. We're investigating her death."

Nina Rivera backed up to the curved, champagne-colored sectional and sat down, her eyes glazed, as if she were in a trance.

"Would you like some water?" Hawkins asked.

"Rum, please. It's behind the bar."

Hawkins went to the bar, carrying Rivera's Glock 19 with her. Santana heard her remove the magazine and eject the chambered round.

"Leave the gun behind the bar," she said. "I like to know where it is when it's not in my purse."

Santana sat down on a large cushioned chair across from the sectional and took out his notebook and pen. "You're Nina Rivera?"

She stared at him without replying, her brunette hair in a long French braid that had fallen over her shoulder, a faraway look in her eyes. Behind the eye shadow, mascara, make-up, and lipstick was the beautiful face of a woman in her late twenties.

"Yes," she said as her eyes refocused. "What happened to Cata?"

"Her body was discovered in a downtown hotel room this morning."

"How did she die?"

Santana preferred to keep the details private, at least in the early stages of the investigation. "We're not sure yet."

Rivera opened her purse, removed a package of Derby cigarettes—a popular brand in Latin America—and lit one with a black lighter, lifting her chin as she blew a small cloud of smoke up and away from her. Santana noted her hand was shaking as she brought the cigarette to her lips. He wondered if she was simply upset about her roommate's death, or if she was afraid of something—or someone.

She took a few more seconds to compose herself and then said, "But you're homicide detectives."

"We investigate many deaths, Ms. Rivera."

"I see."

Hawkins returned with a cocktail glass half full of rum and without the Glock 19. She handed the rum to Rivera, who drank it down in two quick swallows.

Hawkins—always concerned about her health—sat at the other end of the sectional, as far away from the smoke as she could get.

"Do you know of anyone who might want to harm Ms. Díaz?" Santana asked.

Rivera started to speak and then stopped. "No, I don't."

Santana sensed that she did. "Who was she meeting last night?"

She shrugged. "I arrived today. I haven't spoken with Cata in days."

"Arrived from where?"

"Costa Rica."

"And what is it you do for a living, Ms. Rivera?"

Her eyes held his a moment. They were the color of amber and just as hard. "I'm a model. I work for the Lenoir Agency here in town."

"Did Ms. Díaz work for the agency?"

"Yes."

"Have you ever met any of her clients?"

"Clients? What do you mean?"

"I think you know, Ms. Rivera."

"You are mistaken," she said, staring at the empty glass in her hand as though she wanted another drink.

A moment ago her eyes had been hard and focused. Now they were looking inward at something only she could see. Santana suspected she was lying. He decided to push harder. "One of Díaz's clients could very well have murdered her."

"But you said you didn't know if she was murdered."

"I don't. That doesn't mean she wasn't."

She took a long drag on her cigarette and blew out a cloud of smoke. "I'm sorry. I cannot help you."

Santana thought there might be a deeper meaning in her response. "You can't help us because you don't know anything? Or you can't help us because you're worried about your own safety?"

She stood up. "I need another drink."

"I'll get it," Hawkins said, taking the cocktail glass from Nina Rivera and heading for the bar.

"You are worried about the gun, Detective?" Rivera said, looking at Santana.

"You have a permit?"

"Of course. Cata and I both took training. We practiced every month at the range."

"Are you worried about your safety?"

"I grew up worrying about my safety. Nothing has changed."

"Tell me about Catalina Díaz."

"What is there to tell?" she said, sitting down again and crushing out her cigarette in the ashtray on the coffee table.

"What was she like?"

"Cata liked very nice things." She gestured with a hand, indicating the condo. "That's why she lived with me."

"You own this condo?"

She nodded.

Santana glanced at Hawkins, who shook her head in resignation. They hadn't gotten a warrant because they had thought Díaz owned the condo. Santana hoped it wouldn't become a problem in the future.

"Who were Ms. Diaz's friends?" he asked.

"I was."

"No one else?"

"You mean lady friends?"

"I mean all her friends."

Rivera averted her eyes. "I don't know."

Hawkins returned to the sofa and handed her the glass of rum. She drank it more slowly this time—but she still drank all of it.

"You speak English very well," he said.

She smiled. "As do you, Detective Santana. But you still have a slight accent. Where are you from?"

"Colombia."

"Ah, then we are almost neighbors."

Santana let the comment pass. "How did you meet Ms. Díaz?"

"At the modeling agency."

"How long ago was that?"

She thought about it. "Two years ago now."

"Who owns the agency?"

"Why does that matter?"

"I may want to speak to the owner."

"A man named Paul Lenoir."

Santana wrote down the name. "Did Ms. Díaz ever mention a man named Philip Campbell?"

"Not that I remember." Her eyes were a little unfocused now, her speech slightly slurred. It was hard to tell if she was lying.

"Do you own a computer, Ms. Rivera?"

"It's in my suitcase."

"So the one in the bedroom upstairs belongs to Catalina Díaz."

She nodded.

"Did Ms. Díaz have a cell phone?"

"Certainly."

"It wasn't in her purse or anywhere in the hotel room."

"Then someone must've taken it."

"Do you know what service she used?"

"Sprint. The same service I use."

"Her keys were also missing. You might want to have the lock on your door changed."

Rivera's eyes widened with concern. Then she seemed to regain control of her emotions. "I will do that."

"Do you have family here, Ms. Rivera?"

She shook her head.

"How about Costa Rica?"

She hesitated and then shook her head again. Based on what he'd read in the letter he'd found in a dresser drawer, Santana knew she was lying. He wondered why.

"Did Ms. Díaz have family here?"

"In Costa Rica."

"Whereabouts?"

"In Escazú, near San José."

"I'll need the contact information."

She stood and went into the kitchen. Two minutes later, she returned with piece of paper and handed it to Santana. "It's her parents' phone number."

"Did Ms. Díaz ever mention the name of the church she attended?"

Rivera shook her head.

"How about the *barrio* where she lived?"

"I'm sorry, no."

"You'll need to make arrangements to ship the body home once the autopsy is complete."

She sucked in a breath of air and let it out slowly. "I'm not sure how to do that."

"The department can help." Santana placed a business card on the coffee table. "Numbers for a victim advocate and the medical examiner's office are written on the back of my card. Call me if you think of anything you'd like to tell me, Ms. Rivera. In the meantime, it would be best if you would let me know if you're leaving town."

Anger flamed her eyes. "Why? I have done nothing."

"I never said you did."

She stared at him and then at the card, but didn't pick it up.

* * *

Santana dropped off Hawkins at the Law Enforcement Center and drove to the morgue at Regions Hospital. He couldn't recall how many autopsies he'd witnessed in his years as a detective, but it was enough that the sight of a body and the gallery of instruments used for prying, chiseling, and sawing into the dead no longer repulsed him. He'd learned quickly that homicide required a unique level of detachment, an understanding that a body was part of a much larger puzzle, a puzzle that once solved, could lead him to the perpetrator.

Catalina Díaz's hands had been bagged at the scene, and her body had been delivered in a plastic body bag to eliminate any evidence contamination. She'd been x-rayed, photographed, weighed, measured, fingerprinted, and washed before being placed face up on a slanted aluminum table with raised edges. The table had several faucets and drains for washing away blood during the internal investigation. A rubber body block had been placed under her back, causing her chest to protrude, making it easier to cut it open. Later the block would be placed under the neck like a pillow, allowing Reiko Tanabe to remove the brain.

She used cotton swabs to collect specimens of the moisture inside Díaz's mouth, vagina, and rectum as she spoke into a recording microphone above the table. She wore scrubs under her surgical gown and two pairs of surgical gloves along with shoe covers, a face shield, hairnet, and surgical mask to protect her from errant splatters. Santana wore a surgical gown and surgical mask to cut the smell.

He heard Tanabe say, "Two linear surgical scars are found beneath each breast, transversely oriented and measuring two inches in length." Clicking off the microphone above the table, she said, "I've got something here, John."

He walked over to her and stood beside the table. "Díaz had breast implants."

"Correct, but there's also an abrasion about three-sixteenths of an inch wide by one-sixteenth of an inch long on the posterior wall at the entrance to the vagina. I'll remove a tissue sample and examine it under a microscope. It's compatible with a forcible attempt at sexual intercourse."

"Could it have been caused by the dildo?"

"Possible. I couldn't say for sure. No surprise that forensics found semen stains on the bedspread. Given it was a hotel room, they could've been there a long time or deposited as recently as last night. Semen is a pretty resistant substance. Laundering and dry cleaning might not remove all traces of PSA and SAP," she said, referring to the prostate-specific antigen produced by the prostate gland and seminal acid phosphatase enzyme found in sperm.

"I'll send the swabs to the lab," she said. "See if anything turns up. I'll take some vaginal swabs as well."

* * *

Santana left the autopsy suite and drove to his house overlooking the St. Croix River. Sunlight had finally broken through the dissipating clouds, but the back yard stayed in deep shade from the birch and pine trees that studded his property. From the second floor deck, he looked down the slope to the boathouse and along the shore of the river, swollen from the snowmelt and heavy spring rains. A thick border of pine trees stood on the far side of the river, and beyond the pines, large homes sat on the high bluff overlooking the St. Croix, the glass windows reflecting the sun as it sank toward the horizon.

His golden retriever, Gitana—or gypsy in Spanish—licked his face as he bent down and stroked her back.

"Are you my girl? Yes, you are."

Her tail thumped against the hardwood floor as he spoke to her in a high-pitched voice she associated with approval.

He changed into a T-shirt and a pair of Nikes and took her out for a run. Her previous owner had been killed during one of Santana's murder investigations, and he'd adopted her. It had proven to be a wise decision. She was an excellent watchdog and had alerted him to danger on more than one occasion.

Santana enjoyed the scenery along the St. Croix, but he'd purchased the house primarily because of its private location. Assassins from the Cali cartel had continued to hunt him ever since he'd fled Colombia at the age of sixteen. He knew they would never quit and could blend more easily into a city neighborhood. So he'd chosen to live away from the city and to always carry his department issue Glock 25 or his smaller backup Glock 27.

A conventional holster was problematic when jogging because it tended to move around, so instead he carried the Glock 27 in a small perspiration-resistant pouch holster designed to fit compact semi-autos. The holster was comfortable and lightweight and had a narrow belt he could strap around his waist, allowing him noise-free access to the gun under his shirt.

While his Glocks and Gitana's vigilance provided some security, Santana had also upgraded his home security system by adding four high-resolution cameras, strategically mounted to give him a view of all sides of the house. The cameras recorded images in color during the day and switched automatically to black and white recording when ambient light was low. Infrared LED lights surrounding the lenses allowed the cameras to record with night vision capabilities up to fifty feet from the house. The cameras activated and recorded only when they detected motion.

The video streams could be viewed on his computer monitor. A large hard drive on a digital recorder stored the video recorded by the security cameras. When the hard drive was full, Santana had configured the system to back up all footage to an external hard drive, thus freeing space on the DVR. The system was also capable of transferring live video feeds to any computer with an Internet connection.

Unlike many of the uninformed citizenry that purchased alarm systems, Santana never used the protective sticker or signs advertising the name of the alarm company. Most professional burglars had the wiring diagrams to all the major systems. They would know exactly how to pry open the control cover and cut the right wire before the alarm had a chance to send its signal.

Santana considered his security measures preparation rather than paranoia.

Chapter 3

That night Santana had dinner with Jordan Parrish at her condo near St. Anthony Main in Minneapolis. Although they'd been dating for only a short time, he'd felt a connection with her from the moment they'd met. She'd been a Minneapolis cop prior to starting her private investigator business and was taking graduate classes in the evenings to finish her master's degree in psychology.

They were seated at her dining room table, which was perched on a small riser above the walnut floor. Jordan had dimmed the recessed lights in the ceiling and the torchiere-type floor lamps in the corners. The flame from a candle in the center of the table gave off the scent of cinnamon and cast a long, thin shadow on the wall. A Diana Krall CD played softly. Outside the window behind Jordan, lampposts lit a walking path along the Mississippi riverbank, and moonlight glazed the water.

"You seem a little distant tonight," she said.

"Sorry. I caught a new case today."

She drank some Chardonnay and looked at him with her intense hazel eyes. "Want to tell me about it?"

He took his time explaining, but not because he thought she couldn't handle it. Santana knew experience and intellect had taught her what to expect when the yellow crime scene tape went up. But he wanted to review the Catalina Díaz case in his mind one frame at a time as he spoke, hoping that he might see something he'd previously missed.

"Do you think she was murdered?" Jordan asked when he'd finished.

"We'll interview Philip Campbell, the doctor who we believe was with Díaz, tomorrow. Kacie and I thought her roommate, Nina Rivera, was holding something back. I'd like to talk with Paul Lenoir, the head of the modeling agency. See if we can shake something loose."

He finished his pasta alfredo and sockeye salmon, then refilled their wine glasses while Diana Krall sang, "Maybe You'll Be There." As the tension of the day ebbed, the image of a bungee cord suddenly releasing from Catalina Díaz's body flashed in his mind.

"You ever study anything about autoerotic asphyxia in your psych classes at the U of M?"

She nodded. "As I recall, nearly all reported cases of death by autoerotic asphyxia are males and most are under forty years old. But women do participate and often with a male partner. It's called terminal sex or scarving."

"Any idea why someone would get into it?"

She thought about it a moment. "Well, Freudians believe a child passes through several stages of psychosexual development that focus on sexual stimulation, similar to what occurs in autoerotic behavior. But some remain fixated in the phallic stage, which could result in autoerotic behavior as the primary means of achieving sexual gratification."

"What do you believe?"

"I side with the behaviorists who think autoerotic activity is learned through modeling or conditioning."

"You mean by watching videos or movies?"

"Or by reading about it."

"But how does that explain why someone would add in the danger of hypoxia to achieve orgasm?"

"It's an acting out of a masochistic fantasy."

She finished her meal and ran a hand through her ash blond hair. When they'd met, she'd worn it shorter in what is known as a bedroom cut because it could be easily styled in the morning by just running her fingers through it. Her hair was a bit longer now, but it still had a ruffled look that Santana found attractive.

"You study anything about bondage, discipline, sadism, and masochism?"

"Yes, in a human sexuality course where we discussed sexual deviation. Actually, Minneapolis has quite a large BDSM community. From what I remember, the whole idea that it's just about inflicting physical, psychological, and mental pain rather than a mutually agreed upon relationship is a stereotype and has nothing to do with their everyday life."

Santana smiled and thought, like all stereotypes, knowledge kills the myth. "You mean the image of the whip-swinging dominatrix, the sadomasochist in full leather regalia, isn't accurate?"

"Not for the majority of practitioners. Though that's how it's often depicted in magazines and movies. And women are often portrayed as the dominant party."

"The way I look at Catalina Díaz's death, there are three possibilities," he said. "One, she was alone and trying to achieve orgasm through autoerotic asphyxia. Two, someone was with her and accidentally killed her while engaging in the practice. Or someone murdered her and made it look like she accidentally killed herself."

"Consenting parties usually have a safeword they can use if they feel things are getting out of hand, John."

"And if the dominant doesn't stop when asked?"

"That would probably end the relationship and could be considered a crime. Consent is important. And BDSM sessions often require more safety precautions than vanilla sex."

"Is that what we're into?" he said, trying to lighten the mood some.

She smiled. "We and most of the population."

Later, after they'd cleared the dishes from the table, Jordan took him by the hand and led him into the bedroom, closing the door behind her as though she wanted the moment to be especially private and intimate. She kissed him lightly at first, then more passionately, her tongue exploring his mouth. They undressed each other and slipped under the cool covers. As he lay down beside her and she rolled against him, he could feel her body heat, the warmth of her breath, and smell the intoxicating scent of sandalwood and berries in her perfume.

He kissed her eyes, her nose, her breasts, as her hand brushed his thigh and touched his sex. Then, as she straddled him and placed him inside her, he propped his head on the pillows and slipped his arms around her narrow waist. In the silver moonlight filtering through edges of the blinds, he could see that her lips were slightly parted, her head was tilted back, and her eyes were closed as she moved him the way she wanted till they climaxed together.

Afterward, as she lay in his arms, her head resting under his chin, Santana asked the question that had been lingering at the edge of his consciousness. "Have you been sleeping well?"

"Better lately."

"Still have nightmares?"

"Sometimes."

"You don't want to see a therapist?"

Propping herself up on an elbow, she looked down at him and said, "You don't."

She knew that he'd killed in the line of duty. But he'd never told her about the violence in Colombia that had scarred his soul. "I've lived with my nightmares for a long time, Jordan."

"Oh, so you can handle the fact that you've taken a life and I can't."

Hers had been a good shooting and had probably saved both their lives, he thought. But he knew first hand what killing could do to the psyche. He'd never been the same, and he feared that Jordan wouldn't be either.

"I never said that. Everyone deals with it differently. I wish it'd never happened. I wish it would've been me who pulled the trigger instead of you."

"I know." She rolled away from him and sat on the edge of the bed, her back to him, moonlight spilling across the floor beneath the window.

"I'm just worried about you."

She turned toward him. "I suppose you think because I'm studying psychology I'd be more open to therapy."

"Maybe."

"I just want to work through it in my own way."

"I understand."

"Do you?"

"Of course."

"And how would I know that, John? You're unwilling to tell me much about your past. But you expect me to share mine and my feelings with you."

"I can't share everything."

"Because you don't trust me."

"I do trust you."

"Then show me you do." She reached out and took his right hand, tracing the long, jagged scar on the back of it with a fingertip.

He'd cut the hand on a *rienda*, or a sharp spur on a young guadua tree. The scar served as a constant reminder of how he'd nearly lost his life in the mountain forests of Colombia when he was sixteen. Jordan hadn't asked him how he'd acquired it, as if she understood intuitively that it represented something private, something dark, but he suspected she eventually would.

"I think this scar runs deep, John. In order to understand you, in order for us to be close, you're going to have to let me see what's underneath it."

"Why does it matter?"

"If you have to ask that question," she said, "then it's not worth answering."

* * *

Dark clouds shadowed the moon as Santana drove home. He'd wanted to share the ugliness of his past with Jordan, yet he had to keep her safe. He had to keep his sister, Natalia, safe. Assassins from the Cali cartel knew where he was and how to get to him. He'd vowed a long time ago that if they found him he wouldn't run, he wouldn't hide. He'd live his life to the fullest for as long as he could. The cartel didn't know where Natalia was, and Santana would die before he told them. But the more Jordan knew, the more her life and Natalia's would be in danger. That, he reminded himself, was his reason for remaining silent about his past.

But he understood there was a second reason, one that he was reluctant to admit. He cared about Jordan, cared about her more than he had anyone in a long time. And he feared that if he told her what he'd done, it might change her feelings for him. Yet if he didn't tell her, there would always be a familiar distance between them, a distance he'd maintained in previous relationships, a distance that had fractured and ultimately ended all of them.

As always, Gitana was happy to see him when he arrived home, and her excitement brightened his spirits. He took her outside and played tug and fetch for thirty minutes with a squeaky Tugga Wubba, her favorite toy. Then he refilled her food and water bowls and went upstairs and showered and slipped into a robe.

His mind was still wired from his conversation with Jordan. Knowing he wouldn't sleep immediately, Santana sat down at his computer and opened a private e-mail account. Only his uncle, Arturo Gutiérrez Restrepo, in Bogotá, Colombia, and Natalia, who lived in Barcelona, Spain, knew the password to the account. Santana could not risk sending a direct e-mail to her given that it might be intercepted, thus revealing her whereabouts to the Cali cartel. And so he and Natalia had worked out a system in which they would write each other e-mails but never send them. As long as each of them had the password to open the account, they could read the e-mails.

When he'd finished writing the e-mail, Santana did a Google search for Nina Rivera. He found three Nina Riveras currently listed on Facebook, two more on LinkedIn. But only one woman had a cached website page advertising escort services for men, women, and couples.

His cell phone rang. He recognized the number.

"Sorry to call so late, John," Kacie Hawkins said. "You in bed?"

"Soon."

"Well, I thought I'd give you a quick synopsis so we could hit the ground running tomorrow."

Santana figured she was jacked up about the case and couldn't sleep either.

"I typed a warrant for Catalina Díaz's cell phone and sent it to Sprint. I also called them and asked if they'd ping her phone, hoping I could find its location. But the phone has been turned off or destroyed. I'll call Sprint tomorrow and have the phone pinged again just to make sure. If someone took it, they might be stupid enough to use it."

"You never know," Santana said. "Write up a warrant for Díaz's computer. Her e-mails might tell us who killed her."

"Okay. I also have some information on Philip Campbell. He not only attended the conference at the hotel yesterday, he was one of the speakers. He's also an anesthesiologist with an office in St. Paul. He's fifty years old and divorced. He has a daughter and a son, and a stellar reputation."

"Sounds like he has a lot to lose if it got out he hired an escort."

"If he's the Philip on the list you found in Díaz's condo, maybe he knows the other men."

"We're going to find out," Santana said.

Chapter 4

The following morning, Santana sat at his desk in the Homicide Unit and contemplated how he would notify Catalina Díaz's parents that their daughter was dead. He could call them directly using the phone number Nina Rivera had given him. But that seemed cold and impersonal. And he had no idea how they might react.

Death notifications were never easy, particularly when communication was a barrier. Fortunately, Spanish was Santana's first language. But no matter how many times he'd spoken to family members of the victim, no matter how much experience he'd had, it always seemed like it was his very first time.

St. Paul PD procedure dictated that two officers were assigned to a bereavement detail. But Pete Romano wasn't about to approve a ticket to Costa Rica, let alone two. So Santana had to figure out a way to work around the limitations.

He flipped through his notebook till he found the page where he'd written Escazú, the *canton* or county where Catalina Díaz's family lived. Then he searched Google for Catholic churches in the county. He soon discovered that Escazú was considered to be one of the most trendy and upscale suburbs of the San José metropolitan area. That information surprised him. He'd figured that Catalina Díaz had come from a poor family, like most of the prostitutes working in Costa Rica—and everywhere else. She still might have been poor as a child, but Escazú looked much nicer than he'd envisioned.

The county was divided into three *barrios*, or neighborhoods, San Rafael, San Miguel, and San Antonio. Like in all Spanish cities, a Catholic church dominated the central plazas. He found the phone number for the central church in San Rafael and dialed. Costa Rica was on Central Standard Time, so he didn't have to deal with time zones.

He told the secretary who answered that he was a detective from Minnesota. He was looking for a priest who might know a Díaz family that belonged to the congregation and had a daughter in her twenties named Catalina. He considered his request to be a long shot, but one worth taking. If he found a priest who knew Díaz, he could ask him to be with her family when he phoned with the news of her death.

It took a while before a priest came on the phone. Santana explained the situation again. The priest was very understanding, but he knew of no Díaz in his congregation that had a daughter named Catalina. Santana thanked him and dialed the number for the church in San Miguel. He spoke again to a secretary and then to two different priests with the same result.

According to what he'd learned on the Internet, the San Antonio *barrio* was the smallest and quietest neighborhood of the three. The secretary who answered the phone at the church in the central square put him in touch with a priest who, after listening to Santana's story, connected him to a second but older priest named Father Ramirez.

"Yes," Ramirez said, after Santana explained why he was calling. "I am sure we are talking about the same family. They have a daughter Catalina living in the States."

"Do you have a fax machine? I need to be sure. We can't afford to make a mistake."

"Of course."

Santana wrote down the fax number and then sent him a copy of the photo he'd taken from Catalina Díaz's condo.

"It is Catalina," the priest said with regret. "This is terrible."

"What do you know about her family?"

"They are very poor. The mother works as a maid. The father is a custodian at an elementary school."

"I'll give you my cell number," Santana said. "If you could call me when you arrive at the house, I'll phone the family."

"I will leave immediately. It is not far."

Thirty minutes later, Father Ramirez called. Santana thanked him and disconnected. Then he used the landline on his desk to call Catalina Díaz's house. A man answered.

"*Señor* Díaz?"

"Yes."

"My name is John Santana," he said in Spanish. "I am a police officer in St. Paul, Minnesota."

"Father Ramirez told me to expect your call."

Santana could hear a woman weeping softly in the background. "Then you know that Catalina is dead."

"Yes," he said, his voice breaking.

Santana had no clue if her family was aware of their daughter's profession and was reluctant to go into details. Anything he said would be pure speculation until he received the ME's autopsy report. And even then, there might not be a definitive determination as to whether Catalina Díaz had died accidentally or been murdered. He decided to stick to what little he knew, while keeping silent about the possible sexual implications of her death.

"I am very sorry about your daughter's death. We are trying to determine the exact cause of death at this time," he said.

"Do you believe my daughter was murdered?"

Santana was certainly leaning in that direction, despite the lack of concrete evidence. He'd been working homicide long enough to trust his instincts. Still, instincts were not facts. And that's what he needed before giving a definitive answer.

"We investigate all suspicious deaths, *Señor* Díaz. That does not mean that your daughter was murdered. Were you aware she was in Minnesota?"

"Yes. She sent money home every month."

"Do you know her roommate, Nina Rivera?"

"No."

"Well, I have asked her to accompany the body back to Costa Rica. We have a victim advocate who works with the department. She will let you know when the arrangements have been finalized."

"Whoever did this must be punished."

Santana did not reply, though he felt the same. He offered his condolences one more time. Then, as he hung up the phone, Kacie Hawkins strode into the Homicide Unit, her dark eyes wide with excitement.

She came to his desk and said, "We got a hit on the fingerprints in the hotel room. A custodian named Brian Howard."

"He works at the hotel?"

She nodded.

"Well, it stands to reason his prints would be in her room."

"Take a look at this," she said, placing the paper on his desk.

Santana scanned it and then looked at Hawkins. "You have an address?"

She smiled and said, "Follow me."

* * *

Roman shades covered the windows and vintage gas signs hung on one of the walls of Brian Howard's apartment. Bookshelves along a third wall were lined with comic books and vinyl records. Three copies of Superman comic books were splayed like a fan on a trunk table. Santana and Hawkins sat in a pair of deco leather armchairs. Brian Howard sat on a matching sofa across from them.

"You're here about the dead woman in the hotel room, right?"

"That's correct," Santana said, taking out his notebook and a pen.

"Well, I don't see how I can help."

Howard was dressed in a white button-down shirt, creased khaki pants, white athletic socks, and deck shoes. His head and oblong face were shaved clean, and he smelled of musk. Nothing about him or his apartment appeared out of place.

"How long have you worked at the hotel, Mr. Howard?"

"Nearly fifteen years. I have an associate's degree in engineering technology. I've always liked working with my hands. I also have a small custodial cleaning business I run on the side."

"Many employees?"

"Just two right now."

"Did you know or have you ever met Ms. Catalina Díaz?"

"She was the dead woman in room nine eighteen?"

"Yes."

He shook his head. "Absolutely not."

"But you were in her room."

"What do you mean?"

"The desk had a work order for you to replace the faulty thermostat."

His pale face reddened. "I have to enter rooms sometimes when there's a problem."

"You work the night shift?"

"Four to midnight."

"What was the problem with the thermostat?"

"It was sticking."

"And you fixed it."

"Of course."

Santana recalled that the temperature in the room when Díaz's body was discovered was fifty-five degrees. "You're sure the thermostat was working when you left?"

"Absolutely. I know what I'm doing."

"Do you recall what you set the temperature at after you made the repairs?"

"Sixty-eight degrees is standard procedure."

If Howard was telling the truth, then it seemed unlikely that Díaz had turned down the thermostat to an uncomfortably cold temperature. Someone else had turned down the temperature to confuse the ME. "Did you replace the thermostat while Ms. Díaz was in the room?"

"I just told you. I never met her, never even saw her."

"Did you see anyone enter or leave Ms. Díaz's room?"

"No."

"Where was Ms. Díaz while you were replacing the thermostat?"

"How would I know? Maybe she went to a restaurant or bar?"

"Did she know you were coming?"

"Yes. I called ahead and told her when I'd be there."

"And you knocked?"

"Of course. But when no one answered, I used my master key and opened the door."

"What did you see when you entered the room?"

"Nothing out of the ordinary," Howard said. "She wasn't there, so I got right to work and replaced the thermostat."

"And Ms. Díaz never returned while you were repairing the thermostat?"

"No. I left when I finished and notified the desk. The time should be on the work order."

Santana knew it was. He also knew the answer to the next question he was about to ask, but he wanted to test

Howard's honesty. "Ever been in trouble with the law, Mr. Howard?"

He looked down at his shoes. Stalling for time as he weighed his options, Santana thought. Then he looked at Santana again. "Once," he said in a voice just above a whisper.

"I ran your prints through the FBI database," Hawkins said. "Guess what I found?"

Howard let out a breath of resignation. "I don't have to guess. I already know."

"You've got a gross misdemeanor on your record."

"I can explain."

"Go ahead."

"I was caught mooning some girls during high school. It was a prank, just a joke."

"Then why was it classified as a gross misdemeanor instead of a misdemeanor?" Hawkins asked.

"Because there was a minor present at the time. He was a friend of mine, but he was only sixteen. I was eighteen. That automatically bumps it up to a gross misdemeanor."

Hawkins nodded, confirming Howard's correct interpretation of the state statute.

"You've got to keep this quiet, please," he said. "It was a long time ago. I don't want to lose my job."

"How old are you now, Mr. Howard?" Santana asked.

"I'm forty."

"Single?"

"Divorced."

"Your ex-wife lives in town?"

He nodded.

"Any children?"

"One son," he said. "And I'm paying child support, which is why I really need to keep my job."

"Been divorced long?"

"Five years. But I was married six," he said, as if the length of time he was married justified his divorce.

"Still on friendly terms with your wife?"

He shook his head and offered a crooked smile. "Well, Marsha and I talk once in a while, mostly about our son. But I wouldn't call us friendly. Not too many divorced couples are, I imagine."

"Do you know what autoerotic asphyxia is, Mr. Howard?"

He smiled hesitantly and waited for a few beats before replying. "It sounds like something sexual."

Santana could detect no incongruity between his words and body language. But that didn't mean he was telling the truth. "What does your former wife do?"

"She's an elementary principal in St. Paul."

"You have her current address?"

"Why do you want to talk to her?" His voice had climbed an octave and become louder.

Santana wondered if Howard's ex-wife could shed some light on her former husband's sexual practices. But he didn't want Howard to know that. "I'm sure we can locate her," he said. "But you could save us time."

"I'd rather you wouldn't talk to her, Detective. I only get to see my son every other weekend. If she finds out the police have questioned me regarding a murder investigation, she might take me to court. I could lose my custody rights."

"We never said Ms. Díaz was murdered."

He seemed lost for words. "Well, I mean, you're homicide detectives. What am I supposed to think? And I don't want something silly that I did years ago to affect my job or the ability to see my son."

"Your wife doesn't know about your gross misdemeanor conviction?"

"No. And I want to keep it that way."

Santana stopped writing in his notebook. "You had access to Ms. Díaz's room."

"But she could've let anyone in there, including her clients."

Santana glanced at Hawkins. She said, "So you're aware that Ms. Díaz was an escort."

He shrugged. "It wasn't a secret among the staff. Escorts use the hotel all the time."

"Does management know?"

"How could they not?"

"You have a girlfriend?" Santana asked.

"Why? You want to talk to her, too?"

"So you do have a girlfriend."

"No, I don't. I don't even date much."

"You ever use an escort service, Mr. Howard?"

"I don't have the money for that."

Santana pointed to the comic books on the table. "Yet you have money to buy these."

"It's all about priorities, Detective. I'm a pannapicta-graphist, or a collector to you. I prefer to spend my money on my hobbies."

"Is that all you collect?"

"Vinyl records and vintage signs," he said. "And old fur-niture."

* * *

The air near Lake Harriet in Minneapolis was cool and heavy with the rich, loamy smell of earth, the area mostly de-serted save for a few joggers and bikers, the surface of the lake as dull and lifeless as the eyes of the dead. Santana sat beside Dr. Philip Campbell on a wooden bench in front of the castle-shaped band shell. Hawkins sat on a second bench opposite Campbell.

He had a broad, blunt face, thinning blond hair, and pale blue eyes that looked red and irritated. He wore a jogging suit with a zippered front, running shoes and white socks. His unusually large hands were draped over the curved end of a cane. Santana thought he looked at least ten years older than his fifty years.

"Thanks for meeting me here. It's not the best of days, but I hate to miss my daily walk." Campbell patted his right leg. "I shattered my femur in a skiing accident in Vail. Still recovering."

Santana wondered if Campbell's "not the best of days" remark referred to the weather, the presence of the homicide detectives—or both. He took out his notebook and pen. "I understand you were at the medical conference in St. Paul yesterday."

Campbell stared silently at the lake for a time before responding. "I'm sure you've checked."

"Did you know Catalina Díaz?"

His gaze found Santana. "Whenever you're gauging someone's honesty, Detective, I assume you operate under the premise of never asking a question you don't already have the answer to."

"Your business card was in her purse along with your cell phone number."

"Which is how you were able to contact me."

"That's right."

He shook his head in resignation. "That was a bit careless."

"You know that Catalina Díaz is dead."

Campbell lowered his head and his shoulders slumped. He suddenly seemed smaller, as though a mass of bone and tissue had been removed from his body. "I read about her death in this morning's paper. I was very sorry to hear it."

"You paid five hundred dollars to have sex with her."

46

He raised his chin and looked into Santana's eyes. "Yes, I did. But she was alive when I left the room."

"What time was that?"

"Around one a.m. I went back to my room and slept before checking out at six."

"Was that the first time you'd had sex with her?"

He let out a sigh. "No. I've been seeing her for a year or so. But it was nothing serious. Just sex, you know."

"What kind of sex were you having?" Hawkins asked.

Campbell's eyes narrowed in a squint as he looked at her and then at Santana. "What's she talking about?"

"Your sexual practices."

He held out a hand, palm up in a placating gesture. "We had normal sex. I'm not into anything kinky."

"You have a daughter and a son," Hawkins said.

Campbell peered at her. "They're adults now with their own lives. Still, I hope that none of this gets back to them. But you and your partner are going to do what you have to do."

"If you were worried about their reaction, maybe you should've thought of that before," Hawkins said.

"Perhaps I should have. But I'm divorced. I still have . . . needs. Still, I had no reason to kill Catalina. I liked her very much."

"How did you meet her?" Santana asked.

"It's the Internet age, Detective. You can find just about anything you want there."

Santana removed a copy of the list from the inner pocket of his sport coat, unfolded it, and showed it to Campbell. "We found this in Catalina Díaz's condo. I believe it's a client list. Do you know the other men?"

Campbell glanced at the list before returning it to Santana. "You're making an assumption, Detective."

Santana knew most people were only as good as a coin toss in spotting deception. Even the best human lie detectors called "wizards" could spot a lie only eighty percent of the time. But he'd taken Facial Action Coding System, or FACS, training as part of his master's degree in criminology and had spent much of his life interviewing and interrogating practiced liars. He listened carefully for hesitations in speech, slips of the tongue, and lack of detail. He had a better than average success rate at catching facial changes called micro-expressions that lasted less than a second. He believed Campbell was lying in an effort to protect the other men on the list.

"We need a DNA swab," he said.

"Legally, I don't have to provide one."

"No, you don't. But if the ME finds semen inside Catalina Díaz, and we don't have a sample from you, we won't know if it's yours or someone else's."

"I used a condom."

"Maybe someone else didn't."

Campbell stared off into some thoughtful distance. "I'm innocent."

"We never said you weren't."

"I already admitted I had sex with the woman."

"It's up to you."

Campbell hesitated a few seconds longer before he nodded his head in agreement. "Could we step inside the band shell where we'll have some privacy?"

"All right," Santana said.

When they reached the privacy of the band shell, Hawkins slipped on a pair of latex gloves and took a DNA kit out of her purse. Campbell stood silently as she swabbed the inside of his cheek to collect cells. Then she placed the swab in a protective tube and labeled it.

"What happens now?" he asked.

"We're continuing the investigation," Santana said.

"Do I need to contact an attorney?"

"That's up to you. But officially, you haven't been charged with anything." Santana handed Campbell one of his business cards. "You can reach me directly at this number."

"I told you the truth, Detective."

"It's always better that way, Dr. Campbell. Because one way or another, we're going to find it."

Chapter 5

That afternoon in the Homicide Unit, Santana ran into a dead end with the silk scarf found around Catalina Díaz's waist and the bungee cords used to bind her. Both the cords and scarf were common brands that could be purchased with cash from numerous retail outlets. Santana wondered if he might find similar cords and scarves in Philip Campbell's house. But without more evidence linking Campbell to Díaz's death, a judge would never sign a warrant.

Santana was working on the case summary reports and the interviews Hawkins had conducted with those who'd attended the medical conference or stayed at the hotel the night Catalina Díaz died when he received a call from the desk officer in the lobby.

"There's a woman named Sarah Malik and her daughter, Samantha, here, John. She wants to see you."

"About what?"

"She wouldn't say."

"She asked specifically to see me?"

"Yep."

Interior security in the Griffin building prevented anyone from gaining access to the SPPD offices and departments without a card key or escort.

"I'll be right down."

Santana took an elevator to the first floor. A middle-aged woman in a long wool coat, and a young girl no more than five or six years old were sitting in a set of chairs in the small lobby near a large glass case containing one of the first SPPD police uniforms. While the desk officer had identified them as mother and daughter, they could not have looked more different.

Sarah Malik was very tall and thin, with a pale, androgynous face illuminated by blueberry eyes and capped by a brushed-back crop of blond hair. She was dressed conservatively in black jeans and a charcoal pullover worn over a light grey polo turtleneck. She was an unusual-looking woman, the sort of woman you couldn't take your eyes off of.

Her daughter sitting beside her had light brown skin and black hair cut in a pageboy style. Her large, striking eyes were the color of jade. She was dressed in jeans, a white turtleneck, pink jacket, and black canvas shoes with pink laces. Colorful stars, monkeys, and peace signs were stitched on the sides of her shoes.

Santana introduced himself and escorted them to the elevator and up to the Homicide Unit on the second floor. The seven detectives assigned to homicide each had an individual workstation. Six were located in a large common work area, which was separated from the rest of the floor by sound partitions. Only the most senior detective and the commander, Pete Romano, had separate offices. Santana wanted privacy, so he led Sarah Malik and her daughter to one of the interview rooms.

When they were settled in chairs across the table from him, he said, "Can I get you some coffee or water, Ms. Malik?"

"No. Thank you. I'm fine." She set her purse on the table in front of him. The black bag had an embossed leather Ruger pistol and chrome plated metal foliage. A large silver pendant attached to the chainmail strap had a green horizontal figure eight in the center and three phrases scripted around the scalloped edge: There is No Beginning; There is No End; There is Only Change.

Santana looked at her daughter. "What about you, Samantha?"

"You can call her Sammy," her mother said.

"Okay. Would you like some pop or water, Sammy?"

She blinked her large eyes and shook her head.

"You're sure?"

"Uh-huh."

Santana felt an uncomfortable sense of foreboding as he gazed at the child. He never ignored his instincts and wouldn't in this instance. But he kept his expression neutral, not wanting to upset the child or her mother. He turned his attention to Sarah Malik again. "You wanted to see me?"

"Yes," she said. "We saw the news report on television about the death of the woman in the hotel room yesterday."

"Catalina Díaz."

She nodded. "Do you have any suspects besides Philip Campbell?"

Santana was taken aback. "How do you know about Campbell?"

"His name was mentioned in an article on the *Pioneer Press* website."

Santana wanted to know who the hell had leaked Campbell's name to the press. "I really can't discuss the case with you, Ms. Malik."

"But you believe she was murdered."

"Like I said, I can't comment on an ongoing investigation."

"I understand. But Sammy insisted we come and talk to you. The news report identified you as the investigating officer."

Santana glanced at the child who was staring at him as though he was an interesting object she'd never encountered before. "Why did your daughter insist on seeing me?"

"I read an article about you in the *Pioneer Press* when you were awarded a Medal of Valor. You were born in Colombia and understand Spanish." Sarah Malik spoke in a straightforward, matter-of-fact way, as though the answer were obvious.

Santana spread his hands, indicating he didn't understand the connection.

"A young Latina was murdered six years ago."

"In St. Paul?"

"Yes."

"And how would your daughter know that? She doesn't look much older than five or six."

"She's six."

Santana waited.

Sarah Malik let out a breath. "Sammy believes that in a previous life she was a young Latina named Tania Cruz. The woman who was murdered six years ago in the same manner as the young woman in the hotel room."

Santana wasn't sure how he should respond. He'd heard many unbelievable stories in his years as a detective, mostly from gangbangers and murderers. Sarah Malik seemed sincere. He didn't want to dismiss her outright.

"Perhaps your daughter has a vivid imagination."

"This isn't the first time Sammy's mentioned a past life."

"Kids talk," Santana said. "Maybe she heard something about the murder at school."

"Sammy is homeschooled. And from the moment she could speak, she's described another life in a different country."

"What country?"

"Costa Rica," Sammy said.

The little girl's voice startled Santana. He fixed his gaze on her. "Costa Rica?"

She bobbed her head. "I grew up there. *Yo hablaba Español muy bien.*"

"You used to speak Spanish well?" he said.

"*Sí, pero no puedo recordar mucho mi Español ahora.*"

He smiled at her. "Well, you seem to remember quite a bit." He looked at her mother. "Do you speak Spanish, Ms. Malik?"

"No. And Sammy's never had a lesson."

Santana was sure if he saw himself in a mirror right now, his eyes would be bugging out of his head like some cartoon character's. "She's never had a lesson?"

"No. And none of her friends speak Spanish. Yet, from the time she could first talk, she would often speak in Spanish."

"Would you describe your daughter as a bright child?"

"Yes, Sammy is very bright and very mature for her age."

"Then maybe she just memorized a few phrases she heard on television," he said.

Sarah Malik gestured with a hand toward her daughter. "Go ahead. Ask her something in Spanish."

Santana considered asking something simple about school. Then another thought came to him. He was hesitant to ask the little girl about Tania Cruz's death because he thought it might upset her mother. But if he asked her questions in Spanish, her mother wouldn't understand. Still, he was concerned about frightening the child.

"*¿Cuéntame lo qué pasó con Tania Cruz?*" he said, asking if she could tell him what had happened to Tania Cruz.

Sammy tilted her head as though she were trying to understand. Santana thought she hadn't when suddenly she said, "*Tenía una bolsa de plástico en mi cabeza. Yo no podía respirar.*"

Santana was stunned. She'd said she'd had a plastic bag over *my* head and couldn't breathe, as though she were speaking as Tania Cruz and not Sammy Malik.

He wanted to know what else she remembered. "*¿Qué más recuerdas?*"

"*Yo tenía una cuerda alrededor de mi cintura y mi cuello.*"

He tried to mask his surprise, but Sarah Malik saw it on his face.

"What did you ask her? What did she say?"

54

Santana was reluctant to say that Sammy had described having a cord around her waist and neck, in the same fashion as Catalina Díaz. "Your daughter seemed to know some details about Tania Cruz's death that weren't made public."

"I've learned that *bolsa* is the word for bag in Spanish," Sarah Malik said. "Sammy has always had a great fear of plastic bags. She won't even touch them. And she often has nightmares about not being able to breathe."

Santana took a moment to collect his thoughts and calm his emotions. He felt as if he were watching an old episode of *The Twilight Zone.*

"*¿Y entonces qué pasó?* And then what happened?" he asked Sammy.

"*Yo me morí.*"

"You died?"

She nodded.

Santana wondered if perhaps Sammy Malik was a savant like Dustin Hoffman had played in the movie *Rain Man.* Yet she'd displayed no outward signs that suggested she was anything but a normal six-year-old. Except that she could speak fluent Spanish without apparently having had any experience with the language.

"*¿Sabes quién te mató?*" he asked. "Do you know who killed you?"

Sammy nodded confidently.

"*¿Era un hombre?*"

She nodded again, indicating a man had killed her.

"*¿Cómo se llamaba?*"

"*No sé.*"

She either hadn't known him or didn't remember his name. "*¿Podría reconocerlo?* Could you recognize him?"

"*No sé,*" she said again, indicating she didn't know.

"Were you assigned to the Tania Cruz case, Detective Santana?" Sarah Malik asked.

"No. Quite honestly, I don't even know if a woman named Tania Cruz was murdered six years ago."

"Why don't you check?"

Santana mentally debated whether he should say he'd get back to her later. But the little girl's ability to speak Spanish and her description of Tania Cruz's death intrigued him.

"I want you to see something," Sarah Malik said. She turned to Sammy. "Show the detective your birthmark."

"That's not necessary, Ms. Malik."

Sammy used an index finger to pull back her collar, revealing a raised, reddish birthmark that looked like a rope burn on her neck.

"Please," Sarah Malik said again. "See if a woman named Tania Cruz was murdered."

Santana stood. "Wait here. I'll be right back."

He went up to the third floor storage room where the homicide files were kept, his thoughts lingering on the child's birthmark and the improbability of what he'd just witnessed in the interview room. To his surprise, he found the Tania Cruz file. Nick Baker, a retired SPPD homicide detective, had worked the case, along with Tim Branigan, who was now the assistant chief of the Major Crimes and Investigations Division. Santana wasn't sure how important that information was— or if it was important at all—but his instincts told him to remember it.

A photo in the file revealed that Tania Cruz had been a beautiful, dark-haired young woman like Catalina Díaz. But a man named Arias Marchena had been convicted of the murder. His photo was clipped to the investigative report.

The photos gave Santana an idea. He collected an array of five photos of female and male police officers out of uniform. He took the fillers and the photos of Cruz and Marchena back to the interview room, where he sat down at the table and looked at the young girl. He was surprised by her ability to sit still. He hadn't been around many children, but he thought most would be out their seat and roaming the room by now.

"I'm going to show you some photos," he said to Sammy. "I want you to tell me if you recognize anyone. Do you understand?"

She nodded.

Santana knew that photos shown to a witness should be presented individually rather than in a group. The procedure encouraged a witness to compare each person individually to his or her independent memory of the perpetrator's identity. When presented with a group of photos, a witness was more likely to pick the person who merely looked the most like the perpetrator from the group. He'd once read a study conducted in Minnesota that showed the individual procedure improved identification accuracy and reduced the occurrence of false identifications. Detectives in the department had been trained to use the same procedure when presenting a lineup.

Santana put down a photo of a male officer and waited. Sammy peered at it and then looked at Santana again. He'd decided to hold the Arias Marchena photo till last, giving her multiple opportunities to choose the wrong one, thus revealing her unreliability.

He put down a second photo and then a third, pausing between each one. Sammy gave no indication that she recognized the men in the first three photos. He proceeded to set down the fourth and fifth photos, again pausing in between. Finally, he put down the photo of Arias Marchena.

Sammy peered at it for a time, as she had all of them, and shook her head.

"You don't recognize any of these men?"

"No," she said.

That Sammy Malik couldn't recognize any of the men, including Marchena, had proved nothing, because she hadn't met them. Santana collected the photos and followed the same procedure with the female array. As he placed the last of the six female photos on the table, Sammy seemed to hesitate for a moment, as she held a small index finger against her chin. Then she placed the finger on the photo of Tania Cruz and looked innocently at Santana. "That's me," she said.

* * *

That evening Santana drove with Gitana to the St. Croix Marina in Hudson, Wisconsin, where they boarded the used 37-foot Mainship he'd recently purchased. He'd paid what he considered a low price for a boat that would allow him to relax and spend the night on board while cruising the river in his off hours. It was something he'd wanted to do for a long time.

The boat was only ten years old and had been well cared for. It had lots of space and headroom below, which he appreciated, given that he was six-feet two inches in shoes. There was a wide aft deck with a wet bar area and steps up to the fly bridge that offered a 360-degree view. Walkthrough steps led to the foredeck, which meant he and any guests wouldn't have to tiptoe around the sides to go forward. The boat had a large galley and slept six, two in the forward cabin, two on a convertible dinette, and two in the aft stateroom that had a separate shower. The conveniences would allow him to spend a comfortable night onboard, hopefully with Jordan.

He called her on his cell while sitting in the captain's chair on the fly bridge, a cool breeze rippling the surface of the water, the molten sun flaming the edges of the horizon red as it sank in the western sky.

"Want to take a cruise tomorrow evening?" he asked when Jordan answered.

"Your new boat is in the water?"

"As of yesterday."

"I'd love to. But I'm leaving tomorrow for the P.I. conference in San Diego. Remember?"

"I do now. You're going for three days?"

"Yes. And I have to testify at a trial. That might extend the trip. But we could take the boat out when I return."

"All right."

She paused before speaking again. "I won't let you off the hook, John. You can't keep your emotional distance and expect this relationship to go beyond what we have now."

The thought crossed his mind that what they had right now was just fine. Then, like the sea gull that flew quickly across his field of vision, it was gone.

"Call me when you get to San Diego," he said.

"Any progress on the case?"

"Some."

"Be safe," she said and clicked off.

He opened a bottle of Sam Adams and let his thoughts return to the interview he'd conducted with Sarah Malik and her daughter, Sammy, that afternoon. He was well aware that some people believed in reincarnation, particularly in countries such as India that had a large Hindu population. If he remembered correctly, the phenomenon had been heavily researched at the University of Virginia. But Santana had lost his faith in the afterlife years ago after a drunk driver had killed his father and after his mother's murder. The anecdotal accounts of reincarnation were just that, he reminded himself.

But he'd grown up with the stories of Gabriel García Márquez that mixed magic and realism, and in a culture in which religion and superstition were as intertwined as the ecosystem in the river. Ofir, the woman who'd worked as a maid for years in his childhood home in Manizales, had taught him the importance of listening to his intuition and understanding his dreams, which were often populated with the ghosts of those who had died violent deaths.

Yet the logical part of his mind told him he was being fooled. Sarah Malik had lied. She spoke fluent Spanish and had probably taught her daughter the language. Many children were bilingual at a young age, particularly in foreign countries where second languages were often taught in kindergarten. Santana had begun his study of English in Colombia when he was eight years old.

Sarah Malik had probably recalled the news reports of Tania Cruz's murder when she'd heard about Catalina Díaz's death. And Sammy Malik had just gotten lucky when she'd pointed out Cruz's photo, or perhaps her mother had shown her an archived *Pioneer Press* photo of Cruz. The child's birthmark was simply a birthmark—which happened to be on her neck and happened to look like a rope burn and exactly like the marks Santana had seen in the autopsy photos in Cruz's file. But despite all his logic, all his rationalization, his instincts told him that what he'd observed was no parlor trick. Sammy Malik truly believed that she was Tania Cruz reincarnated.

He had no definitive explanation for it.

Chapter 6

Santana ran with Gitana early the next morning when the light was still soft in the trees and dew glistened on blades of grass. His senses were alive with the scent of wild flowers and pine, his thoughts focused on interpreting both the metaphorical and literal elements of the dreams he'd had the night before.

In the first dream, he'd been looking through the windshield of his Crown Vic when a bump in the road had suddenly cracked the glass in a large spider web pattern, making it nearly impossible to see. He'd experienced this dream before and knew that looking through the glass windshield represented what was ahead of him and the choices he would make. The cracks indicated he would experience setbacks in the pursuit of his goals.

The second dream of being unable to open a locked door represented the privacy and emotional distance he'd chosen as a means of protecting himself and those closest to him. He knew that, metaphorically, Jordan wanted him to unlock the door and let her in. The literal elements of the dream, however, were more difficult to interpret—but even more important. Often in the past, his ability to understand the meaning of his dreams had helped him solve cases and had saved his life. He had learned never to dismiss his dreams and always kept a journal on his nightstand to record them.

Initially in the investigation, he'd noted the lock on Catalina Díaz's hotel room and wondered if someone could enter her room without a key or key card, or without her opening the door. No one had been registered in the rooms on either side of hers, nor had anyone been in the room across the hall. Since Philip Campbell was a client, she would have let him in. But if Campbell was telling the truth, then there were only two possibilities. Either Catalina Díaz had accidentally killed herself—or someone other than Campbell had killed her. If that were true, Santana was certain that Catalina Díaz knew the killer and had let him or her into the room after Campbell's departure—or someone with a key card had entered her room.

He was still reflecting on the possibilities as he parked along the curb in front of the Lenoir Studio and directly behind Kacie Hawkins' Crown Vic. The studio was located in an old brick building in Merriam Park, an affluent residential neighborhood on the west side of St. Paul. The area was populated with wood-frame Queen-Anne style houses, small apartments and studios, as well as numerous antique and vintage stores.

"Someone leaked Philip Campbell's name to the press," Santana said as they walked under the arched entrance of the building.

"You think it was Romano?"

"I do," Santana said. "I'll deal with it after we talk to Lenoir."

They went up a set of stairs to the second floor and into a 20 x 40 foot room with a high ceiling and walls painted in a white matte finish. At the far end of the room Santana saw a reflector board, strobe lights, umbrella, and two digital SLR cameras on tripods. The legs were taped to the floor to prevent them from moving or tangling with the heavy-duty electrical cords slithering across the hardwood. A black canvas drop against the far wall was attached to a motorized system mounted to a heavy beam in the ceiling. Framed color and black and white photos of children, families, and beautiful young women were hung on the walls on either side of him.

An open door to Santana's right led into a small dressing room with a full-length mirror. On the corner of a desk straight ahead was a framed photo of a young, light-complected man in an Air Force uniform. He had an angular face, a strong jaw line, and a cleft in his chin.

A tall, muscular, forty-something version of that same man strode toward Santana and Hawkins now, a small digital camera in one hand. He wore pleated khakis, a red polo shirt, and deck shoes, and he had a cocky, wary friendliness about him.

"I'm Paul Lenoir," he said, shaking hands with both of them. He held onto Hawkins' hand a bit too long and let his eyes linger till she pulled her hand away. Then his gaze came back to Santana. "Can I help you?"

Santana showed him his badge and introduced himself and Hawkins.

"You must here about Cata."

Lenoir's eyes, which were as dark and distant as a moonless sky, crinkled in the outer corners. He smiled when he realized Santana was staring. "My irises are smaller than normal. Makes my sclera visible at the bottom of my eyes. John F. Kennedy had the same condition. It's called *sanpaku* eyes by the Japanese and means three whites. I learned that when I was stationed there. Not many people notice the irregularity. It's probably what makes you a good detective. You notice things others don't."

"If you could spare some time, Mr. Lenoir."

He glanced at the Rolex on his wrist. "I've got a photo shoot coming up."

"We'll try not to take too much of your time."

Lenoir nodded and gestured toward a set of three chairs near the desk.

Santana heard someone coming up the stairs. He glanced back and saw a tall blonde in heeled sandals, jeans, and a baggy sweatshirt. She paused at the entrance to the dressing room, an overnight case in one hand, her eyes staring intently at him.

"I'll be with you soon," Lenoir said to the woman.

She nodded and closed the door behind her.

Santana took a chair slightly to Lenoir's right, Hawkins to Lenoir's left. When they were all comfortably settled, Lenoir said, "Please tell me how Cata died."

"We're unsure at this time," Santana said. "Any information you provide might be helpful."

"I'll do whatever I can."

Santana retrieved his notebook and pen. "How well did you know Ms. Díaz?"

"Well, she worked as a model for me the last two years. I do a lot of photo shoots for magazine and catalogue advertising. I've also done some casting for stage production, film, and commercials."

As he was about to write in his notebook, Santana caught Hawkins watching Lenoir. Whenever Lenoir glanced at her, she would look away and pretend she was looking at something else. "Do you know of anyone who might want to harm Ms. Díaz?"

"Absolutely not. She was a terrific person and well liked by the other models." Lenoir held his eyes on Santana and then glanced at Hawkins.

"I understand Nina Rivera also models for you."

"Yes, she does. Nina is . . . I mean, *was* Cata's good friend. Have you spoken to her?"

"We have."

"I should call Nina," he said. "I'm sure she's upset."

Santana regarded the black and white photo on the corner of the desk. "You were in the Air Force, Mr. Lenoir?"

"Yes. I was stationed in Japan shortly after graduating from high school."

"Were you a pilot?"

"No, I worked as a mechanic, but I always had an interest in photography."

"How long have you owned the agency?"

"About fifteen years."

The model who had gone into the dressing room earlier came out and headed for the far end of the room, her lithe body wrapped in a short, white, tight-fitting terrycloth robe, her blond hair combed and touching her shoulders, her makeup and lipstick expertly applied.

Lenoir looked at his Rolex and stood. Santana and Hawkins did the same.

"I'm sorry, Detectives, but that's all the time I have now."

Santana handed Lenoir a business card.

Lenoir smiled good-naturedly and looked at Hawkins.

"We finished here, John?" she said. He nodded, and she headed for the staircase.

"Is your partner always this touchy?" Lenoir said, suppressing his amusement.

"Maybe she didn't like the way you looked at her and shook her hand when we were introduced."

"I was just flirting a little."

"Do it on your own time."

"Maybe I will," Lenoir said.

* * *

One hour later in the Homicide Unit, Hawkins swiveled her desk chair and said to Santana, "What's Cheese want to see you about?" Her eyes were fixed momentarily on the open door to Romano's office before returning to Santana's face.

"He didn't say, but I can guess."

She cocked her head. "The Díaz case?"

"Uh-huh."

"Instead of babysitting us, why doesn't he handle it himself?"

"Maybe I'll ask him."

"Do that," she said, and went back to her paperwork.

When Santana entered, Romano was leaning back in the swivel chair behind his desk, his hands clasped behind his head, his long white sleeves rolled up to his elbows, his eyes staring at the framed photos on his desk of his wife and five children.

"You wanted to see me."

Romano gestured at the lone chair in front of the desk. Santana sat down.

On the large white board attached to the wall behind Romano, Santana could see the open homicides written in red marker in one column. The name of the detective assigned to each case was written in red beside it. The most recent closed cases and the detectives credited with solving each were written in black in a second column to the right. That included solved cold cases whose investigations had become a larger part of the department's operational budget since the advent of DNA technology.

Romano unclasped his hands, sat forward, and placed his elbows on the desk. "Tell me what you've got on the Díaz case."

"Not much more than what I had when I talked to you yesterday," Santana said, trying to keep the sarcasm out of his voice.

Romano opened a file on the desktop in front of him and then a small spiral notebook. Santana couldn't believe that Romano was actually taking notes on the case, as if he were the investigating officer.

"Well, after reviewing your preliminary report, Detective, it seems to me that this is a case of accidental death from auto-erotic asphyxia."

"Don't you think it's a little early to draw that conclusion?"

"I had a similar case when I worked homicide. Usually the vic is nude, sexually exposed, maybe wearing clothing of the opposite sex, or dressed in sadomasochistic clothing if it's a male." He glanced at the notes in the file. "Semen is normally present on the victim, clothing, or ground. But since we're looking at a female here, we can ignore that."

"Forensics found some semen stains on the bedspread, Pete."

"Could belong to anyone."

"Novak is checking the CODIS database for a match."

Romano nodded. "He should. But let's assume the semen doesn't have anything to do with the vic's death. If you look at the profile, many of these scenes have sexually stimulating pictures lying around or displayed on walls to assist in the vic's fantasy. Sexual devices like dildos are often present. According to your report, there were pornographic movies playing on the television and a dildo in her vagina. The scene fits the profile."

"Doesn't mean her death was accidental. Someone could've staged it."

"So maybe she committed suicide."

"Why not just hang herself?"

"Well, I agree that suicide would be a questionable conclusion."

"And isn't autoerotic asphyxia usually acted out in an isolated or secluded location like a basement or closet in order to reach orgasm?"

"Usually," Romano said. He peered at his notes once more and then at Santana. "What about Philip Campbell?"

"We interviewed him."

"And?"

"He admitted he was with Díaz the night she died. We took a DNA sample. Forensics can compare it to the semen found on the bedspread or any found on her body."

Romano nodded and wrote in his notebook. After he'd finished, he peered at his notes for a while, as though he were re-reading what he'd written. Then he looked up and said, "What do you know about Campbell's background?"

"He's a well-known anesthesiologist in town."

"What about family?"

"He's divorced and has a couple of grown kids. And someone leaked his name to the press."

"Are you suggesting I did?"

"It wasn't Hawkins or me."

"Or me either," Romano said, his voice threaded with anger.

"Then who could it be?"

Romano's eyes darted back and forth as he considered an answer. "I have no idea, Detective."

Santana believed he was lying.

Romano took a breath as if to calm down and thought for a moment. "What's your impression of Campbell?"

"My impression is that this dance we're doing has nothing to do with the current case."

Romano dropped his pen on the desktop and stared at Santana with a hard edge in his eyes. "Meaning?"

"Are you planning to show up at every future homicide scene or just the ones I'm assigned?"

"I told you, I'm more hands-on than Gamboni."

"So you *are* planning to be at every homicide."

"It really shouldn't concern you."

"But it does. I think you're still upset about my last investigation."

Romano's complexion darkened. "And why is that?"

"Because two of the cases turned out to be murders and not accidental drownings. And you were originally the I/O on those cases."

"So now I'm looking for payback, is that what you think?"

"Why else would you be showing up at my crime scenes?"

Romano paused as his brain searched for a response. Finally, he said, "You're just being paranoid."

"I don't think so, Pete."

"Daily reports," he said, tapping the desktop with a thick index finger. "On my desk."

"I'll try."

"Don't try, Detective. Just do it."

Santana considered giving Romano the benefit of the doubt. Maybe he wasn't angry about the previous investigation. Maybe he just wanted a high homicide closure rate like Rita Gamboni had achieved as commander. Maybe appearing at departmental crime scenes was his way of offering assistance and support. But another possible reason troubled Santana, one that if true could rock the department and put his career on the line.

* * *

Not wanting to rehash the outcome of his meeting with Romano, Santana was relieved to see that Kacie Hawkins had left the unit when he returned to his desk. But he knew she would ask him about the meeting as soon as she saw him again.

He poured himself a cup of hot chocolate from his thermos and sat down at his desk in front of Tania Cruz's case file. Questions about her death had been crowding his mind ever since his interview with Sammy Malik and her mother. He'd pulled the murder book from the archives, knowing that he would never be satisfied till his questions had been answered.

The reports Nick Baker and Tim Branigan had filed six years ago were in chronological order and neatly typed. The preliminary report indicated that a friend had discovered Cruz's body in the victim's apartment. As in the case of Catalina Díaz, Tania Cruz had been naked and bound in a way that indicated she'd died of autoerotic asphyxiation. Santana skimmed the supplemental reports on the victim's prior arrests for prostitution and focused his attention on the details of the autopsy report.

Removal of the bungee cord around Tania Cruz's neck had revealed a ligature mark below the mandible. Reiko Tanabe had made a notation that this mark would be known throughout the report as Ligature A. It was approximately 1.5 inches wide and encircled the neck. Minor abrasions were present in the area of the ligature, but lack of hemorrhage surrounding it indicated the injury to be post-mortem. There was evidence of recent sexual activity. But no semen had been recovered from the vagina, and there was no indication that Cruz had been raped.

Following removal of her blouse, a second ligature mark, listed as ligature B, was observed on the victim's neck. The mark was dark red and encircled the neck, crossing the anterior midline just below the laryngeal prominence. Ligature B was not consistent with that which caused Ligature A. The absence of abrasions associated with Ligature B, along with the variations in the width of the ligature mark, were consistent with a soft ligature, such as a length of fabric. Trace evidence recovered from Ligature B indicated that it matched the silk scarf bound around the victim's waist. Subsequent autopsy revealed a fractured hyoid bone. Hemorrhaging from Ligature B had penetrated the skin and sub-dermal tissues of the neck.

There were ten autopsy photographs in the file, along with swabs taken from various body locations and samples of blood, bile, and tissue. Lab and drug screenings were negative.

The time of death was estimated to be between 9:30 p.m. and midnight. The immediate cause of death was listed as asphyxia due to ligature strangulation. Manner of death was listed as homicide.

In the remarks section of the report, Tanabe had noted that the decedent had originally been presented to her office as a victim of accidental death. However, the presence of the post-mortem ligature mark suggested that accidental death in this case was highly improbable. SPPD detectives were notified of her finding immediately upon conclusion of examination.

Based on the evidence that strangulation had occurred after death, and that there had been no conclusive evidence of rape, Santana reached the same conclusion as the ME. Someone had attempted to disguise the crime by making it look like an accidental death.

Next, Santana reviewed the summary reports of the interviews conducted during the investigation with residents of the apartment building where Tania Cruz had lived, and with her friends and acquaintances. Two names in the report caught his eye.

Paul Lenoir and Nina Rivera.

Tania Cruz had worked as a model for Lenoir's agency. Nina Rivera was identified as a friend of Cruz. She'd pointed Baker in the direction of an illegal immigrant named Arias Marchena. He'd worked as a custodian at the modeling agency. According to Rivera, Marchena had made suggestive remarks to Cruz and had asked her out. She'd refused and had told Rivera that she considered him to be "creepy."

Marchena had had no alibi for the time of Cruz's death and had a deep fingernail scratch across his cheek. A DNA swab taken from him was later matched to tissue cells found under Cruz's fingernails. Marchena had been arrested, charged, tried, and convicted of her murder and sentenced to twelve years in Stillwater prison.

* * *

Nick Baker lived in a small one-and-a-half story stucco-sided bungalow in a quiet residential neighborhood near Lake Como in St. Paul, not far from the Como Zoo. The house had a low-pitched roof with a wide overhang and a protruding enclosed porch that stretched partway across its width. A large willow tree grew in the front yard, but the stumps of two ash trees that had been cut down due to the emerald ash borer infestation were all that remained of the trees along the curb.

As Santana walked up the sidewalk and rang the doorbell, his mind was still back at the station with Tania Cruz's autopsy report.

"Hey, John!" Baker said, pushing open the screen door. "Long time no see." A big smile spread across Baker's face as they shook hands. "Come on in. Hope you don't mind the mess. The housekeeper only comes once a month. You off the clock?"

Santana nodded.

"How 'bout a beer?"

"Sounds good."

Santana sat on a worn fabric couch in the small living room while Baker went into the kitchen. An ashtray on the coffee table was filled with crushed cigarette butts, the smell of smoke still lingering in the stale air.

A silver-framed photo of Baker and his wife, Carol, sat on an end table beside the couch. In it, Baker's hair and mustache were not yet white, and Santana saw no sign of the age marks that currently spotted the retired detective's face.

Santana had visited the house on occasion when Baker was still with the department. He remembered that Carol had always kept a very clean home and had never allowed her husband to smoke indoors. Now the smoking ban had been lifted, a housekeeper came once a month, and the place looked as though it hadn't been cleaned in weeks. Something had happened.

Baker came into the living room with two cans of Michelob Golden Draft. His six-foot frame was noticeably thinner since he'd retired. He handed a can to Santana. "Didn't have time to pick up some Sam Adams," he said. "I know it's your favorite."

"This'll do just fine, Nick." Santana raised his can in a toast. "To old times." They drank.

Baker sat across from Santana in what looked like a newly purchased black leather recliner. He noticed Santana looking at the framed photo of Carol. "I miss her," he said, his eyes tearing.

"When did she die?"

"You didn't know?"

Santana shook his head. "Not until I walked in here today."

"You were in the hospital with the gunshot wound, John. I figured someone told you. But you had enough to worry about at the time."

"I'm sorry, Nick."

Baker drank some beer and wiped his eyes with the back of a hand. "Heart attack. She went quickly. Only sixty-two. Thought we'd have more time together after I retired. But I've got a couple of grandchildren that keep me busy. Refrigerator door is filled with pictures." He smiled at the thought.

In the uncomfortable conversational lull that followed, Santana could hear the ticking of a grandfather clock.

"You said on the phone, John, that you thought the Tania Cruz murder case might be connected to a current investigation."

Santana nodded, thankful that Baker had initiated a different conversation. "The crime scene photos in her murder book were remarkably similar to Catalina Díaz's scene. And the methodology with the bungee cords, the presence of a silk scarf, and position of the body were virtually the same."

Baker drank some beer before answering. "Problem is, the guy who murdered Tania Cruz is doing a twelve year stretch in Stillwater Prison on a second degree murder charge."

"Arias Marchena."

"Uh-huh. And once he's finished doing his time, he'll be deported back to Costa Rica."

"Catalina Díaz and Tania Cruz were both from Costa Rica."

"Lot of coincidences."

Santana could see the inquisitive gleam in Baker's eyes. *Once a detective, always a detective*, he thought. "You figure Marchena was good for it, Nick?"

"Tough to dismiss his skin cells under her fingernails and the DNA match. Plus, he worked at the modeling agency where Cruz was employed. Marchena had talked to her on numerous occasions. A friend of hers testified that he'd made suggestive remarks about Cruz in the past."

"Nina Rivera."

"Right. Plus, Marchena had no alibi for the time of the murder."

"But you didn't answer my question, Nick. Do you think he was good for it?"

Baker shrugged. "You know how you get a sense of the perp, John. Everything pointed to Marchena, but it never felt right."

"Why?"

"I hate to say he wasn't the type, 'cause you know that's a crock of shit. Sometimes the weakest looking, church-going nerd can be a cold-blooded killer. Marchena always claimed he was innocent. But you ask most cons and they're going to deny guilt. Still, if there was ever a guy I thought was innocent, despite the evidence, it was Marchena."

"You worked the Cruz case with Tim Branigan."

"I did. Not too long after that he was promoted to commander of the Narco/Vice Unit. Three years later, he's behind the desk in the AC's office."

"Did Branigan feel the same way as you did about Marchena?"

"Not that I remember."

"There were no eyewitness statements in the file, Nick."

"Because we couldn't find any. Nina Rivera got worried when she couldn't get ahold of Cruz. She convinced Cruz's landlord to open the door. Cruz had been dead for two days."

"Was she hooking?"

"Definitely."

"Working the streets?"

Baker shook his head. "She was using her website and craigslist before they shut down the adult section."

"Who defended Marchena?"

"Alvarado Vega."

Santana made a mental note. "Vega doesn't lose many cases."

"You got that right."

"The name Philip Campbell ever surface in your investigation?"

Baker thought for few seconds and then shook his head. "Not that I recall."

"You discover the names of any of her clients, Nick?"

"No one wanted to talk much about her."

"How come?"

"I think they were afraid."

"Of what?"

"Someone," he said.

"Anyone from the department ever try and get you to back off the Cruz investigation, Nick?"

75

His hazel eyes narrowed. "Not that I remember. Why do you ask?"

"Just covering all the bases."

Baker leaned forward and rested his forearms on his knees, the beer can still in his hand. But the gleam had gone out of his eyes now. "What are you thinking, John?"

"Bad things," Santana said. "Very bad things."

Chapter 7

The next morning Santana drove to Stillwater prison to see Arias Marchena, the man convicted of murdering Tania Cruz six years earlier. The prison was the state's largest close-security, level four institution for adult male felons. It was actually located in Bayport, a small town a mile south of Stillwater, on the St. Croix River. A smaller Supermax facility at Oak Park Heights two and a half miles away housed level five male offenders—those classified as extreme risks to the public—transferred primarily from other institutions.

A column of white smoke billowed from the tall smoke stack at the X-cel energy power plant across the road from the prison and rose toward the dome of gray and black clouds covering the sky. Santana parked along the curb in front of the main entrance and went up the steps and into the building through the two glass doors. He left his gun with the turnkey and was escorted through a metal detector and into the visitor's area, then through a door near the back of the room and into the non-contact area, where he could meet privately with Arias Marchena.

Santana sat on a stool facing a wall of Plexiglas and waited until a correctional officer brought Marchena through a door on the other side of the glass. Marchena wore the standard state-issue attire: white T-shirt, denim trousers, and tennis shoes, the clothing hanging on his bony shoulders as though on a wire hanger. He shuffled to the stool and sat silently until the CO exited and closed the door behind him. Santana picked up the telephone handset on his side of the glass and waited for Marchena to do the same.

As a child, Santana had vacationed with his parents once in Liberia near the Pacific coast of Costa Rica, before it became a booming tourist attraction. He remembered that the *Ticos*, as Costa Ricans were called, were a very polite and happy people. But the eyes that looked through the glass at him now were as dark and as empty as a gun barrel. A long, thin, pink scar on Marchena's pale skin extended from just below his left eye to the corner of his mouth.

"What do you want?" he asked, his voice a harsh whisper, his gaze direct and glaring.

"*Hablar.*"

Marchena hesitated and rubbed the short dark hair on his head. "Talk about what?"

"Tania Cruz."

His eyes roved over Santana's face. "*¿De dónde eres?*"

"Colombia. And we can speak in Spanish or English. Whatever you prefer."

"Why do you want to talk about Tania Cruz?" Marchena said, continuing to speak in Spanish.

"Because I am investigating the death of someone who died in a similar manner. A woman named Catalina Díaz."

"You are a homicide detective?"

Santana nodded.

"Well, I did not kill this Díaz woman." He punctuated the reply with a short, bitter laugh. "Unless you think I leave here at night."

"You claim you did not kill Tania Cruz either."

"What does it matter now?" Marchena said with a shake of his head. "I am here and the one who killed Tania Cruz is free. Perhaps the same one who killed this Díaz woman."

"Did you ever meet Catalina Díaz?"

"Why do you ask this question when I could not have killed her?"

"I am not trying to implicate you in her death, Mr. Marchena. I am trying to establish connections."

"Then do it on your own time," he said, starting to rise. "And quit wasting mine."

"Maybe you did not kill Tania Cruz," Santana said. He had no evidence suggesting Marchena wasn't guilty, but he needed to offer him something, even if it might be false hope.

Marchena stood by his stool, the phone still pressed against his ear, and stared at Santana. "Don't jerk me around," he said, switching to English.

"I'm asking the same of you. Sit down and answer my questions. Right now, I may be your only hope of getting out of here."

The CO opened the door. "You finished here?"

Santana looked at Marchena. "Are we?"

After some thought, Marchena lowered himself onto the stool again.

"Give us a few more minutes," Santana said.

The CO nodded and closed the door again.

"Tania Cruz and Catalina Díaz were both from Costa Rica, like you. And they were both involved in prostitution."

"I never was with Cruz," Marchena said.

"But your DNA was found under her fingernails."

"I don't know how it got there."

"What about that scar on your cheek? It looks like it could have come from a fingernail."

"It did. I was mugged the night before Cruz was killed. The jury never believed me. They thought Cruz had scratched me."

"I take it you couldn't identify the mugger?"

"It was dark."

79

"Did you ever meet a man named Philip Campbell?"

Marchena shook his head.

"What about Paul Lenoir?"

"Yes. He owned the modeling agency where Tania worked, and where I was a custodian."

Santana had wanted to get a sense of Arias Marchena. He knew the man staring at him was not the same man that Nick Baker had remembered from six years ago. Santana believed the man he saw now was fully capable of committing murder. Whether that impression was due to Marchena's time in prison or his nature, he couldn't be sure.

"Okay," Santana said.

"Okay what?"

Santana stood. "I'll get back to you."

"You going to get me out of here?"

"If you're innocent."

"You have to get me out, Santana." He pressed a palm against the glass. The CO quickly came out from behind the door and grabbed Marchena by the elbow. "I have to get out."

Marchena's eyes had the desperate look of a man who believed death was coming—and very soon.

* * *

After leaving Stillwater prison, Santana drove to the Hindu temple on the outskirts of Maple Grove, a suburb west of Minneapolis, an hour's drive from the prison. The large white temple stood like a lonely sentinel under the dark gray sky amid vast soybean fields and silos. Pre-cast concrete panels on the building's exterior reminded Santana of the ancient stone temples he'd seen in photos of India. A ceremonial gateway topped with hand-carved stucco figurines marked the transition into the temple.

A long processional concrete path passed through a secular one-story wing of the building and led to a lobby, where a middle-aged, attractive woman approached Santana. In her bare feet, she moved with the easy grace of a cat.

She shook his hand and offered a warm, friendly smile. "I'm Indira Khan, the woman you spoke to on the phone. It's very nice to meet you, Detective Santana. I hope I can be of help."

"I'm sure you can."

She wore a red and orange patterned silk sari and a pair of gold bangles on each forearm. She had a *bindi*, or perfectly round drop of red vermillion powder, between her eyebrows and a powdered red line, a *sindoor*, on the middle part of her long black hair, signifying that she was married.

"Would you like to see the temple first, before we begin?"

"I would," he said.

He followed her through two glass doors on the opposite side of the lobby.

"You can leave your shoes in the coat room," she said.

"How about my socks?"

She smiled. "You can wear them if you'd like."

Santana removed his shoes but left his socks on. Then he followed her up a long set of stairs leading to the main temple and its gleaming tile floor.

Mini-temples lined all four walls of the expansive room. Each temple had elaborate carvings and designs and was set off by its own ceiling and floor pattern, hand-carved columns, and skylight. The tallest one nearly touched the ceiling. Santana guessed it was close to fifty feet high.

"The temples are beautiful," he said.

"Thank you. There are twenty-one in the hall. Many are replicas of famous temples in India. Each is dedicated to a different Hindu god. It's a diplomatic way of managing the tangled politics of religion."

"I've lived in Minnesota for many years and never realized there was a Hindu temple here."

"Where did you live before coming to Minnesota?"

"Colombia."

"You were born there?"

"Yes."

"Well, this temple was completed only a few years ago," she said. "It serves the thirty thousand Hindus who live in and around the cities."

"I guess I didn't realize there were that many Hindus here either."

"We've had to make some building adaptations due to the weather, as I'm sure you've made coming from Colombia."

"I've made quite a few."

She made a sweeping gesture with a hand. "This temple is one of the largest Hindu places of worship in North America. In keeping with Vedic guidelines, architects oriented the entrance to face east and set it on the highest point of the site. Now, if you'll follow me, we can find a place to talk."

She led him down the stairs again, where Santana retrieved his shoes, and then across the lobby to a small conference room located in the secular wing of the building. A round table sat in the center of the room, surrounded by bookshelves and pictures of divinities on the walls. The blinds on the window facing the lobby were closed.

Indira Khan sat across the table from him. "How much do you know about Hinduism, Detective Santana?"

"Not much."

"Well, there is a great deal of misinformation and ignorance about Hinduism among the general population."

"Such as?"

"There's no concept of conversion. Hinduism preaches acceptance of all other faiths, not simply tolerance. We believe in oneness and equality of all, regardless of the age, gender, race, or ethnicity. Each soul is free to find his or her own spiritual path."

"What about heaven and hell?"

"Hindus believe there is a divine spirit, but no eternal hell or damnation. Contentment comes in understanding the true nature of the self."

"And how does one discover one's true self?"

"Through truth, consciousness, and bliss."

"Can't argue with that," he said. "What about karma?"

"Ah, yes, karma. It is the one concept that most non-Hindus are familiar with. The belief that one's current position is a natural consequence of her or his past actions in the present life and the many before."

If there was such a thing as karma, Santana wondered what he'd done in a previous life that had led to the problems he'd experienced in this one.

"Hindus believe that the soul survives after death until it enters a new body," she continued.

"Reincarnation is really what I've come to talk to you about," he said.

"Are you a believer?"

"I'm afraid not."

She nodded as though she'd expected the answer. "Well, you're in the majority, Detective Santana. But the idea that our mind or soul continues after we die is certainly appealing for many, regardless of their faith."

"It's a comforting thought," Santana said. "But difficult to prove."

"Very true. Though William James once remarked that our desire to believe in survival after death does not automatically negate its possibility. Wouldn't you agree?"

"Perhaps if people focused more on doing the right thing in this life instead of wondering about the next, it would make my job easier. Might even put me out of business."

She smiled. "Would it surprise you to learn that many of us who believe in reincarnation would prefer not to?"

"Why?"

"For us, life is as fleeting and illusory as a dream, a constant cycle of births and deaths in which we are doomed to struggle and suffer until we have reached perfection and can finally escape."

"And how might you reach perfection?"

"By letting go of the desire to be reborn or to be in a body, which, sadly, can never bring lasting happiness or peace. The true self is the immortal soul and not the body and the ego that seeks the pleasures of the world. Only when we let go of earthly desires can the soul attain happiness and peace by realizing our souls are part of God."

"Any idea as to why your culture has so many more reported cases of reincarnation than the West?"

"It may be because we have more time to reflect on our lives and remember our dead more than western societies. We have strong family ties. To us there is no such thing as random fate. Everything happens for a reason, and that reason often has to do with someone who wishes us well or harm. We also believe much more than the West in telepathy, the paranormal, and that dreams foretell the future."

I can identify with that, Santana thought.

"But I doubt that surviving death is what inspired your interest in reincarnation, Detective Santana."

"My primary interest stems from a case I'm working. During the course of my investigation, a woman not connected to the case brought her daughter to see me. She struck me as a remarkable child. The woman told me that before her daughter was born, the little girl had lived as a woman named Tania Cruz."

"And you believed the mother?"

He shook his head.

"Yet here you are."

"The little girl was very . . . convincing."

84

"So you believe she is telling the truth."

"At least as she sees it. But there are connections. Tania Cruz was murdered six years ago in the same manner as the woman in the case I'm currently investigating. And the child knew things about the murder that only Cruz or the perpetrator would know."

"The perpetrator was never found."

"He was."

"Then I don't understand the problem."

"There's a possibility that the man thought to be the perpetrator isn't. I want to be sure."

Indira Khan nodded her head slowly.

"I was hoping you might shed some light on cases of reincarnation."

She sat silent and still for a time before speaking. "Most children who talk about a past life are very intelligent. They begin talking about it at a very early age, typically between the ages of two and four. How old is the child?"

"Six."

She nodded again. "The lives that children describe tend to be very recent ones. The median time between the death of the previous personality and the birth of the subject is generally fifteen to sixteen months. Exceptions do exist, of course. Almost all the children describe only one previous life. Most stop talking about the past life around the age of six or seven and go on to lead normal lives."

"Seems sort of pointless, then, doesn't it?"

"I don't understand."

"Well, suppose that reincarnation were true. Wouldn't it be important to remember a past life or lives, so that you could improve upon this one? Not make the same mistakes you made before. But if you can't remember anything after the age of six or seven, then might we not make the same mistakes all over again?"

After a long silence Indira Kahn replied. "Perhaps forgetting is essential to successfully living in the present, Detective Santana. If we always were to remember how we failed in the past, whether in relationships or occupations, we may be too fearful to try again. People may say they envy children who remember previous lives, as if these children had special wisdom. In fact, it makes more sense to look upon them as suffering from an abnormality, almost a defect. The memories they have are often more of a handicap than a blessing. Nearly all of them become happier as they grow older and forget their previous lives."

Santana looked at his notes. "The little girl had a birthmark on her neck."

"Many children describe the way they died in their previous life, and many of the deaths are described as violent or sudden. Birthmarks or birth defects that match wounds on the body of the previous person are very common. Many are not small discolorations but are often unusual in shape or size and are often puckered or raised rather than simply flat. And they are noticeable immediately after birth."

"The little girl's birthmark is like that," Santana said. "Very unusual. And as crazy as it sounds, her birthmark appears to match the marks recorded in Tania Cruz's autopsy report."

"Given my experiences and belief, that doesn't sound crazy to me at all."

"No offense meant."

"None taken, Detective. Some children mimic the occupation of the previous personality and some act out the death scene from the previous life," Indira Kahn continued. "Phobias are also common. Many children have an intense fear related to the method of the previous personality's death. And children frequently remember or seem to recognize members of the previous family."

Santana recalled Sarah Malik mentioning that Sammy had a fear of plastic bags. "Has a belief in reincarnation made any difference?" he asked.

"How do you mean?"

"You still have crime in India and amongst Hindus."

"Unfortunately, yes. We have as many criminals in India as you have in the West."

Santana's cell phone buzzed. He recognized the number. "Excuse me. I have to take this call. What's up, Kacie?"

"Where are you?"

"I'll explain later. Why?"

"Philip Campbell apparently took his own life," Hawkins said. "Gunshot to the head."

Chapter 8

Yellow crime scene tape was strung across the sidewalk leading to Philip Campbell's south Minneapolis home. Santana and Hawkins showed their badges to one of the uniforms manning the area and signed their names on the Crime Scene Attendance Log an officer held on a clipboard.

"We're looking for Detective Reynolds," Santana said.

The uniform gestured toward the house, and Santana and Hawkins slipped under the tape. Near the front door, they placed each foot separately into a Bootie Box containing protective shoe coverings before gloving up and stepping inside the house.

Philip Campbell was slumped to his right in a cushioned chair facing a brick fireplace in the living room. His chin rested on his chest, his left hand in his lap. His right arm extended over the arm of the chair. A .22 caliber, five-shot mini-revolver with a red and black wood-grained grip lay on the carpet just beneath his right hand.

"Bullet's probably still in the skull."

Santana looked to his left at the sound of the voice and saw a heavy-set, jowly man in a checkered sport coat approaching. The man moved purposefully, but with wearied effort.

"You Reynolds?"

The man nodded. He looked at each of the detectives and then let his gray eyes wander to the body. "Doubt we'll get any

GSR because of the small caliber. But it looks like Dr. Campbell blew out his brains."

Santana squatted so he could get a better look at the circular wound in Campbell's right temple. The wound had ragged, blackened, and seared margins, but didn't have the stellate appearance typically found in higher caliber contact wounds to the head.

He stood. "Not much noise with a small caliber."

"Nope," Reynolds said. "We canvassed the neighborhood. But no one heard the shot."

Santana was thinking the noise factor was the reason .22 caliber revolvers were frequently used for mob hits. If the killer could get close to his target, even though it was a pretty weak cartridge, it was very effective. Up close, a .22 caliber bullet would penetrate the skull but usually wouldn't come out. Instead, it often spun around the curved interior of the skull, creating massive damage and assuring almost instant death.

"Who found the body?" Hawkins asked.

"Campbell was supposed to meet a friend for lunch. When he didn't show, the friend stopped by. Front door was unlocked, so he came in and discovered the body."

"Who's the friend?"

"A man named Matthew Singer."

Santana looked at Hawkins, whose eyebrows were raised in recognition. Matthew Singer was one of the names on the list Santana had found in the hidden drawer in Catalina Díaz's bedroom.

"Is Singer still here?" Santana asked.

Reynolds shook his head. "No reason to detain him."

"Kind of odd that Campbell would plan to meet a friend for lunch and then kill himself."

"Hey," Reynolds said. "When you make up your mind to off yourself, you don't worry about missing lunch."

"Any suicide note?" Hawkins asked.

"Not that we found. But you know most suicides don't leave notes." Reynolds hiked up his trousers and said to Santana, "So what's your interest in Campbell?"

"We interviewed him the other day regarding the death of an escort in a hotel room."

"Well, there you go. Campbell murdered the hooker. When you questioned him, he figured it was only a matter of time before he went down for it and decided to check out."

"Maybe," Santana said.

"No maybes about it. Let's not make a federal case out of this, Santana. Besides, Campbell had a thing for escorts."

"How so?"

"I found a brochure in his bedroom for a resort in Costa Rica called Erotic Tours. They provide hookers while you're vacationing."

"You get a phone number?"

Reynolds gave it to him.

"You run the gun's serial number through NCIC?" Hawkins asked.

"We will," Reynolds said with a little laugh. "We're not a bunch of amateurs on this side of the river, you know. But then, we don't have the reputations that you and your partner have."

"And what reputation is that?" Santana asked.

"You're closers."

"Really?"

Reynolds nodded.

Hawkins stepped closer to Reynolds. "How's your clearance rate?"

"Just fine, Detective. But don't you worry. You'll be able to wrap up the hooker murder real quick. Keep your reputations intact."

"Yeah," Hawkins said. "Our reputations have always been our primary concern."

Reynolds was about to respond when Santana cut him off. "We'd like a copy of Campbell's phone records."

Reynolds looked at him blankly.

"You were planning on running Campbell's cell phone records and the landline record as well, if he has one?"

Reynolds nodded. "You bet," he said.

* * *

Back at the station later that afternoon, Hawkins swiveled her chair so that she was facing Santana.

"What did Cheese want to see you about yesterday?"

"He thinks Díaz's death was accidental. And he denied leaking Campbell's name to the press."

"If it wasn't Romano, then who's the leak?"

"I don't know, Kacie."

"What's your take on Campbell's suicide?"

"Convenient."

"I agree. But we've got no evidence indicating he was murdered. And with the MPD in charge of the case, it's going down as a suicide."

"Unless Reynolds finds something to the contrary."

"How's he going to do that, John, when he isn't looking? And what's with the bullshit at Campbell's house?"

"Detectives don't like other departments meddling in their investigations."

"How were we meddling?"

"Just by being there."

"Jesus," she said, with an angry shake of her head. "We wouldn't act that way with a detective from the MPD."

"Wouldn't we?"

Hawkins smiled and shrugged. "Well, we might, but only if the detective was an asshole. And Reynolds sure qualifies."

Santana thought there might be something more than territorial issues behind Reynolds' attitude toward them. It was an attitude Santana had come to expect from even those within his own department. He and Hawkins were treated differently, but not because they were minorities. Rather, they had been wounded in the line of duty and survived. For that, they were mostly admired and respected, particularly by the younger officers and detectives. But the light of admiration and respect he saw in his older colleagues' eyes had been shadowed with jealousy and resentment. He'd seen something similar in the eyes of those who'd never served in battle when told of someone's war experiences.

Santana understood the conflicted feelings of his fellow officers in the way only someone who had an intimate relationship with death could understand. Many wanted a chance to perform a heroic act, to look into the eyes of death, to survive the sharp cut of the Grim Reaper's scythe. But like those who had served in battle, Santana had to live with the physical and emotional scars of violence and death, scars that those who wished for a similar fate could never understand.

"Reynolds is probably competent enough," Santana said. "I'll give him the benefit of the doubt. If he turns up something, I think he'll let us know. Regardless, we've got to work Catalina Díaz's death from our side of the river. If Campbell did her, then we have no problem."

"And if not?"

"Then we'll have to find out who did, no matter what Reynolds or anyone else thinks."

"I talked with Brian Howard's ex-wife," Hawkins said. "I got the sense that she doesn't have any feelings left for him, but no great animosity either."

"Let's keep him on our radar, Kacie. You have a chance to look at the hotel security tapes?"

"Nothing definitive there, John. Cameras cover the lobby and pool area, not the hallways. If we get photos of each of the men on the list, I could compare them with the guests in the lobby."

Santana's cell phone rang. He recognized the ME's number.

"Have you met with Romano yet about Catalina Díaz's autopsy?" Reiko Tanabe asked.

"No. Why?"

"He phoned me yesterday and wanted a copy of her autopsy report. I told him I was sending the report to you."

"But he wanted it first."

"Correct," she said. "I'll e-mail you a copy right now."

"Anything interesting?"

"Looks like an accidental death, John."

Once Romano read the autopsy report, he'd want the case closed and off the board. But Santana felt he was missing something, something that could connect Tania Cruz's murder with the death of Catalina Díaz. And until he knew what that something was, he could not let either case go.

"Is there a way that someone could've strangled Díaz and not left any external marks, Reiko?"

"It's possible if the perp used the palm of the hand to apply downward pressure to the neck, compressing the blood vessels. In the cases I've seen, the vic was unconscious, usually from alcohol intoxication, and wouldn't struggle."

"Isn't sphincter incontinence a characteristic of strangulation?"

"Yes, but it's not an absolute finding. Unless I have something more concrete, I have to rule Díaz's death as accidental."

"Okay. Thanks for the heads up, Reiko."

Santana waited for Catalina Díaz's autopsy report. When he got it, he printed a copy. Then he sat down at his desk again and carefully read it.

An examination of the neck had revealed a pale ligature mark above the larynx, 5x1cm wide, with mottled looking hemorrhages of the right neck lymphatics. Similar elastic strap marks were evident on the body along with binding marks visible on the neck. No evidence of erythematous marks, contusions, or fingernail marks common in manual strangulation was detected. The skull was intact, but the thyroid cartilage in Díaz's neck had been fractured. No fractures of the hyoid bone, usually seen in cases of strangulation, were detected. No lubricants had been spread over the plastic bag. Tanabe had detected no injuries to the anus, and no fingernail marks at or around the neck suggesting she'd tried to escape the ligature. There was no evidence of defensive wounds or any other injuries on her body.

Díaz had widespread petechial hemorrhaging in her eyes. Santana knew petechiae often occurred in cases of sexual assault, but Tanabe had found no evidence supporting that conclusion. No psychoactive substances had been found in the blood and no semen in the vagina, which made sense if the perp had used a condom. Tanabe had considered the possibility that the small vaginal abrasion could have been caused by a forcible attempt at sexual intercourse or an attempted penetration with an inanimate object such as the dildo. But there was no way to determine what had caused the injury with any degree of certainty.

Tanabe estimated the TOD to be between midnight and five a.m. The cool room temperature had slowed decomposition, making the estimate more difficult. Philip Campbell had stated that he'd left the room at one a.m., which meant he certainly could have killed Díaz. But based on an analysis of the death scene, an external examination, and forensic and psychological autopsy findings, Tanabe had concluded that Catalina Díaz had died of accidental autoerotic asphyxiation caused by neck strangulation and suffocation with a plastic bag.

Santana had just finished reading the report when he and Hawkins were called into Pete Romano's office.

They sat in cushioned hardback chairs placed strategically in front of Romano's desk, facing the commander.

Romano pointed to the manila folder on the desktop. "I've got the ME's report on Catalina Díaz. Accidental death by autoerotic asphyxia."

He stood, erased Catalina Díaz's name from the red UN-SOLVED column, and rewrote it in black in the SOLVED column to the right. Placing the eraser in the metal lip of the whiteboard again, he turned and faced the two detectives, a smile on his lips. "Good to get that first one out of the way, even if it wasn't a homicide."

He sat down again, placed his elbows on the desk, and clasped his hands. His expression was that of a satisfied man.

Santana could feel Hawkins staring at him, waiting for him to object. "You might be jumping the gun, Pete," he said, making sure he kept the emotion out of his voice.

Romano's expression quickly changed to skepticism. "Do you and Detective Hawkins have evidence indicating Díaz was murdered?"

"We know she was with Philip Campbell the night she died."

"The doctor who committed suicide."

"Yes. And by the way, thanks for running interference for us with your counterpart at the MPD."

Hawkins let Santana know that she was aware of his phony attempt at praise by clearing her throat. *Whatever works*, he thought.

"No problem," Romano said.

"I think there might be."

Romano cocked his head. "What do you mean?"

"If Catalina Díaz's death was accidental, why would Campbell kill himself?"

Romano gave it some thought. Finally, he said, "We might never know exactly what happened that night. But unless you have evidence to the contrary, I'm agreeing with the ME's ruling and taking Díaz's name off the board."

"What about the list of apostles?" Hawkins said.

Santana's heart skipped a beat.

"What list?" Romano asked.

Santana had had no intention of revealing the list to Romano until he had something concrete. But now that Hawkins had mentioned it, he had to respond.

"When we searched Díaz's condo, I found this." Santana handed Romano the copy he'd made.

Romano unfolded the paper and peered at it. "What's this?"

"We think it's a list of her clients."

Romano raised his chin and looked at each of the detectives. "But Hawkins called it a list of apostles."

"Same first names, Pete. We've spoken with Campbell. Singer found Campbell's body."

Romano peered at the list again and then at Santana. "Did you ask Campbell about the list?"

"Yes."

Romano raised his heavy eyebrows and waited.

"He never admitted knowing the other men."

"What about Singer?"

"I haven't spoken to him yet."

Romano held his palms out and shrugged. "Then we don't know exactly what we have here, Detectives—and if it means anything at all."

"The list was well hidden," Hawkins said.

Romano looked at her for a long time. Then his gaze shifted to Santana. "I'd like a copy, Detective."

"What for?"

"Because I want a copy."

"All right."

"Before tomorrow."

"What about Díaz?"

Romano made a hitchhiking motion with his thumb. "Her name stays in the solved cases column. But go ahead and talk to Singer. See if it leads anywhere. And I want those daily reports I haven't been getting."

"I'll get them to you," Santana said.

"Make sure that you do."

Chapter 9

Matthew Singer lived in a large Italianate-style home in the Crocus Hill neighborhood near downtown St. Paul. Built by the wealthy robber barons that founded the city, the neighborhood of large homes and stately mansions was a testament to the excesses of the Gilded Age.

The study had dark mahogany paneled walls, shelves filled with thick medical texts, a red oak floor, and a heavy smell of vanilla blend tobacco. Singer opened one of the stained-glass windows and then faced Santana, who was seated on the leather couch, spiral notebook and pen in hand.

"Could I get you something to drink, Detective?"

"I'm fine. Thanks."

Singer went to a small liquor cabinet in a corner and poured himself a glass of Jameson Vintage Reserve Irish whiskey over ice. Then he settled his lean frame into a leather recliner near the fireplace, smoke from his briar pipe swirling in the air above his close-cropped black hair that was salted with gray. His small, dark eyes were set under a hard brow, and a thin slash of a mouth was nearly hidden by the thick, graying mustache under his sharply ridged nose.

"This was the only place my wife let me smoke my pipes," he said with a nostalgic smile. "Still, I always had to open a window. She's been gone for nearly three years now," he said, a note of melancholy in his voice. "But old habits die hard."

"She must've died young."

He nodded. "She was forty-seven. Died of brain cancer."

Santana thought of Nick Baker's late wife, Carol, and how she'd felt about Nick's smoking in the house. Then he gestured toward the two dozen pipes displayed in the red oak cabinet mounted on the wall next to a roll-top desk. "My father was a pipe smoker. He had quite a collection as well."

Singer drank some whiskey and stared at the cabinet, as though he hadn't realized it was there. "Not many men smoke a pipe nowadays," he said, setting the cocktail glass gently on a coaster on the end table beside him. "I find the practice very relaxing, though I know what you're thinking, Detective."

"Do you?"

"Sure," he said, with a wry smile. "Doctors shouldn't be smoking. But I started in college and was never able to stop completely. Probably shouldn't be drinking either."

"You grow up in the Twin Cities, Dr. Singer?"

"In St. Paul. My father worked for the state health department. Probably why I developed an interest in medicine, though I chose to specialize in plastic surgery."

Santana pointed to the large blue and silver fish mounted on the wall behind the bar. "That's a black marlin, isn't it?"

"A ten-footer. Very few can tell the difference between a blue and black marlin, Detective. I'm impressed."

"I fished with my father off the Pacific coast of Costa Rica when I was young."

"Costa Rica has some of the best sport fishing in the world," Singer said, his face creasing as he smiled. "I caught that marlin off the coast of the Guanacaste Province. Tough shipping it home, though. The pectoral fins on an adult black marlin are rigid and can't be folded flat against the body. I had the fins shipped unattached and then reattached them with a nut and washer after I hung it on the wall."

"Mind if I take a closer look?"

"Be my guest."

Santana stood and walked to the wall where the fish was mounted. He was more interested in the framed color photo hanging beside the black marlin than the fish itself. He pretended to look at it and then let his eyes wander to the photo of three men standing on a dock beside the same marlin, which was hanging upside down from a hook.

Santana recognized Matthew Singer and Philip Campbell, but not the third man. He was a few inches taller and darker complected.

Turning to Singer, Santana said, "Were you and Philip Campbell with a fishing guide?"

Singer stared at the mounted fish as though reliving the day he'd caught it. Then he turned his attention to Santana again and let out a small laugh. "No, Detective. That's Nathaniel Burdette."

Santana felt his heartbeat kick up a notch. He peered at the photo again, hoping Singer hadn't noticed his reaction. Nathaniel Burdette was the third name on Catalina Díaz's apostle list. When he'd regained control of his emotions, Santana looked at Singer again. "What does Mr. Burdette do for a living?"

"He's a plastic surgeon at our clinic."

"And what clinic is that?"

"The Genesis Clinic in St. Paul."

"You said 'our' clinic, Dr. Singer."

"Yes. Philip, Nathaniel and I own it."

Santana waited for more details, but Singer offered none.

A second framed photo hanging on the wall showed Singer in a bar with his arm around a pretty young woman. She wore a blue T-shirt with the words "Blue Marlin" stitched in large white letters across the front.

"I understand Costa Rica is quite a magnet for single men looking for female companionship."

Singer's eyes remained locked on Santana's. "I'd love to discuss big-game fishing, tobacco pipes, and the night-life in Costa Rica with you, Detective, but you're here to talk about Philip's death." He smiled.

"I appreciate your cooperation."

"It's no problem," Singer said with a wave. "I'm just saddened that Philip took his own life."

Santana returned to his seat. "Did Campbell strike you as suicidal?"

"Well, he was in considerable pain. He had a horrible skiing accident a few months ago in Vail. The leg wasn't healing well. He'd been somewhat depressed of late."

"How long had you known him?"

"Since medical school."

"He was one of your classmates?"

"Yes, he was."

"Was Nathaniel Burdette one of your classmates as well?"

Singer's dark eyebrows arched momentarily in surprise. "Yes, he was. We all had an interest in big-game fishing."

And probably escorts, Santana thought.

Singer drank more whiskey and set the glass on the table again. "You do realize I've spoken with Detective Reynolds about Philip's death."

"I know he talked with you. But I'm not here specifically about that."

"Then what is your interest?"

Santana concentrated his gaze on Singer's face prior to asking the question. "I'm investigating the death of a young woman named Catalina Díaz."

Singer's dark eyes opened wide in shock. The emotion quickly disappeared. But Santana saw that his lower eyelid had remained raised and tensed for a second in a show of fear.

"We believe Philip Campbell might've been involved in the young woman's death."

Singer smoked his pipe and then pointed it at Santana. "Knowing Philip as I did, I find that hard to believe, Detective."

"I spoke to him prior to his death. He admitted being with Ms. Díaz the night she died."

"Do you have solid evidence linking him to her death?"

Santana ignored the question. "Did Campbell ever talk to you about his sexual habits?"

Matthew Singer smiled and shook his head, as if Santana had asked a ridiculous question. "What in the world does that have to do with your investigation?"

"Catalina Díaz was an escort."

"I see. Well, the days of sharing sexual exploits with friends have passed, Detective."

Santana debated whether to reveal the list of names he had. Like most men, Singer wouldn't want it known that he'd sought the company of escorts, particularly if one of them had possibly been murdered.

"Did you ever meet Catalina Díaz?"

"No," he said, his face devoid of emotion or tells.

"How about Nina Rivera?"

He shook his head.

Singer, Campbell, and Burdette had all traveled to Costa Rica, purportedly to do some deep-sea fishing. But given the brochure found in Campbell's bedroom, Santana figured the men had gone there for another reason as well.

"Just for the sake of discussion, Dr. Singer, where were you last Saturday evening?"

Singer set his pipe in the glass ashtray on an end table beside the chair and leaned forward. "What are you suggesting?"

"I'm just asking a question."

"I doubt that very much. I suspect there's a purpose behind every question. Why would you ask it?"

"Catalina Díaz was from Costa Rica. You've fished there."

"Costa Rica is a big country, Detective. And, I believe, it's time for you to leave."

* * *

Santana had once read that the key to evolutionary survival was parsimony, the ability to accomplish more by doing less. He wasn't sure what he'd accomplished by talking to Matthew Singer, other than to provoke him. Still, if he'd read the man's body language and responses correctly, he was certain that Singer had known Catalina Díaz—and perhaps had had sexual relations with her. And his conversation with Singer had led to Nathaniel Burdette.

Santana was able to arrange a meeting with Burdette at the University Club. It was located on Summit Avenue in a large Tudor building that sat high on a bluff overlooking downtown St. Paul and the Mississippi River Valley. Since it first opened in 1913, its members had included the wealthy and powerful of St. Paul.

Brass chandeliers hung from the ceiling and Audubon prints hung on the walls of the fireside room adjacent to the bar where Nathaniel Burdette was waiting. The room reminded Santana of similar lounges in clubs built in the early twentieth century—before women were allowed to be members.

Burdette rose from one of the overstuffed chairs near the fireplace with the easy elegance of a man accustomed to the finer things in life. He was tall and slender, with a perfectly symmetrical face and thick brown hair, graying on the sides. Though he had to be the same age as his medical school classmates, Philip Campbell and Matthew Singer, his tan skin was perfectly smooth, except for the tiny creases in the corners of his eyes that were like those in a tightly folded sheet of paper.

"Detective," he said, shaking hands firmly, his close-set indigo eyes steady and unblinking, as if taking Santana's measure. "Would you like something from the bar?"

"No, thank you."

He motioned for Santana to sit in an overstuffed chair facing him. "I thought it would be best if we talked here. It's quieter and more private than the bar or restaurant."

Santana retrieved his pen and spiral notebook and flipped it open to a clean page. "I understand you were Philip Campbell's friend."

"That's correct." Burdette paused, as if collecting his thoughts. "I've known him for over twenty-five years."

"Since medical school."

"Yes. Hard to believe time has passed so quickly," he said with a shake of his head. "Philip was a good man. I can't believe he's gone." He drank from his martini glass.

"You originally from the cities, Dr. Burdette?"

"Actually, I was born in Chicago."

"Your parents still live there?"

"My father passed away. My mother lives there. I have a sister in California."

Santana wrote some quick notes and moved on. "Had you spoken to Philip Campbell recently?"

"We spoke a few days ago."

"Did he seem depressed?"

"Not any more than usual."

"You mean he was often depressed?"

Burdette pursed his lips and stared at the glass in his hand as though it held the answer. Then his eyes drifted to Santana. "Philip was always very active and loved the outdoors. His recent skiing accident had limited his activity."

"You and Campbell and Singer deep-sea fished together."

His eyes widened and then quickly narrowed. "You spoke with Matthew?"

"He discovered Campbell's body."

"Yes, but in Minneapolis where Philip lived. I'm surprised the St. Paul Police Department is involved in the death investigation, particularly when it appears to be a suicide."

"How do you know it was a suicide, Dr. Burdette?"

"Well . . . Matthew told me."

"Recently?"

"Why, yes. He called just before . . ." Burdette's voice tailed off.

"And Dr. Singer is an expert on matters of suicide."

Burdette shrugged. "Perhaps Matthew was merely speculating." He swallowed the last of his martini. "Still, I fail to see why the St. Paul police are involved."

Santana felt no obligation to respond. "Have you done quite a bit of deep-sea fishing, Dr. Burdette?"

He shook his head. "I'm not really the adventurous type. Matthew always booked the trips."

"Did he use an agency in town?"

Burdette nodded and started to speak and then abruptly stopped.

"You were about to say?"

"I'm sorry. The name escapes me, Detective Santana."

"Really."

He nodded his head again.

"But the agency is here in town."

"You'd have to ask Matthew."

Santana made a note before asking the next question. "Are you married, Dr. Burdette?"

"Never have been."

"Ever heard of a woman named Nina Rivera?"

Burdette failed to match Santana's stare and averted his eyes. "No, I don't believe so."

"How about Catalina Díaz?"

"No, why?" His gaze returned to Santana's face.

"Campbell had sex with Ms. Díaz two days before he died."

"I didn't know Philip was seeing anyone."

"Ms. Díaz was an escort. Campbell had been seeing her for over a year. She was found dead in a downtown hotel room two days ago. He saw her the night she died."

"My, God! Do you think Philip killed her and then committed suicide?"

Santana ignored the question. His thoughts were focused on a previous scenario, the same one Matthew Singer had proffered. Burdette had admitted that he'd spoken with Singer. Perhaps they'd speculated over the phone about Campbell's death and arrived at the same conclusion. But Santana had purposely not asked Burdette if he'd *known* Catalina Díaz. He'd asked Burdette if he'd ever *heard* of Díaz. Burdette had said no, despite the fact that he'd talked earlier with his good friend, Singer. Santana figured the two men had discussed Campbell's relationship with Díaz. So why had Burdette lied about it?

* * *

After leaving the University Club, Santana stopped for a cup of hot chocolate at Starbucks. While there, he used Google's search engine to look for information on Erotic Tours. He found that the company billed itself as a full service travel agency specializing in pre-designed adult companion packages to all regions of Costa Rica.

For $1895, we'll put you up in one of our luxury rooms for three nights and offer you the private company of South American women who could satisfy even the most active imagination in one of the world's great adult travel vacation destinations.

Santana called Erotic Tours using the number Dave Reynolds, the Minneapolis cop, had given him at Philip

Campbell's crime scene. When he discovered the business phone had been disconnected, he typed the disconnected phone number into the Google search engine.

The number was linked to Paul Lenoir.

Santana drove to Lenoir's studio, where he found the photographer seated behind his desk, his black, tight-fitting T-shirt showing off his good-sized biceps.

"Hey, Detective," he said, his smile more of a reflexive facial gesture than an expression of welcome. "What can I do for you?"

"I understand you're the man to see if I'm interested in some female companionship while I'm in Costa Rica."

The smile on Lenoir's face faded and his cheeks colored. His lips moved, but it took a few seconds before the words finally spilled out. "Where'd you hear that?"

"From Philip Campbell. Recognize the name?"

He nodded. "But I thought he was dead."

"You knew him?"

Lenoir's eyes slid off Santana's face as he figured out what to say.

Santana saved him the trouble. "You did know Philip Campbell, didn't you, Mr. Lenoir?"

He lifted his eyes and gathered his thoughts before replying. "Actually I did."

"And you know Matthew Singer and Nathaniel Burdette as well."

"Yes."

"Do you have one of those brochures you gave to Campbell?"

Lenoir's pupils widened, and his lips parted slightly. "No, I don't."

"So tell me about Erotic Tours."

"Well, from what I understand it's a private luxury resort in Costa Rica."

"Have you been there?"

"Why, yes. I have."

"Then you do know the resort, Mr. Lenoir."

"I suppose I do."

"Why did you give Campbell a brochure?"

"He was going big game fishing and was looking for some . . . companionship. But that was a couple of years ago."

"Who owns the resort?"

Lenoir shrugged. "I assume some businessmen in Costa Rica."

Santana wondered what Lenoir's definition was of "businessmen." "Where did you meet Catalina Díaz and Nina Rivera?"

"At the Blue Marlin Bar in San Jose."

"And Tania Cruz?"

Lenoir narrowed his eyes. "I met Tania there as well."

"And then you hired them as models."

"That's right. But I don't understand what you're after, Detective."

Santana sat forward and leaned into Lenoir's personal space. "I'm looking for the man who murdered Catalina Díaz and Tania Cruz."

Lenoir released a small, nervous laugh. "I don't know anything about that."

"I think you know much more than you're telling me, Mr. Lenoir."

"I assumed Philip Campbell killed Catalina and then killed himself."

"Why would you assume Campbell killed her?"

"Well, according to the newspaper reports, he was with her that night. Then he killed himself after the police questioned him. It seemed like a logical conclusion."

"It's been my experience, Mr. Lenoir, that most murders have little to do with logic."

* * *

As Santana came out of the arched entrance to Lenoir's studio, a dark panel van with HOWARD CUSTODIAL SER-VICES stenciled on the side pulled up alongside his Crown Vic, which was parked at the curb, and backed into an open spot behind it. Santana saw a large, heavyset African-American man in a khaki shirt and pants get out of the van and head for the rear doors.

Santana walked toward him. "Excuse me."

The man turned, eyeing Santana with suspicion.

"Do you work for Brian Howard?"

"Who's askin'?"

Santana took out his badge wallet, flipped it open, and held it up so the man could see it.

The man offered an embarrassed smile. "Sorry, Detective."

"No problem."

"Am I in some kind of trouble?"

"No, sir, you're not. I just have a few questions. Maybe you can help me."

"I'll try," he said hesitantly.

Santana returned the badge wallet to his pocket and closed the distance between them. "By the way, I'm Detective Santana." He held out his hand. "What's your name?"

"Tyrone," the man said. His hand was big, his grip firm.

"So do you work for Brian Howard, Tyrone?"

He nodded. "Sure do."

"And you do custodial work at the Lenoir studio?"

"That's right. Been workin' here for six years now, ever since the last guy got in some trouble."

Santana had a hunch. "Do you recall the guy's name?"

"Well, normally I probably wouldn't remember. But he ended up in prison. It was in all the papers. Maybe you heard, Detective. Man's name was Arias Marchena."

109

Santana had no idea if the information he'd just learned was relevant, and if it had any bearing on his current case. He'd known that Marchena had worked as a custodian at Lenoir's studio, but not that he'd worked for Brian Howard. He knew now that Howard was connected to Marchena and, by extension, to Tania Cruz. He'd seen nothing in Cruz's case file indicating that Marchena had worked for Howard, or that Nick Baker and Tim Branigan had interviewed Howard in the course of their investigation into Cruz's death. Yet Brian Howard, if only peripherally, was linked to the deaths of two escorts. Was it just unfortunate luck or golden opportunity that had led to this connection? Santana wouldn't rest till he knew the answer.

Chapter 10

The next morning at the Law Enforcement Center, which housed both the SPPD and the Ramsey County Sheriff's Department, Santana told Hawkins about Paul Lenoir's connection with Erotic Tours. Then he told her about his conversation with Tyrone outside of Lenoir's studio.

"Sweet Jesus," she said. "Brian Howard is connected to Arias Marchena and Tania Cruz. You think Howard murdered Cruz and Catalina Díaz?"

"We can't rule it out."

"What about Howard's wife?"

"What about her, Kacie?"

"Maybe she can tell us something about her ex-husband."

"He has joint custody of their son. If she has an axe to grind, our visit might affect the custody arrangement."

"If he hasn't done anything, then there shouldn't be a problem. She's an elementary principal in St. Paul, right?"

Santana nodded.

"Why don't we drop by her school?" Hawkins said. "She can always tell anyone who asks why we're there that it's a student privacy matter and she can't divulge information."

Brian Howard had asked Santana not to interview his ex-wife. Still, Santana thought, if he and Hawkins discovered something during the interview that helped solve the case, the fallout from Howard would be worth it. However, Santana had no desire to cause problems for him. And talking to Howard's ex-wife could do just that. Plus, it was a long shot at best. But they were at a point in the investigation where something needed to be shaken loose.

"All right," he said. "Let's see if we can turn up something."

* * *

Santana was pleased to see that security was tight in the school. Once inside the outer doors, they showed their badges to a uniformed officer seated behind a second set of inner doors. He hit a buzzer that allowed them to enter the lobby, where they proceeded to the office near the main entrance.

"How can I help you?" asked a middle age, dark-haired woman seated behind a high counter. A nameplate on the counter identified her as Sharon.

"We're here to see the principal."

She typed something on her computer and then looked at Santana. "I'm afraid I don't have you on the schedule. Do you have an appointment?"

"I'm afraid not," Santana said, showing her his badge.

The pupils in her brown eyes grew large. She started to speak and then stopped, as if she didn't know what to say.

"If you could tell her we'd like to speak with her as soon as possible, we'd appreciate it."

Sharon sprang out of her chair and disappeared through a door leading to Marsha Howard's inner office.

"Good to know the sight of a badge still concerns some people," Hawkins said with a slight smile. "I get real tired of the bored reaction we get from bangers when we show them the badge."

The secretary came back a few moments later and said Principal Howard would be with them shortly and to please have a seat. They sat in two chairs along the wall and waited. A minute later, a young boy around seven emerged from the principal's office, his chin on his chest, his eyes downcast, and a yellow hallway pass in his hand.

"I remember one of those visits," Hawkins said, watching the kid as he trudged down the hallway, in no apparent hurry to return to his classroom.

"You were a naughty child?" Santana said, a half-smile on his face.

"I was framed," she said.

Marsha Howard stepped out of her office and shook their hands as she introduced herself. "Please, Detectives, come in."

"Hope you don't have any unpleasant flashbacks," Santana whispered to Hawkins as they entered Howard's office.

Hawkins punched him lightly on the arm.

The three of them sat down at a round table in the small, but nicely furnished office.

"Are you here about one of our students?" Marsha Howard asked.

She wore a black silk scoop neck top under a black pants suit. Her auburn hair was parted in the center, and the soft waves that touched the tips of her shoulders matched the freckles that were sprinkled on her pleasant face. Santana had the feeling that she and her ex-husband must've made an odd-looking couple.

"Actually, we're here about your ex-husband, Brian," he said.

A hand went to her mouth. "Has something happened to him?"

"No, he's fine."

"Then what's the reason for your visit?"

"Perhaps you heard there was a death in the hotel where your ex-husband works."

Her honey-colored eyes shifted back and forth as she considered a response. "What type of detectives are you?"

"Homicide," Santana said.

The color drained from her face. "Do you suspect Brian is involved in the woman's death?"

"Then you heard about the incident."

"Yes. It was in the paper."

"We're interviewing a number of people who were in the hotel that night."

"But I wasn't there," she said. "You must think Brian had something to do with it. Otherwise, why would you be here?"

Her logic was sound, Santana thought. He wondered if it helped any in dealing with elementary students.

"We spoke with your husband," Hawkins said.

"Ex-husband."

"Sorry. Ex-husband."

"And?"

"We'd like some more information and thought you could help us."

Marsha Howard's eyes were wary. "What kind of information?"

Hawkins looked at Santana. He said, "Was your husband ever in any trouble during your marriage?"

"You mean with the police?"

"With anyone."

She shook her head. "Not that I was aware of."

"So there was nothing unusual about his behavior."

"I'm not sure what you mean by unusual. But Brian has always been a little . . . different."

"How do you mean?"

"He's a loner. Communication is not his strong point. While that characteristic might be a plus when it comes to self-sufficiency, it can cause difficulty when you're sharing the same space with a wife."

Santana thought for a moment about his relationship with Jordan. Outside of his reluctance to share his past with her, he considered himself to be a good communicator. He wondered if Jordan felt the same.

"What did he do in his spare time?" he asked.

"Work," she said. "When he wasn't working at the hotel, he was busy with his cleaning business. He never had much time for us."

"How is he with your son?"

"Good, if he doesn't miss his scheduled weekends."

"Does he frequently miss those?"

"Yes. He claims he's busy with his business. But it upsets Daniel—and me." She paused and let out a sigh. "What is it you're really after, Detective? It would save us all some time if you'd get to it."

"Did your husband have any unusual habits?"

Marsha Howard looked silently at both of them. "Habits?" she said.

"Uh-huh. Habits."

She remained silent for what seemed like a long time. Santana thought she might not want to answer the question when she said, "The woman who was found dead in the hotel was an escort."

"That's correct," Santana said.

"So by 'habits' you mean, did Brian seek out the company of escorts during our marriage?"

"It could mean that, yes."

"I don't believe so."

"But you're not sure."

"No wife is ever one hundred percent sure that her husband is faithful, at least none that I've met. But Brian never gave me any reason to think that he was unfaithful. He was too busy working."

"Any other habits you can think of?"

She bit her lower lip. Santana and Hawkins waited.

"You mean sexual habits, don't you?"

"I do," Santana said, relieved that the subject was finally out in the open.

"What kind of sexual habits?"

"Was your ex-husband into any type of bondage?"

"No," she said. "And neither was I."

"I have one more question," Santana said. "Did your husband ever mention the name Arias Marchena?"

She thought about it. Then her eyes widened with recognition. "He worked for my husband. I don't remember exactly how long ago, maybe five or six years. But he was convicted of killing a . . ." She stopped abruptly.

"Thanks for your time," Santana said, starting to stand.

"Wait a minute," she said, touching him lightly on the forearm. "Are you suggesting that my ex-husband murdered two escorts?"

"We're not suggesting anything, Ms. Howard. We're just asking questions."

"I don't believe that for a minute, Detective."

As they left the building, Hawkins said, "You think we'll be hearing from Brian Howard?"

"We can count on it."

"Ever hear about the Boston Strangler who killed a number of women back in the sixties, John?"

"I read something about it."

"The strangler was a maintenance man and worked in a lot of apartment buildings where he had easy access to women. Maybe Brian Howard has more skeletons in his closet than just the gross misdemeanor charge for mooning."

* * *

After they had returned to the Homicide Unit, Hawkins rolled her chair closer to Santana and picked up the list of apostles on his desktop. She stared at it awhile and then looked at him again. "What did Matthew Singer have to say when you questioned him yesterday?"

Santana explained.

"What was your impression of him?"

"Singer knows more than he's telling."

"And you didn't show him the list of apostles because he might tell Burdette."

"Exactly. I'd rather have the element of surprise on our side."

"But you showed the list to Campbell. Maybe he told Singer and Burdette that we had it. Maybe . . ." Hawkins stopped suddenly.

"I know what you're thinking, Kacie."

She shrugged her shoulders. "Maybe it got Campbell killed."

"I've considered the possibility. There was a photo on the wall in Singer's study of Campbell, Singer, and Nathaniel Burdette fishing together in Costa Rica."

"They were probably doing more than fishing."

Santana nodded.

"You talk to him?"

"At the University Club. He and Campbell and Singer went to medical school together. Singer and Burdette both denied knowing Catalina Díaz, but I believe they're lying."

"You think it's because she was an escort?"

"They could be concerned about their reputations. But my sense is they're worried about something else."

"Like what?"

Santana shook his head.

Hawkins thought for a moment. "Why do you think Cheese wants a copy of the list?"

"I don't know. But it makes me really curious, Kacie."

"Me, too."

"There's a second possible connection," Santana said, figuring it was time to bring Hawkins up to speed.

"Who?"

"A young woman named Tania Cruz. Let me explain."

Santana began with the day Sarah Malik and her daughter, Sammy, had come to see him. He summarized his visit with Nick Baker and Arias Marchena. He left out any mention of his visit to the Hindu temple.

Hawkins let out a heavy sigh when he finished. "Why didn't you tell me this earlier, John?"

"Because all I know is that Tania Cruz died in virtually the same way as Catalina Díaz."

"And Marchena went down for it."

"He did."

"But you have doubts."

"Not just me. Nick Baker still has them as well."

"You talked with Nick?"

Santana nodded.

"How's he doing?"

"Not so well since his wife died."

"That was kind of sudden."

"Did you hear about it when she died?"

"I heard about it later."

"How come you never told me?"

"I thought you'd heard."

"No. It really threw me when I talked with Nick."

Hawkins remained quiet for a time. Then she said, "You don't really believe that Sammy Malik is a reincarnation of Tania Cruz?"

"She's been accurate about everything she's told me so far."

"Come on, John. It can't be true."

"But everything about the Christian faith can be?"

"I didn't suggest that." Her eyes were fixed on his as she spoke again. "That's why you didn't tell me about this Malik kid till now, isn't it? You were embarrassed."

"Skeptical might be a better term, Kacie."

"So why now?"

"My instinct tells me that whoever killed Tania Cruz killed Catalina Díaz."

"But why kill them both in the same way? That's like leaving a calling card."

"Maybe the perp is into kinky sex. Maybe both deaths were accidental. But even if the deaths were intentional, I doubt that the perp thought we would connect them. They happened six years apart. And I wasn't aware of the similarities until Sarah Malik brought in her daughter."

"Well, if Brian Howard or one of the apostles is guilty, then Marchena was framed."

"Probably. And speaking of the apostles, I didn't want Romano to know about the list we found, Kacie, at least not yet."

"We had to give him something."

"You could've checked with me first."

"Romano was about to close the case."

"That's true."

"And how was Marchena framed? You told me his DNA was found under Tania Cruz's fingernails. How would it have gotten there?"

Santana thought about it. "Marchena had a long scar on his cheek. During the trial, the prosecution argued that Cruz had scratched him when he attacked her. But Marchena claimed he was mugged the night before Cruz was murdered."

"It might be helpful to find the mugger," Hawkins said. "If Marchena is telling the truth."

"I'll look into it. You get Díaz's cell phone records?"

She nodded. "I'll look for regularly occurring numbers, then use the reverse searches to find the names and addresses connected to the phone numbers."

"What about Campbell's phone records?"

"I've got a call into Reynolds at the MPD."

"All right. Let's see if Bobby Jackson found anything on Catalina Díaz's computer."

"Bobby?" Hawkins said, her voice rising in alarm.

"Are the two of you still dating?"

"Not really."

"So you're uncomfortable talking with him?"

She shrugged. "Why don't you fill me in later."

"Okay. I'll talk with Jackson."

*　*　*

The SPPD's computer forensic room was located on the third floor of the Griffin Building in the LEC complex. The computer room, like the main lab adjacent to it, required a key card for entry. The carpeted room was the size of a large master bedroom. It had laminate counters and cabinets along three walls and a center island in the middle. Intake report forms were neatly stacked on the center island beside hard drives and empty shells of seized computers. Jackson, a light-complected African American and the department's computer forensics examiner, always had mellow jazz playing on a CD player.

"Hey, Santana," he said as Santana entered the room.

"You find anything on Catalina Díaz's computer?"

"Take a seat."

Santana rolled a cushioned chair next to Jackson and sat down.

"Díaz's MacBook Air is the newest model and has the latest OS software installed. But there was nothing on her hard drive."

"How can that be?"

"Data recovery software is only effective when files have been deleted, not overwritten. Díaz—or someone else—used a very sophisticated data wipe program like those used by the Department of Defense. The hard drive is rewritten and covered with random patterns. With each wipe, the deleted data becomes harder to piece back together. The DOD sets the wiping standard, which requires seven passes."

"What about e-mails?"

"They're gone, too, just like the names and erased files, all traces of activity, and recently opened files and applications. If the files and e-mails had just been deleted, I'd be able to recover the information on the hard drive and show times and dates of downloads, e-mails, and all content."

"But you can tell a wipe program was used."

Jackson nodded. "But that's all I can tell."

* * *

When Santana returned to his workstation, he saw that Kacie Hawkins was using different colored highlighters to mark patterns of phone numbers on Catalina Díaz's cell phone records.

She looked up as he sat down at his workstation next to hers. "Anything interesting?"

"Nothing," he said. "And I mean that literally. Whatever was on her hard drive has been totally wiped clean using sophisticated software."

"You think Díaz did that?"

"No. I think someone took the keys from her purse at the hotel and used them to gain entry to the condo."

"So they could erase evidence from her computer. More indication Díaz was murdered."

"Yes."

"Someone on the list of apostles would have to be familiar with the software, John."

"Or know someone who was."

Hawkins paused before speaking again. "So maybe one of Díaz's clients killed her and wanted to make sure his name didn't appear anywhere."

"If Campbell killed Díaz and wanted to cover his tracks, he wouldn't have left his business card in her purse. And he wouldn't have waited to check out until early the next morning."

"And if he wanted to wipe her hard drive clean," Hawkins said, "he would've taken her keys and gone to the condo immediately."

"Yes. I think whoever wiped the hard drive came to her hotel room after Campbell left, killed Díaz, and then left evidence implicating him."

"Are you're thinking that same someone killed Campbell and made it look like a suicide?"

"That would wrap up everything nice and neat, wouldn't it?"

"But the perp didn't know about the list of apostles."

"I don't think so," Santana said. "But even if he suspected there was a hard copy and searched her condo, he didn't find it."

"Why would Díaz make a hard copy, John?"

"She was probably concerned that someone might gain access to her computer. And she may have suspected that one of the apostles was a murderer."

"You were lucky to find it in that hidden drawer."

"Not lucky. Good."

Hawkins smiled. "Okay, good."

Santana phoned Alvarado Vega, Arias Marchena's attorney.

"You miss me, Santana?"

"I need information concerning one of your former clients, Arias Marchena."

"He still *is* my client. I'm working on a second appeal."

"You don't think he's guilty."

"None of my clients are guilty, Santana," he said with a laugh. "You should know that."

Vega reminded Santana of Geraldo Rivera in both looks and personality. He'd built a reputation defending clients accused of murder, and drawn the ire of the SPPD in the process. Still, if Santana ever needed an attorney, Alvarado Vega would be the first one he'd call.

"Why the sudden interest in Marchena?" Vega asked.

"I'm investigating a case similar to the murder he was charged with."

"Tell me about it." There was no humor in Vega's voice now.

"I can't do that."

"Yet you expect me to give you information, Santana."

"It may help your client."

"How?"

"Marchena told me he'd been mugged the night before Tania Cruz was murdered. It was how he got the scratch on his cheek."

"That's right. But he couldn't identify the perp."

"There were no witnesses?"

"No."

"Anything taken?"

"*Nada.*"

"Marchena must've fought back."

"That's the strange part," Vega said. "He was knocked immediately to the ground and claimed he didn't resist because the man had a gun. Yet, outside of the skin he lost on his cheek, nothing was taken."

"Marchena was sure it was a man who attacked him?"

"Positive. But the perp wore a mask."

"What if it was a setup?"

"I like how you think, Detective."

"Any ideas as to who might be behind it?"

"No. But maybe you have one."

"Not yet," Santana said.

When he hung up, Hawkins said, "What did Vega have to say?"

Santana told her.

She nodded and then gestured toward a page from Catalina Díaz's cell phone records. "Take a look at the numbers highlighted in yellow."

Santana slid his chair next to hers.

"They're all calls to and from Philip Campbell. He and Díaz spoke twice the night she was killed. But there are no other incoming or outgoing calls recorded that night."

"Whose numbers are highlighted in green and pink?"

"Matthew Singer's and Nathaniel Burdette's."

"What about the numbers highlighted in red?"

"They belong to a man named James Elliot."

Santana gazed at the phone numbers in front of Hawkins once more, his eyes unconsciously scanning the paper till they locked on a number that stunned him. He tried to calm himself, but he knew that Hawkins had picked up on his change in body language.

"Something wrong, John?" she asked.

"No, Kacie," he said, as his heart thumped in his chest and a sound like ocean waves crashing against the shore rushed through his eardrums.

* * *

Santana and Hawkins left the LEC and drove to Holman Field in downtown St. Paul. The small airport had a flight training school and served aircraft operated by corporations in the area and the Minnesota Army National Guard aviation unit, as well as transient general aviation aircraft.

The Mississippi River that bordered the three asphalt runways smelled of mud and wet earth as they walked toward the hangar and the white Learjet inside. Near the open door and entry steps on the left forward side of the jet cabin stood a big, heavy-set man in a blue ball cap, checkered flannel shirt, and jeans.

"Excuse me," Santana said. "Are you James Elliot?"

He looked at the two detectives, his mahogany eyes filled with caution, his beefy face flat and expressionless, his red hair curling off the back of his neck, his shoulders wide and sloping like a weight lifter's.

"You the detective that called about Catalina Díaz?"

Holding out his badge, Santana nodded and introduced himself and Hawkins.

"Like I told you on the phone, Detective, I knew Díaz, but that doesn't mean I had anything to do with her death."

"You from here originally, Mr. Elliot?"

"Pretty much from all over," he said.

"Where were you a week ago Saturday?"

Elliot retrieved a logbook from the plane and flipped through it till he found the page he was searching for. "I flew some businessmen to Arizona. Flew back that evening." He held out the logbook so Santana could see it and then handed it to Hawkins.

"Can you fly this plane alone?"

"I could," he said with a grin, "but that would be illegal. I always have a co-pilot."

"And who would that be?"

"Depends on the flight and the day." Elliot gave Santana the names of another captain and two co-pilots.

Santana wrote the names in his notebook. "You fly many businessmen?"

"Sure do. I fly athletes and politicians, too. Heck, I've even flown some folks from the police departments."

"Ever flown any escorts?"

He smiled. "Sometimes executives might bring a companion along on a business trip. It's not my place to question their morals."

"Uh-huh," Santana said. "That how you met Catalina Díaz?"

He nodded. "I take it you think her death was intentional, Detective."

Santana didn't answer.

"Well," Elliot said, "there's a lot of risk in her line of work."

"You married, Mr. Elliot?"

"My last wife divorced me a few years ago."

"How many wives have you had?" Hawkins asked.

"Three," he said without a trace of embarrassment. "Seems I keep making the same mistake."

"Maybe they're the ones making the mistake," she said.

He smiled good-naturedly. "There's some truth to that, Detective. Don't think I'll try marriage again."

"Your wives live in the area?" Santana asked.

"I married my first wife while I was in flight school in Laughlin, Texas. Don't know where she is now. My last two wives were Japanese. I imagine they're still in Japan."

"You know Philip Campbell, Matthew Singer, or Nathaniel Burdette?"

"I attended med school with them. But before I graduated, I decided to enlist in the Air Force. Flying was always my first love."

"So you never actually practiced medicine."

"Nope. Never did."

"Ever meet an escort named Tania Cruz?"

Elliot hid his facial expression by peering down at his shoes. "I don't recall the name."

"Are charters your primary source of income, Mr. Elliot?"

126

"It's my only source," he said. "But it pays the bills."

"Business must be good," Santana said, tapping the fuselage and noting the number on the tail. "Pretty expensive plane unless you're a millionaire."

"Well, I just fly it. I don't own it."

"Who does?"

"The Genesis Clinic," Elliot said as his cell phone rang. "Excuse me a minute, Detectives. I'm expecting a call about a charter." He retrieved the phone from a pocket in his jeans and walked toward a workbench on the opposite side of the hangar as he answered.

Santana wrote the jet's tail number, or "N" number, in his notebook and said, "Let me see the logbook, Kacie."

She handed it to him.

The words Pilot's Flight Log and Record were embossed in gold lettering on the rectangular, leather-bound black cover.

"What're you looking for, John?" Hawkins asked.

"I don't know. But see if you can keep Elliot busy for a few minutes when he's off the phone."

Elliot stood near a workbench, talking in a soft voice, the cell phone pressed against his ear. Hawkins headed in his direction, her eyes gazing nonchalantly at the framed black and white photos hanging on the walls of jet fighter planes and Elliot in a judo gi and black belt.

Santana stepped closer to the plane, using it as cover as he opened the logbook. He started with the most recent charter and worked backwards, scanning each page quickly before flipping to the next. He focused his attention on the ARRIVAL column and on the passenger names under the REMARKS column.

A third of the way through the book he came across a familiar name that sent a shock through him. But he had no time to reflect on the name or its implications. Santana closed the book and set it on a toolkit just as Elliot and Hawkins came around the tail of the plane, engaged in conversation. As they came to a stop, Elliot pushed up the bill of his cap that was embroidered with an Air Force insignia and the words U.S. AIR FORCE VETERAN.

"You know a man named Paul Lenoir?" Santana asked.

"He was one of my mechanics when I was stationed in Japan."

"Seen him recently?"

Elliot shook his head. "We've sort of lost touch with one another."

"But you're aware he lives in town."

"Last time I heard, yeah."

"What's the range on this jet?"

"Around thirteen hundred nautical miles, depending on the weight and weather conditions."

"So you could fly out of the country."

His eyes narrowed. "Sure."

"What about customs?"

"Holman Field has custom officials on call."

"Ever fly to Costa Rica?"

Elliot's gaze shifted quickly to the logbook on the toolkit and then returned to Santana. "I've flown charters there. Lots of good fishing."

Santana nodded. "You have to refuel?"

"In Dallas."

"And you'd go through customs there."

"Yes."

"Your cell phone number the primary one where you can be reached?"

"Don't have a landline anymore."

"How about your home address?"

Santana wrote it in his notebook as Elliot recited it. Then he handed Elliot a business card. "Thanks for your time," he said. "We'll be in touch."

* * *

As they drove back to St. Paul, Hawkins looked away from the view outside the Crown Vic's passenger side window and focused her gaze on Santana. "Did you find anything interesting in Elliot's logbook?"

"He's been making frequent trips to Costa Rica."

"Probably flying men who are looking for some cheap sex," she said, her voice filled with disgust.

"Probably."

"As sick as that is, there's nothing illegal about it," Hawkins said. "Plus, he's got an alibi for the night Díaz was murdered."

"Even if it's written in his flight logbook, we don't know if he flew that night, Kacie. And if he did, are the times correct?"

"He'd have to file a flight plan."

"If we need to, we can check it out."

"I heard Elliot talking on the phone, John. He's flying to Costa Rica in two days."

"Did he mention a specific destination?"

"San José. But how does all this relate to Catalina Díaz's death?"

"I don't know that it does."

Hawkins went quiet for a while. Then she said, "You find anything else in the logbook?"

"One familiar name." Santana paused.

"Well?"

"Tim Branigan," he said.

"The AC?"

Santana nodded. "He's flown with Elliot to Costa Rica."

"Maybe he went there to fish?"

"And maybe I'm the Pope."

Hawkins looked out the passenger side window again.

"Something bothering you, Kacie?"

She shifted her gaze to his face and nodded.

"Want to tell me?"

"It's about Branigan. I finished checking all the numbers on Catalina Díaz's phone records. His cell number was on it."

Santana didn't acknowledge that he'd recognized Branigan's number the day she was highlighting the phone record. "It might be the reason why Romano was all over this case from the beginning, Kacie."

"Romano said he wanted to be more hands on."

"No," Santana said. "He was getting pressure from Branigan."

"What're we going to do?"

"I'll go to Branigan."

"But what if we're wrong, John?"

"I'll keep you out of it."

"Hey, do me a favor and quit trying to protect me. I'm your partner. We're in this together."

Santana looked at her. "No matter where this case leads?"

"No matter where it leads," Hawkins said.

Chapter 11

Before leaving the LEC that afternoon, Santana called Sarah Malik and arranged a meeting. Then he did a Google search and learned that her surname was Indian and that she'd written a book entitled *Past Lives*. According to her website, she had an M.S. in counseling and was an author, lecturer, counselor, and therapist who practiced past life regressions.

She lived in the University Grove neighborhood just west of the University of Minnesota's St. Paul campus in the suburb of Falcon Heights, ten minutes north of St. Paul. Many of the homes along the neighborhood's oak-lined streets had been designed by well-known Twin City architects and built for U of M faculty and their families between the 1920s and 1980s. Malik lived on a corner in a large French country-style house.

Santana was seated on a small leather couch in the second floor office opposite Sarah Malik, who wore a double-breasted gray jacket and pants. White floor-to-ceiling bookshelves fronted the sage green walls, and a bay window let in natural light.

He set his briefcase beside him on the dark hardwood floor. "When you brought your daughter to see me, you neglected to mention that you had written a book on past lives."

"Would that have made a difference?"

"Possibly."

"In what regard?"

"Maybe you're just seeking publicity?"

"If I wanted publicity, Detective, I could've gone to the media with my story. I'm sure they would love it. But I don't need more publicity. My business is doing just fine, thank you. However, I do need to protect Sammy. So what I've told you will stay between you and me."

"That's fine with me," he said. "I'm here more to get a sense of what you do."

"Perhaps it's best if we start with the premise that a past life regression is not the same as a psychic reading. I don't *tell* clients about their past lives. Rather, I serve as a guide to help them remember past life memories and relate them to their present lives. It's an active, not a passive process. The goal, of course, is spiritual healing."

"Does regression work for everyone?"

"Unfortunately, no. And I have no way of predicting for whom it will work."

"Maybe the success rate has to do with a belief in reincarnation and how much you want it to work."

"First of all, I welcome everyone, skeptics as well as the curious. I choose to believe an unsuccessful regression may have more to do with a soul's readiness or my rapport with a particular client. Would you consider yourself a skeptic, Detective Santana?"

"It's my nature."

She nodded as though confirming a belief and leaned back in the leather swivel chair. "Given your line of work, I suppose skepticism is a healthy trait to possess. I imagine you've been told many things by many people that prove to be untrue."

"I'm accustomed to hearing lies."

"Do you consider past life regressions to be a lie?"

"Maybe these past life memories of which you speak are not lies exactly, but simply memories from experiences in this life or products of the imagination. Or . . ." Santana paused.

"Or what?"

"Perhaps they're not memories at all, but intentional or unintentional suggestions, false memories if you will."

"As I said at the beginning of our discussion, I don't tell my clients about their past memories, they tell me."

"Still, isn't there a danger of creating delusions or false memories that might be harmful?"

"That hasn't been my experience—or the experiences of my clients."

"But if memories exist in the brain, and the brain is destroyed at death, then wouldn't memories be destroyed, too, as they are with a disease such as Alzheimer's?"

"You forget about the spirit, Detective. It exists independently of the brain."

Santana hadn't "forgotten" about the spirit or soul. He'd just lost his belief in one. "What about children?"

"I won't do regressions with children under the age of twelve," she said. "But I often consult with parents who feel that their child is experiencing a past life memory and need more help understanding what's happening."

"So you haven't done a regression on your daughter?"

"No," she said. "And I don't plan to."

"I'd like to speak to her again."

"Why? According to the paper, Philip Campbell was likely responsible for Catalina Díaz's murder."

"Truth and news are not always the same thing, Ms. Malik."

"What is it that you'd like to ask my daughter?"

"Before speaking with her, I wonder if you could answer a few questions?"

"What questions?"

He could hear the concern in her voice. He'd seen framed photos of Sarah Malik and Sammy placed strategically throughout the living room downstairs and figured he knew the answer to his first question. But he asked it anyway. "What does Mr. Malik do?"

"I was about to say there is no Mr. Malik, and technically that's true. I was married to a Malik for two years, but we divorced right after Sammy was born."

"And he was from the States?"

"No. He was from India. He returned to his country shortly after we divorced. He was never comfortable here, but my biological clock was ticking, and I wanted a child. Does that seem cold to you, Detective?"

It did, but Santana said, "People marry for a lot of reasons."

"Yes, they do. But I kept his name." She offered a small, quick smile.

Santana moved on. "Was your ex-husband Hindu?"

"As a matter of fact, he was."

"And you?"

"I embraced Hinduism before I married. I've always been fascinated with the culture of India and have visited it on a number of occasions."

"But you were born here."

"Yes. In Minneapolis, actually."

Santana looked at his notes a moment. "You said that in her previous life your daughter grew up in Costa Rica."

"That's correct."

"And she's never been there?"

"No."

"Has she ever described the place in Costa Rica where she lived?"

"I don't remember the details, but I've written everything down since Sammy first began describing her past life. It's all in my journal."

She retrieved a leather-bound journal the size of a trade paperback from amongst the hardcover books on the shelves.

Santana waited while she sat down and flipped through the journal pages, her excitement almost palpable.

"Here," she said, pointing to a page with her index finger. She looked at him, her eyes gleaming with excitement. "Sammy lived in a town called Zarcero. She said her father grew lettuce and cilantro, which her mother sold in the town square. Are you familiar with the town?"

"No, I'm not."

"I want to visit. I want to know if Sammy's recollections about her childhood and the people in her neighborhood are accurate."

"Did she say anything else about the place?"

Sarah Malik looked at her journal once more. "Sammy said there was a swing set and slide in the yard. Across the road was a small factory that made cigarettes."

"What about her family?"

"She said she had an older brother. And the neighbor that lived next door worked in the factory."

Santana nodded and wrote the information in his notebook.

"You still have doubts that my daughter is the reincarnation of Tania Cruz, don't you, Detective Santana?"

"Yes."

"Then why are you here?"

"I try and keep an open mind."

"I wasn't certain it was true either," she said. "But when Sammy started talking specifically about her past, and began speaking Spanish, I couldn't ignore it. You spoke to her. You know she picked out Tania Cruz's photo from all the ones you showed her."

"Maybe it was a lucky guess."

She stared at him for a long moment before responding. "You don't think it was luck, Detective."

"Can I talk to Sammy now? I'd like her to look at a few more photos."

"Of suspects?"

"If you wouldn't mind," he said.

Sarah Malik stood up and went downstairs.

While she was gone, Santana opened his briefcase, picked up an 8 1/2" x 11" manila envelope, and removed the black and white photos he'd downloaded off the Internet of Philip Campbell, Matthew Singer, Nathaniel Burdette, and Paul Lenoir and stacked them together.

A minute later, Sarah Malik returned, holding Sammy by the hand. "You remember Detective Santana, don't you, Sammy?"

She nodded her head and peered at him with her large, curious eyes. She wore a grey hooded sweatshirt with a dark moon on the front, a pair of jeans, and the black canvas shoes with pink laces she'd worn before.

"Hello, Sammy," he said.

She smiled.

Sarah Malik squatted on her haunches in front of her daughter. "The detective would like you to look at some photos again. Can you do that for him?"

Sammy looked over her mother's shoulder at Santana. He smiled at her again, and she nodded her assent.

"I'd like you to look at each of these photos," he said, "and tell me if you recognize any of these men."

Her mother stood and directed Sammy gently toward the coffee table.

Sammy held her eyes on Santana for a few seconds longer. Then she focused her gaze on the photo of Philip Campbell.

"Take your time, Sammy," he said.

The little girl had surprised him when she'd correctly identified Tania Cruz's photo. Now, Santana suspected one of the men on the list of apostles had killed both Catalina Díaz and Tania Cruz. He was hoping the child might surprise him again by picking out a photo of the man who'd killed her. He knew it was a long shot. And even if Sammy identified one or more of the men, it would prove nothing, other than he might be crazy for trying such a stunt.

"Do you recognize this man, Sammy?" he asked again, pointing to the photo of Philip Campbell.

She shook her head.

He placed Campbell's photo in his briefcase and asked her if she recognized the photo of Matthew Singer.

She shook her head.

"How about this man?" Santana asked, showing her Nathaniel Burdette's photo.

Again, she shook her head.

The last photo Santana showed her was of Paul Lenoir.

Sammy shook her head and looked at her mother. "Can I go and play now?"

"Are we all finished here?" Sarah Malik asked Santana.

"Yes," he said. "Thank you, Sammy." The little girl turned and hurried downstairs.

Sarah Malik sat down across from Santana again and gestured toward the photos. "Who are these men? Was one of them responsible for Tania Cruz's death?"

"I really can't say right now, Ms. Malik." Santana gathered up the photos and returned them to the envelope in his briefcase. "Can I see Sammy's room?"

"Why?"

"I'm not really sure. I'm just trying to get a better sense of your daughter."

"And you think seeing her room will help."

"Possibly."

She paused for a moment and then said, "All right."

Santana followed her downstairs and into a room with white furniture and storage bins, sky-blue walls, and a large earthen brown rug. There were mossy green leafy prints on the pillows and window cushion, framed photos of horses, and a stenciled, dark blue tree-branch mural on the wall beside the bed. It was a beautiful bedroom.

"Your daughter like horses?"

"Yes. She loves to ride."

"I used to as a kid," he said.

Her eyes shifted off him and focused on something in the room or in her mind. "It's what you do with the dead, isn't it?"

"What do you mean?"

Her gaze found his again. "You look through their things, through their past. You use what you find to help you solve the case."

"Yes."

"Maybe that's why Sammy trusts you," she said.

Santana shook his head, indicating he didn't understand.

"Because my daughter senses your relationship with the dead."

Suddenly a hysterical scream outside the bedroom window pierced the silence. Sarah Malik bolted out of the bedroom. Santana followed her as she sprinted through living room and kitchen and out the back door, racing toward Sammy, who was running toward the house, her eyes wide with fright, a small, stuffed doll clutched in one hand.

Santana quickly scanned the yard, looking for something or someone that had frightened the child—but he saw nothing out of the ordinary.

Sarah Malik caught her daughter in her arms and picked her up. She held the back of her daughter's head as Sammy pressed her face against her shoulder. "It's okay now," she said. "I've got you."

Santana could see that Sammy was trembling with fear, but she wasn't crying. "What is it?" he asked.

"There," Sarah Malik said, pointing toward a tall oak tree in the yard.

Santana could see nothing out of the ordinary. "I don't—"

"The bird," she said.

Santana saw a bald eagle perched on a branch near the top of the tree, its black, beady eyes focused on the three of them. It sat perfectly still for a time. Then it flapped its expansive wings and lifted off, its shadow tracking across the lawn and passing over them like a dark cloud.

"Sammy's afraid of birds?" he said.

"Not birds," Sarah Malik said. "Eagles. Sammy's deathly afraid of them." She turned and carried her daughter into the house, leaving Santana alone in the fading twilight.

* * *

Santana called Nina Rivera after he left Sarah Malik's house. He told her he had a few questions to ask and wondered if he could stop by. She told him to give her thirty minutes.

At the appointed time, she ushered him into the condo. "Could I get you a drink, Detective?"

"I'm fine," he said, sitting on the couch.

"I do have non-alcoholic beverages."

"I'll take a Coke," he said. "No diet, please."

"What's with men and Diet Coke?"

Besides the lousy taste, Santana wasn't sure.

"Would you like ice?"

"Please."

Nina Rivera went to the bar and poured a glass of Coke over ice and carried it to the couch. She handed him his drink, brushing her fingers against his, and sat down close beside him.

She wore a red V-neck sweater, tight designer jeans, and low-heeled sandals. Her brunette hair was side-parted, and long rolling curls fell to one side of her face. What little makeup and lipstick she wore was lightly applied, as was the hint of roses, wood, and powder in her perfume.

"You know many things about me, Detective Santana. But I know so little about you."

"This isn't a social call, Ms. Rivera."

"I never assumed it was."

Santana thought the low light and soft Brazilian jazz in the background suggested otherwise. He drank some Coke and placed the glass on a coaster on the coffee table, beside her wine glass half-filled with white wine. He felt uncomfortable having her seated so close to him. He could move or ask her to, but that might upset her. Then she might refuse to answer the questions he'd mentally prepared.

He took out his notebook and pen, trying to keep the interview as formal as possible, and looked at her.

She brushed her long, side-swept bangs and stared at him, her amber eyes glowing like the sunset beyond the window. He'd heard that eyes that color were called wolf eyes.

"I found your cached website, Ms. Rivera. But I'm not concerned with your past, or what you're doing now."

She picked up her glass and drank the wine slowly.

Santana waited.

"This is a very puritanical country," she said at last. "Especially when it comes to women involved in a certain . . . business."

She set down her drink and reached for the package of Derby cigarettes and the black lighter on the coffee table, tapped out a cigarette, and lit it. Then she set the lighter and package on the table and leaned back on the couch again as smoke swirled like a crown above her head.

"Habits are hard to break," she said.

"You're not just speaking of smoking."

"No."

Santana was curious about another aspect of Nina Rivera's life. "I noticed you have a statue of *Santa Muerte* in your bedroom."

Her posture stiffened. "When were you in my bedroom?"

"The day Detective Hawkins and I were here. The day Catalina Díaz's body was found."

She nodded and drew in some smoke. As she blew it out, her body relaxed again like a cat curling up for a nap.

"I'd expect to see that statue in a Mexican household," he said, probing for a more detailed response.

"We all have to come to terms with death, Detective, wherever we live."

"Have you come to terms with it, Ms. Rivera?"

A faraway look came into her eyes. "When I was a young girl, my parents took me to visit an aunt who lived in Mexico City. It was during the Day of the Dead celebration. We went to the cemetery, and my aunt spoke to the dead. When I was older, I returned to Mexico City and saw the *Santa Muerte* shrine. These events had a profound influence on me."

"Do you believe you can speak to the dead?"

She shook her head. "But there are those who can."

Santana was aware of the uniqueness and the familiarity of death in Mexican culture, and of the worship of *Santa Muerte,* especially among the poor and illiterate. But he did not understand all of it. "Is there a meaning behind the votive candles on your nightstand?"

"Red represents my wish for love, gold prosperity, and purple health."

"And the black candle?"

"Protection."

"From whom?"

"My enemies."

"Many drug traffickers and gangbangers worship *Santa Muerte*."

"I am aware of this. But no matter who you are, when you ask *Santa Muerte* for something, you have to promise her something in return. If you don't make that promise, she can take away one of your loved ones."

"And who are your enemies, Ms. Rivera?"

She smiled. "I hope you are not one, Detective Santana."

"Then don't make me one. Be honest. Tell me the truth."

"What do you want to know?"

"Have you ever met a man named Matthew Singer?"

She peered at the space in front of her without speaking. Her silence was his answer. "You met him in Costa Rica?"

"Originally, yes. Then again after I came here at one of his parties."

"How did you meet him?"

"Through Paul Lenoir."

"Did Singer often have parties?"

"A few times a year."

"What about Nathaniel Burdette and James Elliot?"

"I met them, too," she said.

"And Philip Campbell?"

"I don't ever recall meeting him."

"Campbell had an appointment with Catalina Díaz the night she died."

"Do you believe Cata was murdered?"

"I'm leaning in that direction. But I need evidence to support it. You can help me out. Catalina was your friend."

"You don't have to remind me."

"Apparently someone does."

A flush of color spread across her cheeks. "Now you are being cruel."

"Campbell is dead, Ms. Rivera."

"How?"

"It appears to be a suicide."

She stared at him without speaking, as though she hadn't understood his statement. Then she leaned forward and crushed out her cigarette in the ashtray on the table. "Why do you say *appears* to be?"

"I'm waiting for the forensic results." Even then, he thought, Campbell's manner of death might not be any more conclusive than Catalina Díaz's had been. But Santana wasn't about to express his doubts, particularly when he had her off-balance.

"Tell me about Tania Cruz," he said.

Her eyes widened with surprise. "Who?"

"Tania Cruz. The woman you knew who died six years ago."

She lowered the glass into her lap, her eyes fixed, as if she were without sight.

"Why didn't you mention Cruz's death, Ms. Rivera?"

"I didn't think it was important."

"Even though she and Catalina Díaz died in the same manner."

Nina Rivera shrugged. "We worked at the Lenoir Agency together just after coming to St. Paul."

"How did you get your job at the agency?"

"We met Paul Lenoir in Costa Rica. He took some photographs and offered us jobs."

"As models?"

She let out a sigh. "Yes, as models."

"Where did you meet Lenoir?"

"In a bar called the Blue Marlin. It is where many of the gringos go to have sex with women."

"How did you become escorts?"

"How does anyone become an escort, Detective Santana? Later, we left the Blue Marlin and went to work at Erotic Tours. The pay was better and so were the men."

"So it was your own decision?"

"No one forced us into it, if that's what you are asking. We were never sexual slaves."

"Did Catalina Díaz follow a similar path?"

"Yes. As many women have."

"Did Tania Cruz attend the parties?"

"Sometimes."

"Were the women at the parties from Costa Rica?"

"Some."

"Were they all Latina women?"

She nodded.

"Do you have a client list?"

She shook her head. "Our clients are very wealthy and important men. Discretion is important."

"But you and Díaz and Cruz must've shared information."

"We were told from the beginning that we should never keep written records, never talk about our clients."

"By whom?"

"Paul Lenoir."

Santana wrote the information in his notebook. "Why did you tell the police that you thought Arias Marchena killed Tania Cruz?"

"Because he did."

"How could you be so sure?"

She shook her head as if she had no answer.

"When you were working as an escort, did any of these men ever ask if they could tie you up?"

She stared at him without responding.

"Anyone ever mention the term autoerotic asphyxia?" He let the silence sit there awhile. "What are you afraid of, Ms. Rivera, or maybe I should say *who* are you afraid of?"

"No one."

She drank the last of her wine, stood up, and went to the bar. She poured herself more wine and raised the glass to her lips, holding it still a moment without drinking. Then she turned and looked at him, her back resting against the bar.

Santana knew the fear of meeting death at the hands of another was as primal as is the fear of fire or drowning. He wondered if that fear was behind Nina Rivera's silence.

"Why did you come here tonight, Detective Santana?"

"To ask you some questions."

"Couldn't those questions have waited until tomorrow?"

"Well, I suppose—"

"Do you have a woman?"

"Excuse me?"

"Do you have a woman? Someone you're involved with?"

He thought so, despite the fact that he and Jordan had argued. "Without sounding rude, Ms. Rivera, I really think it's none of your business."

Her smile indicated that she wasn't terribly offended. "Perhaps not."

He stood and walked to her. "I think you know more then you're telling me, Ms. Rivera."

She looked into his eyes without speaking. Her eyes were softer now, and up close, Santana thought there was a damaged beauty behind the tough facade.

"Tell me what you know," he said.

"I know that you are a brave man, Detective Santana, but a foolish one. You need to be very careful."

"Of what?"

Her amber eyes remained locked on his. He could feel her sweet breath against his face, the faint smell of nicotine and tobacco. Holding the wine glass in both hands, she leaned forward to kiss him, but he placed an index finger on her lips and stopped her.

She leaned back slightly, her eyes staying locked on his. "You don't want me to kiss you?"

"I'm involved with someone."

She tilted her head as if he'd said something strange. "Your woman doesn't have to know."

"But I'd know," he said.

She smiled a little. "A man with principles. How unusual."

"You need to tell me what you know."

Her eyes remained on his for another moment before she stepped around him. "I'm going to bed now, Detective Santana. I'd like it very much if you stayed." She set her glass on the bar and walked down the hallway, her body swaying seductively, as graceful as smoke.

He watched her as she went into the bedroom and closed the door. She never looked back.

Santana stared at the empty space where Nina Rivera had stood a moment ago, listening to sweet sounds of Brazilian jazz and thinking about the many choices each of us has to make in our lives.

Then he let himself out, locking the door behind him.

* * *

That night, Santana awoke suddenly from a dream, his senses triggered by a sound. He wasn't sure what he'd heard, but he was positive that he'd heard something.

As he lay in the dark stillness of the night, he recalled his dream in which an eagle had been feeding on what he'd thought was a dead animal. But as Santana had approached, he'd realized the eagle was not feeding on a dead animal, but on a small doll, like the one Sammy Malik had been carrying. He wondered now if the shock of seeing the doll and not a noise had awakened him.

He didn't know why Sammy Malik was so afraid of eagles, and apparently neither did her mother. But he'd known instinctively that the child was in danger the moment that he'd met her. It was that instinct that was motivating him now, even more than his curiosity about her supposed reincarnation.

He took a deep breath, trying to relax, trying to clarify the image that was lurking at the edge of his consciousness. Then he heard the sound again, as though someone or something was scratching the side of the house.

Perhaps it was a branch blowing in the breeze, or a small animal, or perhaps it was Gitana. She usually slept at the foot of the bed and was rarely allowed in it. He whispered her name, but received no response.

Throwing back the covers, he stood, pulled on a pair of jeans and a sweatshirt, and removed the Glock-27 from the nightstand drawer. The clock's green numbers glowed 3:17 a.m. Ashen light glimmering faintly through the partially opened blinds on the slider created strange shadows that huddled in the corners of the bedroom.

Any movement behind the house would trigger a bright set of motion detector lights. They had no switch and could only be turned off if the main power supply was shut down. Anyone attempting to enter the house through a door or window would trigger the "stay" alarm, which had backup batteries if power was lost. Because Gitana was often home alone, Santana had set zoned alarms. She'd quickly learned to stay in the kitchen and in the laundry area where her bed, food, and water dishes were located whenever the "away" alarm was on, thus avoiding the interior sensors that were set off by movement.

There was only one area Santana considered vulnerable. That was the dog-door near the kitchen. It was large enough for a small man, woman, or animal to squeeze through. To prevent that from happening, an electronic chip in Gitana's collar activated the door that gave her access to an enclosed dog run Santana had constructed in the backyard. The door automatically locked shut once she'd exited or entered. But it wasn't like her to venture out at night. His instincts told him something had happened to her.

He went to the computer on the desk and touched a key to awaken it. Then he clicked on the application for the security cameras mounted around the house. Four separate rectangular black and white boxes appeared, representing the sides of the house. He felt a rush of anger when he saw the white image of Gitana lying still on her side outside the dog run. Someone must've opened the gate and let her out. He inhaled a deep breath and exhaled slowly, willing himself to remain calm. Emotion would only cloud his judgment and slow his reactions.

He tried the switch on the desk lamp. Nothing. The main power source had likely been disabled, though the alarm system and computer would run on batteries.

He wondered if an assassin from the Cali cartel was lurking in the darkness, or if it was someone related to the case he was currently working. He doubted it was a burglar. Someone wanted him out of the house. Gitana was the bait.

From the bottom desk drawer, he removed a pair of thermal vision goggles. They had a range of 1,000 to 1500 feet, used two AA alkaline batteries, and worked for 45-90 minutes. Unlike the green-cast images seen through night-vision goggles, these goggles relied on heat rather than light to create clear white images that contrasted sharply with the background, like the thermal cameras mounted around the house. Not even someone wearing camouflage could avoid detection.

Santana put on his running shoes and made certain they were tightly laced. Then he started down the staircase, staying close to the wall, where the steps were less likely to squeak, just in case someone had breached the security system and entered the house.

At the bottom of the stairs, he paused and listened, his senses acute, a cold tightness in his chest, the barrel of the Glock pointed skyward as he held it firmly in one hand.

The house was as silent as a tomb.

The steady red light on the keypad near the front door indicated the alarm was still operating on batteries. He entered the code to deactivate it, but kept the door closed. If someone was out there waiting for him, Santana wanted the element of surprise on his side.

In the basement, he opened a small window that led to a seven-foot deep, concrete window well on the side of the house. There was enough room for him to squeeze through the window, and enough cover to make sure he wasn't seen. Crouching in the dark well, he strapped the thermal goggles on his head. Then he climbed up the iron ladder anchored in the concrete and peered cautiously over the lip of the well.

He focused his vision on the birch and pine trees studding the property, slowly scanning the area around each one till he saw a figure lying flat on his stomach in a prone position to the right of a tree, thirty yards in the distance. A bipod was attached to the front of a rifle stock, the butt pressed against the figure's right shoulder. Santana couldn't tell if the shooter had his own pair of night or thermal vision goggles.

He climbed out of the well and crept along the ground toward his target, his Glock clutched in his right hand. He was tempted to see if Gitana was still alive. But he knew he might be detected. Instead, he gave the dog a wide berth, moving in a counter-clockwise direction, hoping to come in behind the shooter.

Santana was sweating as he moved along in the cool night air that smelled heavily of wet soil and pine. A slight breeze rattled the leaves on the trees and covered any noise he made as he moved. Still, he stopped every few yards, gauging his position and that of the shooter. He figured he'd been crawling for no more than three or four minutes.

As he came to a stand of trees that provided him cover but momentarily blocked his vision, he took a few seconds to adjust his goggles. When he moved around the stand of trees, a shot of adrenaline jacked up his heart rate. The shooter had disappeared. Santana paused and hunkered close to the ground, scanning the area, fearing the shooter might have him in his sights. It was then that he felt the rifle barrel pressed against the back of his head.

His heart was thumping hard in his chest, his mind swirling with thoughts as he waited for the bullet that would end his life. Had he stayed in the house or called 911, the scenario might have worked out differently. His options now were slim and none. If he made any sudden movement, he would be dead before he could aim and pull the Glock's trigger. He'd known since he was sixteen that this day would eventually come. He just hadn't known how he would die. In his mind's eye he saw the faces of Jordan and his sister, Natalia. Then a strange thought crept into his head. He wanted to know who was about to kill him.

"Who are you?" he asked, trying to keep his voice steady.

"Your worst nightmare."

The shooter's voice had been altered to sound like a robot, probably through the use of a portable voice changer, Santana thought. "You kill me and a shit storm is going to rain down on you."

Santana knew it wasn't true. The shooter was a professional. When the job was finished, he would disappear into the netherworld of assassins from which he'd come. It would be difficult to find him and to identify whoever had hired him. Santana felt the weight of the rifle barrel press tighter against his skull. He knew his time was up. He squeezed his eyes shut and held his breath, as if by sheer force of will he could stop the bullet from entering his skull and shutting down his brain.

Then he felt a rush of wind and heard a low growl and a *thump*, as though an object had hit the shooter. When he realized the weight of the barrel had lifted from his head, Santana rolled onto his back, stripped off his thermal goggles, and pointed the Glock at the empty space in front of him, ready to fire.

That's when he realized that Gitana had leapt out of the night and knocked the shooter on his back, like a linebacker sacking a quarterback. She had the assassin's right forearm locked in her jaw, her bared teeth ripping at the sleeve of his camo outfit.

Santana stood and leveled the Glock. He called off Gitana, and she immediately let go of the shooter's arm and stepped back, her teeth still bared.

It was difficult to see clearly in the dim light. But Santana could tell that the shooter was a stocky man with broad shoulders and a thick neck. The kind of man who was comfortable using his body and fists to impose his will on those who were weaker and less skilled. Santana motioned with the Glock for him to stand and take off the ski mask.

"You have a good dog," he said, staring at Gitana as pale ribbons of vapors steamed in front of his face. "I should have used more tranquilizer in the dart and not have let her live."

"Life is full of should haves," Santana said.

"Sadly, that is true. But I am an animal lover." His voice was clear and steady now and had a thick Hispanic accent.

Santana motioned with the Glock again. "Get up."

"I do not think so, *señor*." Still sitting on the ground with his legs stretched in front of him, the shooter pulled a KA-BAR out of a sheath strapped to his leg.

"Drop the knife or I'll kill you."

The man looked directly at Santana. "I believe you would." Then he lifted his chin and in one swift move he drew the sharp edge of the knife across his own throat, severing the carotid arteries in his neck.

Chapter 12

Sunlight pierced a thin layer of clouds, lighting the fog that floated over the St. Croix River like a spirit over a grave. White-suited forensic techs scouring the grounds and woods around Santana's house reminded him of the images he'd seen through the lenses of his thermal goggles just hours before. He drank from his cup of hot chocolate and turned away from the window that was running with moisture.

Kacie Hawkins was seated on a leather recliner near the fireplace, facing Pete Romano. He was sitting on the couch.

"Is your dog going to be okay, John?" Hawkins asked.

"I spoke with the vet. He thinks so. But he wants to observe her for a while. She was still wobbly from the tranquilizer."

After the gangbanger had taken his own life, Santana had placed Gitana in a quiet, darkened room in the house and kept her as quiet and comfortable as possible till a canine officer he knew and trusted had driven her to a twenty-four hour veterinary hospital. He would have preferred to take her himself, but he couldn't leave the scene.

"She saved your life."

"It isn't the first time, Kacie."

"That's all well and good," Romano said. "But who the hell was this guy?"

"He had no ID. But his whole body was tattooed with Mara Salvatrucha gang symbols."

"The MS 13 doesn't have much of a presence here."

"No. But they could be hooking up with the SUR 13s."

"Maybe we can match his prints," Hawkins said. "Or get a line on where he got the portable voice changer."

Romano nodded his head and looked at Santana. "Any idea why he'd want to kill you?"

"Because I'm getting too close."

"Close to what?"

"If I knew that, we wouldn't be having this conversation."

Romano shook his head in frustration and rubbed his eyes that were rheumy from lack of sleep.

"It's the list," Hawkins said. "Someone on that list is panicking."

Romano stared at her, a quizzical look on his face. "About what?"

"Catalina Díaz's murder."

"What would the men on the list have to do with Díaz's death or with the MS 13?"

"We're going to find out, Pete."

"Tanabe ruled Díaz's death accidental."

"She's changed her mind before," Santana said. "And we might be looking at a second murder."

Romano looked in Santana's direction. "What?"

Santana told him about Tania Cruz's murder, leaving out any mention of Sarah Malik and her daughter Sammy.

"I don't recall that being an unsolved."

"Technically, it isn't. A guy named Arias Marchena was convicted of her murder."

Romano spread his hands. "If I look like I'm confused, Detective, it's because I am."

"I think Marchena might've been framed."

"By who?"

"The same guy who killed Díaz."

"How'd you make the connection to Cruz?"

Hawkins glanced at Santana, a slight grin tugging at the corners of her mouth. She knew he'd avoid telling Romano anything about Sammy Malik and Tania Cruz's alleged reincarnation if he could.

"I talked with Nick Baker," Santana said. "He investigated the Cruz murder. Cruz and Díaz were both murdered in a similar manner. And Baker thinks Marchena was framed."

"When did Baker come out of retirement?" Romano's voice was leaden with sarcasm. A long moment of silence followed before he let out a sigh. "Let me see that damn list again."

Santana sat down on the couch beside Romano and handed it to him.

"What do you know about Matthew Singer and Nathaniel Burdette?"

Santana told him what he knew.

"This is just guess work, Detective."

"Oh, I think it's more than that, Pete. Someone hired a Mara 13 to kill me. That makes it personal."

"I don't want any vendettas driving this investigation. Right now, we've got Marchena in prison for the Cruz murder and Díaz's death listed as accidental."

"Think about it, Pete. The shooter tries to take me out. When he fails, he kills himself. What does that tell you?"

Romano shrugged. "That he was probably insane."

"I think he was afraid for having failed," Santana said. "So afraid that he preferred to take his own life rather than face his gangbanger buddies."

"Come on, John. You've made enemies. This attempt on your life might have nothing to do with the Díaz case or any of the names on this list."

"I can't take that chance," Santana said. "And neither can you."

* * *

After Hawkins, Romano, and the forensic crew had cleared out, Santana slept for three hours before awakening from a nightmare in which he'd felt the cold steel of a rifle barrel pressed against the back of his head. He sat on the edge of the bed, listening to the cry of the wind and waiting till his heart rate slowed. He called the vet and learned that Gitana was still doing fine. Then he ate lunch, took a long hot shower, and dressed. In order to better conceal his compact Glock 27, he slipped on a DeSantis shoulder rig, which fit comfortably under his jacket.

He took a cup of hot chocolate and his binoculars onto the deck off his bedroom. Sunlight had burned away the morning fog. Long, wispy cirrus clouds smeared the high blue sky, and a cool breeze created small whitecaps in the river.

He trained the binoculars on the bald eagle nest in the tall dead oak along the shoreline. The nest grew in size every year. Santana had seen two grayish chicks with wobbly legs earlier in the spring, but he saw only one now. He figured the larger eaglet was female and had killed the smaller one since females were consistently larger than males. He'd also noted that neither parent had made the slightest effort to stop the fratricide.

He finished his hot chocolate, went inside, and checked the Sun Country website for Jordan's flight arrival time from San Diego. Then he called the Genesis Clinic and asked to speak to Nathaniel Burdette. A receptionist said she'd take a message—till Santana told her he was a homicide detective. Thirty seconds later, Burdette came on the line.

"Has something happened?" he said in a voice filled with concern.

"I'd like to speak to you as soon as possible, Dr. Burdette."

"Is this about Catalina Díaz?"

"Yes."

Silence.

"Are you free at all this afternoon?"

"I'm very busy with patients today, Detective Santana."

"I'd hate to have to ask you to come downtown."

"Yes. Well . . . I'm hosting a fundraiser tomorrow night for breast cancer research. I do quite a bit of breast reconstructive surgery. Why don't you come by? And feel free to bring your wife or significant other."

"I doubt that a fundraiser would be a good place for a conversation."

"We'll be able to find some private time, Detective. And if you'd like, you could make a small donation to breast cancer research."

Burdette's invitation could provide some much needed time for him and Jordan, Santana thought.

"Eight o'clock," Burdette said. "By the way, it's black-tie." He paused, as though waiting for a response.

"No problem."

"Fine. I'll add your name to the guest list. It'll be crowded, but ask anyone. They'll point you in my direction."

"I found you once, Dr. Burdette," Santana said. "I can find you again."

* * *

Later that afternoon, Santana called a Drug Enforcement Agent he knew.

Mike Rios answered his cell phone on the third ring. "Who's this?"

"John Santana."

"I take it you want something."

"I'll buy you dinner at Mancini's," Santana said. "Meet me there and find out."

Rios had collaborated with the SPPD on a number of drug busts, though Santana had never worked directly with him. But Rios also had some baggage.

When he'd begun working for the DEA, his job had been to "cold stop" those he suspected of smuggling drugs or money through the Minneapolis/St. Paul International Airport. A "cold stop" was based solely on an agent's observation of a passenger, in contrast to a "hot stop," where an individual was stopped based on prior investigative information. Rios had been accused of cold-stopping only African-Americans, none of which were found to be carrying drugs or money. One of those he'd stopped had brought a racial profiling lawsuit against him and the DEA. It was eventually settled out of court for a substantial amount of money.

A second lawsuit involving Rios had occurred when he and members of the SPPD Narco/Vice drug task force had raided a house in St. Paul. After breaking down the front door and shooting the family dog, they'd handcuffed three children and forced them to sit next to the carcass of their dead pet for more than an hour while they searched for drugs—even after they realized they'd raided the wrong house. The family sued the DEA and SPPD for $10 million for civil rights violations and $20 million in punitive damages. The lawsuit was still pending.

Because of these incidents and his somewhat abrasive personality, Rios had been passed over for promotion. Santana knew that Rios still had an axe to grind with DEA administrators. He thought he could use that knowledge to extract information.

Mancini's Char House was on West 7th Street near downtown. The family-run restaurant was famous for its steaks and had been a staple in St. Paul for over forty years. Art Deco lamps in the low ceiling softened the light, and ceiling fans circulated cool air. Santana sat at a table across from Rios in the carpeted dining room, near the open kitchen and small serving bar. Out of habit, he made sure his chair faced the arched brick entrance.

"Thanks for the invitation," Rios said as they waited for their order. "But you didn't offer to buy me dinner because of my winning personality."

Santana looked across the table at the husky but fit Latino with his dark complexion, shaved head, and deep-set brown eyes. He was in his mid-thirties but could easily pass for a mid-twenties gangbanger.

"I need some information."

Rios shrugged. "You think because you offered to buy me dinner, I'm going to give it to you?"

Santana shook his head. "If I thought you were that shallow, I wouldn't be asking."

"Praise isn't going to get you any further than dinner," he said. "I don't know if I should even be talking to you."

"Why's that?"

"Our conversation wouldn't have anything to do with a death that occurred at a house along the St. Croix early this morning, would it?"

"Word travels fast."

"That it does."

"Why not wait till you hear what I have to say, Rios? Then you can decide whether or not you want to help."

"Seems fair enough," he said and drank some red wine. He held up the glass. "I'm not too much of a wine guy, but this is good."

"One more thing before I begin."

Rios's eyes narrowed in suspicion. "Let's hear it."

"Whatever I tell you stays between you and me."

"I'll make that decision after I hear what you have to say, Santana. Take it or leave it."

Santana knew he had little choice. Rios had the upper hand—for now. Santana was hoping to reverse that position soon. "You heard about Catalina Díaz, the escort found dead in the downtown hotel?"

"I heard."

"I think she was murdered."

"Too bad. But what's that have to do with me?"

"Before I answer, I need some information."

A pretty, friendly waitress named Vicki brought their filet mignon dinners and refilled their wine glasses from the bottle of red named after the restaurant. They ate in silence for a time till Rios spoke again. "So what exactly do you want, Santana?"

"Tell me what you know about the MS 13."

"Why are you interested?"

"Because one of them tried to kill me last night."

Rios stopped cutting a piece of steak and stared at Santana. "An MS 13 tried to off you?"

"That's right. I think something is going on with the Maras and DEA knows what it is."

"You've got your wires crossed, Santana. The Mara Salvatruchas aren't operating in the Twin Cities."

"What about a Mara and SUR 13 connection?"

"You're crazy."

"Is Ricky Garza still running the SURs?"

He nodded.

"What is it you're not telling me, Rios?"

"Uh-uh," he said. "Your turn." He drank his wine, set the empty glass on the table, and pushed it to the side as though moving a chess piece.

Santana told Rios what he knew about the men on the list and their association with the escorts from Costa Rica and from Erotic Tours.

When Santana finished, Rios wiped his mouth with a napkin and slid out of the chair. "None of what you've told me is worth shit, Santana, but thanks for dinner. I'll pick up the check next time. If there is a next time."

"I'm going to find out what's going on one way or another. If this is what I think it is, it could turn things around for you."

"I'm not in it for the glory."

"Nobody said you were. But I know you believed you got screwed when it came time for a promotion. Nothing is sweeter than revenge."

"You know all about that, huh?"

"I do," Santana said. "Revenge is never as sweet as you think it'll be. But it's better than nothing at all."

Rios stood beside the table, looking down at Santana, his eyes focused inward as he considered whatever scenarios he imagined in his mind. "Good luck," he said and headed for the front door.

* * *

Santana found Ricky Garza on the porch of his Craftsman-style house on St. Paul's East Side with three of his *eses*, or homeboys, all clad in blue LA Dodger jerseys, their gang colors. Garza was sitting in a canvas chair with his legs stretched out and the backs of his ankles resting on the chipped and peeling white porch railing. The four men were drinking from 40-ounce cans of malt liquor and listening to a *narcocorrido*, or drug ballad, on a large boom box. The Mexican music with the accordion-based rhythm celebrated the criminal activities of the cartels the way some rap music glorified American gangbangers.

Like the majority of SUR 13 members in St. Paul, Garza and his homeboys were loosely connected to Southern California's *Sureño*, or southern gangs, the term used to describe various Latino street gangs that paid tribute to the Mexican Mafia while in federal and state correctional facilities. Once inside the prison system, the *Sureño* gangs suspended their traditional rivalries and turf wars and aligned themselves with the Mexican Mafia, or *La EME*, against the *Norteños*, or northern gangs connected to the *Nuestra Familia*.

Many of the SUR 13 bangers in St. Paul were either Mexican nationals or natives of other Central American nations who traveled through the illegal immigration pipeline primarily controlled by the MS 13. They were involved in a wide variety of criminal enterprises, including homicides, drug trafficking, prostitution, and kidnapping. Having been born in St. Paul twenty-eight years ago, Garza could not be deported for his previous crimes.

Santana parked behind Garza's familiar red Chevrolet Silverado lowrider. Two beefy Rottweilers leashed to thick oak trees in the front yard—one on each side of a crumbling sidewalk—began barking loudly when he got out of his Crown Vic and started toward the house, their eyes bulging and their thick bodies straining to break loose.

Garza yelled, "*Cállense el hocico,*" and the dogs shut up.

A bank of thunderclouds had rolled out of the west as dusk settled over the landscape. Santana could smell ozone in the air as he stopped in front of the porch.

Garza glanced at Santana, his obsidian eyes as cold and indifferent as a shark's, his smile as relaxed as a lizard on a sunny log. His close-cut hair was shaved into the shape of an arrowhead, and the ends of a thin, dark mustache curved like small blades at the corners of his mouth. The Roman numeral XIII was tattooed on his right hand, the numeral representing the thirteenth letter of the alphabet, the letter M, in order to pay allegiance to the Mexican Mafia.

"What'd you want, Santana?" he said with a slight Spanish accent.

"Information about Tania Cruz."

"I don't know any Tania Cruz. You're wastin' your time."

"I have plenty of it."

Garza snickered. "I don't have to talk to you."

"No, you don't. But I'm sure I could convince the gang unit to drop by and pay you and your *eses* a visit."

"It wouldn't be the first time."

"You ever meet Arias Marchena?"

He shook his head and drank some malt liquor.

"How about Catalina Díaz?"

"No," he said, his eyes revealing nothing.

"Maybe you know something about the Mara who tried to kill me last night?"

"Hey, Santana. I'm really sorry to hear that. I guess being a homicide detective is a dangerous profession."

His gangbanger buddies all laughed.

Through the screen door, Santana could hear a baby crying inside the house and a television commercial in Spanish.

Garza stood up. "My woman is working. I have to look in on my kid."

"I didn't know you were married, Ricky."

"I'm not, Santana. But maybe you don't know a lot of things."

* * *

From his SUV, Santana called the veterinary clinic and was happy to learn that he could pick up Gitana tomorrow. Then he called Kacie Hawkins.

When he got her cellphone voicemail, he decided to drive by the house she'd recently purchased, a small stone Tudor located on St. Paul's East Side.

Rain fell in gray sheets as he parked behind a silver Nissan 370Z sports car. He waited ten minutes till it let up before exiting the Explorer and striding up the sidewalk leading to the house. He could smell the sweet scent of wet grass and feel the evening air, sharp as the touch of a cold blade against his skin.

Santana pushed the doorbell and waited.

He was about to press the bell again when the inner door swung open and Santana found himself face to face with Paul Lenoir.

"Detective Santana," Lenoir said. "How're you doing?"

Santana was speechless.

"Kacie is in the bathroom. Want to come in?"

Santana stepped back as Lenoir swung open the screen door. "No," he said, "I'll talk to her later."

As he headed back to his Explorer, he heard Kacie's voice. "Wait a minute, John!"

Santana turned and saw her hurrying toward him, an exasperated look on her face. She stopped just in front of him. "What are you doing here?"

He could smell the beer on her breath and, over her shoulders, see Paul Lenoir standing behind the screen door, a grin on his face. He waited till Lenoir closed the front door and then nodded toward the house. "What is *he* doing here?"

Hawkins gave an embarrassed shrug. "He came by for dinner."

"Why?"

"I asked him to," she said.

"He may be a murder suspect."

"Since when?"

Santana knew he had nothing to stand on, so he changed the subject. "I thought you didn't like Lenoir."

"I never said that."

"No, but I thought after that first meeting—"

"He called and apologized."

"So how long has this been going on?"

"Not that it's any of your business, John, but tonight is the second time I've seen him."

"I think this is a bad idea, Kacie."

"Oh, like it was a good idea when you were seeing Grace Chandler," she said, reminding Santana that he'd been involved with a suspect in a previous murder investigation.

"Okay," he said. "I see your point."

"I'm not sure that you do. As partners, I defer to you on most things. But that deference doesn't extend to my private life." Her tone was firm, but Santana detected no anger in her voice.

He held his hands up in a gesture of surrender. "I was out of line, Kacie."

She looked at him for what seemed like a long time. "Are you really concerned about Lenoir because you think he's a suspect, or is something else bothering you?"

"What do you mean?"

She stared at him a moment longer. "Forget it," she said.

Her meaning suddenly became clear to him. "Look, Kacie. I'm concerned about you because you're my partner, my friend. I've lost a partner before and don't want to lose another."

"For God's sake, John. I know what I'm doing. I don't trust Lenoir any more than you do."

"Then why are you dating him?"

"It isn't a date," she said. "At least from my perspective. I knew Lenoir was attracted to me. I figured I might get some information if I got closer to him. I'm sure he knew you'd tell me about his involvement with Escort Tours. He's trying to build trust with me."

"Or find out how much we know."

"So what was so important that it couldn't wait till Monday?" she asked.

Santana told her about his conversations with Ricky Garza and Mike Rios.

"Garza knows something," she said. "But he won't talk."

"Not unless we find some leverage."

"What about Rios?"

"We'll need leverage with him as well."

"By the way, the prints taken from the banger who tried to kill you weren't in the AFIS database. And I've got nothing yet on the voice changer he was wearing."

Santana nodded and turned to leave. Then he hesitated. "Just be careful with Lenoir, okay?"

Hawkins placed her hands on her hips. "How about cutting me some slack, John?"

"Have a nice dinner," he said.

* * *

Jordan's flight landed at 11:00 p.m. By the time they'd collected her luggage and Santana had driven her back to her condo near St. Anthony Main, it was well after midnight. They showered together, then made love. Afterwards, they lay together in Jordan's bed, her head resting in the hollow of his shoulder.

She'd recapped her trial testimony in San Diego and the highlights of the PI conference. Now she wanted to know how Santana's current case was proceeding.

He knew she would eventually hear about the attempt on his life. He'd already withheld information concerning his past. He was worried that withholding further information could drive a permanent wedge between them.

"You need to know about something that happened when you were out of town."

"Okay," she said.

He could think of no delicate way to phrase it. "Someone tried to kill me."

Jordan sat up. "What?" Moonlight filtering through the slats in the blinds formed a pattern of dark bars across her naked torso.

Santana went through it, leaving nothing out, including the list of men he'd found in Catalina Díaz's condo.

"My God," she said. "How's Gitana?"

"She's at the vet's. I'll pick her up today. She'll be fine."

"You hope."

"Yes," he said. "I do."

She looked down at him without speaking. Then she placed a hand gently on the dimpled scar near his heart, courtesy of a bullet that had nearly taken his life. "Why would the MS 13 want you dead?"

"I haven't put it all together yet, but I think it has something to do with the men on the list."

"But why, John? Why would a group of successful men be dealing with gangbangers like the MS 13?"

"I don't know. But one or more of them might also be connected to the murder of Catalina Díaz and another escort murdered six years ago named Tania Cruz."

"How?"

Santana told her about the visit he'd received from Sarah Malik and her daughter Sammy. When he'd finished, Jordan got out of bed and put on a silk robe. "You want something to drink?"

"No," he said. "I'm fine."

She went out of the bedroom and came back two minutes later with a glass full of orange juice. Sitting on the edge of the bed, the glass in her hand, she stared at him awhile before speaking. "Do you believe Sarah Malik is telling the truth?"

"Maybe as she sees it."

"Suppose she's right, John? Suppose Sammy Malik is the reincarnation of Tania Cruz?"

"It doesn't seem possible."

"But imagine how things would change if it were true."

"How would things change, Jordan? Would there no longer be violence in the world?"

"Maybe not."

Santana shook his head. "Millions of people in the Far East believe in reincarnation. Yet the violence continues."

"So you're saying we can't learn from our mistakes?"

"Some can," he said. "But some never will. It's human nature."

"That's a very pessimistic view."

"No. It's realistic. That banger who tried to kill me was probably baptized as a Catholic. He went to Mass as a child and was told about heaven and hell and what would happen if he chose the wrong path. Despite all the teachings, all the warnings, he became a killer. And because he feared retribution in this life more than the next, he committed suicide."

Jordan drank some juice while she considered what he'd said. "Are you afraid of death, John?"

"I don't think I could ever be happy if I was thinking about it all the time."

"But you think about it some. We all do."

"If there's nothing after death, Jordan, it'll be like a dreamless, painless sleep. If Sarah Malik and the Hindus are correct, then I probably won't remember my past life or lives anyway."

"And if there's a heaven and a hell?"

"Where do you think I'd go, Jordan?"

"The same place as me," she said with a little smile.

"Then that would be heaven," he said.

She leaned over, kissed him, and stared into his eyes for a long moment. "You're not backing off."

"Would you?"

"No," she said. "I was going to ask you to be careful, but I know you will. At least as careful as you can be when someone is trying to kill you."

"I don't come with a lifetime warranty."

"None of us does," she said. She set the glass on the nightstand, slipped out of her robe and lay beside him, her head once again in the hollow of his shoulder, an arm draped lightly across his chest.

Santana could feel her breath against his cheek, hear the sound of a distant siren, its appeal irresistibly sad but sweet, like the Sirens of Greek mythology, whose enchanting songs lured sailors to the rocky coast of their island—and to their deaths.

Chapter 13

On Saturday evening, Santana stood beside Jordan as they rode a crowded private elevator up to Nathaniel Burdette's penthouse on the 25th floor of the Landmark Towers. Santana was surreptitiously admiring Jordan's black, floor-length evening gown with the cowl neck and open back, appreciating the way the dress clung tightly to her curves. He leaned into her, inhaling the scent of her Wonderstruck perfume.

"Why don't we skip the party?" he whispered in her ear.

She smiled shyly without looking at him and held his hand as the elevator doors slid open, revealing an ornate grand rotunda with a crystal chandelier.

A long corridor led to a large sunken living room with a cherrywood floor. The room was filled with elegantly dressed men and women whose jewelry glittered in the indirect lighting. A sectional, three cushioned chairs, and two coffee tables made of exotic wood were centered on a Persian rug around a marble gas fireplace. Floor to ceiling windows offered a magnificent view of the city lights.

Santana saw Matthew Singer and two other distinguished-looking men huddled in the far corner of the room near a grand piano. They were drinking champagne out of tall crystal flutes and were engaged in an animated conversation with three beautiful, dark-haired women no more than twenty-five years of age.

"Good evening, Detective."

Santana turned. Nina Rivera stood in front of him, a glass of champagne in one hand. She wore a strapless satin floor-length gown and a wide diamond collar necklace. Her lipstick matched the fuchsia color of her dress. Her thick brunette hair had been styled like it was the last time he'd seen her, side-parted with long rolling curls falling to one side of her face.

Santana introduced her to Jordan.

"Pleased to meet you," Jordan said, holding out a hand.

Nina Rivera shook it but didn't reply. Her amber eyes quickly shifted their focus to Santana again. "It's nice to see you, Detective, especially in a more relaxed environment."

"Have you seen Nathaniel Burdette?"

"I'm right here," Burdette said, sidling up beside Rivera. He shook hands with Santana, smiling broadly, his grip firm, his demeanor confident and his gaze steady. "I asked Nina to let me know when you arrived." Turning to Jordan, Burdette offered his hand and said, "This must be the lovely Mrs. Santana."

"Jordan Parrish," she said without missing a beat.

"Ah, it's so good of you to come." He looked at Rivera. "Nina, why don't you show Ms. Parrish around while the detective and I chat?"

Nina Rivera's tight smile indicated she wasn't thrilled with the idea. But she said, "I'd be happy to."

As the women departed, Santana noted an icy white, four-foot tall sculpture of a three-headed dog near the fireplace. It had a serpent for a tail and heads of snakes running down its back.

"You like it?" Burdette said, following Santana's gaze.

"It's Cerberus, isn't it?"

"Yes. Are you familiar with the Greek myth, Detective?"

"It's the beast that guards the entrance to Hades. It allows only the spirits of the dead to enter the underworld and none to leave."

"A literate detective. I'm impressed. Do you recall what the three heads represent?"

"The past, the present, and the future."

"That's one interpretation. Other scholars suggest the heads represent birth, youth, and old age."

"What do you think, Doctor?"

"Well, as a plastic surgeon, I choose to believe that youth is never lost."

"You bought the statue because it represents youth?"

"That's part of it. Looking good on the outside allows one to feel good on the inside. Wouldn't you agree, Detective?"

"Many beautiful people are depressed, Doctor. Look at Hollywood."

"Perhaps that has more to do with the pressure of fame. Come," he said, gesturing toward two sets of double doors that opened from the living room to a large terrace. "Let's get some fresh air." Burdette grabbed two flutes of champagne off a tray as a server passed by and handed one to Santana.

They walked out to a terrace that reminded Santana of an Italian palazzo. The city was aglow with lights, the night air as crisp and cool as the champagne. From the terrace, Santana could see Rice Park and what appeared to be miniature versions of the state capitol and the St. Paul Cathedral.

"So, Detective," Burdette said, leaning against a railing near a terrace lamp, "what can I do for you?"

"You know why I'm here."

"Hopefully to enjoy the evening and support a worthy cause."

"Besides that."

Burdette drank some champagne. "Catalina Díaz."

"Correct. You lied to me, Dr. Burdette. You were seeing Díaz."

"Lie is a disturbing word, Detective."

"So is murder."

Burdette swallowed some champagne. "I was seeing Catalina strictly on a professional basis. I had nothing to do with her death."

"How long had you been seeing her?"

"A year or two."

"Where were you the night she died?"

"Here," he said, gesturing toward the living room.

"Can anyone verify that?"

"I'm afraid not. I had a long day in surgery. I was exhausted and came straight home. I do recall that the Twins were playing the Tigers that night. I ate a light dinner and went straight to bed. Didn't even finish the game."

"Most people can't remember what they did two days ago," Santana said. "You have a very good memory, Dr. Burdette."

"Let's be honest, Detective. I knew you'd ask me if I had an alibi. I had some time to remember one."

Or concoct one, Santana thought.

In the night sky over Burdette's shoulder, Santana could see a ring of ice crystals around the full moon. He remembered hearing in his childhood that a ring signified that bad weather was coming soon.

"Tell me about Tania Cruz," he said.

Burdette's mouth fell open and his complexion darkened. "Who?"

"Tania Cruz."

"I don't know the woman."

"You're sure?"

Burdette nodded and drank more champagne.

"She was a young escort who died six years ago in the same manner as Catalina Díaz."

"I'm sorry to hear that."

Santana stared at Burdette till the doctor broke eye contact. "You were in medical school with Philip Campbell and Matthew Singer."

Burdette's gaze drifted back to Santana's face. "That's right. We've been friends ever since."

"And you've taken trips to Costa Rica together. And James Elliot, a former medical school classmate of yours, runs a charter service you use."

He nodded.

"What about Paul Lenoir?"

"I know Paul." Burdette finished his champagne and gestured with his glass toward Santana. "You don't like the champagne, Detective?"

"It's fine."

"But it isn't fine that I've been seeing escorts?"

"What isn't fine is that one of Catalina Díaz's clients might have murdered her, Dr. Burdette."

"Normally, I'd be shocked. But Matthew told me of your supposition. Frankly, I believe you are mistaken and are wasting your time."

"Finding a murderer is never a waste of time."

"You don't believe Philip killed her?"

"No. Despite the best efforts of someone to make me think so."

"Why would any of us want to murder Catalina Díaz?"

"I'll know that soon enough," Santana said.

* * *

Santana and Jordan left the fundraiser at ten p.m. Thirty-five minutes later they were driving on a side road off Interstate 94 toward Santana's house amidst a thick fog that rose from the lowlands along the riverbank like smoke from a smoldering fire.

"We should've gone to my place," Jordan said.

172

"We're almost there. Besides, I need to check on Gitana. I picked her up from the veterinary hospital after leaving your place this morning."

"How is she?"

"Better than when she went to the vet's. But I feel uncomfortable leaving her alone for long stretches."

"Did you learn anything from Burdette?"

"He claims he was home the night Catalina Díaz died."

"Since he lives alone," she said, "it'll be difficult to verify."

"He might be telling the truth about that night, Jordan, but he lied about not knowing Tania Cruz."

"You're thinking the same man murdered both women."

"I am," Santana said, straining to see beyond the fog lit headlights. "So what did you think of the party?"

"Lots of rich, middle-aged men with young, beautiful Latina women."

"You're just as beautiful."

"I'm pleased you think so."

"Still, I get the feeling I'm missing something."

"I'm too old for you?"

He laughed. "I mean I'm missing something about the case." He braked lightly, dropping the speed from 25 to 15 miles an hour, and leaned over the steering wheel and peered straight ahead till he saw the end of his driveway.

Once inside the house, they first checked on Gitana. She wagged her tail furiously and licked both their faces. Santana praised her in the baby voice she loved as she leaned against his legs, asking to be stroked. Then, while Jordan laid a fire, Santana made two cups of *canelazo* by mixing a shot of *aguardiente* with brown sugar and boiling cinnamon water.

"Mmm," she said, as they sat on the couch in front of the fireplace. "This is good."

"And good for you, too," he said.

"I'll bet."

The lights were dim, the music soft. Gitana sat on the floor and placed her head in Santana's lap. He petted her sun-kissed coat gently and thought about all those who'd sat in front of fires before him, and all those who would sit in front of them after he was gone.

"What are you thinking, John?"

He didn't want to spoil the moment by confessing that he was thinking about death. "How much I enjoy the fire."

"It's nice," she said, resting her head on his shoulder. "Makes me feel warm and comfortable."

"And sleepy?"

"Not yet."

Gitana stretched out in front of the fireplace, yawning as she relaxed her body. He heard the snap of the birch logs and saw the flames twist up the chimney. The fire triggered a memory of the votive candles around the statue of *Santa Muerte* he'd seen in Nina Rivera's bedroom.

"What was your impression of Nina Rivera?"

"She likes you."

Santana felt his heartbeat kick up a nervous notch. "Did she tell you that?"

Jordan lifted her head off his shoulder and looked at him, her hazel eyes glittering in the firelight. "No, she didn't."

"Then how do you know?"

"Trust me. I know."

"But I'm with you."

"I know that, too," she said, kissing him gently on the lips.

Santana wondered how much Nina Rivera knew about Catalina Díaz's death and the death of Tania Cruz. He wondered who and what was behind her fear of the truth. He wondered if she feared the men on the list or something else.

Jordan angled her body toward him, her expression thoughtful, her pretty face filled with tenderness and quiet strength. "What else is on your mind, John?"

He knew she could read the disturbed thought on his face no matter how hard he tried to conceal it. "Sammy Malik."

She rested an elbow on the back of the couch and brushed his dark, wavy hair with her fingertips. "You're having trouble with the idea of reincarnation."

"I don't believe Tania Cruz's soul has returned from the dead, Jordan."

"But you want to know for sure."

"Someone once wrote that death is the only promise kept."

"There are other promises kept," she said.

"I hope so."

She touched his cheek. "There is no way of knowing for sure if reincarnation is true, John."

"That's frustrating."

"Because it conflicts with your belief?"

"It's more than that," he said. "It muddies the case."

"How?"

"Without Sarah Malik and her daughter, I wouldn't have considered the possibility of a murder link between Tania Cruz and Catalina Díaz."

"That's a good thing."

"It is. But it's based on a falsehood."

"Reincarnation?"

He nodded.

"There are many who'd disagree with you."

"It wouldn't be the first time," he said.

She smiled.

"You don't believe in the afterlife any more than I do, Jordan."

"I try not to think about it much. But then we probably spend too much of our time thinking about the future and what's going to happen, or thinking about the past and what might have been. We should spend more of our time living in the present, enjoying this life, especially if it's all we have."

"That's easy to say."

"I know it's harder for you to ignore death, John, given your job. Plus, you've nearly died yourself. It gives you some perspective."

Reflecting on the significance of his life and what gave it meaning had helped Santana come to terms with his own eventual death and the deaths of those he hunted. He'd learned that when it was time, death never negotiated. It always had its way. But the deaths of the innocent still troubled him and always would.

An oak log shifted in the grate and the fire increased in intensity, turning its attention to a birch log just above it, the bark quickly succumbing to the flames. The sudden shift in the fire reminded him of those whose defective personalities were impulsive and dangerous. Like fire, they had no fear or doubt, no mercy or shame. They would destroy everything in their path and could only be stopped when they burned out—or when they were extinguished.

* * *

Two hours after Santana had fallen asleep, he awoke to the sounds of Jordan moaning and thrashing about. He rolled over and spoke quietly to her, but she lashed out at him, throwing punches wildly, as if fighting for her life.

"Jordan!" he said, grabbing her wrists in his hands to ward off the blows. In the dim light he saw her eyes open wide. "It's John. You're okay." He waited till her breathing slowed and her body relaxed. Then he let go of her wrists and turned on the lamp on the nightstand. He sat on his haunches beside her and gently touched her face with a hand. "You were having a nightmare."

Her eyes teared and she turned her head away from him. "I'm sorry."

He lay down beside her, took her in his arms, and held her close. He could feel her tears on his chest as he stroked the back of her head.

After a time she said, "I've been having more nightmares lately."

"Why didn't you tell me?"

"I'm embarrassed."

"Don't be," he said. "I've had them since I was a teenager. It's nothing to be ashamed of."

She sat up and looked down at him. "Why?"

"Why the nightmares?"

She nodded.

With a thumb, he wiped away the damp tears under her eyes. "When I was sixteen, two men murdered my mother."

Her face twisted in anguish. "Oh, John," she said. "I'm so sorry."

He knew he had to share the rest of it with her now. Take his chances that she'd understand. And maybe if he told her, it would help her deal with her own sense of guilt, her own inner demon.

"That's not all of it," he said.

She cocked her head and waited.

"I found out who the men were, and then I killed them. But not before one of them nearly killed me." He showed her his hand with the long jagged scar. When she didn't react, he continued, hoping that a further explanation would help her understand, help her retain the feelings she had for him. "They were the twin sons of Alejandro Estrada, the former head of the Cali cartel."

"Bad men," she said.

"Yes. They'd killed before. But the cartel was powerful. The police would do nothing."

"That's who's after you, isn't it? The cartel."

He nodded. "Estrada is dead, but the remaining family members want me dead, too. They won't stop, Jordan. And neither will my nightmares."

"But you've learned to live with them."

"Mostly," he said.

"How?"

"By trying to figure out what they mean. I've been doing it since I was a kid. An old woman named Ofir lived with my family and worked in our home. She would help me interpret my dreams." Santana picked up the journal on the nightstand. "Writing down my dreams and nightmares, even if they seem to make no sense, helps me understand them and sometimes helps me solve cases."

"Maybe journaling is something I should try."

"It wouldn't hurt. And I know a therapist named Karen Wong. She works with the department on officer-involved shootings."

"You've seen her before?"

He nodded. "The department requires at least one counseling session after every OIS."

"The Minneapolis PD had the same requirement when I was an officer," she said. "But if you relied too much on the Employee Assistance Program, colleagues started to worry about your mental health. No one wanted to partner with you. I knew officers who ended their careers on the rubber-gun squad."

Santana had heard the term used at the SPPD as well, often disparagingly, for an officer who had been stripped of his service weapon for his own safety or the safety of others and placed on restricted desk duty.

"I know Karen Wong is very good, Jordan."

"You didn't continue seeing her."

"But I've worked with her on cases. Why not give her a try?"

"I can work through this, John."

"I know you can. But seeing Wong isn't an admission of weakness."

"I'll bet that's not how you interpreted it when the department had you see her."

Santana knew she was right. He tried another tack. "Do you feel differently about me now that I've told you about my past?"

"No. What you did when you were sixteen hasn't changed my feelings. I know you're a good man."

He felt a sense of relief. "I know you're a strong woman, Jordan. I know you can handle yourself. Hell, you saved our lives. So seeing a therapist isn't a sign of weakness in my eyes. And it won't change my feelings toward you."

She looked at him for a long moment. "And what are your feelings, John?"

Oh, oh, he thought. *I walked right into that one.* But as he looked into her hazel eyes, he knew how he felt. "I'm in love with you," he said.

She smiled shyly. "You're not just saying that because I put you on the spot?"

"No. I wouldn't do that."

"No," she said. "You wouldn't." She leaned down and kissed him softly. Then she whispered in his ear, "I love you, too, John Santana."

Chapter 14

Before Santana left for the LEC on Monday morning, Dave Reynolds called him from the Minneapolis PD.

"I might have something for you, Santana," Reynolds said in a husky voice.

"I'm listening."

"The bullet the ME took out of Philip Campbell's brain came from the .22 caliber mini-revolver we found at the scene."

"So the ME is ruling Campbell's death a suicide."

"Don't get all amped up," he said. "I'm not finished."

Santana waited.

"I questioned Campbell's family."

"You have an address for the ex?"

Reynolds gave it to him. "She goes by Nancy Greely now. Neither she nor the two kids figured Campbell for a suicide. Now that doesn't mean much."

"But it means something," Santana said.

"Yeah. It means something. So does the fact that the gun wasn't registered in the NCIC database. Campbell's son told me his father never owned a mini-revolver. The only guns Campbell ever owned were a twelve-gauge shotgun and an old Colt forty-five. And there's one other thing."

"I'm listening."

"The palm of Campbell's hand and the grip of the gun were both bloodstained."

Santana knew that the insides of the hands and corresponding parts of the grip of the gun were usually bloodless in a suicide. "That doesn't prove he was murdered."

"No, it doesn't. But the blood marks on the hand and on the grip of the gun don't match. And we found a print that wasn't Campbell's."

"You run the print through AFIS?"

"Yeah. No match. So whoever the print belongs to doesn't have a record."

"So what's the plan, Reynolds?"

"I'll keep looking."

"I'll do the same," Santana said.

* * *

That afternoon, Santana considered calling Nancy Greely, Philip Campbell's ex-wife, but he decided to take a chance that she would be home. He preferred an in-person interview rather than a phone conversation.

She lived in a nicely furnished condo just off 50th street and France Avenue in Edina, an affluent first-ring suburb southwest of Minneapolis. Santana sat on a couch with leafy green print across the room from a gas fireplace with an oak mantel. Nancy Greely was on a matching love seat facing him, a cocktail glass filled with Scotch and water on the glass-topped coffee table between them. She was dressed in slacks and a V-neck tunic blouse and reminded Santana of a younger version of the English actress Helen Mirren.

"I'm afraid I can't tell you much more than I told Detective Reynolds," she said. "I hadn't spoken to Philip in quite some time. But I must say, I was shocked by his death."

"I understand he'd had surgery recently and was depressed."

"Perhaps. But depressed is not the same as suicidal."

Santana silently conceded the point. "How long were you married?"

"Twenty-one years. We divorced four years ago."

"You met in college?"

"Yes. Philip was in medical school. I was studying journalism. Once we were married and our first child was on the way, I gave up my ambition of becoming a journalist." She let out a sigh that Santana interpreted as regret.

He could think of no easy way to approach the subject of her ex-husband's involvement with an escort and his possible implication in her death. He wasn't sure whether Nancy Greely knew about Catalina Díaz, and if she didn't, whether knowing about Díaz now would hurt her.

"I guess I'm unclear as to why you're investigating my husband's death when he lived in Minneapolis," she said, giving Santana an opening to the unpleasant subject matter.

"It's not your husband's death that I'm investigating, Ms. Greely."

Santana glanced at his notebook, as though simple instructions were written on how to proceed with the interview. "A young woman was found dead in a hotel room in St. Paul earlier this week," he said. "Your ex-husband admitted that he'd been with her. I'm investigating her death."

Nancy Greely looked at him with steady eyes that were as gray as an overcast sky. "The escort," she said.

"Yes, the escort."

She smiled slightly, as though to herself. "I was aware of Philip's . . . indiscretions during our marriage. I hoped he'd grow out of it after we had children. I believe he did for most of our married years. But he became restless again when he turned forty, a time when so many men become nostalgic about their youth and sexual prowess. I put up with his philandering for as long as I could before I asked for a divorce."

Like most men, Philip Campbell had probably figured his wife wouldn't find out about his affairs. And, like most men, he had been proven wrong. Given her cold, emotionless responses to his questions, Santana figured that cheating had not only destroyed the marriage, but also any feelings Campbell's ex-wife had concerning her husband's sudden death.

"Having told you about Philip's indiscretions," she went on, "I don't for one second believe that he had anything to do with the woman's death. What was her name?"

"Catalina Díaz."

She nodded.

"I don't mean to pry, Ms. Greely."

"But you're going to," she said.

"Yes, I'm afraid so."

"I'd better have another, then." She stood and went into the kitchen where she mixed a second Scotch and soda. "Sure I can't get you anything, Detective?"

"I'm good."

She returned to the love seat and placed the full cocktail glass on a napkin on the coffee table. "Go ahead with your questions."

"When you were married, did your husband ever ask you to try bondage?"

"My," she said with a little smile. "You do get personal."

"I'm sorry."

"No need to apologize. And no, Philip was pretty conventional when it came to our sex life, much to my disappointment, actually."

"You must know Matthew Singer and Nathaniel Burdette?" Santana said, moving quickly to his next question.

"Of course."

"Paul Lenoir?"

"No, I don't recognize the name."

"How about James Elliot?"

"James went to medical school with Matthew, Nathaniel, and my husband. They were inseparable." Her smile was tinged with melancholy.

She stood and pulled a book off the bookshelf behind her. Santana could see a large gold University of Minnesota M on the maroon cover and realized it was a yearbook.

Nancy Greely set the book in her lap and flipped through the pages till she found what she was searching for. She placed the yearbook on the table and turned it so Santana could see the photo of Philip Campbell, Matthew Singer, and Nathaniel Burdette standing in front of a fraternity house, Greek letters prominently displayed in a second story window behind them. Their arms were slung over each other's shoulders. They wore sweatshirts and jeans, and the confident smiles of young, well-educated men who knew what they wanted and how to acquire it.

"They were smart and handsome, and they all liked women," Nancy Greely said. "Too much, I'm afraid. I urged Philip to abandon the group when we got engaged, but it was like asking a captain to abandon his ship. Still, the group broke up for quite a few years after they graduated."

"Do you know why?"

She shook her head. "Something happened between them, something that soured their relationship. I'm not sure what. Philip never talked about it. But then the fishing trips started."

"You mean the trips to Costa Rica?"

She nodded and drank some Scotch.

"Who organized the trips?"

"Matthew Singer. He was always the leader of the group. The one, I suspect, who had the most affairs."

"Did his wife know about the affairs?"

"Certainly. It was ironic, actually. Our marriages were going to be different than our mothers'. But for some of us, it was hard to give up the comforts that being married to a wealthy, successful physician provided. Kathy and I chose to look the other way."

"Kathy?"

"She was married to Matthew. I think the stress caused by Matthew's affairs contributed to her developing cancer."

"How well did you know these men?"

"Not well enough to tell you about their sexual practices, Detective Santana. But well enough to be surprised if one of them is found to be a murderer."

* * *

Monthly copies of *Police Chief Magazine* were neatly arranged on a mahogany coffee table in Assistant Chief Tim Branigan's office. As head of the Major Crimes and Investigations Division of the St. Paul PD, he oversaw operations in Homicide, Narco/Vice, Crimes Against Property, Family and Sexual Violence, Juvenile, Internet Crimes Against Children, and the Gang Unit.

Branigan glanced up from the paperwork on his desk when Santana knocked on the open office door. "I'll be with you in a minute, Detective," he said, waving Santana in.

Santana closed the office door behind him and sat down in a comfortable leather chair facing the desk.

Besides the ceremonial plaques, awards, and family photos on the office walls, Branigan had a life-sized sculpted raven on the corner of his desk, a reminder to all who entered that his surname had come from a very famous Irish clan and meant the descendent of the son of the raven.

Santana waited quietly. He'd been in this position before and knew that Branigan wasn't actually reading the report on his desk. Rather, the prolonged wait time was purely intentional, designed to unnerve Santana and everyone else who came into the office. Santana wondered if the silence actually intimidated anyone. Still, he was concerned about what he had to say to Branigan and worried about how he would say it. The back of his shirt was damp with sweat, and it clung like tape to his moist skin.

Branigan had actually been a very competent detective when he'd worked in Fraud and Forgery and later in Homicide. Santana wasn't sure why the AC believed that detectives would be more productive if they worked in an atmosphere of fear and intimidation. But he suspected the police department was no different from many businesses and public institutions where people were promoted based more on favoritism and ass kissing than on leadership skills and an ability to work with a variety of people.

"So, Detective," Branigan said at last. "What can I do for you?" He signed the paper in front of him with a flourish, capped his gold-plated pen, and looked at Santana for the first time.

Branigan had the dark hair and eyes associated with the Black Irish and their Iberian ancestors, rather than the stereotypical fair hair, pale skin, and blue or green eyes. He favored black and navy blue suits and dark colored shirts with vertical lines, the choice of clothes designed to boost his inflated ego and self-confidence, and make his thin, five-foot-eight-inch frame appear taller than it actually was.

Before Santana could reply, Branigan said, "How's the transition with Commander Romano going?"

The big smile on Branigan's face indicated that he only wanted to hear positives. He would view a negative appraisal of Romano's job performance as a breach of protocol—or worse yet, outright heresy.

"Fine," Santana said.

"Good." Branigan slapped his hands together and then rubbed his palms as though trying to keep them warm. "Commander Gamboni did a terrific job in homicide, but things are constantly changing. I've found it's best to embrace change. Fighting the inevitable just wastes time and energy."

Santana figured Branigan's comment about change, though presented as a general statement, was a not-so-subtle threat directed at him.

"I need to talk with you about a case I'm working, Chief."

Branigan's eyes narrowed with concern. "Have you spoken with Commander Romano?"

"No, I haven't."

"And why is that?"

"Because I thought you should hear this before he did."

"Hear what?"

Santana reached into an inner pocket of his sport coat, removed a copy of the list he'd found in Catalina Díaz's bedroom, and handed it to Branigan. "I'd like you to take a look at this."

Branigan took the folded paper and held it in his hand for a time, his eyes locked on Santana. Then he sat back in his leather chair, unfolded the paper, and peered at it.

Santana watched him intently, looking for a reaction, but he couldn't detect any. That didn't surprise him, since he knew Branigan had learned how to hide his emotions, something cops often could do.

After what seemed like a long time, Branigan raised his chin and gazed at Santana. "What is it I'm supposed to be seeing here, Detective?"

"Do you recognize any of the names, Chief? Matthew Singer, Philip Campbell, or Nathaniel Burdette?"

"Well, I believe Philip Campbell recently committed suicide in Minneapolis."

"How about the other names?"

"Can't say that I recognize them." Branigan folded the paper again and held it out over the desk, waiting for Santana to reach for it.

"Take another look," Santana said.

Branigan hesitated and then retracted his arm, unfolded the paper, and looked at the list once more. "Who are these men?"

Santana took a deep breath and said, "The men on that list were seeing a high-priced escort named Catalina Díaz."

Branigan jerked ever so slightly, as though a small insect had bitten him. He continued to peer at the paper for a while until his eyes gradually shifted to Santana.

"As I'm sure you're aware, Chief, Díaz was found dead in a downtown hotel room earlier this week."

Branigan's tongue darted across his thin lips like a snake's. He set down the paper and sat forward, resting his forearms on the desktop. "What are you suggesting, Detective?"

"I believe you were seeing her, too," Santana said.

Branigan leaned farther forward, as if he were about to reveal a secret. "You are treading on thin ice here, Detective," he said in voice not much louder than a whisper. "My advice is to leave this office now, before you find yourself swimming in very deep water."

"You asked Romano to monitor the progress of the Díaz investigation and urged him to shut it down once he had the ME's report," Santana said. "You've also been leaking information about Philip Campbell to the press. Romano doesn't know who's leaking the information or why you wanted the Díaz case off the board, but he isn't going to ask questions."

Branigan stood and pointed toward the door. "I'll be speaking with your commander about you, Detective Santana. I'm certain there will be disciplinary measures. In fact, I wouldn't be surprised if you found yourself out of Homicide and back on the streets in uniform before very long."

Santana remained seated, fished a second folded paper out of his pocket, and set it on the AC's desk. "You might want to take a look at that first."

"What is it? Another list of random names?"

"Actually, it is a list. But of phone numbers, not names."

Santana could see the color drain from Branigan's cheeks. Tiny beads of sweat appeared on his brow. He adjusted the Windsor knot on his red striped tie and sat down.

"The phone numbers highlighted in orange are from your cell phone, Chief. I know that because I've called you on occasion."

Branigan reached for the paper and unfolded it. He sat stiffly in his chair, staring at the paper without comment.

"How long had you been seeing Catalina Díaz?" Santana asked.

Branigan exhaled as if he'd been holding his breath. "I was going through a bad time. My wife and I had separated. I saw Díaz a few times. It was a mistake."

"How many of the men do you know on the list?"

"None," he said, setting the paper on his desk.

"That's a lie."

Branigan looked like he was about to leap out of his chair and over the desk. Santana saved him the trouble. "You flew to Costa Rica with them on a plane piloted by James Elliot."

Branigan's nod was nearly imperceptible. "I attended a fund raiser for the department at Matthew Singer's house while I was separated. He invited me to his fishing tournament in Costa Rica."

"But it was more than fishing."

"I didn't know that at the time."

"And you asked Romano to monitor the Díaz investigation."

"But I had nothing to do with her death, Detective. And according to the ME's report, no one else did either. She died of autoerotic asphyxiation."

"I believe someone killed her and made it look like an accidental death."

"I was home all evening the night she died. In fact, I hadn't seen her for weeks. It was so stupid of me to call her." He spoke rapidly, blurting the words out as if he feared Santana wouldn't believe him. "But I never expected that . . ." His voice trailed off, the words tinged with regret. He gave a meek shrug.

The date of Branigan's last call on the phone log indicated that it had been three weeks since he'd called Díaz, unless he'd used another phone. But Santana doubted that Branigan had used his home or office phone.

"You and Nick Baker were the I/Os on the Tania Cruz murder case," Santana said.

Branigan seemed to think for a long time. "I remember it."

"Didn't it strike you as coincidental that Cruz and Díaz died in the same way?"

"But we arrested the perp who killed Cruz."

"Arias Marchena."

"Yes," he said.

"What if Marchena didn't kill Cruz?"

"You have proof that he didn't?"

"Not yet."

"Who else knows about this, Detective?"

"You mean that you were seeing Díaz?"

He nodded.

"My partner, Kacie Hawkins."

"What are you planning to do?"

"Solve the case," Santana said.

"You know what I meant."

"I haven't decided yet."

"What about Hawkins?"

"She goes her own way. But neither one of us is looking to destroy your marriage."

"So what do you want?"

"Nothing but the truth. And perhaps your authorization to travel to Costa Rica."

"Why?"

"I'm looking for answers. I might find some there."

"I don't have money in the budget for that."

"I'll bet if you searched real hard, you'd find some."

Branigan started to protest and then changed his mind. "My wife and I are back together again, Detective. I don't have to tell you how this information about Díaz would affect my family and my career if it ever became public."

"No," Santana said. "You don't."

Chapter 15

After leaving Branigan's office, Santana returned to the Homicide Unit and debriefed Hawkins about his conversation with the assistant chief.

"Branigan admitted it?"

"He did."

"Jesus," Hawkins said with a shake of her head. "What else did he say?"

"He's worried his family might find out. But I told him neither one of us wants to break up his marriage."

Hawkins sat silently in the chair, a questioning look in her eyes.

"We can't say anything, Kacie."

"Why not?"

"What would we gain?"

"This isn't about us, John. What about Branigan's wife and family?"

"And how would telling his wife help?"

"I don't know," she said with a shrug. "But he cheated on her."

"Not anymore."

"Oh, so everything is forgiven now because Catalina Díaz is dead."

"It never was all right, Kacie. But we're going to need Branigan's cooperation and backing."

"Why?"

"Because I'm thinking of traveling to Costa Rica."

"What for?"

"There's something about this case that we're missing. Maybe the answer is there."

Hawkins released a frustrated breath. "I hate it when men cheat."

"Is this personal?"

"Damn right it is. My father used to cheat on my mother till she threw him out."

"Was Bobby Jackson cheating on you?"

Her gaze slid away from him as she gave a reluctant nod.

"I'm sorry, Kacie." Santana thought Jackson's cheating might be the reason why Hawkins had decided to see Paul Lenoir despite her protestations that she was only seeking information from him. But he wasn't about to suggest it—at least not while Hawkins was armed.

"Okay," she said, looking at him again. "So what's our next move?"

"There's one angle I'd like you to pursue."

"What's that?"

"I want you to go back in the archives and see if there were any deaths of prostitutes around the time of the apostles' graduation from medical school, especially deaths involving autoerotic asphyxia."

"You think this goes back that far?"

"I do."

"Why?"

"Nancy Greely, Campbell's ex-wife, told me that something had happened between Campbell, Singer, Burdette, and Elliot before graduation. Something that soured their relationship."

"Murder would certainly do that," Hawkins said.

"In the meantime, Kacie, let's see if we can find out more about Matthew Singer."

Santana logged on to his computer. Like a driver on a foggy stretch of road, he was struggling to see something about the Díaz investigation that he sensed was right in front of him. He found the Entertainment section of the *Pioneer Press* and then a link to a weekly column written by Gloria Whitaker.

"The newspaper's gossip columnist?" Hawkins said, peering over Santana's shoulder.

"She knows a lot."

"Yeah. Most of it isn't worth shit."

He clicked on the archives and then typed Matthew Singer's name in the search box. Numerous photos and articles immediately appeared. Santana wasn't surprised to see that Gloria Whitaker had attended parties at the Singer mansion. Nor was he surprised to see that she'd managed to get herself photographed with local sports celebrities, actors, and politicians, some of whom she'd written about in unflattering prose. He saw no recent photos of the men on the list besides Nathaniel Burdette, who was photographed on a number of occasions with a much younger and very beautiful blonde. It took Santana a minute to place her. She was the model he'd seen at Paul Lenoir's studio the day after Catalina Díaz's death.

"You see anyone you recognize besides Singer?" Santana asked.

"No," Hawkins said.

Santana clicked out of the newspaper website and logged on to the Minnesota DMV website, where he found Gloria Whitaker's address and phone number.

"Give me a few minutes," he said, dialing her number.

Whitaker answered on the first ring.

"Well, well," she said after Santana had identified himself. "Detective John Santana. I'm flattered that you called. Do you have something juicy you'd like to tell me?"

He could hear the anticipation in her voice. "Sorry, Ms. Whitaker. I'm calling because I hoped you might help me with something."

"Me, help you?" she said with a hearty laugh. "Now there's a switch. What is it you think I can do? Solve a murder?" She laughed again, but when Santana didn't respond in kind, she abruptly stopped. "Is this serious?"

"Before I tell you, I need you to agree to keep anything we talk about off the record."

"And why should I agree to that? After all, I am a gossip columnist."

"Because I might be able to give you a major scoop in the future."

"Might?"

"I try not to make promises I can't keep."

"I wish there were more men like that. But why should I trust you?"

"It's a two-way street, Ms. Whitaker."

"So it is." There was a moment of silence followed by a sigh of resignation. "All right, Detective. You've piqued my curiosity. What is it you'd like to know?"

"Tell me about the parties you attended at Matthew Singer's mansion."

"And why do you want to know about the parties?"

"I'm afraid I can't tell you that just yet."

"But you will if I keep my part of the deal."

"I will."

"Okay. I trust that you'll keep your word, Detective."

"As I trust that you'll keep yours."

"Of course. Well, Matthew's parties are always lavish, catered affairs, usually black-tie for the men and expensive gowns for the women. They're well-attended by many of the wealthy and connected in the Twin Cities."

"How well do you know Singer?"

"Not well."

"You're familiar with his background."

"Oh, yes."

"How about his friends, like Nathaniel Burdette and Philip Campbell?"

"Is that what this phone call is about? Philip Campbell's death?"

"I can't comment on that."

"I see. Well, I'm aware that Campbell was in business with Burdette and Singer. Their plastic surgery clinic is recognized as one of the best in the country. The men are well thought of and respected—and very wealthy."

"What about a man named Paul Lenoir?"

"The name doesn't ring a bell."

"James Elliot?"

"I haven't heard of him either," she said.

"Are most of the men who attend these parties near Singer's age?"

"Hmm," she said. "Now that you mention it, I believe they are. But that shouldn't be surprising since many of the guests were friends of Matthew's."

"What about the women?"

"Most are much younger," she said with a small laugh, as if she hated to acknowledge she wasn't in that age group. "Surely you've heard the term trophy wives."

"Are many of them Latina?"

"Yes, they are."

"Are the majority of the men single?"

"I'm not sure about that."

"In the newspaper's archives, I saw photos of Nathaniel Burdette photographed with a young blond woman."

"Off the top of my head, I don't know who that would be," she said. "I'd have to see the picture or look in the archives."

Santana took a second to review the scenario he was building in his mind before he said, "You've been very helpful, Ms. Whitaker."

"When will you be in touch again, Detective Santana?"

"I hope soon," he said. "Very soon."

* * *

Early that evening, Santana drove to Matthew Singer's mansion and rang the doorbell.

"Detective Santana," Singer said, holding open the door. He wore jeans, a white shirt open at the collar, and a pair of black cowboy boots. "I take it this isn't a social call."

"Not exactly."

"Well, come in."

Santana stepped into the entryway and followed Singer into the living room.

"I just brewed some coffee. Could I get you some, Detective?"

"No, thanks."

He directed Santana to one of the two burgundy tufted sofas on opposite sides of an Italianate coffee table. "Well, let me get a fresh cup for myself. I won't be a minute."

Heavy, burgundy-colored drapes were drawn over the windows. A Tiffany lamp on an end table lit the room and exposed the shadows along the walls.

As Santana took out his notebook and pen, his eyes were drawn to the painting above the fireplace. It was a reproduction of the Rokeby Venus painted by Diego Velázquez in which a naked Venus, the goddess of love, was gazing at herself and at the viewer in a mirror held up by her son Cupid.

Matthew Singer reentered the room carrying a mug of steaming coffee and sat across from Santana. "What can I do for you this evening, Detective?"

Santana took out a copy of the list and laid it on the table so that Singer could read it. "These men were all having sex with Catalina Díaz."

Singer sat forward, his elbows on his thighs, and peered at the paper. "Philip's name has been crossed out, Detective," he said, fixing his gaze on Santana. "Why is that?"

"I no longer consider him a suspect."

"A suspect to what?"

"Catalina Díaz's murder."

Singer inhaled a long breath and released it slowly. "If you believe that Ms. Díaz was murdered, then surely you can connect the dots to Philip's suicide."

"I figure someone wants me to see it that way."

"But you have your doubts."

Santana nodded.

"Which is why you've crossed his name off the list."

"Correct."

"Well, then, Detective, you must believe one of the other men on the list killed Ms. Díaz."

"Which includes you, Dr. Singer."

"That it does. Are you here to arrest me?"

"Only if you're about to confess."

His face creased in a tight smile. "That would be foolish, even if I were guilty."

"Then perhaps you can answer some questions."

"I could try."

"I understand you often host parties here."

Singer sipped his coffee and looked at Santana, his small dark eyes blank and without emotion. "And where did you hear that?"

"I have my sources."

He nodded and stroked his thick, graying mustache with a thumb and forefinger.

"Tell me about the parties," Santana said.

Singer shrugged and set the mug on a coaster on the coffee table. "They're simply social gatherings. Nothing more."

"Let's start with the young women."

"I'm afraid I don't understand."

"I think you do, Dr. Singer."

"Is there something illegal about inviting pretty young women to social gatherings?"

"There might be. If two of them are dead."

Singer cocked his head and narrowed his eyes. "Two?"

"That's right. Catalina Díaz and Tania Cruz."

Singer screwed up his face. "Who's Tania Cruz?"

"An escort who was murdered six years ago; an escort who was a friend of Catalina Díaz; an escort who attended your parties," Santana said.

"I don't recall any Tania Cruz attending my parties. But then, I often have a large gathering. I don't know everyone's name."

"What goes on at one of your parties?"

"Conversation, mostly."

"And introductions?"

"Of course. As I said, not everyone knows everyone else."

"Do you know Paul Lenoir?"

"As a matter of fact, I do know Paul. A great guy and photographer."

"Have you spoken to him recently?"

Singer thought about it and then shook his head. "Not that I recall."

"How many times have you traveled to Costa Rica, Dr. Singer?"

"A few. I can't say for certain."

"And you've flown with James Elliot, your former med school classmate."

"Yes."

"Tania Cruz and Catalina Díaz were both from Costa Rica."

"Meaning?"

"Are other women who attend your parties from there?"

"Some."

"Are these women here legally?"

"I believe so."

Santana pointed to the list. "You know everyone who's a suspect in Catalina Díaz's death, Dr. Singer."

He peered at the paper and nodded.

"Why didn't you tell me that before?"

He spread his hands and sighed. "What happened to Philip Campbell and Catalina Díaz was tragic. But simply knowing these men is no crime."

"That remains to be seen, Dr. Singer."

Ten minutes after leaving Matthew Singer's home, Santana received a call from Kacie Hawkins. Paul Lenoir was dead.

* * *

Paul Lenoir's naked calves and feet stuck up out of the water at the far end of an old cast iron tub with short claw-footed legs that looked like animal paws. Headphones covered his ears. His mouth was frozen open in a silent scream. His eyes stared blankly at some distant point. Looking into the dead man's eyes, Santana was reminded of Nietzsche's quote: "If you look long enough into the void, the void begins to look back through you." There was no sign of a struggle, no sign of blood, no electrical burns on the body.

He looked at Hawkins. "You all right, Kacie?"

"Yeah."

"What were you doing here?"

"Lenoir asked me to stop by. He said he had something to tell me. I rang the bell, but he didn't answer. I walked around the side of the house and looked in the windows and saw him lying in the bathtub. Guess we'll never know what it was he wanted to tell me."

"How long ago did he call?"

"Forty-five minutes."

"You have his cell number?"

She nodded.

"Dial it."

Hawkins took out her phone and tapped in Lenoir's number. "His phone's ringing," she said, "but I don't hear anything in the room or house."

"Did you check the place?" he asked.

"Quickly."

Santana knew they were still on solid legal ground without a warrant. Hawkins had seen Lenoir's body when she looked in the window. They were also allowed to conduct a protective sweep in the house to make sure the perpetrator wasn't hiding somewhere. But they couldn't legally seize any evidence without a warrant.

"Call forensics," he said. "Then check the place again." He pointed to the router on the desk. "There's a wireless connection. Get your laptop and write up a search warrant."

"Okay," she said, and headed out of the bathroom.

Santana opened the medicine cabinet above the sink, looking for any medication that might have contributed to or caused Lenoir's death. Then he squatted on his haunches and opened the two doors to the cabinet under the sink, where he saw a set of red bungee cords similar to those used on Catalina Díaz. Next to the cords was a hair dryer. As he lifted it, a single drop of water fell from the barrel.

He figured Paul Lenoir had likely been electrocuted in the bathtub. Older houses often had no ground fault circuit interrupters. Without a GFCI, the electricity would've kept flowing. When Lenoir was dead, the perp had unplugged the hair dryer, taken it out of the tub and wiped it off, but had left some water inside that hadn't dried yet.

He stood and went into Lenoir's bedroom. It was small and cluttered. He scanned the room for secrets. File folders, newspapers, and photography magazines were scattered on the desk, window ledges, and double bed. Two rows of framed black and white photos of women who looked like models hung on the wall above the headboard.

On the desk was a framed photo taken of a younger Paul Lenoir and James Elliot standing in front of a Buddhist temple in Japan. Santana opened the bottom desk drawer. His eyes were immediately drawn to a box containing a computer program entitled Shredit X for Mac OSX. According to the description on the box, the program was designed to wipe a hard drive clean. In a second drawer Santana found a credit card.

At that moment he heard the sound of a car engine out back. His gaze locked on Hawkins, who was just entering the bedroom. They both ran toward the living room and out the front door.

As they came around the back corner of the building and into an alley, Hawkins pointed toward a dark sedan ten yards in front of them. Waving her arms as the car backed away from them into the alley, she hesitated for a second, her body silhouetted in the high beams suddenly spearing the gathering darkness.

Santana cupped a hand above his eyebrows, trying to see in the blinding light. The engine revved and the car leapt forward. "Kacie!" he yelled. Dashing toward her, he shoved her out of the way as the car flew by them in a rush of wind.

"What the hell was that all about?" she said, her hands fisted on her hips, her eyes glaring at the taillights fading in the distance.

It was fear rather than anger Santana heard in her voice. She could've been killed, and she knew it. Now she was trying to cover.

"You okay?"

"I'm fine," she said. "But that asshole isn't."

Santana grabbed her by the elbow as she headed for the front of the building and her Crown Vic. "Hold it, Kacie."

"Why?" she said, shaking loose of his grip.

"We'll never catch him now. Did you get a license number?"

Hawkins shook her head. "It was too dark to see the make, too. How about you?"

"No."

She stood in the shadowy darkness breathing heavily, her breath misting in the cool air. "I searched Lenoir's place carefully," she said, glaring at Santana.

"I never said you didn't. Maybe the perp was hiding in the garage?"

"Whoever he was, he's going to wish he'd never seen me," she said.

Santana had no doubt of that.

* * *

Floodlights lit the alley behind Paul Lenoir's house. Santana watched as Tony Novak, from the SPPD crime lab, used dental stone to take tire cast impressions of the car that had nearly hit Hawkins.

Looking up at Santana, he said, "I'll compare the tire pattern crime scene photos with the tire and tread patterns available in the TreadMate database."

Santana was aware that the database matched crime scene and reconstructed tire images to potential tire models. It also contained information on typical tire wear, damages, and slight differences like waves, curves, blocks, and zigzags embedded in the tire design.

"If I find some individual characteristics present in the impressions," Novak said, "it'll help me distinguish the crime scene impressions from the mass produced ones. I'll also measure the track width between the front and rear tires."

"You mean the distance between the center line of each tire?"

"Technically, it's the distance between the two axle mounts. Most of the makes and models have common brands of tires, but they have slightly different track widths. The measurement isn't unique to any particular vehicle, but it should eliminate possible vehicles. Still, it'd be better if we had the exact measurements of the suspect's vehicle. But you'd need a warrant for that, John."

"Not if it's parked in a public place."

"Nice to be aware of the loophole. By the way, the DNA sample Hawkins took from Philip Campbell didn't match any of the DNA found on the bedspread in Catalina Díaz's hotel room or on her body. And I found no match in CODIS."

Santana had figured as much. He thanked Novak and returned to the house, where he found Hawkins.

"Anything on Lenoir's family?"

She shook her head. "I called James Elliot, figuring he might provide some information. He thought Lenoir had grown up on the East Coast, but he wasn't sure where."

"Let's see what Tanabe found."

Reiko Tanabe was leaning over the tub, examining Paul Lenoir's body, when Santana and Hawkins entered the bathroom.

"Anything, Reiko?"

She straightened up. "Well, the presence of petechiae in the eyes could've been caused by a combination of venous congestion due to cardiac arrest and a sudden rise in blood pressure induced by muscle contractions."

"Meaning?"

"It's a non-specific but typical finding in electrocution."

"My gut and the wet hair dryer tell me Lenoir didn't die of a heart attack, Reiko."

"I'll see what else I can find," she said.

"One other thing," he said. "We're having trouble locating Lenoir's next of kin. Could you place an obituary in the paper? Maybe a relative or family member of Lenoir's will see it and respond."

"I'll make sure I do that," she said.

* * *

Sometimes in his dreams, Santana finds himself in the cloud forests of Colombia at the age of sixteen. He sees the night sky veined with lightning, sees the trees bending in the wind and driving rain, sees the glint of a steel blade poised above his chest.

Sometimes he dreams of his dead partner and sometimes of his dead parents, but not tonight.

An eagle rides the thermals high above a river valley, its eyes focused on a distant prey. Santana watches as it descends toward the river's surface, its huge wings spread wide, its speed increasing, its razor-sharp talons outstretched as it closes in on the small child walking toward him along the shoreline, a doll held against her chest. He attempts to run toward her, but his legs are too heavy. He points to the eagle swooping out of the sky, trying to warn her. She glances over her shoulder and then turns toward him, her eyes wide, her lips stretched tight, her brows raised, and her mouth slightly open, as though it's forming the letter O. She starts to run to him, but it's too late. Santana watches helplessly as the eagle buries its talons in her back and lifts her off the ground, her screams echoing off the valley walls before gradually dying away.

Chapter 16

When Santana woke the following morning, he sat for a long time on the side of his bed, rubbing his head with his hands as if he could cleanse his mind of the dream. He had no doubt that the little girl in the dream was Sammy Malik, but he had no idea if the bird of prey represented a person or simply her fear of eagles. He described the dream in detail in his journal. Then he ran with Gitana, lifted weights, and worked out for thirty minutes on the heavy bag and on the speed bag till his arms felt like a pair of five-pound dumbbells and the memory of the dream had retreated to the edges of his consciousness. After a shower and shave, he drove to Ricky Garza's house.

A young woman who appeared to be no more than eighteen opened the door a crack and hesitantly peered around it, the chain lock stretching across the opening.

He held up his badge wallet so she could see it through the screen door. "I'm Detective John Santana from the St. Paul Police Department. I'd like to speak to Ricky Garza."

"He is not home," she said in a heavy Spanish accent.

"Perhaps you could help me?"

"I no think so," she said.

"What's your name?"

"Lucita."

"Lucita what?"

"Lucita Sánchez."

"Do you have any identification?"

Even through the screen door, Santana could see the panic in her eyes. He was well aware that Minneapolis and St. Paul had "separation ordinances," meaning police couldn't ask residents they interacted with about their immigration status unless it pertained to a crime. He'd asked for her ID just to gauge her reaction—and her status.

"Never mind," he said. "You're Ricky's girlfriend?"

She nodded.

"Do you know where he is?"

She shook her head and then looked behind her at the sound of a baby crying. "I have to go," she said.

"Is that your daughter?"

"My son."

"Tell Ricky I stopped by."

She closed the door and turned the bolt, as though a locked door could protect her from all the dangers that lay beyond it.

* * *

Hawkins was waiting for Santana when he arrived at the LEC. "Cheese wants to see us."

"I'm not surprised."

"Neither am I," she said.

When they were seated in his office, Romano shuffled some papers, found what he was looking for, and said, "I see by your reports that a search of Paul Lenoir's house and studio turned up evidence linking him to Díaz's murder. Nice work, Detectives. Seems we were initially wrong about her death."

"*We* were wrong?" Hawkins said.

"Yes. The ME as well."

Santana thought that Romano was still looking to close the Díaz case as quickly as possible and was deliberately ignoring the conflicting evidence in the report he'd written.

"My report also indicates someone else was in Lenoir's house around the time of his death, Pete. They nearly ran down Kacie as they were fleeing."

"I'm aware of that, Detective."

"What if the person driving the car killed Lenoir and planted the evidence in his house?"

"Since you don't know who was driving, that amounts to guess work."

"But we need to follow up."

He gave a reluctant nod. "By all means. Follow up. But keep me informed."

"Absolutely," Santana said.

As he and Hawkins left Romano's office, Santana received a call from Bobby Jackson, the SPPD's computer forensic analyst.

"You have something for me, Bobby?"

"That card you found at Paul Lenoir's place is a stored value card."

"Meaning?"

"It's not quite the same as a credit card, or a gift card, for that matter. Gift cards are considered to be a closed type of card in that you have to use them at specific merchants such as a Macy's or Target. An SVC is an open type of card. There's no recorded account and no money on deposit with an issuer like a debit card. SVCs are connected to the global ATM networks and can be used anywhere without restrictions. The card's embedded computer chip contains the value."

"Why would Lenoir have one of those?"

"Hard to say. Did he travel a lot?"

"Between here and Costa Rica."

"I don't know all the details about the cards, but ships and military bases in the U.S. and overseas typically use them to limit the circulation of cash and reduce the expense and administration of processing credit cards and checks."

"How much money was on the card?"

"We'd need a PIN to access the amount, John. Security is one of the advantages of that type of card. They use multi-layered, integrated chip circuitry to control access to funds. It's more secure than the mag-stripe technology used to authenticate credit and debit card transactions."

"Thanks, Bobby." Santana disconnected and told Hawkins what Jackson had found.

"Why would Lenoir have one of those cards?"

"I don't know, Kacie."

"You're not convinced that he's responsible for the murders."

"Are you?"

Hawkins shook her head. "Someone wants us to think so."

"Probably the same perp who wanted us to think Philip Campbell killed Catalina Díaz and then took his own life."

"You think Lenoir was electrocuted?"

"Tanabe didn't find any marks on his body. She'll do a complete tox screen. That won't cover all the possibilities. But the hair dryer under the bathroom sink was wet. Still, it'll be hard to prove without burn marks."

"It's all we've got, John."

"For now," he said.

* * *

Later that afternoon, Santana and Hawkins sat on the couch in Nina Rivera's condo. She sat down across from them, tucking her bare feet under her, one arm draped casually along the back of the cushioned chair. She wore a red velour hoodie over a white T-shirt, and her long brunette hair was in a ponytail.

"What is it that you wanted to see me about this time, Detectives?"

Without her makeup, Santana could see the shadowed puffiness under her amber eyes, as if she had insomnia.

"Paul Lenoir is dead, Ms. Rivera. We need answers."

Her complexion paled and the hard amber light in her eyes suddenly softened. "Paul is dead?"

"We found his body last night."

"Was he killed?"

"We're still trying to determine that. But we found evidence linking Lenoir to Catalina Díaz's death."

She shook her head. "That's impossible. Paul had no reason to harm Cata."

"What if they were into autoerotic asphyxia?"

"Cata wasn't into that and neither was Paul."

"How do you know?"

Nina Rivera started to answer and then stopped.

"So you had sex with Lenoir," Kacie Hawkins said.

"Since when is that a crime?" Her gaze slid off Hawkins.

When she looked at the detectives again, Santana said, "The last time I was here, you mentioned you'd attended some parties at Matthew Singer's."

Out the corner of his eye, he could see Hawkins looking at the side of his face. He hadn't told her about his last visit with Rivera. He was certain she would ask him about it the minute they were out the door.

"Which one of your clients is into autoerotic asphyxiation, Ms. Rivera?" he asked.

"How would I know?"

Hawkins glared at her. "Maybe you were into the practice yourself?"

Rivera let out sigh. "No. Never."

"You recruited Catalina Díaz, didn't you?" Santana said.

"Recruited?"

"For the parties."

"I only went to the parties. Nothing else."

"Have you made arrangements to ship the body?"

She nodded.

"Are you accompanying it to Costa Rica?"

"Yes. The funeral is in two days."

"When are you leaving?"

"Tomorrow. Is that going to be a problem?"

"I hope not," Santana said.

* * *

As they exited the condo, Hawkins said to Santana, "Tell me about you and Nina Rivera."

"There's nothing to tell."

"You stopped by to see her."

"I had some questions that needed answering."

"Did she answer them?"

"No."

"You and Rivera aren't . . ."

"No. I'm with Jordan."

"That's good. But we should bring Rivera in, John. Put more pressure on her."

He shook his head. "I want her to go to Costa Rica with Díaz's body."

"Why?"

"So I can follow her. See what she's up to."

"Romano isn't going to approve money for the trip."

"No. But Branigan will."

Hawkins stopped and grabbed Santana by the arm. "You're blackmailing him?"

"I wouldn't call it blackmail."

"Is that the only reason you're going?"

"No."

Her eyes suddenly lit with recognition. "You want to visit the place where Tania Cruz was born."

"Yes," Santana said. "I do."

* * *

Santana drove Hawkins back to the station and then called DEA agent Mike Rios. "We need to talk."

"About what?"

"Meet me at the Ten Twenty-Nine in thirty minutes," Santana said. Then he disconnected.

Known for its lobster rolls, shrimp po' boy sandwiches, and mac and cheese, the 1029 was located in a small two-story stone building in Northeast Minneapolis. The neighborhood bar was decked out in cop patches, badges, license plates, flags, bullet-riddled car doors, and brassieres hanging from the rafters and on the walls.

Rios was seated alone at a square table in a corner, a half-empty glass of Grain Belt Premium and an empty shot glass in front of him. He looked up when Santana entered and pushed the empty chair opposite him away from the table with his foot.

Santana sat down and ordered a Blue Moon draft after the waitress told him the bar didn't serve Sam Adams.

"What do you have for me?" Rios asked.

"I need information first."

"You're running out of favors, Santana."

"I didn't realize there was a limit."

"Keep up the smartass routine and you'll find out."

"You know anything about stored value cards?"

Rios appeared to perk up. "Why?"

"I found one at Paul Lenoir's place."

"Who's Paul Lenoir?"

"A photographer who died last night."

"Died?"

"I don't know if he was murdered, but I'm leaning in that direction."

Rios thought about it and drank some beer before he spoke. "SVC cards are the latest way to move large sums of drug money between countries."

"How so?"

"Service companies generally require no credit checks and keep few records on user activity and personal information. Anyone can apply online and a minimal amount of personal information is required. Hell, you could easily use a false name."

"That'd be an advantage for drug dealers," Santana said.

Rios nodded. "And there's a huge legal loophole that allows companies to get around the requirement that anything in excess of ten grand must be declared on a CTR when entering or leaving the U.S."

"CTR?"

"A Cash Transaction Receipt. Anyone laundering money has to keep cash transactions under ten grand. Amounts over that have to be reported to the IRS through a CTR. But it's perfectly legal to carry larger amounts on a SVC. Dealers and cartels use the cards to funnel large amounts of cash into the financial system."

"Can't you seize the cards?"

"They're not subject to the same rules, Santana. It's like a shadow banking system. And Congress won't close the loophole because it would anger the lobbyists from the banking industry and probably bring down the whole economy. It's all about virtual currency now."

"You mean currency that exists in electronic form."

"Exactly. It is not physical like printed paper money or minted coins. Most national currencies today are hybrid currencies that exist in both physical and electronic form."

"Maybe there'll come a time when physical currencies are no longer used."

"Some people are already there. They move their money around electronically with credit cards, debit cards, stored-value cards, and even make electronic payments to pay all of their bills and debts."

"What drugs are coming out of Costa Rica?"

Rios sat back, a grin at one corner of his mouth. "Why should I tell you anything else?"

"Because your career went off the rails, Rios. Because the state is being overrun with cheap heroin. It's over ninety-three percent pure, some of the strongest in the country. Heroin deaths have skyrocketed. Maybe the DEA noticed?"

"Like I said, Santana, sarcasm is a winning strategy. It really makes me want to help you."

The waitress appeared with Santana's glass of Blue Moon and another glass of Grain Belt and a shot of Jack Daniels for Rios. After she'd departed, Santana said, "Figuring out how the smack is coming into the cities has the potential to put your career back on track, Rios."

"You think I give a shit about a promotion?"

"Uh-huh."

Rios drank from his glass of beer as he considered his options. "Okay, here's what I can tell you. Costa Rica is the key transit point for coke along the drug route from Colombia to the U.S."

"What about heroin?"

"Same thing. Most of the drugs from South America are shipped, flown, or driven through Costa Rica on the way to Mexico, and then to the Pan-American Highway to the States. The Costa Rican government has a lot of coastline to cover on the Caribbean and Pacific Ocean. The roads are poorly patrolled, there's a lack of border security in the south, and limited police resources in rural areas. In other words, it isn't difficult for the cartels to get the shipments through to Mexico."

After draining his shot of whiskey and chasing it with a swallow of beer, Rios wiped his mouth with a napkin and said, "So what've you got for me?"

"There's something else I need."

Rios shook his head in frustration. "Come on, Santana. You haven't given me shit."

"I will."

"Remind me not to hold my breath."

"You have contacts in Costa Rica?"

"Yeah," he said hesitantly.

"I need you to connect me."

"What does Costa Rica have to do with a hooker's murder?"

"There might be four murders, Rios."

"I thought you were working the Díaz case."

"I am. But I think her death is connected to the death of another escort and possibly to Philip Campbell's and Paul Lenoir's. And the SVC might indicate Lenoir and his escorts were dealing drugs."

"All right. I'll make a call and get back to you."

Santana stood. "Thanks."

"Where're you going?"

"Costa Rica."

"What about the information you're supposed to give me?"

"I'll call you when I get back. Provided you give me your contact information."

"Like I'm supposed to trust you."

"Who else have you got?" Santana said.

* * *

A silky mist fell from the black sky as Santana left the bar and drove toward Tim Branigan's house, the rain swirling in the air and glazing the hard surfaces of the city with a thin coating of moisture that shimmered in the muted glow of streetlights.

Santana had considered calling Branigan, but decided he could pressure the AC more if he visited him at his home. He wasn't interested in Branigan's personal life or whether he'd cheated on his wife. He was only interested in discovering the truth about the deaths of Tania Cruz and Catalina Díaz. He'd been dealt an ace when he'd discovered that Branigan had been seeing Díaz. He'd use that ace and whatever resources he had at his disposal if it led him to the truth. He figured any good detective would.

Standing under the eave on the screened-in front porch, Santana rang the doorbell. Seconds later, a light above him came on and the front door swung open. Branigan, still dressed in his white shirt—minus the tie—and his slacks and shoes, stared at Santana as if he'd seen the walking dead. In the background a television was tuned to a baseball game.

"What're you doing here, Detective?"

"I need to talk to you."

"It couldn't wait till tomorrow?"

"I wouldn't be here if it could."

Branigan looked behind him and hollered to his wife. "I'm stepping out for a moment, hon. I'll be right back." He grabbed a windbreaker from a closet and closed the front door behind him. "Let's sit in your car," he said.

When they were settled in the Explorer's front seats, Branigan said, "I don't appreciate you coming to my house, Detective. I want to make sure you understand that." The words were spoken in a voice that was as flat and as hard as the glass surrounding them.

"I figured you wouldn't."

"Yet you came here anyway."

"I wanted to make a point."

"You have. Now what the hell do you want?"

"A ticket to Costa Rica."

Branigan, whose face was partially bathed in shadow, shook his head in disgust. "You've got a lot of nerve. If you think I'm going to take money from my already thin budget to send you on a vacation to Costa Rica, you're crazy, Santana. I don't care what you know about my private life or what you plan to do with that information."

"This isn't about a vacation, Chief. It's about the murders of Tania Cruz and Catalina Díaz."

"Are we going through that again?"

"We are. And we're going to keep going through it till I'm satisfied. I think the answers to their deaths are in Costa Rica."

"Romano told me you'd found evidence implicating a man named Paul Lenoir in Díaz's death. So why should I send you to Costa Rica?"

"I think Lenoir is being set up. I think these deaths might be about heroin."

"You sure?"

"I will be by the time I return."

"I can't afford to send Hawkins, too."

"I understand that."

Branigan released a frustrated sigh and peered out the windshield that was beginning to fog. "If it's about heroin, why not turn it over to the DEA?"

"Because their number one priority is drug smuggling. Not a homicide investigation. But I've already spoken with Mike Rios."

Branigan looked at Santana. "Rios? That fuck-up?"

Santana ignored the comment. "The MS-13 are running drugs into St. Paul. One of them tried to kill me. That indicates I'm on the right track."

"Yeah," Branigan said. "A track that can get you killed. How much is this trip going to cost me?"

"The plane fare and hotel. Everything else is on my dime."

"Make sure it isn't a first class ticket or five-star hotel."

Branigan knew he'd never book a first-class ticket or a five-star hotel, Santana thought. But he understood the AC had to feel like he still had some power, some say over the matter.

"I'll give you my receipts."

"Damn right you will." The raindrops sounded heavier now as they drummed on the roof and hood of the sedan, driven by a gusty wind. "What do you know or think you know, Detective?"

"Only that the deaths of the two women were staged to look like accidents—and that Philip Campbell wasn't responsible."

"You're sure of this?"

Santana nodded.

"What if this guesswork all goes south?" Branigan said. "Who's going to cover my ass?"

"You'd better hope that it doesn't, Chief."

"We'd both better hope that, Detective." He let out another sigh. "When do you want to leave?"

"As soon as possible. You'll have to clear it with Pete Romano."

"I'll fill out the paperwork in the morning and talk to him." Branigan got out of the car and slammed the door behind him.

Through the moisture clouding the passenger window, Santana could see him trudging toward his house, his gait slow, yet purposeful, undeterred by the rain or the storm that had befallen him.

* * *

Later that evening, as Santana was on the Internet searching for a reasonably priced airfare and hotel package and information on travel in Costa Rica, he received a phone call from Brian Howard.

"I didn't appreciate you interrogating my ex-wife about me, Detective Santana."

"I wouldn't call it an interrogation, Mr. Howard."

"Well, I asked you not to talk to her and you did anyway."

"We're investigating a possible murder."

"And that excuses everything."

"Tell me about Arias Marchena."

Howard went silent.

"Marchena worked for you, Mr. Howard."

"Yes, he did."

"For how long?"

"Approximately a year and a half, if I remember correctly."

"Did you testify at his trial?"

"I did."

"Marchena was accused of murdering an escort named Tania Cruz."

"I believe so," Howard said, his tone quieter now, more subdued.

"You never mentioned the Cruz case the first time Detective Hawkins and I interviewed you."

"There was no reason to."

"Marchena worked for you and was accused of murdering a young escort. And now we have the death of another escort that died in a very similar manner in a hotel where you worked. Coincidence?"

"What else could it be?"

"I think you know the answer to that question, Mr. Howard."

"Marchena was tried and convicted."

"Yes, he was."

"I had nothing to do with either death."

"But now you know why we questioned your ex-wife," Santana said. "And why we'll question her again if we need to."

Santana closed his cell phone, shut down his computer, and phoned Jordan. "I'm going to Costa Rica for a few days."

"The case?"

"Yes."

"When are you leaving?"

"Tomorrow afternoon."

"Does this have something to do with the MS 13?" she asked.

"It's more about finding out who murdered Tania Cruz and Catalina Díaz."

"But you think the Maras are part of it."

"I do."

"They tried to kill you once, John. If they know you're coming to Costa Rica, they'll try again."

"I don't know that for certain."

"Yes, you do," she said.

"You'll take care of Gitana while I'm gone."

"Of course. You gave me a key and the code for the alarm. Remember?"

"I don't want you staying at my place," he said. "It's too dangerous. If the Maras think I'm home, they might send someone else to finish the job."

"I can take care of myself, John."

"I know that. But please bring Gitana to your place."

She let out a sigh. "Okay. If you insist."

"I do."

There was a pause before she said, "Have you ever given a key and your alarm code to anyone before?"

Santana knew it was a question that had only one correct answer. Problem was, he had given a key and the code to his former partner and homicide commander, Rita Gamboni. They had also once been lovers.

"Don't answer that," she said. "It's none of my business."

He was thankful for the reprieve, not because he wanted to avoid the truth, but because honesty was sometimes painful. "Be careful when you come out here, Jordan."

"Quit worrying about me," she said. "Just take care of yourself."

Chapter 17

The Delta flight had a stopover in Atlanta before landing in San José, Costa Rica at 11:00 p.m. Santana hailed one of the orange taxis at the airport and took it to the Adventure Inn, a reasonably priced hotel with an indigenous Mayan theme, ten minutes from the airport and from the heart of the city. He used the phone in his room to call Jordan and let her know that he had landed safely. He promised he would call her again soon.

Early the next morning, he ate breakfast in the hotel's Moon Glow bar and grill. Then he called Rodolfo Murillo, the contact Mike Rios had given him, and set up an appointment. Murillo worked for the Judicial Investigation Organization (OIJ), a police agency of the Ministry of Justice, created to investigate and fight crime. Within the organization was a small anti-narcotics group that concentrated on international cases. They cooperated with other law enforcement units and with DEA agents, routinely sharing information and conducting joint operations.

Santana grabbed a poncho out of his suitcase in the event it rained and took a taxi to the OIJ building to meet Rodolfo Murillo.

Murillo's secretary opened the office door to let Santana in. A tall, gray-haired man in a green striped button-down shirt and plain yellow tie came around his desk.

"Welcome to Costa Rica," Murillo said in excellent English, shaking Santana's hand. He gestured to the empty chair in front of his desk.

Santana hung his poncho over the back of the chair and sat down.

Murillo sat in the chair behind his desk and adjusted his brown-framed glasses. "I hope you had an uneventful flight."

"It was smooth," Santana said.

"Would you care for some coffee?"

"I'm good."

Murillo looked at Santana for a time without speaking, as if he were trying to get a sense of him. "I understand you are originally from Colombia."

Santana nodded.

"And you are investigating the suspected homicides of two Costa Rican women in Minnesota."

"Tania Cruz and Catalina Díaz. Did you know them or their families?"

Murillo shook his head. "There are so many who sell their bodies to the sharks."

"Sharks?"

"It is what Costa Rican prostitutes call the men who come here looking for sex."

"Is there anyone who might have known Cruz or Díaz?"

Murillo thought about it. "Eva Miranda. She has worked at the Blue Marlin for many years. She is from Colombia as well. Ask a bartender to identify her."

"I understand prostitution is legal here."

"We call them sex workers in Chepe. It is what the locals call the city. Sex workers must have a medical ID card to even enter the hotel."

"It's the same in Colombia," Santana said.

Murillo nodded and drank some coffee from the cup in front of him. "The *chicas* in the Blue Marlin will not bother you unless you want them to. You have to make eye contact, let one know you are interested."

"Thanks for the tip." Santana wrote Eva Miranda's name in his notebook. "What do you know about a place called Erotic Tours?"

"It is a resort near Jaco along the coast where rich Americans go to enjoy the waters and the beautiful women. We believe the resort is owned by members of the Sinaloa cartel."

Santana was more familiar with the Colombian cartels that had controlled much of his country when he was a teenager. But through his investigative work, he'd learned that the Sinaloa cartel was now considered to be the most powerful drug trafficking organization in the world. They were primarily involved in the smuggling and distribution of Colombian cocaine, Mexican marijuana, methamphetamine, and Mexican and Southeast Asian heroin into the U.S.

"I understand they've formed an alliance with the Gulf cartel."

"Yes," Murillo said. "The Sinaloa and Gulf cartels are competing for the drug trade with the Juarez and Tijuana cartels and Los Zetas, who have joined forces. It is a bloody business. The Sinaloa cartel has begun moving some of its operations south into Costa Rica. Obviously, we are concerned."

"A large increase in the amount and quality of heroin has been showing up in Minnesota."

Murillo stood and pointed to the Costa Rican map on the wall behind his desk. "The Sinaloa cartel has been expanding into our parks." He pointed to the long, jagged Pacific coastline. "It is part of the balloon effect of the narcotics trade. You squeeze the balloon in the south in Colombia," he said, closing his fingers in a squeezing gesture. "Then you squeeze the balloon in the north in Mexico. What you get is pressure in the center, which is where the cartel is extending its operations in Central America." He pointed again to the map. "Traffickers bring large amounts of cocaine out of Colombia's Pacific port of Buenaventura. From there they can sail straight into parks like Manuel Antonio, which has large stretches of Pacific beach. Then they can continue their route north on the Pan-American Highway," he said, tracing a line on the map with his index finger, "or organize further trips up the Pacific coast. Colombians come and leave the drugs and Mexicans come and pick them up. We are the waistline of the Americas."

He sat down in his chair again and folded his hands under his chin. "With the decline of local fisheries and new catch restrictions, fishermen have turned to running million-dollar coke packages for the cartels. Locals bring drug loads to shore or deliver gasoline out to sea for traffickers coming north from Colombia in high-powered speedboats. And, of course, the pay is much more than a fisherman can make."

"I suspect the heroin is coming from here through the MS 13."

Murillo nodded slowly. "The Sinaloa cartel has been known to use the MS 13 to carry out murders and other crimes."

Santana wondered if the Sinaloa cartel had hired the MS 13 banger who'd tried to kill him.

"It is good that you checked in with me," Murillo continued. "I do not want police detectives wandering around my country unsupervised, especially if you are dealing with the Sinaloa cartel or MS 13. Gambling is something to enjoy, but not when it involves your life."

Murillo picked up a map on his desktop and unfolded it. "The Blue Marlin bar is located in the Hotel Del Ray, in the heart of what we call 'Gringo Gulch'—so named because of the hundreds of North American men who come to the city for cheap and easy sex with beautiful young women from all over

Central and South America. In the neighborhoods bordering Gringo Gulch are districts that include brothels catering to rich westerners, homosexual and transvestite districts, and seedier clubs. I recommend that you avoid those areas."

Santana noted that Murillo had failed to mention the trafficked young women in the brothels, who'd come from the surrounding poorer Latin American countries, or the gangs of children called *chapulines*, or grasshoppers, that roamed the streets. Many were easy prey for traffickers, pimps, and drug dealers.

"What about Nina Rivera?"

Murillo removed a small notebook from his shirt pocket and opened it. "She arrived yesterday and is staying at the Hotel Grano de Oro near the museum. My men are watching her."

"I don't want her to know I'm in Costa Rica. But I'd like to speak with her mother today. I believe she lives in Heredia. I don't know where."

"I thought you did not want Nina Rivera to know you are here in Costa Rica."

"She told me she had no family, Lieutenant. But I found a letter from her mother. I believe she's estranged from her family and has no plans to visit them."

"You better hope so," Murillo said.

"I need to turn Rivera. But I need some leverage. Right now, she's too frightened to talk."

"If she is working for the cartel, then talking to the police would mean a death sentence."

"I understand. Still, I believe she knows more about the murders than she is telling."

"I will check my sources, Detective. For now, I ask that you let me and my men handle the investigation while you enjoy your stay with us."

"No problem."

Murillo offered a thin smile. "Let me give you one more piece of advice. Licensed taxis are red and have the license plate number painted in the middle of a yellow triangle on both doors. Orange-colored cabs serve the airport. Any other color is illegal. Identification has to be visible in the cab, including the driver's name and photograph. Still," he shrugged, "cabs are inexpensive. I recommend them in the city where traffic is a major problem."

"You have to be careful with taxis in Colombia as well, Lieutenant."

Murillo reached into an open desk drawer and came out with a cell phone. "I cannot offer you a gun, Detective. But I can offer you something that will keep you safe—as long as you stay in contact."

Santana knew that in order to carry a gun in Costa Rica he needed a carry permit, and permits were only issued to legal residents. If he were caught illegally carrying, he'd lose his Glock and be quickly deported.

Murillo handed him the phone. "This phone uses a three-G system. It is much more reliable than the GSM system that we also have here." He leaned forward and rested his elbows on the desktop and his eyes on Santana. "Make sure that you keep it charged and the power on."

"Of course," Santana said.

* * *

Santana took a cab back to the airport and rented a Toyota 4 x 4. Then he followed the Pan American Highway out of San José. Thirty minutes later, he took the Naranjo exit and headed north toward Zarcero, where Tania Cruz had been born.

The landscape became greener, lusher, and cooler as the road climbed through gently meandering slopes of orchids, coffee trees, mosses, and wild blueberries, the deep emerald color of the hillsides reminding Santana of the vegetation of his boyhood home in Manizales, Colombia, high in the Andes Mountains. Cattle grazed on the hillsides, and a light mist fell from the low hanging clouds that rolled over the landscape, giving it a mystical, otherworldly feel.

Zarcero was perched on the edge of the Central Valley in the San José Highlands. In the town square, near a surreal topiary garden in which shrubs and trees were cut and trimmed to look like animals, was a long tunnel of tall, wavy arches carved from conifer trees. The tunnel led to the double doors of a beautiful pink and blue cottage-style church, where Santana got directions to the house in which Tania Cruz had once lived.

Just outside town, he stopped the Toyota on the opposite side of the asphalt road from a one-story cement block home. The house had a small tile patio open on three sides. Cilantro grew in the cultivated dark soil out front. A metal slide and swing set stood on one side of the house. Colorful plastic bins used for collecting vegetables were stacked along the opposite outside wall. Directly behind him was a small factory.

He took out his notebook and turned to the page where he'd written the information Sarah Malik had given him regarding Sammy's recollections of her home in Zarcero. The cilantro, the slide and swing set, the small factory, all matched what he'd written.

A knock on the driver's side window drove Santana's heart into his throat. He took a deep breath to slow his racing heart before opening the window. He found himself staring into the face of a very thin man Santana estimated was in his early thirties. The man wore a white T-shirt and jeans that were as wet as his short, dark hair. He didn't seem to mind.

"*¿Te puedo ayudar?*" the man asked, bending slightly to peer into the SUV.

Santana wasn't sure if he needed help, but perhaps the man could save him some time. "Do you know if Tania Cruz used to live in this house?" he asked in Spanish.

"Why do you want to know?" There was a sharp edge in his voice.

Since he wasn't technically assigned to Tania Cruz's case, Santana wanted to avoid any discussion of it. So he asked a question of his own. "Who are you?"

"I am Tania's brother, Gonzalo. And you have not told me who you are, *señor*."

Santana showed him his badge wallet and introduced himself.

"My sister's killer is in jail in the States."

"How did you know that?"

"A friend of Tania's told us years ago."

"Was the friend's name Nina Rivera?"

Gonzalo nodded.

"How did you know Rivera?"

"I do not know her. She called six years ago and told us what had happened to Tania."

Santana pointed to the house across the road. "Do your parents still live there?"

"They are both dead." His gaze momentarily slid away from Santana and toward the house.

"Are they buried here?"

"In the cemetery up the road. But what business is it of yours?"

"Is Tania buried there, too?"

"I want to know why you are here, *señor*."

"*Gracias por su ayuda*," Santana said.

He touched the button to raise the window and then stopped when the young man placed his hand on Santana's shoulder.

"Let my sister rest in peace, *señor*."

"She will," Santana said. "Soon."

* * *

It didn't take Santana long to locate Tania Cruz's headstone. It was less weathered than most of the simple stone markers around it, save for those of her parents. The headstone was near a cypress tree. A resurrection fern clung to the trunk of the tree, the fern deriving its name from its ability to survive long periods of drought by curling up and appearing dead. Once moisture was again present in the soil and air, the fern uncurled and reopened, appearing to resurrect and return to life.

Santana knelt beside the headstone and pulled up the hood of his poncho as a rain rattled off the fabric and clouds fogged the mountainsides. Written underneath Tania Cruz's name and the dates of her birth and death were the words:

HASTA QUE NOS ENCONTREMOS DE NUEVO
(UNTIL WE MEET AGAIN)

Given what Sammy Malik had told him—and what he'd seen with his own eyes—Santana found added significance in the chiseled words. But he found little solace in the inscription written on a tombstone, or in a religion that believed an immortal soul would return in the body of another. Justice was what he believed in now; justice not only for himself, but also for the many victims whose cases he investigated.

He reached out and touched Tania Cruz's gravestone, gently running his hands over the rough stone as if it were her face. "I will find the person who took your life, Tania. That is my promise to you."

* * *

After leaving Zarcero, Santana called Murillo. "Any information on where Nina Rivera's mother lives in Heredia?"

Santana heard him shuffling some papers before he recited the location, which was an hour's drive from his present location.

The manicured gardens, tropical landscaping, and the size of the Spanish style house located in the beautiful city of Heredia at the foothills of the extinct Brava volcano surprised Santana. He'd expected the house to look more like Tania Cruz's home in Zarcero. He knocked on the thick wooden door and waited in the shade of the huge *Guanacaste* tree in the front yard till a tall, tan, very thin woman with chestnut-colored hair cut short and straight on the ends opened it.

"Can I help you?" she asked in Spanish.

"*Señora* Rivera?"

She nodded.

"My name is John Santana," he said, continuing to speak in Spanish.

She held out a hand. "Nice to meet you."

Shaking hands with her was like gripping a piece of bone.

"I am a detective from Minnesota." He showed her his badge. "I would like to speak with you about your daughter, Nina."

Her eyes enlarged and a hand went immediately to her mouth. "Has something happened to her?"

"No. She is fine."

"You have seen her recently?"

He nodded.

She let out a relieved sigh. "Thank God."

"Forgive me," Santana said. "I did not mean to startle you."

She stared at him a moment, as if seeing him for the first time. "Then what is this about?"

"If you could spare some time."

She hesitated and then said, "Please, come in."

Santana stepped onto a foyer floor, which was made of rose-colored marble. She closed the heavy door and led him through a formal dining room with a vaulted ceiling and indirect lights, and into a large open living area that had a wood beamed ceiling, a stone fireplace, and a rustic, copper-colored slate floor. He sat on a soft leather couch directly across from a set of wrought iron and glass doors that gave onto a Spanish style terrace and fountain.

"I am sorry my husband is at work."

Santana was pleased that she was alone. He'd gathered from the letter he'd read that Nina Rivera had a closer relationship with her mother than with her father. He figured that meeting with the mother would be more productive.

"What does your husband do?"

"He is a politician." She attempted a smile that came off as lopsided grin.

"And you?"

"I taught school. But when Nina was born, I decided to stay at home."

"You're an American," he said. "Yet your Spanish is excellent."

"Thank you. I have lived in Costa Rica since graduating from college with a degree in Spanish. But I would prefer if we conversed in English, if you do not mind. I have few chances to speak it anymore." Her eyes were the color of moss, and they slid off his face, as if she were embarrassed by the request.

"All right," he said, switching to English.

"You said you were here about Nina."

"Yes. I'm investigating the death of her roommate, Catalina Díaz."

"You're a homicide detective?"

"That's correct."

"Is Nina in any danger?"

"To be honest, I'm not sure."

She let out a heavy sigh and shook her head in resignation.

"Have you spoken with your daughter recently?"

"I'm afraid not."

Obviously, Nina Rivera hadn't wanted her parents to know that she was coming to Costa Rica for Catalina Díaz's funeral. Santana wondered why.

"Have you ever met Catalina Díaz?" he asked.

"No. But if she was in the same profession as my daughter, then there were probably many men capable of doing her harm." She gestured with a hand, indicating the surroundings. "Nina had a good upbringing. She came from a good family. She was a model child." Tears glistened in her eyes. She paused a moment and wiped her eyes with the back of a hand.

Santana waited.

She let out another sigh before continuing. "I can't begin to tell you how disappointed we were when Nina left the house."

"And when was that?"

"When she turned sixteen."

"Where did she go?"

"We didn't know at first. So my husband hired a private investigator. He discovered that she was working at the Blue Marlin and living with a girlfriend."

"What was the girlfriend's name?"

She thought for a moment. "Tania," she said.

The name hit Santana like a punch. "Tania Cruz?"

"Do you know her?"

"I've come across her name during my investigation." Santana didn't want to tell her that Tania Cruz was also dead. He changed the subject before she asked more questions about her. "What happened after the investigator located your daughter?"

"She disappeared again."

"And you were unable to find her?"

"Unfortunately, yes. But two years later, she came home for her grandmother's funeral."

"Were you aware your daughter was in Minnesota?"

"Her grandmother had mentioned it. She gave me Nina's address. I sent her a letter, but she never replied."

Santana figured it was the letter he'd found in Nina Rivera's bedroom. "Was your daughter very upset about her grandmother's death?"

"They were very close and kept in contact. I only spoke to Nina briefly. But she looked so mature, so different."

"How do you mean?"

"Well, for one thing, she'd had breast implants."

Santana remembered from the autopsy that Catalina Díaz had also had implants. He looked at his notes and processed all that he'd heard. Something was off. He could feel it.

"You said your daughter was a model child, Ms. Rivera."

"Things changed when she was fourteen."

"Did something happen?"

"Not that I was aware of."

Santana thought it was an odd answer. "Not that you were aware of?"

She shook her head.

He noted that all expression, all emotion, had disappeared from her face, as though she were wearing a blank mask. He wondered if she was taking any medication. "How was your daughter different?"

"She became very withdrawn. That was so unlike her."

"Did you ask her if something had happened?"

"Of course. But she said there was nothing wrong."

"Was she dating?"

"No. My husband refused to allow her to date."

Given his Colombian upbringing, Santana understood how overprotective Latino fathers could be with their daughters. Still, he sensed there was something much darker than adolescent rebellion in Nina Rivera's sudden change in behavior, in the same way he sensed the presence of danger in an unlit room.

"Is Nina your only child?"

"No. We have a younger daughter."

"How old is she?"

"Ten."

"And how is she doing?"

Susan Rivera stared at Santana without replying for a long time before she spoke. "Why are we talking about my younger daughter?"

Santana heard the front door open. An olive-complected man with a broad, big-boned body that had a look of sedentary softness lumbered into the room.

"What are you doing here?" the man said in Spanish, glaring at Santana. He had dark, arrogant eyes and hair the color of a shadow.

"We were talking about Nina," his wife said. Her eyes found Santana. "This is my husband, Victor."

Santana stood and offered his hand. "Detective John Santana."

Victor Rivera's hands remained on his expansive hips. "My question still stands. What are you doing here?"

"Learning something about your daughter."

"What is your interest?"

"I am investigating the death of your daughter's roommate."

"Was it suicide?"

Santana thought it was an unusual question. "There is no indication of that."

"I want to be kept informed of any developments in the case, Detective Santana."

Santana could hear the insistence in the man's voice, as if he were issuing an ultimatum. "What is the phone number here?"

"Call me at my office," Victor Rivera said. "I will let my secretary know that I am expecting your calls. You can also contact me through my e-mail." He handed Santana a business card.

Santana slid the card into his notebook.

"There will be no further need to come to my house and question my wife behind my back."

"We were just talking, Victor," Susan Rivera said.

He looked at her as he would something on the bottom of his shoe.

"Thank you for your time, *Señora* Rivera," Santana said, setting a business card on the table. He turned to leave and felt Victor Rivera's hand on his forearm.

"We need to talk, Detective."

Santana let his gaze slide to the hand on his forearm before looking directly into the man's eyes. Rivera removed his hand quickly, as if he'd touched a hot iron.

"Do not do that again, *Señor* Rivera."

He offered a conciliatory smile. "I just want to know about my daughter. I . . . we miss her very much."

"Maybe someday you and I will talk more about your daughter."

He shook his head. "I do not understand your meaning, *señor*."

"Sure you do," Santana said.

* * *

Santana had a hollow feeling in his chest as he left the Riveras' residence. Though the mountain air felt cool, his skin burned hot. He had all he could do to tame the inner demon that urged him to return to the house and beat the hell out of Victor Rivera. He knew why Nina Rivera had run away and turned to a life of prostitution at sixteen.

He sat behind the wheel of the Toyota and took some deep breaths to calm himself. He'd considered driving to the San Antonio *barrio* in Escazú to see Catalina Díaz's parents but rejected the idea. They were grieving and preparing for the funeral tomorrow. Plus, he had nothing concrete to tell them regarding their daughter's death.

He called Rodolfo Murillo. "Your men still watching Nina Rivera?"

"Yes. She is at a medical clinic in Heredia, north of San José."

"I am in Heredia now. What is the name of the clinic?"

"The Calderón Cosmetic Center."

"Where is it located?"

"My man is watching the clinic, Detective."

"I would like to see it as well."

"For what purpose?"

"I can find it on my own, Lieutenant. But you could save me time."

"As you wish."

Santana wrote down the directions as Murillo recited the location. Then he broke off the connection. It took him ten minutes to drive to the clinic.

He parked across the street from the two-story adobe building near the University of Costa Rica and thought about his next move. If Nina Rivera were having anything but minor surgery, she would probably be in the clinic all night. He could return to his hotel and wait till Murillo contacted him. But he wanted to keep moving. Sitting in his hotel room would accomplish nothing—though he was uncertain what he'd accomplish by watching the clinic.

Then he saw Nina Rivera come out of the front entrance of the building, an arm draped around the shoulders of another young woman he recognized as the blonde model he'd seen at Paul Lenoir's studio and again in the newspaper clipping with Nathaniel Burdette. At first glance, Santana thought she was supporting Rivera. But he soon realized it was the other way around.

Nina Rivera escorted the blonde to the curb just as a black van pulled up and stopped. The side doors slid open and the two women got in. Santana followed as the van drove off. He stayed two cars back as they drove south along Route 3. He thought they were headed for the main airport, but when they passed the Pan American highway and kept going south, he wasn't sure where the van was headed. A few miles past the highway, the van turned right onto *Calle* Alexander Humboldt. Santana realized they were headed for the smaller Tobias Bolaños International Airport in Pavas. He called Murillo on his cell.

"What are you doing following Nina Rivera?" Murillo asked.

Santana glanced in his rearview and saw a second van. "Your man is behind me."

"Exactly. And you did not listen to me."

"Tell me what you know about the airport."

"I know you will not be allowed to pass through the security without a ticket for a flight."

"What about your man?"

"He has a badge."

I do, too, Santana thought. But he knew his SPPD badge carried little weight in Costa Rica. "What else can you tell me?"

"Pull over and let my man do his job."

"I will. But what about the airport?"

"It is the hub for Natural Air as well as corporate and eco-tour charters. The rich and famous also use it so they can avoid the main airport and the crowds."

"So it handles mostly small charter flights."

"Yes, primarily from Nicaragua, Granada, and Panama. Since it is only a few miles from the U.S. Embassy, diplomats also like to use it."

Santana saw that a high chain-link fence surrounded the field. A black Lexus was stopped in front of the small kiosk and gated main entrance. Two uniformed guards were check-ing the occupant's papers. A third guard with a drug-sniffing German shepherd on a leash stood farther back behind the fence.

The van carrying Nina Rivera pulled up directly behind the Lexus. Santana drove past and looked in his rearview. Murillo's man pulled in and stopped behind the van.

"Are you still there?" Murillo asked.

"Still here," Santana said. "But I'll call you back."

He clicked off and made a U-turn and drove back toward the main gate, pulling to the side of the road before he reached it. From this position, he had a clear view of the main entrance, runways, passenger terminal, and control tower.

His phone vibrated. When he saw that it was Murillo calling back, Santana shut off his phone.

The lieutenant had neglected to mention that the airport had a reputation for drug running and loose security. By the looks of things, they had tightened things up. Santana figured the increased security had something to do with the small chartered plane filled with kilos of cocaine that had recently crashed in a nearby neighborhood. It might also have some-thing to do with the growing presence of the Sinaloa cartel and the Mexican government's crackdown of the cartels. Since Costa Rica had no standing army and a very limited police force, it was easy to see how the Colombian and Mexican cartels could stockpile drugs for shipments north—and why Costa Rica was fast becoming the new hub for drug traffic.

Santana watched as the van carrying Nina Rivera passed through the security checkpoint, followed shortly by Murillo's man in the van. Thirty minutes later, Santana saw a Learjet taxi into position for takeoff. He quickly checked his notebook. The jet had an "N" registry from the U.S. and the same tail number as the plane flown by James Elliot.

Chapter 18

Santana returned his rented Toyota to the airport and took a taxi to his hotel. The high temperatures and humidity in the center of the city had left his clothes as damp as the landscape, so he showered and shaved again. He ate a late lunch of black beans and rice called *gallo pinto*, then phoned Jordan and gave her a rundown of his progress. Then he took a taxi to the Blue Marlin Bar at the Del Ray Hotel, a seven-story, pink neo-classical building topped with the Del Rey logo.

As he stepped out of the taxi and into the rain, Santana spotted one of the new Bestum 500 model police cars the Chinese had built and donated to Costa Rica. The white sedans with the blue *Fuerza Publica*, or Public Force, decals on the front doors looked like the Ford Fusion. He figured Murillo's men were still keeping an eye on him.

Inside the Blue Marlin, Santana could see three rows of tables and chairs between the windows fronting the street. A wooden rail kept customers from falling off the raised platform holding the large main bar that was shaped like an upside-down U. TVs were bolted to the walls and tuned to sports channels. Mounted above the liquor shelves and dangling from the ceiling were stuffed, carved, and sculpted fish. A wrinkled American flag was taped to one wall, and dozens of shoulder patches, left behind by American cops and firemen, were tacked up behind the bar. Speakers were pumping out calypso music.

Two young Americans in tank tops sat at one of the tables. Seated at the bar was a sixty-something man wearing socks with his sandals and a Yankee cap on his head. A graying middle-aged guy in a floral-print shirt sat five stools down. The cute, dark-haired bartender wore a ball cap, a short skirt, and a halter top that hid very little of her large breasts. A handful of young women were sitting on stools in the back corner, smoking cigarettes and looking bored. Santana figured they were working—but not very hard. He imagined that when the cocktail hour began the place would be jammed. Murillo had told him that a prostitute from Colombia named Eva Miranda might've known Tania Cruz or Catalina Diaz. He wanted to talk to her and then move on before the bar became packed.

He found a vacant seat at one of the high tops by the bar rail and ordered a Bavaria Dark. When the waitress brought him his beer, he asked her in Spanish if she knew Catalina Díaz.

She shook her head.

He paid for his drink and then held up a twenty-dollar bill. "Do you know Eva Miranda?"

"*Sí.*"

"This money is yours if you tell me when she arrives."

"*Sí, señor,*" she said with a big smile.

The more the crowd grew, the louder the music became. Santana noted that every few minutes one of the young prostitutes, who were mingling with receptive young men, would head for the hotel lobby. Still, the supply of *chicas* never seemed to diminish. They always outnumbered the *gringos*.

Santana ordered a second beer. He'd finished half of it when he noticed a woman looking at him. She had shoulder-length curly black hair and copper-colored skin. Her short white low-cut dress was as tight as a snake's skin. She was pretty, but her complexion had started to show the wear and tear of her profession. He guessed she was at least ten years older than the majority of prostitutes in the bar. Despite her age, most of the men couldn't take their eyes off her as strode across the floor and sidled up to Santana. She had a cigarette between her fingers and asked in Spanish if he had a light.

"Sorry."

She looked at him with her large eyes that were the color of coffee beans and just a little too cold for her warm smile. "You wanted to talk to me."

"Eva Miranda?"

"Yes," she said, placing a hand on his forearm.

"Do you know Catalina Díaz?"

She nodded and cocked her head in a questioning gesture, running a long red fingernail up and down his forearm.

"I would like to ask you some questions about her."

"How come?" she asked, a seductive, playful quality still evident in her voice.

Santana wanted her to lose the attitude, something that wouldn't happen as long as she viewed him as a potential client. He showed her his badge wallet. "I am a homicide detective from Minnesota investigating Catalina Díaz's murder."

The smile faded from her lips, the glimmer from her eyes.

"We should go someplace where it's quieter," he said. He stood, but she hesitated. "I will pay you for your time."

They took a cab to her apartment on the outskirts of the city. Eva Miranda didn't speak or ask about Catalina Díaz's death. Rather, she sat staring silently out the window as they drove into a *barrio* where residents were caged into ironwork-enclosed homes surrounded by high fences topped by barbed wire or broken bottles cemented atop walls.

"It is not only the wealthy that now live in gated communities," she said.

Two guards armed with bolt action rifles and a German shepherd patrolled the gated entrance where Eva Miranda lived.

The security around Eva Miranda's apartment reminded Santana of Colombia, and to some extent, what he was seeing in the States with the gated communities. Gangs and cartels were illegally obtaining high-powered weapons, many from the U.S., and pushing into the southern states like an invading army. It was illegal to possess military-style weapons in Costa Rica. Santana wondered how long it would be before the Costa Rican courts realized that their police forces would soon be overwhelmed by firepower.

As they got out of the cab, Eva Miranda greeted the guards. Santana followed her to the door of her ground-level apartment. He sat on the unforgiving couch in the living room furnished with rustic wood furniture and drank from a bottle of Heineken she offered. In the kitchen, she mixed soda with *guaro*, which was made from sugar cane.

When she sat down in the living room in a cushioned chair across from him, she said, "You are Colombian?"

"As are you," he said. "Your accent tells me you are from Cartagena."

"And you are a *paisa*," she said, using the Colombian term that described people from the northwest region of the country.

"From Manizales," he said. "How did you end up here?"

"You mean how did I become a prostitute."

"Your profession is not my concern."

She considered his response before answering. "I worked in the fashion industry in Colombia. When the economy began to slow, I came to Costa Rica to find similar work. But I could not find a job here. I made enough money through prostitution to buy a small house and to get out of the trade. Eventually, I found a job in a factory, but it paid less. When I got laid off earlier this year, I had no choice but to return to what I know. But it is much harder now. There are many more girls working here than before. And most of them are foreigners like me. Before it was mostly *Ticas* from here and *Nicas* from Nicaragua," she said. "And many of the men seem more interested in viewing than in paying for a service. It is disappointing."

"I can use your help."

She lit a cigarette and sipped her drink. A breeze blew in through an open window, billowing the thin white curtains out across the room. "You came a long way."

"I go where the case takes me."

She nodded.

"How long had you known Catalina Díaz?" he asked.

"Perhaps a year, perhaps a year and a half."

"You worked with her at the Blue Marlin."

"Yes."

From a pocket, Santana removed the 3" x 5" photos he'd run of Philip Campbell, Matthew Singer, and Nathaniel Burdette and placed them on the coffee table. "Catalina Díaz met these men at the Blue Marlin. I believe one of them killed her. Do you recognize any of the faces?"

Eva Miranda leaned forward and peered at the photos for what seemed like a long time. Then she leaned back in her chair and shook her head. "I meet many men. But I do not really know them."

"These men come here often."

"So do others."

Another thought came to him. "Catalina Díaz also worked at a resort in Jaco called Erotic Tours."

Eva Miranda's body suddenly stiffened.

"You know this place?"

She took a long drag on her cigarette, the smoke leaking out her nostrils and between her lips. "Of course," she said, exhaling.

"Have you ever worked there?"

"No." She crushed out her cigarette and stared at him silently for a time before speaking again. "How did Catalina die?"

"She was strangled."

Eva Miranda's face twisted as if she'd felt a sharp pain.

"What do you know about autoerotic asphyxia?" Santana asked. "It's sometimes called terminal sex or scarving."

She was looking right through him now.

"Ms. Miranda," he said.

Her eyes refocused. "Yes?"

"I asked you a question."

She swallowed the rest of her drink and shook her head. "I know nothing about it."

"Did you know Tania Cruz?"

Her eyes widened with recognition.

"You did know her."

She shook her head.

"You are lying, Ms. Miranda."

"No. I speak the truth."

"Tania Cruz died six years ago in the same manner as Catalina Díaz."

She stood and pointed toward the front door. "You need to pay me for my time and then go."

Santana remained seated, thinking through the possibilities, trying to understand what he was missing.

"I charge one hundred dollars an hour, Detective." She took out her cell and called him a cab.

Santana removed two fifty-dollar bills from his wallet and set the money on the coffee table. "Two young women have been murdered, Ms. Miranda," he said, gesturing at the photos on the coffee table. "One of these men might have killed them. Think about that. Think real hard."

"You can wait outside the door."

He picked up the photos. "If you change your mind, I'll be at the Adventure Inn." He set his business card on the table and wrote the cell number for the phone Murillo had given him on the back.

"Detective," she said as he headed for the door.

He turned and looked at her.

"Because you are Colombian like me."

Santana waited.

"There are more," she said.

"You mean more women who have been murdered?"

She nodded.

"How many?"

"More," she said. "That is all I know."

"*Gracias.*"

"*Vaya con Dios*, Detective."

Santana closed the door behind him and stood under the portico, waiting for the cab that would take him back to his hotel. His thoughts were focused on the last words uttered by Eva Miranda telling him to "go with God" and her statement that more young women had met the same fate as Tania Cruz and Catalina Díaz. He was more determined now than ever to find the perpetrator and bring him to justice.

A cab pulled up in front of the gate. One of the security guards leaned into the open driver's side window and spoke to the driver. Then the guard straightened up, turned toward Santana, and gestured for him to come. But Santana wasn't going anywhere. The cab was neither red nor orange in color and had no yellow triangle sticker on the front doors with the plate number. Instinctively, he knew that Eva Miranda had set him up, either by choice or by threat. He tried the handle on the front door to her place. It was locked. If he made a scene the guards would be on him, and for all he knew, they could be paid off as well.

"*Señor*," the security guard called. "*El taxi está aquí.*"

Santana told him in Spanish that he wanted another taxi.

"There are few taxis at this hour, *señor.*"

"Then I will walk."

"It is five kilometers back to the city. And it is dangerous walking alone."

Santana wished he had his Glock. Still, he figured the odds were better in the street than in the cab. "I will take my chances," he said.

"As you wish, *señor*." The guard motioned for the cab to leave.

Santana waited another minute before walking out the gate. He wondered if the guards would attempt to stop him, but they let him go.

He was alone and unarmed now—but at least he was alive.

* * *

Santana ran two to three miles four times a week to keep in shape. Five kilometers was equal to a little over three miles. If he ran at an eight minute pace—something he was accustomed to—he could make it to the city central in less than thirty minutes, even if he had to push himself the last mile. Once there, he was certain he could hail a cab to drive him to his hotel. He'd paid close attention during the cab ride from the Blue Marlin to Eva Miranda's house and knew it would be a straight, flat run in a westerly direction. He was wearing his running shoes and figured he needed a workout.

He settled into a comfortable stride, arms pumping easily, his heart rate easing as his muscles warmed, running against the flow of traffic through pools of white light and night shadows cast by trees. The night air felt cooler in the *barrio* and smelled less of diesel fuel, but it was thick with humidity, which typically increased as darkness enveloped the Costa Rican landscape.

Like much of San José, the outskirts of the city was an unsightly collection of dilapidated infrastructure, potholed streets, and crumbling sidewalks that snaked through a confused mixture of corrugated metal and plaster. Santana kept alert for any gangs roaming the streets, and for the cab that had come to pick him up. Whoever had sent it would no doubt be searching for him.

Checking his watch periodically to gauge his time and distance, he calculated he was a third of the way to his destination when he spotted the cab he'd seen at Eva Miranda's house. It was parked along the curb on his side of the street near a dimly lit intersection up ahead.

As he approached, he saw two men get out of the car. He increased his stride and veered to his right, dashing across the road between traffic to the opposite side of the street. He wanted to stay on the main road. A legal cab might come by, or if he was lucky, a police car. If he were forced down a darkened side street or alley, the odds of escape would shift considerably.

He was thankful that he'd paced himself and had something left in his tank. Out of the corner of his eye, he could see the two men stepping out into traffic, hear horns honking as they tried to cross the road in the narrow space between speeding cars. Santana tucked his arms close to his side and his chin to his chest and sprinted, going for speed now rather than endurance, hoping to make the intersection before the two men crossed the street and cut him off.

He was nearly to the intersection when an SUV pulled up alongside and the passenger window came down. He was expecting to see a gun, but instead, Rodolfo Murillo stuck his head out the window and said in Spanish, "Quit running and get in the backseat."

Santana did.

"What about the guys who are chasing me?" he said.

Murillo made a hitchhiking motion with his thumb as the SUV pulled away from the curb and shot through the intersection.

Santana looked out the rear window and saw red lights flashing and policemen pointing guns at the two men, who had their hands held high above their heads. Then he looked at the back of Murillo's head. "You have been following me."

"Of course. I knew you would never take my advice."

"Would you if you were me?"

"Probably not." Murillo held out a hand, and the driver gave him a handful of *colones*.

"What's the money for?" Santana asked.

"We bet on your time. I thought you would run each mile in eight minutes or less. My colleague here, Enrique, thought you were more of a nine-minute man. He lost."

His body sheathed in sweat, his breathing still labored, Santana didn't know whether to be grateful or angry. "Why didn't you pick me up sooner?"

"Then there would have been no bet, Detective." Murillo looked at the driver—a big-boned, cement block of a man— and both men laughed.

"Hilarious," Santana said. "Thanks for betting with my life."

Murillo half-turned in his seat so that he was facing Santana. "Your life was never in danger."

"Says who?"

"My men were always in position to protect you."

"What if I'd gotten into the cab?"

"You are not a stupid man." Murillo smiled and glanced at Enrique. "I won that bet, too."

Enrique gave him the finger.

Murillo shook his head and sighed. "Unfortunately, my colleague is a sore loser."

"Well, now that you two have had your fun," Santana said, "how about telling me who those men were?"

"We suspect they work for the Sinaloa cartel."

"Why kidnap me?"

"We believe the two men will provide us with some answers."

"I would like to listen to the interrogation."

"I am afraid that is not possible, Detective. We are driving you back to your hotel. You can catch a flight home tomorrow."

"What if I am not ready to leave?"

"The subject is not up for debate," Murillo said.

* * *

Before going to bed that night, Santana called Jordan.

"How are you and Gitana doing?"

"We're fine. But she does want to sleep in my bed."

"Don't spoil her. Make her sleep on the bedroom floor."

"We're still negotiating," she said. "When are you coming home?"

"Soon."

"Have you found what you're looking for?"

"I think so. But I want to give it one more day."

"You're being careful, right?"

"Absolutely."

"And you won't do anything foolish."

"You know me."

"It's the reason I'm asking," she said.

"You sound like Murillo."

"Who's Murillo?"

"A police lieutenant I'm working with."

"I like him."

"You don't even know him."

"I know he's giving you good advice. I hope you take it."

"I'll be careful."

"You'd better," she said.

Chapter 19

The next morning, instead of taking a cab to the airport as Murillo had urged, Santana took one to the Calderón Cosmetic Center in Heredia, the clinic he'd seen Nina Rivera and the blond woman exiting yesterday before they left the country on James Elliot's Learjet. He asked the taxi to wait and then went inside the spacious, contemporary lobby and spoke to the receptionist seated at a desk behind the counter.

"I am afraid you have just missed Dr. Calderón, *señor*. He left for a short vacation."

"I really wanted to speak to him."

"Well, he usually calls in once a day to check his messages. If you would like to leave your name, I am sure he or one of his assistants will contact you."

Santana thought for a moment. "Is that Dr. Calderón?" he asked, pointing to a large framed poster hanging on the wall behind the desk of a handsome, silver-haired, fifty-something man.

"Yes, it is."

"Actually, I am leaving for a short vacation myself this afternoon to Jaco. Probably not the same place the doctor is vacationing." He gave her his best smile.

She smiled back. "No, the doctor went to Puerto Caldera."

"Thank you," Santana said, heading for the door and the waiting cab.

"You are not going to leave your contact information, *señor*?" she called after him.

"I will see the doctor soon," Santana said over his shoulder.

The cab driver explained that the drive to Puntarenas from the Juan Santamaria Airport took about an hour on the paved highway. From there it was another ten minutes south to Puerto Caldera. Santana returned to his hotel and used the free wi-fi and computers to look for hotels in Puerto Caldera. He jotted down the phone number for the Costa del Sol. Then he packed a small bag and made sure he had his passport and the Bushnell binoculars he'd brought with him.

He hailed a cab that took him to the airport, where he rented another Toyota 4x4 that could handle the rough, pot-holed roads. The young woman at the rental counter advised him to exchange at least five U.S. dollars' worth of Costa Rican *colones* for the tolls on the highway. Then she gave him directions for Route 1 west, just past the airport.

The first eight miles was along the old, bumpy route toward San Ramón. But once Santana made it to the highway, the road was much better and faster. His cell phone rang twice. He recognized Murillo's number and switched off the phone. He figured it was embedded with a global positioning system chip, which could calculate his coordinates to within a few yards by receiving signals from satellites. A phone without batteries installed or turned off would not make contact with the cell towers or satellites. He didn't want Murillo tracking him via GPS. But even without the phone, Santana was sure Murillo's men were trying to tail him, as they had the previous evening when he'd gone to Eva Miranda's house. Just because he hadn't spotted a tail didn't mean there wasn't one.

It was a question of trust. Despite Murillo's intervention last night, which had saved him from a possible deadly confrontation with members of the Sinaloa cartel, Santana wasn't sure he could fully trust Murillo. The lieutenant had given

Santana no reason to doubt him. But Santana had grown up in a culture in which trust was earned over time. In his present position, he could not afford to make a mistake—a mistake that could cost him his life.

Shortly after passing signs for Jaco/Quepos, he saw the Pacific Ocean open up before him, blue and endless and glittering with sunlight. Two minutes later, with the ocean on his left, he spotted the exit sign for Puntarenas and headed north into downtown.

The mostly run-down port city sat on a long, narrow ten-mile peninsula that jutted out into the Nicoya Gulf. He could see a cruise ship docked at the pier and souvenir stands and *sodas*, or informal lunch counters, setup to greet passengers. Tourists with their cameras were walking along the Paseo de los Turistas, a tree-lined promenade of restaurants, cafes, bars, and hotels adjacent to the beach. He was surprised to see that the water along the beach was murky, which was probably why few people were swimming.

Santana continued driving south ten more miles to Puerto Caldera on the Gulf of Nicoya. He nearly missed the Costa del Sol Restaurant & Hotel as he passed through town. The small European-style hotel was the only one in the tiny port city, and it sat across a lagoon.

He asked at the front desk if Dr. Calderón had checked in yet and was pleased to hear that he had indeed. A standard room was inexpensive and included breakfast. Santana figured Branigan wouldn't object to paying the tab for the hotel. Plus, Santana hoped his stay would be short. His room was comfortable and clean and had a good, functioning shower, which he quickly used.

After changing into a fresh set of clothes, Santana located Dr. Luis Calderón in the restaurant. Calderón was seated at a table with a short, thin Asian man who wore dark-framed glasses and appeared to be Chinese. Santana took a table under a ceiling fan near a large tank of live lobsters. He was close enough to keep an eye on the doctor, but far enough away to go unnoticed. The crowded restaurant was open on one side and overlooked a lagoon, where jet skiers were racing across the water. Santana could hear nothing that the two men discussed. But he doubted they were talking about the weather or a tour to the rainforest.

Santana had just finished his meal when Calderón and the Asian man got up to leave. He waited till they passed and then followed them to the parking lot, where they got into a white Nissan Pathfinder, the Asian behind the wheel. The temperature outside felt much hotter than in San José, despite the ocean breeze. Santana flipped the switch for the air-conditioning as soon as he was inside the Toyota and had started the engine.

He followed the two men south, staying well back, fearing he'd be spotted, but keeping the Pathfinder in sight. Traffic was light. The mountains were dotted with cattle, coffee, and cocoa farms, the ocean sparkling like expensive diamonds. He tailed the men for twenty minutes before their SUV turned onto a side road leading into the rainforest. Santana pulled onto the shoulder and waited. He knew it was risky to follow. He had no weapon and no idea where the two men were headed. He felt like a man clinging to a docking line of a rapidly rising hot air balloon. He knew if he didn't let go soon, he would have no choice other than to stay with it, possibly endangering his life in the process. Still, the momentum of the case was driving him forward. He sensed it was important to find out where they were going. Driven by curiosity and by the darkly attractive thrill that facing death gave him, he decided he'd follow for another ten minutes. If nothing turned up, he'd head back to the hotel and formulate a new plan.

The side road was rutted and made of dirt as it wound upward through the dense rainforest. Santana was thankful that he had rented a 4 x 4 with plenty of power and clearance.

The rough terrain meant slow going, and he soon reached his allotted ten minutes. He considered turning back when he saw another dirt road just ahead and off to his right. He stopped and shut off the engine and got out. Grabbing his binoculars off the seat, he closed the driver's side door quietly and walked ahead till he came to the intersection. One hundred yards down the side road he could see a large, corrugated metal warehouse nestled in a clearing. A ten-foot fence topped with razor wire surrounded the building.

He moved closer and squatted near the trunk of a *guayabón* tree. Peering through the binoculars, he saw signs on the fence in English and Spanish warning that it was electrified and that guard dogs patrolled the premises. Two security guards armed with AK-47s manned the gated entrance. Their heads were shaved, their faces marked with gang tattoos. *Maras*, Santana thought. The warehouse windows were dark empty sockets. Video cameras attached to the three corners of the building were visible from his vantage point. He watched as the Pathfinder conveying Calderón and the Asian man entered the compound through a sliding gate and stopped beside two soft top Land Rover Defenders. Calderón and the Asian man got out and entered the building through a side door.

A few minutes later the same door opened and a man came out accompanied by two massive shorthaired Fila Brasileiros. They had big, heavy heads with deep muzzles. Their droopy ears were large and thick and tapered, their necks and backs well muscled, their chests broad and deep.

Because of their aggressive nature, it was illegal to own them in some countries, but not in Colombia, where he'd first observed them as a child. A neighbor from Brazil who owned one had told him once that the Brazilian army preferred to use the dogs in extreme jungle conditions instead of Dobermans and German shepherds.

Santana figured his chances of getting inside the warehouse had diminished considerably. Once inside the fenced compound, he'd have to face the two dogs without a weapon —a very unpleasant and possibly suicidal prospect.

Using poisoned meat or meat filled with sleeping tablets was something used successfully only in Hollywood movies. A well-trained guard dog would ignore food given to it by anyone except his trainer or owner. And the dogs were probably trained to avoid the electrified fence as well.

He checked the time on his watch. It was 4:00 p.m. It would be dark in two hours along the equator. He figured the dogs handled after hours security. He knew how he would get inside the compound. The urinating dogs had given him an idea as to how he might avoid them.

* * *

Santana drove back to Puntarenas, where he purchased a black T-shirt, ball cap, and pants. He also bought a flashlight, a screwdriver, and a fishing knife with a four-inch stainless steel blade and four-inch wooden handle. Then he bought a newspaper and looked in the classified ads for dog breeders. Using the cell phone Murillo had given him, he called breeders in the area. It took him four tries before he found one that had a female in heat. He got directions and drove to the farm, located on a landscaped ridge overlooking the Central Valley.

The owners were an American couple named Bill and Rosanne George. Rosanne explained in excellent Spanish, spiced with a southern accent, that she and her husband had retired to Costa Rica from Arkansas five years ago and had built their dream farm. They had a stable for their two horses and outbuildings for chickens and turkeys. There was a pond stocked with wild bred and self-breeding tilapia fish. They grew organic bananas, pineapples, lemons and limes, cacao, blackberries, and three varieties of avocados.

"We've got two small spring-fed streams on the property," Rosanne said. "We have a filter system for sediment and an ozonator. No need for chemicals or water treatment. The streams have fresh water shrimp and water crabs. And we have a forty-foot saltwater pool."

From where Santana was standing he could see and hear the ocean. "You've got a great view."

She nodded. "It's a bird watcher's paradise, too. There are lots of parrots, hummingbirds, and occasionally macaws, along with wild turkeys and a variety of monkeys, though we have to lock up because they're smart as hell and can get into just about everything. But you're here about our Cane Corsos."

"Specifically the female in heat," Santana said in English.

She pushed the bill of her sun hat back and cocked her head. "You're an American?"

"From Minnesota. But I'm originally from Colombia."

"And you're not looking for a pup?"

Santana shook his head. He wondered if dealing with an American would be easier than dealing with a Costa Rican. "I'd like to borrow your female for a few hours."

"What for?"

"Normally, I wouldn't ask you to do this, Rosanne. But I'm in Costa Rica investigating the deaths of two young women."

"You're a police officer?"

"I'm a homicide detective." Santana showed her his badge. "I can't get into specifics. But I'll make sure the dog is returned to you safely and unharmed."

She squinted at Santana for a time without speaking, her face tanned from hours in the sun. "Well, you're an American and a police officer, so I want to help you out. My husband went to San José this morning. He should be back first thing tomorrow. I'd like to discuss it with him."

"I really need the dog tonight. I'd be happy to reimburse you."

"It isn't the money, Detective. The secrecy is the problem."

"You're better off not knowing." Before she could offer another objection, Santana said, "What's the dog's name?"

"Annie," she said with a smile. "I named her after my late mother. I come from a family of nine girls. All of us grew up healthy and strong. My mother lived to be ninety-five. Annie's had two litters. The pups were all strong and healthy, too."

"How's she with strangers?"

"Very good."

"Where is she in her estrous cycle?"

"She's in the first stage and just started bleeding. Not much. She's not receptive to breeding, but you've got to watch her closely."

"I'll keep a close eye on her," Santana said. "No harm will come to her."

"I could go with you."

"That would be a bad idea."

She nodded and thought some more. "Maybe you should meet Annie. See how she takes to you."

"Absolutely."

Roseanne started toward the house and then stopped. "You'll bring her back tonight, Detective?"

"I will," Santana said, hoping he was making a promise he could keep.

* * *

Annie sat in the front seat next to Santana. She was two feet tall at the withers and black in color, with small white markings on her chest and toes. Her tail had been docked and her ears cropped to look like equilateral triangles standing upright. She was affectionate and appeared to have a sweet, well-trained disposition. But the wide, long muzzle above her hanging lip and her well-muscled body projected a sense of power, balance, and athleticism. Santana knew she had a powerful bite. He wouldn't want her jaws clamped around any part of his body.

He turned on his phone and listened to his three voice mail messages, all from Murillo asking him to return his call. Murillo's tone had grown stronger with each message. Santana decided he'd call him after he'd been to the warehouse. Maybe he could find something that would temper the lieutenant's anger.

The bloody glow of sunset had seeped out of the horizon, and shadows had hardened into night. The trees outside the windows of his SUV were black against the sky. The ocean was glazed with moonlight. His return trip through Puntarenas and then through Puerto Caldera took longer in the darkness. He nearly missed the dirt road leading into the rainforest. He made a U-turn and parked the SUV along the shoulder so that it was facing Puerto Caldera. If he had to make a swift exit, he wanted the Toyota headed toward his hotel and not Panama. He figured he could walk the potholed road as fast as he could drive it. Plus, being on foot gave him more options for escape—if it came to that.

The dog grew excited as Santana shut off the engine. "We're going for a walk," he said, petting her head. She leaned forward and licked his face. "Sure, you love me now, but will you love me later?"

He made certain her leash was hooked tight on her collar and secure in his right hand before opening the driver's side door and exiting the vehicle. He'd changed into his black outfit in a gas station. Now he pulled on his ball cap and grabbed the flashlight and screwdriver before shutting and locking the car doors.

The green glow of his watch indicated it was nearly 7:00 p.m. The sky was clear, the moon nearly full, the air heavy with humidity. He could hear the nighttime chirps, squeaks, flutters, shrieks, knocks, and clicks of the rainforest. The ruts in the road forced him to move carefully behind the beam from the flashlight. One misstep and he could twist an ankle or break a bone. Annie had been trained well. She followed closely at his side and did not pull on the leash as they moved steadily along the soft, muddy road. The slow trek to the side road leading to the warehouse took fifteen minutes.

Santana could hear the two Fila Brasileiros whining now. They could sense a bitch in heat from as far as three miles. Annie became agitated.

"Easy, girl," Santana said.

A twelve-foot lamppost near the front gate and the full moon provided some light. The grounds looked completely deserted except for the guard dogs. Santana waited to see if someone came out to check on the whining dogs. When no one did, he moved down the road, holding the leash tightly, talking calmly to Annie. The males' whining grew louder and more intense as Santana and Annie neared the compound. The two dogs were desperate to get to her, but fearful of the electrified fence.

When Santana was within ten yards of the fence, he secured the leash to a tree. He could hear the electric buzz of the wires in the fencing. The Fila Brasileiros were beside themselves with excitement now, all their attention focused on Annie. Santana hoped he was the last thing on their minds.

He moved quickly to the operator box located at the bottom of the gate. Using the screwdriver, he popped open the cover. In the beam from the flashlight, he studied the inner workings, looking for the gate's manual release switch. Instead, he found a small handle that fit over an "L" shaped lever. By changing the position of the lever, he disengaged the mechanism, allowing the gate to move freely.

The dogs, the electrified fence, and the razor wire were all designed to keep people out of the compound and the warehouse. Santana saw no evidence of an alarm system, though there certainly could be one. The video cameras might relay information to off-site computers monitored by security. They could be here in minutes depending on how much distance they had to travel. Or perhaps the cameras were connected to a digital recording system that was only monitored periodically or checked if there was physical evidence of a break in. Still, Santana had come this far. He had no intention of turning back now.

It took him only moments to slide the gate open far enough to squeeze through. He hesitated and glanced at the guard dogs. Their attention was focused on Annie. He hoped it wouldn't change once he stepped through the gate. If they attacked, he wondered if the fishing knife he'd bought would be enough to save him.

He slipped through the opening in the gate and made his way toward the warehouse, his cap pulled down on his forehead so that the video cameras couldn't record his face. His eyes were fixed on the two male Fila Brasileiros, who were pacing back and forth in front of the fence, trying to find a safe way to Annie.

Suddenly, one of the males could no longer resist the temptation. He leapt onto the fence, setting off a series of sparks. Stung by a jolt of electricity, he dropped to the ground like a stone and lay still. Santana thought the shock had killed him. Then the dog raised its large head and looked around, as though he had no idea where he was. He struggled to his feet and stood with his head lowered and his legs wobbly. The other male, paying no attention to the plight of his companion, continued to whine and to pace like a caged lion, his gaze locked on Annie.

When Santana reached the warehouse, he focused the light along all four sides of the door, making sure there were no wires or vibration tape that could trigger an alarm. He listened, but could hear only the soft rumble of a generator that supplied power to the building. He removed the knife from the sheath strapped to his belt and slid the blade between the crack in the door and the doorframe where the latch was located. He applied pressure against the knife, jiggling the blade to find the best angle while pushing the latch back into the door, till he felt it release.

The inside of the warehouse was wrapped in darkness and smelled strongly of fish. Santana directed the beam of light to a desk on his left that was cluttered with paperwork. On closer inspection, he saw that the clutter consisted of purchase orders from a shipping company in Taiwan and invoices from a Costa Rican company called Global Services, which Santana suspected was a front for the Sinaloa cartel. The Taiwan shipping company reminded him of the Asian man he'd seen with Dr. Calderón earlier that day.

He shined the light over the top of a series of tables to his right and saw what he thought were dead fish. As he stepped closer to the nearest table, he realized he was looking at piles of shark fins.

Santana followed the beam from the flashlight to the back of the building, where he found a large walk-in freezer with a padlocked handle. He'd opened locks in the past using his picks, but he hadn't brought them to Costa Rica. The padlock on the freezer was an inexpensive Master Lock. He would have no problem opening it if he could find what he needed.

He returned to the desk and removed a large paper clip from a stack of invoices. He broke the paper clip in the middle and then bent the two pieces open so that he had two similar-looking "L"s. One he could use as a pick and the other as a torsion wrench.

He went back to the padlock on the freezer, held the flashlight under an armpit, and forced the hook end of the wrench about 1/2 inch into the lower part of the keyway, bending the clip in his hand down as he did so to get some torque. He slid the straight end of the other half of the paper clip into the lock under the pins. Then he used the wrench clip to turn the keyway clockwise till it clicked open.

His breath clouded as he entered the freezer. There were additional tables here, but these were covered with the bodies of frozen sharks—minus their fins. Why, he wondered, would the cartel keep the carcasses? Usually after cutting off a fin with a hot blade, a fisherman would let the shark sink to the bottom of the ocean, where it would soon die. It took another moment before Santana put it together.

He took out his knife and slit open the belly of a shark. Inside it he found a small garbage bag. And inside the garbage bag he found black tar heroin.

Santana locked the freezer and made sure the warehouse door was closed behind him. As he headed for the front of the warehouse, he cast the light around the room and then stopped as a spike of adrenaline jolted his heart.

In a corner was a 4' x 4' altar with a statue of *Santa Muerte* and six unlit black candles. Leaning against the statue was a black and white photo of him. *Muerte a mis enemigos*, death to my enemies, was written in red marker across the photo. By the grainy look of it, the photo appeared to have been copied from a newspaper article rather than taken with a camera and lens. Santana stepped closer and played the light over the statue.

She wore a long hooded robe, though her black skull face and skeletal hands were clearly defined. In her right hand she held an hourglass. Her left hand was touching her chest and held the handle of a scythe that was resting on her left shoulder. Around the base of the statue were seeds, legumes, and other amulets depicting her worldly powers. Santana thought the statue was made from obsidian, but the longer he stared at it the more it appeared to be composed of pure shadow.

He inhaled a deep breath and released it, hoping to slow his rapidly beating heart. Sweat leaked from his pores. His nerve endings felt like vibrating wires. He did not believe in curses or black magic. Still, he wondered how the cartel had acquired his photo, and if they knew he was here. Without his Glock and with only a knife and a dog, he'd have to rely solely on his instincts and intellect to survive.

He exited the warehouse and closed the door. The dog that had received the jolt of electricity had recovered. He and his companion were yelping and whining, still trying to figure out a safe way to get to Annie. Santana crossed the yard quickly and squeezed through the gate.

Once he was safely outside, he returned the lever in the operator box to its original position and replaced the cover. He'd just untied Annie's leash from the tree when he heard the roar of turbocharged engines and saw shafts of light on the rough road that ran perpendicular to his current position, the headlight beams jumping as tires hit potholes.

"Come on, girl," he said to Annie.

He held the dog tightly by the leash and took off running into the dense underbrush of the rainforest surrounding the compound, branches tearing at his clothing, his sight limited to the cut of his flashlight. Concerned that someone might spot the beam, he switched it off. He stayed close to the edge of the forest while remaining hidden, worried that if he were forced to run deeper into the woods, he could lose his sense of direction.

He shielded his eyes with the palm of his hand as headlights swung toward him and the vehicles powered down the road to his right, heading for the compound and the barking dogs. Santana figured that once security had checked the warehouse and grounds and found them secure, they would let the two Fila Brasileiros loose. He needed to put some distance between them before that happened, or they would easily run him, and Annie, down. He'd vowed to bring her back safe and sound. He wanted to keep that promise.

He counted three Land Rovers and six heavily armed men as the vehicles raced by him. When they had passed, he exited the forest and ran to the crossroads. It had taken him fifteen minutes to walk here from his SUV. If he could cut that time in half, he figured he could make it safely to the Toyota.

He ran along the left edge of the road where the ground was smoother, holding the leash tightly in his left hand, the flashlight in his right, following the narrow blade of light. Annie easily kept pace alongside him. He could hear the thud of his feet, the dog's panting, and the sound of his breath. The moon was high in the sky now, and its luminous glow glossed the road in a soft pale light. He could see the silhouettes of tall trees, their leaves as black as funeral shrouds. He switched off the flashlight and tucked it in a pocket.

They'd nearly made it to the main road where his SUV was parked when Santana smelled cigarette smoke. He yanked on the leash and slowed to a stop. Annie responded, as though sensing the danger that lay ahead. Standing silently in the shimmering lunar glow, the trees like tall dark shadows around him, Santana could hear two men conversing in Spanish. They were talking about a woman and laughing softly. He figured they were ten yards away and were there to watch his SUV while the other security guards searched the compound.

Santana was certain the two men were heavily armed and willing to kill without regard. His concern was sharpened by the fact that all he had was a knife and the dog. He didn't want to put her in harm's way. He reached for the knife in the sheath on his belt and felt a sudden chill when he realized it was missing. He must've lost it when he first ran into the dense underbrush. In the distance, he heard the yelp and whine of the two Fila Brasileiros. They were coming. He needed a plan—and quick.

He tied Annie's leash to the trunk of a nearby tree, patted her on the head and whispered, "Shhh." He found a good-sized rock that fit comfortably in his hand. Then he made his way to the end of the road, staying in the shadows close to the tree line. He squatted behind a clump of shrubs where he had a view of his SUV.

The two men wore sleeveless white T-shirts, camo pants, and ball caps. Each had a semi-automatic rifle slung over his shoulder. They were leaning against the hood on the driver's side of the Toyota, their cigarettes glowing red in the darkness. Santana figured his only chance was to take them by surprise. He knew that killing anyone in a foreign country, even if he was a cop and they were gangbangers and drug dealers, would cause problems. Killing would have to be a last resort.

He crept forward, his knees bent and his body low to the ground, thankful that he could use the vehicle for cover. When he was positioned at the rear end of it, he removed the key fob from his pocket, took a breath, and let it out slowly. Then he peered out from behind the driver's side taillight and pushed the alarm button.

The Toyota's horn blasted and the lights began flashing. Santana could see the two men standing shoulder to shoulder, staring at the SUV, their hands spread in a helpless gesture as they shouted at one another in Spanish. The guard closest to Santana attempted to open the driver's side door. As he did so, Santana moved forward. At the last second, the man sensed his presence and turned to face him, his eyes wide and unblinking.

Santana struck him hard in the face with the rock. The guard's eyes rolled up in his head and he went down quickly. The second man tried to get his rifle sling off his shoulder, but it was too late. Santana hit him between the eyes with the rock. He stumbled backward. Santana hit him again. The guard fell against the hood and slid to the ground. Santana pushed the key fob, quieting the alarm, and unlocked the car doors. In the sudden silence, he heard the yelps of the two Fila Brasileiros. They were close now. He had little time.

He opened the driver's side door, threw the two rifles onto the backseat, climbed in, and started the Toyota, shoving the gearshift into reverse and pressing the accelerator down in one motion. The vehicle shot backward. Santana turned the steering wheel clockwise, swinging the rear end onto the side road, keeping his foot on the gas pedal.

When he reached Annie, he slammed on the brakes and jammed the gearshift into park, exiting the car as it lurched to a halt. He glanced down the road as he ran to her. The two Fila Brasileiros were fifty yards from him, running hard, their tongues hanging from their mouths, two black shadows under the bright moonlight.

Santana untied the leash and pulled Annie toward the SUV. He got her inside, slammed the door, and sprinted around the front of the vehicle. The dogs were fifteen yards from him. He could sense their desperation and hear their snarls and the sound of each panting breath.

He jumped into the front seat and jerked the door shut just as one of them leapt at the driver's side window, splattering it with spittle. Santana felt a second thump as the other dog hit the window, growling as it bared its teeth.

Santana shoved the gearshift into drive and punched the accelerator. The tires spun briefly in the soft dirt before the Toyota sped forward. The front end jumped as the tires hit the asphalt pavement. The dogs kept coming, and Annie began to whine.

"Easy, girl," he said. He kept both hands clamped on the steering wheel as he turned hard to the right, regaining control as the rear end fishtailed, and the SUV sped off into the night.

Chapter 20

Later that night, in the elegant restaurant of the Hotel Grano de Oro in San José, Santana was seated at a courtyard table opposite Lieutenant Rodolfo Murillo. The tropical Victorian mansion had been converted into a 40-room hotel with gleaming marble in the lobby and polished mahogany woodwork. The hallways were lined with period photographs, original art, and lush tropical flower arrangements.

They were drinking mojitos under a clear sky and full moon, the evening breathless as Santana explained why he'd gone to Puerto Caldera and what he'd discovered in the warehouse in the jungle. But all of Murillo's attention had been focused on Santana's failure to leave the country. If it were possible, Santana was certain he would have seen steam coming out of Murillo's ears.

"You had no business in Puerto Caldera, Detective. No business at all."

"Dr. Luis Calderón is involved in drug running, Lieutenant, along with an unidentified Taiwanese man. I would think that is more important than whether I left the country yesterday or tomorrow."

Murillo inhaled a deep breath and let it out slowly. "We have had that warehouse under surveillance for nearly a month, Detective, hoping that it would lead us to the bigger fish, as the Americans like to say. Now," he said with a shrug of his shoulders, "due to your unwillingness to follow my directive, the whole operation has been compromised."

"My face was hidden."

"It does not matter. The cartel knows that someone has been in the building. Logically, they will assume it was someone from law enforcement."

"Not necessarily. They might assume it was someone casing the place from a competing cartel."

"We can only hope."

A waiter appeared. It was nearly 10 p.m. and the restaurant was closing, but it was apparent that the manager and staff were not about to rush the lieutenant and his guest.

Murillo waved the menu at Santana and said, "If you enjoy good beef, I would recommend the *Chateaubriand con tres salsas*."

"Sounds good."

"Perhaps you could choose the beverage, Detective," Murillo said. "The restaurant has a wonderful wine list."

Santana selected a Don Melchor cabernet sauvignon from Chile.

"Excellent choice." Murillo recited the order to the waiter, handed him the menus and wine list, and watched him depart.

"Will you be able to arrest Dr. Luis Calderón?" Santana asked. "And the man from Taiwan?"

"They are not your concern, Detective."

"Look, Lieutenant, had I known that the warehouse was under surveillance, I would have checked with you first. But I go where the case takes me."

"Regardless of the consequences?"

"It is all about justice, Lieutenant."

"Your justice or the law's justice?"

"It is usually one and the same."

"But not always."

Santana shook his head. "Not always. But you know that."

Murillo considered Santana's response. "You have a code."

"Every good detective has one, Lieutenant."

"Are you suggesting I am not a good detective?"

"Not at all."

Murillo raised his cocktail glass in a toast and said, "*Comamos y bebamos, porque mañana moriremos*, Eat and drink, for tomorrow we die." Murillo finished his mojito and ordered another. He'd been drinking one when Santana had arrived and had ordered a second, which he'd drunk in three swallows.

"Luis Calderón may be involved in the murder of two women from Costa Rica, Lieutenant."

"We have no proof of that."

"Yet," Santana said. "What did the two men who tried to kidnap me tell you?"

Murillo looked silently at Santana.

"Okay. So you're not telling me. But you certainly have proof that Calderón is involved in drug running with the man from Taiwan."

Murillo nodded his head slowly.

"So why are the Taiwanese involved?"

Murillo glanced at the fountain in the center of the courtyard and then rested his tired brown eyes on Santana again. "The Taiwanese mafia dominates the shark finning industry in my country. They operate private docks in the Puntarenas area where the majority of all catches are brought in, transported by truck to San José, and flown mostly to Hong Kong."

"All this because of the market for shark fin soup?"

"A single fin from a whale shark or basking shark can cost as much as ten to twenty thousand dollars."

"It must be a hell of a soup," Santana said.

"Actually, the fin adds no flavor, only texture."

"And you have tried to stop the practice."

"Of course we have. Shark finning has been banned in Costa Rica for years. But the fisherman can make more money collecting shark fins than fishing."

"So what's preventing you from acting?"

"Besides your carelessness?"

"Besides that," Santana said.

"Unfortunately, there were loopholes in the law. But the president has issued a new executive order."

"Why shark finning in Costa Rica?"

"Because we have the largest longliner fleet in the hemisphere."

"Longliner?" Santana said.

"Sharks are caught by a horizontal dragline with many baited hooks. And," Murillo said with a shake of his head, "we allow international vessels that trade shark fins to land here. But since the executive order, we have delegated more funds to tracking down and arresting those responsible. We had hoped that the current undercover operation that you, in your overzealousness, have now compromised, would lead us to members of the Taiwanese mafia and the Sinaloa cartel. Many of the same criminals involved in illegal shark finning are also involved in the drug trade."

The waiter set Murillo's third mojito on the table and left.

"Tell me about a *Mara Salvatrucha* connection with the Sinaloa cartel, Lieutenant."

"Why?"

"One tried to kill me in Minnesota. When it didn't work out, he killed himself."

"Then you know all there is to know, Detective. They are cold-blooded killers. You should watch your back. Taking you out would mean no more to them than swatting a fly."

"You know who these people are, Lieutenant."

"Knowing is one thing. Prosecuting is another." He drank more rum and let a few seconds pass before speaking again. "In order to break them, I have to think like a great white shark that gets close enough to watch its prey, yet stays far enough away so it cannot be easily tracked."

Santana noted that Murillo's voice had suddenly become flat and emotionless, as though he were speaking directly to himself. "This sounds personal."

"Oh, it very much is."

Santana waited for an explanation while Murillo drank more rum. "The cartel murdered my wife and child." His distant eyes were suddenly filled with moisture.

"I am sorry," Santana said. He wanted to ask Murillo how they had died but thought better of it. "Perhaps I can help you, Lieutenant."

"How?"

"I think Dr. Calderón is your connection to the cartel."

"Perhaps."

"He is not just involved in running drugs through the sale of shark meat, Lieutenant."

"What do you mean?"

Santana told him.

* * *

Santana's flight from Costa Rica landed late Friday evening. By the time he'd gone through customs, retrieved his SUV from the Park & Fly lot and driven home, it was after midnight. Jordan was happy to see him, Gitana even happier.

"We both missed you," Jordan said as she embraced him and gave him a kiss.

"I didn't expect to see you here."

"Don't worry. I've been staying at my place. But I thought I'd surprise you. Are you disappointed?"

"Oh, no. You smell good. And taste good, too."

"You need a shave," she said, running a palm across the dark shadow on his face.

"First thing tomorrow," he said.

Jordan smiled seductively. "Maybe shaving should be the second thing."

"If you insist."

"I do."

"Thanks for taking care of Gitana."

At the sound of her name, Gitana's tail began wagging furiously again.

"How was your trip?"

"Enlightening," he said. "I know how heroin is being smuggled into the cities."

"Does the DEA know?"

"They will soon enough."

Early the following morning, Santana closed the blinds on the bedroom slider and turned toward Jordan, who was still sleeping, her naked body entwined in the rumpled sheets. She'd slept quietly most of the night, though his sleep had been troubled with thoughts of the MS banger who'd attempted to kill him.

He went downstairs and filled Gitana's water and food dishes. Then he made scrambled eggs, whole-wheat toast, fresh-squeezed orange juice, and hot chocolate, and brought two trays of food up to his bed. He spent Saturday with Jordan, catching up on his sleep—and other activities.

On Sunday he and Jordan and Gitana cruised the river in his boat, the water glittering in the sunlight, the white clouds scudding across the blue sky, the sailboats skimming along the river's surface, their white sails billowing in the breeze. Gitana showed no ill effects from the tranquilizer. That his dog had saved him from a certain death reminded Santana again of the tenuous links in the chain of his life.

Jordan seemed happy and relaxed. Then, after they'd returned to the dock and were driving back to Santana's house that evening, she grew quiet. As she was packing her cosmetics and clothes in an overnight bag, she said, "I've decided to schedule a therapy session with Karen Wong."

Santana nodded. "It's a good idea."

"Maybe therapy will help stop my nightmares."

"It can't hurt."

She wrapped her arms around his waist and laid her head on his shoulder. "Thanks for your support."

"You'd do the same for me."

She raised her head and looked at him. "I would, you know."

"Yes," he said. "I know." He kissed her and then held her close, her body warm, her scent intoxicating, and her face like a light in a world full of darkness.

* * *

Hoping to complete his paperwork and expense reports while the Homicide Unit was quiet, Santana had come in early Monday morning. He'd called Hawkins last night after Jordan had left and debriefed her about his trip. He needed to debrief Tim Branigan and Pete Romano as well, but he wanted to delay the meeting with the two men till he'd spoken to Nina Rivera and James Elliot. But Romano had arrived shortly after Santana and had motioned for him to come into his office.

"Have a seat, Detective."

Santana sat in a chair facing the desk.

Romano removed his sport coat and the top to a Starbucks coffee cup and lowered his heavy frame into his chair. He rolled up the sleeves of his white shirt, sipped some coffee, and looked at Santana. "Tell me about your trip."

"I'd like to debrief you and the AC at the same time, Pete."

"Is that right?" He leaned back in his chair and clasped his hands across his ample belly. "You went over my head, Detective. I didn't appreciate that." His forced smile was filled with menace.

Santana couldn't tell Romano why he'd gone to Branigan to approve his trip. He had to improvise. "I didn't think you had the budget to send me to Costa Rica."

"So you went directly to the AC?"

"Branigan controls the purse strings."

"Uh-uh," Romano said with a shake of his head. "There's another reason. And I want to know what it is."

Santana saw a way he could regain the advantage and put Romano on the defensive. "Why would you think there's another reason, Pete?"

Romano started to speak and then stopped and took a sip of coffee. "Call it a hunch, Detective."

"Branigan asked you to shut down the Díaz investigation, didn't he?"

"Of course not."

Santana knew he had Romano boxed in now. "Why would Branigan do that?"

"I just told you he didn't."

"That's strange, because Branigan told me he did."

Romano's eyes grew large with disbelief.

Santana knew he was hedging the truth. Branigan hadn't actually told him he'd wanted the Catalina Díaz investigation shut down. But given the AC's relationship with Díaz, it was clear that he had an interest in closing the case before that fact was disclosed. Santana was certain Branigan had conveyed the message to Romano—if not explicitly, than certainly implicitly.

"Why would the AC tell me to shut down the Díaz investigation, Detective?"

Santana stood. "Why don't you ask him, Pete?"

He turned and walked out of Romano's office, closing the door behind him. Santana figured Romano would never ask Branigan why he wanted the investigation shut down. The AC was Romano's boss, and Romano would do what he was told without question, especially if he wanted the next promotion. Still, Santana breathed a sigh of relief. Had he not been able to regain the upper hand in the conversation, he would've been forced to tell Romano why he'd gone to Branigan. In so doing, he'd lose Branigan's trust and the hold he had over him. And Santana didn't want to lose either one.

Hawkins was at her desk. She waved to him. He sat down at his workstation next to her.

"What did Romano want?"

Santana told her.

"You didn't give up Branigan?"

"No."

"Thank God. But Branigan will want to know what you found in Costa Rica."

"I'll set up a meeting soon, but there're a few things we need to do first."

"Like what?"

"You told me last night that you had something for me."

Hawkins smiled. "Remember you asked me to look into any deaths from autoerotic asphyxiation that might've occurred around the time the apostles graduated?"

"You found something?"

Hawkins lifted a manila folder off her desktop and opened it. "There were two deaths in the Twin Cities classified as autoerotic during that timeframe. One involved a white male, age thirty-one. The other was a woman, age twenty-three. Both died of neck compression, but only one displayed evidence of bondage."

"The woman."

Hawkins nodded. "There was evidence of masturbation and sexually stimulating paraphernalia present at both scenes. After interviews with family members and friends, and based on the evidence collected at the scene, the ME concluded that both deaths were accidental."

"What was the woman's name?"

"Glenda McCarthy. She was a medical student."

Santana leaned forward. "Where was her body found?"

276

"In a house she rented in the Cedar-Riverside area near the University of Minnesota. The house was razed and replaced by a parking lot."

"What about family?"

"I haven't been able to locate any current information about her family. Bottom line is, we don't know if Glenda McCarthy's death is connected to the apostles."

"But they don't know that, Kacie. Maybe they'll recognize her name. Maybe it'll be enough to break one of them."

Hawkins nodded her head slowly. "If these murders began years ago, maybe Brian Howard had nothing to do with them."

"It's possible," Santana said. "But let's keep him on our radar."

* * *

Later that morning, Santana phoned Dave Reynolds, the Minneapolis detective investigating Philip Campbell's death.

"You have anything new for me, Santana?"

"Not yet."

"Then why are you wasting my time?"

"Philip Campbell was murdered."

"The ME disagrees. He's ruling Campbell's death a suicide."

"He's making a mistake."

"You should tell him that. I'm sure he'd love to see your evidence."

"I'm working on it."

"Let me know if you find something."

"Hang on, Reynolds. I need a favor."

"It better have something to do with Campbell's death."

"I believe it does."

"All right. What do you need?"

"Twenty-five years ago, a medical student named Glenda McCarthy was found dead in a house near the U of M, apparently from autoerotic asphyxia. I want to see her case file."

"Because the hooker with Campbell died the same way?"

"Her name was Catalina Díaz."

"Right. You think Campbell killed McCarthy and Díaz?"

"No. I think someone else is responsible for both deaths."

"You're chasing ghosts, Santana."

"What about the information?"

A few seconds passed before Reynolds said, "I'll get back to you."

* * *

In Santana's mind, the fact that Glenda McCarthy had died in the same manner as Tania Cruz and Catalina Díaz, and that she was a medical student at the U of M with Philip Campbell, Matthew Singer, and Nathaniel Burdette, made her death significant. If and how McCarthy's death fit in with the deaths of Cruz and Díaz still needed to be determined.

He called James Elliot's cell phone number. Elliot agreed to meet him at the Kodokan Judo Club, located in a one-level rectangular building on University Avenue in the Midway area of St. Paul. Blue mats covered the floor of the large open room where the workouts took place, and white tiles and fluorescent light panels covered the low ceiling.

Santana watched Elliot as he and the forty or so students in the class, who ranged in age from young children to senior citizens, attacked and defended against different opponents and then performed a series of stretches to cool down. A handful of students, like Elliot, had black belts tied around their gis. Santana was surprised by Elliot's agility and conditioning. No doubt his years of judo had kept him in good shape. Santana had learned a few throws and escapes at the academy during his police training, but he didn't consider himself an expert.

When the class ended, white towels were handed out. Elliot wiped off his sweat as he walked to the corner of the room where Santana was standing. It was the first time Santana had seen him without a cap, and he realized that Elliot's red hair was receding.

"The class ran a bit long tonight," he said. "Hope you didn't mind waiting."

"I'm used to it."

Elliot smiled as his eyes wandered over Santana. "You look like you're in good shape, Detective. Care to take a few falls with me?"

"Maybe some other time, Mr. Elliot. I just have a few questions for you."

"I'll take a quick shower and change and meet you outside."

* * *

Santana leaned against the Crown Vic's hood as he waited for Elliot. The late afternoon temperature was in the mid-seventies, the blue sky dotted with puffy clouds with gray underbellies, the wind cool and breezy. Santana wished he were cruising in his boat on the river instead of waiting in a parking lot.

Elliot, dressed in jeans and a blue long-sleeved chambray shirt, emerged from the dojo carrying a small black athletic bag.

"Thanks again for waiting," he said. "I take it this is important."

"Tell me about your recent flight to Costa Rica, Mr. Elliot."

The glimmer in Elliot's eyes darkened like sunlight suddenly dimmed by a passing cloud. "My flight to Costa Rica?"

"That's right."

He nodded his head as if he were trying to convince himself that he'd been there. "I flew down and back the same day," he said. "What's to tell?"

"You picked up Nina Rivera and a blonde woman. What's her name?"

"Why is that important?"

"The name," Santana said.

"Isabel," he said. "Isabel Soto."

"Why was she there?"

"Hey, Detective, I'm just the pilot."

"Anyone else fly back with you besides Ms. Soto and Ms. Rivera?"

He shook his head.

"What can you tell me about Ms. Soto?"

"Nothing besides her name."

"You've never flown her before?"

"I didn't say that."

"How about Nina Rivera?"

"I've flown her back and forth to Costa Rica a few times."

"But you have no idea why she makes the trips."

He shrugged. "Maybe she has family there."

"Expensive way to travel, Mr. Elliot."

"Apparently, she can afford it."

"Strange that you knew Catalina Díaz, but not Nina Rivera, since they were roommates."

"I never said I didn't know Rivera, Detective. I said I don't know why she flies to Costa Rica."

"But you know she's an escort."

"If you say so."

"You're aware that Paul Lenoir is dead."

"Yes. I was sorry to hear that, Paul being so young and all. But I guess heart attacks occasionally strike young people."

"How do you know Lenoir died of a heart attack?"

He shrugged his heavy shoulders. "I guess I don't. I just assumed someone dying that young and that quickly must've had a heart attack."

Santana looked directly at Elliot. "You went to medical school with a young woman named Glenda McCarthy."

Elliot looked away, but before he did Santana saw a shimmer of recognition in his dusky eyes, like a flicker of light across a blade. "I don't recall the name, Detective. It was a long time ago."

"There's no statute of limitations for murder in Minnesota," Santana said.

Elliot's eyes met Santana's again. "What's that supposed to mean?"

"I think you know."

"I wish I could help you, Detective."

"Perhaps you already have, Mr. Elliot."

Sometimes it's not what you say to a suspect, but how you say it that matters. Santana was certain that James Elliot had recognized Glenda McCarthy's name. Whether he had had anything to do with her death was a lingering question. But Santana operated under the belief that where there was smoke, there was fire. He'd lit one under Elliot. Now he'd wait to see how quickly it would burn, and how much damage it would cause.

* * *

Rain clouds were building on the horizon as Santana drove to Sarah Malik's house. He waited on a chair in the living room while she heated some tea in the microwave and then returned to the room and sat down on the couch across from him, cradling a mug in both hands.

"What is it you want to talk to Sammy about?" she asked.

He took the photo of Nina Rivera he'd had enlarged out of his briefcase and handed it to her. "I'd like Sammy to look at this."

"Who is she?"

"A friend of Tania Cruz."

"And you're hoping Sammy will recognize her."

He nodded.

She handed the photo back to him. "So you do believe my daughter is the reincarnation of Tania Cruz."

If Sammy Malik were able to identify Nina Rivera, it would add to the mounting evidence that she was Tania Cruz's reincarnated soul. But there were still too many doubts lingering in Santana's mind. He said, "I don't know that for certain."

"Yet you persist, Detective Santana."

"I'll use whatever works."

"Even a child?"

"You came to me, Ms. Malik. Remember?"

She lowered her gaze for a moment and drank some tea. "Why do you want my daughter to identify this woman?"

"I believe the woman has information that might be useful in helping us solve a case." *Perhaps more than one case*, he thought.

"Are you any closer to solving Tania Cruz's murder?"

"I don't have solid proof that she *was* murdered. But perhaps Sammy can help."

"Sammy," Sarah Malik called, setting her cup on the coffee table. "Could you come out here, please? Detective Santana would like to speak to you."

Sammy smiled at Santana as she walked into the room, her large jade eyes wide with curiosity. She plopped on the couch beside her mother and held her right index finger against her bottom lip, her gaze never leaving his face.

Santana showed her the photo of Nina Rivera. "Do you know this woman, Sammy?" he asked.

She took the photo from him and peered at it. Then she held it tightly against her chest, as she would her favorite stuffed bear. "She's my best friend."

"Do you remember her name?"

282

"Nina," she said.

Santana tried to control his heartbeat and the collection of thoughts racing through his mind. Was this just another lucky guess? What did it really prove? Could he use the information to help him solve the case?

"I want to see Nina," Sammy said, looking at him with pleading eyes.

"I don't think that would be a good idea, Sammy."

"Why not?" Sarah Malik asked. "It's obvious my daughter knows her." She glanced at Sammy, the expression on her face a mixture of pride and satisfaction.

"I just don't think it would."

"Please, Mommy," Sammy said. "I want to see Nina."

"Would my daughter be in any danger, Detective?"

Santana stood and picked up his briefcase. He considered asking for the photo back and then let it go. "Thank you both for your time."

"Mommy," Sammy said. "I want to see Nina."

"Please, Detective Santana," Sarah Malik said. "Sammy has done everything you've asked. Won't you just grant her this one request?"

He let his gaze wander to a living room window and to a dead leaf tumbling helplessly across the long blades of green grass. The leaf caught on a small, severed branch for a moment, till a sudden gust tore it from its tenuous moorings and blew it away.

Chapter 21

The next morning, Santana sat down beside Mike Rios in Mickey's Diner, located in downtown St. Paul in a railroad dining car designed in the Art Deco style. Rios was seated on a stool at the counter eating pancakes, eggs, and steak.

"I'll buy you breakfast if you're hungry, Santana."

"I already ate."

"Coffee?"

"I don't drink it."

"A Colombian who doesn't drink coffee."

"We're not all the same, Rios."

"I suppose not. So what'd you find in Costa Rica?"

Santana told him about the heroin he'd discovered hidden in the shark meat.

"I've heard the cartels ship drugs that way," Rios said. "But the import restrictions in Minnesota on shark meat are really tough. You can't find it here."

"That's not how heroin is being smuggled into Minnesota."

Rios held his eyes on Santana. "Okay. So how's it coming in?"

"I'll tell you at the meeting."

"What meeting?"

"The one we're going to have with your supervisor."

"When is this meeting supposed to take place?"

"This afternoon."

"Why not tell me now?"

"Because I'm trying to solve four possible murders. I need a bargaining chip with the DEA."

Rios stayed quiet and stared at his half-empty cup of coffee. Then his gaze shifted to Santana again. "Suppose you do know how the smack is smuggled. Where's the connection to the Maras?"

"You know what it is, Rios. You've known since the first time we talked. It's Ricky Garza. And I'm going to squeeze him."

"How?"

"Five years ago an inmate in Stillwater prison named Arias Marchena took the fall for the murder of an escort named Tania Cruz. I believe Garza helped set him up."

"What proof do you have?"

"None. But I've got leverage. Garza's girlfriend is an illegal Mexican named Lucita Sánchez. A state trooper arrested her recently for driving without a license. She was taken to the Ramsey County jail and her prints were sent to the Department of Homeland Security, which ran a check on her immigration status."

"But ICE didn't detain her."

"No. They're concentrating on the gangbangers and serious crimes. Sánchez is low priority. She was released the same day."

"So where's your leverage?"

"She and Garza just had a son. We threaten to deport her, Garza will talk."

Rios chuckled. "Well, sometimes you need a snake to control your rat problem."

"I'm not interested in deporting Garza's girlfriend. I'm interested in finding out who murdered two escorts and possibly Philip Campbell and Paul Lenoir."

"Hey, don't go bat shit crazy on me," Rios said. "I'd do the same thing if I were in your shoes."

Santana didn't take much comfort in that.

Rios finished off his pancakes and washed it down with coffee. "It all sounds good, Santana. But right now, everything you've got is speculation."

"Tell your supervisor that my AC will be calling to set up a meeting."

"You think Branigan will go along?"

"I'm sure of it."

Rios smirked. "You've got a lot of confidence."

"I've got more than that," Santana said.

* * *

Ricky Garza stared at Santana and Hawkins across the table in an interview room in the Homicide Unit, his eyes as dark as a grave.

"We need some information from you, Ricky. If you cooperate, we'll do what we can for you. If not . . ." Santana let Garza fill in the rest of the sentence.

"What information?"

"Let's start with your relationship with Paul Lenoir."

Garza wagged his head as if this were a waste of time. "You got a reputation as a smart DT, not some *pendejo*, Santana. I don't know Lenoir. But even if I did, I wouldn't tell you." He smoothed his thin mustache with a thumb and forefinger and grinned at Hawkins in the way a sexual predator smiles at a child. "I might tell your partner, though. Maybe save some *micho* for her," he said, using the Latino slang contraction for *mi chorizo*, meaning sausage, or in this case, penis.

Hawkins leaned forward. "Get this straight, douchebag. You're going to cooperate or wish you had."

"Ouch," he said.

"You think you can take the heat?" she asked.

"No problem."

"Maybe you can," Santana said. "But I doubt Lucita can."

286

Garza jerked his head toward Santana. "What you talking about, man?"

"Your girlfriend's status, Ricky. It'd be a real shame if she were deported. You think you can raise your son alone? Or maybe she'll take your son with her? How would you like it if you never saw him again?"

The coals that were Garza's eyes were glowing with anger now. "You're a real *pinche cabrón*, Santana."

"Now you've gone and hurt my feelings, Ricky."

"I don't have to listen to this," Garza said, rising out of the chair.

"You walk out that door, and before you hit the street, I'll have notified ICE."

"Fuck you, man."

"Think about your choices, Ricky. Think about them real carefully."

Garza stood stiffly beside the chair, his eyes wide and darting back and forth with desperation.

"Sit down, Ricky," Hawkins said in a soothing voice. "Help yourself and your girlfriend."

"You use people, Santana. You got no conscience."

"Let me get this straight, Ricky. You sell illegal drugs to kids that turn them into junkies. But I'm the one with no conscience."

He shrugged. "So you say. And even if I did, man, it wouldn't be the same."

"You better believe it isn't. I might use someone to get information I need to put away a killer. But I'm not in it for the money."

"Then why do it?"

"Justice," Santana said. "Something you wouldn't understand."

"You got that wrong, Santana. Me and my *eses* understand justice."

"That's not how the law defines it, Ricky."

"Or maybe how you define it, Santana." Garza glanced at the door. Then the tension went out of his body and he lowered his thin frame into the chair and let out a breath of air.

"Tell us what you know about Paul Lenoir."

Garza spread his hands and looked at Santana with a confused, innocent expression. "I don't know a *gringo* named Paul Lenoir."

Hawkins let out a loud, frustrated breath. "I'm getting real tired of this, John," she said. "How about you?"

"I'm feeling the same."

"I think I'll make a phone call to ICE. What do you think?"

"Might as well."

"Go ahead," Garza said. "I don't give a shit. Besides, ICE won't deport Lucita. She's got no record."

"Oh, ICE might change their mind if we tell them she's involved in a heroin smuggling operation," Santana said.

Garza shifted his weight in the chair. "She's not involved."

"But you are, Ricky. Now's your chance to help yourself and your family."

"No way, man, I'm no *chivato*."

"Say *adios* to Lucita."

Garza sat perfectly still, staring blankly at the wall.

"Here's what I think, Ricky. Paul Lenoir was supplying heroin for the SUR 13."

Garza looked at Santana but said nothing.

"Lenoir had you set up Arias Marchena for the murder of Tania Cruz. You mugged Marchena and planted the DNA from his cheek under Cruz's fingernails."

Garza shrugged. "If you think you know how it went down, why ask me?"

"Because I want an innocent man freed from prison."

"That all?"

"Not quite," Santana said. "I don't think Lenoir killed Tania Cruz. I want to know who did."

"You're askin' the wrong person, Santana." Garza stood. "You or your partner taking me downstairs, or do I leave on my own?"

After escorting Ricky Garza out of the building, Hawkins returned to her workstation and sat down beside Santana. "Garza is a real piece of work. He doesn't care about his kid or his girlfriend."

"He's more concerned about his life, Kacie."

"Meaning?"

"If we're right and the SURs are running heroin for the MS 13, then he'd have a large target on his back. Especially if he became a *chivato* and ratted them out."

* * *

That afternoon Santana and Hawkins met with Tim Branigan, Pete Romano, Mike Rios, and Rios's DEA supervisor, Gina Cody, in Branigan's office. Santana had never met Cody, but he'd heard she was well respected within the DEA. Born on a reservation in northern Minnesota, she had a degree in criminal justice and had been a police officer in Los Angeles before joining the ranks of the DEA as a special agent, eventually heading the district office in charge of operations in Minnesota and North Dakota.

Santana, Hawkins, and Rios were seated on chairs on one side of a large coffee table. Cody, Romano, and Branigan were seated on the couch on the opposite side of the table. Copies of *The Police Chief* magazine were arranged neatly beside five Starbucks coffee cups and a bottle of spring water that Santana had requested.

"Thank you for joining us," Branigan said, his eyes focused on Gina Cody as though she were the only person in the room. Black-haired with high cheekbones and reddish brown skin, she was dressed in a gray pants suit with an American flag pin on her lapel.

"I'm doing this strictly as a favor to you, Tim." She gazed intently at Santana with her dark, almond-shaped eyes. "I'd like to hear what your detective has to say."

Santana began with Catalina Díaz's murder. Then he told of the list of men he'd discovered in the hidden drawer and the stored value card he'd found at Paul Lenoir's house. "Detective Hawkins and I found Lenoir dead in the bathroom of his house and studio. It appears he was electrocuted in the tub. Lenoir had met Díaz and her roommate, Nina Rivera, in San José, Costa Rica. Later, he got them a job working in Jaco, Costa Rica, at Erotic Tours, a resort run by the Sinaloa cartel that caters primarily to American men looking to have sex." Santana glanced at Branigan, whose cheeks reddened as he averted his eyes. "But I believe Lenoir was involved with heroin smuggling."

"How?" Gina Cody asked.

"Through a plastic surgeon in San José named Luis Calderón. He has connections to the cartel."

"I don't understand," Cody said.

"The escorts Lenoir hired are smuggling heroin in their breast implants."

Gina Cody sat forward. "What?"

Santana nodded at her. "It's been done in Colombia. When the escorts arrive here from Costa Rica, their heroin implant is replaced with saline or silicone. The heroin is then sold to the SUR 13s, who distribute it."

"You have proof of this, Detective?"

"I know a woman who I believe will testify that she's smuggled drugs—if she's granted immunity."

"We'd have to clear that with the Ramsey County attorney," Branigan said.

"If you figure there are about thirty cubic centimeters in an ounce," Rios said, "then a three hundred cc implant would be about ten ounces. Multiply that by two and you've got twenty ounces of smack. That's about five hundred seventy grams and a street value of roughly two hundred twenty-six thousand dollars. You go with larger implants, you could probably double that amount."

Santana and everyone else in the room looked at Rios.

He shrugged. "I'm good with numbers." He grinned. "Kind of gives a new meaning to the phrase drug bust, huh?"

"I don't find that amusing," Cody said, glaring at Rios.

He lost the smile and looked at his shoes.

A long silence ensued before Gina Cody spoke. "Well, Detective Santana, that's quite a story. But as far as I can tell, you have no evidence implicating any of the men on the list with heroin smuggling or murder." She looked at Branigan. "Wouldn't you agree, Tim?"

"It is a bit thin," he said, offering her a grin that looked more forced than natural.

Cody's gaze returned to Santana. "It's very difficult for me to believe that the prominent men you're talking about are involved in something as disturbing as heroin smuggling."

"A woman named Isabel Soto is having surgery soon. She recently flew back from Costa Rica on a plane piloted by James Elliot."

"And where is the surgery taking place?"

"I believe at the Genesis Medical Clinic."

"You believe?"

"I don't know for sure," Santana said, hating to admit it.

"The DEA appreciates the tip," Cody said. "But this is our responsibility now, Detective."

"You're looking for the pipeline. I'm looking for the murderer of two women. Finding the source of the heroin might lead me to the perp."

"We can handle this."

Santana gave Branigan a look.

"Our departments could work together on this, Gina," Branigan said, offering Santana and the department a life-line.

"Your detectives would just be in the way."

"I wasn't in the way when I figured out how heroin was being smuggled into town," Santana said, staring at Cody.

Her lips were tightly pressed together, causing a wrinkling of her chin. She looked at Branigan as though waiting for him to discipline his detective.

Branigan smiled crookedly. "Technically, he's correct, Gina."

"What if your detective is wrong?"

"I don't believe that's the case," Romano said, surprising Santana. He'd never expected Romano to verbally support him.

"We could bumper-lock Ricky Garza," Mike Rios said, referring to a surveillance technique in which Garza would know he was being tailed. "Put some pressure on him."

Cody gave him a dismissive look. "I'll be in touch." Her words signaled that the meeting was over.

As Santana left Branigan's office, Rios sidled up to him. "We need to talk, Santana. Privately."

"We could use one of the interview rooms."

"Not here."

"Where then?"

"I'll call you," Rios said.

* * *

Later that afternoon, Santana and Hawkins sat on the couch across from Nina Rivera. She wore a bright red pullover, tight jeans, and sandals, and was smoking a cigarette. "So," she said with an exasperated sigh, "what is it you wanted to discuss?"

"Your trip to Costa Rica," Santana said.

"It was a very sad occasion."

"I'm sure Catalina Díaz's funeral was a very sad occasion. But I'm interested in knowing more about the time you spent with Isabel Soto."

Rivera blushed and her gaze moved quickly off his face.

"Isabel Soto flew back with you from Costa Rica, Ms. Rivera, after you picked her up at Luis Calderón's plastic surgery clinic."

"How do you know this?"

Santana could hear the surprise in her voice and see it in her eyes. "I followed you from the clinic to the airport where you and Soto boarded James Elliot's Learjet."

"You were in Costa Rica?"

He nodded.

She started to speak and then abruptly stopped.

"Escorts have been smuggling heroin, Ms. Rivera."

"You have no proof of this."

"I will have soon. I suggest you cooperate."

She remained silent for a time, lost in the false and fearful world she'd created for herself. "How do I know I can trust you?"

"You'll have to take me at my word when I say I'll do what I can to help you."

"That is all you can offer?"

"It is. Take it or leave it."

She considered her options before speaking again. "I don't know where Isabel is. But I do know she's having surgery tomorrow."

"Who's performing the surgery?"

"I don't know."

"You had it done."

"Yes. But Paul gave me a pill that put me to sleep. When I woke, it was over."

"So you never saw the doctor?"

She shook her head. "Never."

"When was the last time you saw Isabel Soto?"

Rivera's amber eyes seemed to lose focus for a moment. Her hand started to shake. She sat forward and crushed out her cigarette in the ashtray on the coffee table.

Santana played a hunch. "Ricky Garza picked up Soto at the airport, didn't he?"

Her eyes grew larger, as though she'd seen something frightening.

"Tell me," Santana said.

"It was Garza."

"Lenoir was selling heroin to him."

"Yes."

"And the SURs have been working with the MS 13."

She nodded her head slowly.

"You've smuggled heroin, too, Ms. Rivera."

"Only once."

"But you've recruited young women like Tania Cruz, Catalina Díaz, and Isabel Soto."

"I had no choice. Ricky said he would kill me if I refused."

"We believe the Ramsey County attorney will give you immunity if you testify, Ms. Rivera," Hawkins said.

"And in the meantime?"

"We'll protect you."

Rivera laughed. "You cannot protect me. No one can."

Her cell phone rang. She answered, listened for a short time, and then cupped her hand over the phone and looked at Santana. "It's a woman named Sarah Malik. She dialed my three-digit code on the entrance panel in the lobby. She says she knows you."

"As part of the investigation," he said.

"She also said her daughter knew Tania Cruz. She wants to talk to me."

"Did she tell you how old Sammy was?"

Rivera hesitated. "Why, no. I assumed she was Tania's age."

"Tell her I'm coming down."

"I can push nine on my phone to let her in."

"I want to talk to her first," Santana said.

Thunderclouds slid across the sun and a solitary drop of rain shattered on the pavement as Santana exited the building and went to the red Honda Accord parked directly in front of the Crown Vic, where Sarah Malik was releasing Sammy from a rear car seat.

"What are you doing here, Ms. Malik?"

"I'm going to see Nina," Sammy said, her eyes gleaming with anticipation, a wide smile on her face. She jumped onto the sidewalk and headed for the entrance to the building, as if she knew exactly where she was going.

"This isn't a good idea, Ms. Malik."

"I think it is," she said.

Santana caught up to Sammy and said, "Have you been here before, Sammy?"

She nodded her head. "Nina lives here."

The sudden chill he felt was not due to the wind.

Inside the elevator, Sammy attempted to reach the call buttons.

"What number should I push?" her mother asked.

"Ten," she said.

Sarah Malik gave Santana a look of smug satisfaction.

When Sammy Malik walked into the living room, Hawkins smiled at her, but Santana noted it was a hesitant smile, as though she wasn't sure what to make of the child. Sammy went straight to Nina Rivera and crawled up in her lap.

"What a beautiful child," Rivera said, as Sammy peered up at her with round, unblinking eyes.

Sarah Malik sat down across from her daughter and Rivera.

"I missed you," Sammy said, looking up at her.

Hawkins was standing beside Santana. He felt her hand grip his forearm. He wasn't sure where this was going—and if it was a huge mistake.

Rivera peered at Sammy once more and then at Sarah Malik. "Have we met before?"

She shook her head and offered a smile, though her thin red lips were like two tight rubber bands that were suddenly stretched.

Rivera gazed at Sammy and then her eyes settled on Sarah Malik again. "I don't understand why you're here. When you called earlier, you said your daughter was a friend of Tania's."

"She is."

"But she's only a child. Tania has been dead for six years."

"Tell her why you wanted to see her, Sammy," Sarah Malik said.

Rivera looked at Sammy, waiting for a response.

"Because I'm Tania," Sammy said in a matter-of-fact voice.

Rivera inclined her head as if she didn't understand. "I thought your name was Sammy."

"It is now."

Rivera's gaze swept across the room and came back to Sammy. "Tania?" she said. "Tania who?"

"Tania Cruz."

Rivera gave a small laugh and looked at everyone. "Is this some kind of joke?"

"Oh, no," Sarah Malik said. "My daughter was Tania Cruz before she was murdered." She spoke in a confident, straightforward tone, as if there could be no doubt.

"You know nothing about me," Rivera said. "And neither does your daughter."

"*¿Recuerdas cuando solíamos rezar a la Santa Muerte?*" Sammy said, asking Rivera if she remembered when they used to pray to *Santa Muerte*.

Rivera stared at the child in her lap with the stunned, frightened expression of someone who'd just awakened from a nightmare. Then she picked up Sammy, set her on the floor, and stood. "All of you need to leave now."

"Tell her what you told me, Sammy," Sarah Malik said. "Tell her you know why she ran away from home."

"*Por tu padre,*" Sammy said.

Rivera's complexion paled. She fixed her eyes on Sammy. Her bottom lip quivered.

"What did she say?" Hawkins whispered.

Santana could see tears welling in Rivera's eyes and her head slowly shaking back and forth, as if she could not comprehend what she'd just heard. He was having a difficult time understanding it as well. He leaned toward Hawkins and said, "Because of her father."

"You never told anyone what your father did to you, Ms. Rivera," Sarah Malik said, "except your friend, Tania Cruz."

Rivera sank into a chair. Her face was very still. No one spoke. No one moved. Then Sammy stepped forward and laid her head in Rivera's lap.

Santana said, "You need to tell us who killed Catalina Díaz and Tania Cruz."

Rivera looked at Santana, her cheeks wet with heavy tears. "I wish I knew," she said.

Chapter 22

The following morning, Santana met Mike Rios at the Uptowner Café on Grand and Lexington, a small neighborhood restaurant that looked like a converted corner bar. They sat in a burnt orange booth near the grill and the front counter.

"I'm buying, Santana."

"They have steak and lobster here?"

"Breakfast. I'm buying breakfast."

Rios ordered the Cajun with andouille; Santana scrambled eggs, bacon, and hash browns.

When the waitress departed with the order, Rios leaned forward and said, "Something's going down. Something big."

"You want me to guess?"

"Hey, I'm doing you a favor."

"Okay. Let's hear it."

"Rumor has it that a shitload of government agencies are about to crack a huge money laundering network headquartered in Costa Rica. That's why Cody wants you out of it."

"How do you know this?"

"The DEA has been tracking SUR 13 money."

"Which is why you were so interested when I mentioned the stored value card."

Rios nodded. "Cybercrime, Santana. It's the Wild West of illicit Internet banking. Organized crime and terrorist groups are financing their operations through anonymous payment systems."

"Banks no longer have a monopoly on moving capital around the world."

"You got it. A handful of men in Costa Rica incorporated an unlicensed money transmitting business. Users only had to provide a name, address, and date of birth. But they weren't required to validate their identity."

"So the accounts could be anonymous."

"Or fictitious," Rios said. "Essentially, all a customer needed to open an account was an e-mail address. The firm didn't take or make cash payments directly. They used third-party exchangers instead."

"The advantage being?"

"The exchangers would take and make payments and then credit or debit an account. That meant the firm didn't have to collect any banking information on their clients and wouldn't leave a financial paper trail. Estimates are they've funneled six billion dollars, most of it drug money."

"Why you telling me this, Rios?"

"Cody isn't exactly sold on your story. She's not going to look for Isabel Soto with as much enthusiasm as you will."

"It'll be a good career move for you, Rios, if everything works out."

"Take it from me, Santana. Nothing much does."

* * *

As Santana was working on his reports later that morning, he received a call from Dave Reynolds.

"I'll fax you copies of Glenda McCarthy's case file."

"I appreciate it, Reynolds. I'll let you know if anything breaks."

"Make sure you do," he said, and hung up.

"What did Reynolds want?" Hawkins asked.

Santana told her.

"Check the fax machine, Kacie. I'll call the Genesis Clinic. See if Singer and Burdette have a surgery scheduled for this afternoon."

"You think Isabel Soto is there?"

"The SURs and Maras want their heroin, and Soto wants her new breasts."

Hawkins shook her head in disgust. "Jesus."

The receptionist at the Genesis Clinic told Santana that Dr. Burdette had no surgery scheduled that day, so he had taken the day off. Dr. Singer had taken the day off as well.

"Let's drive by Singer's house," Santana said as Hawkins dropped the faxed copies Reynolds had sent on his desk. "Have a talk with the doctor."

* * *

The sun was warm and the oak trees in the front yard of Matthew Singer's house full of sparrows and finches as Santana stood on the front step with Hawkins and rang the doorbell. After a minute had passed, he rang the bell again and waited another thirty seconds. He glanced at Hawkins and then tried the door handle. It was unlocked. He opened the door.

"Dr. Singer?"

From where he stood, Santana could clearly see Singer sitting in a wing chair in his living room, his arms hanging over the armrests, the back of his head resting against the leather padding, his face angled upward, his eyes wide open, as though he were watching something on the ceiling. Santana could smell the stench of vomit.

"Dr. Singer?"

No response.

Santana stepped into the entryway, Hawkins right behind him. They walked carefully into the living room. One look into

Singer's vacant eyes told Santana that Singer was dead. A check for a pulse confirmed it.

Hawkins returned to the Crown Vic for a Bootie Box while Santana walked outside and called the watch commander. He wrote down the time they'd arrived in his notebook. Then he and Hawkins unrolled crime scene tape and established a secure perimeter. Santana gave the first uniformed officer on the scene a clipboard and the Crime Scene Attendance Log. When Reiko Tanabe and Tony Novak and his two forensic specialists arrived, the six of them entered the house.

"No sign of a struggle," Tanabe said, bending over to examine the body. "Perhaps he had a heart attack, though the vomit on his shirt suggests he may have ingested something." She straightened up.

"You'll run a thorough tox screen?" Santana said.

"There's an old adage in medicine," she said. "'Common things occur commonly.' Most people die from natural causes. But I'll screen for alcohol and common drugs."

"So now what, John?" Hawkins asked.

"Let's get a warrant and look around."

They started in the kitchen, where they found a pan of beef stew on the stove and a dirty dinner plate on the table. After alerting Novak to save a sample of the stew for testing, they spent the next hour searching—but found nothing incriminating.

On the sidewalk outside of the house, Santana's gaze went from the reporters who were shouting at him from behind the crime scene tape to a large crow that was picking at the remains of a dead squirrel down the street. The crow reminded him of how frightened Sammy had become when she'd seen the eagle in her backyard. It also triggered a memory of the dream he'd had of an eagle feeding on a small doll.

"What are you thinking, John?" Hawkins asked.

Santana's eyes found hers. "Let's stop by Paul Lenoir's house."

"Why?"

"There's something I want to check again."

As they headed for the Crown Vic, Santana saw Pete Romano lumbering toward them.

"Oh, brother. It's Cheese," Hawkins said under her breath.

"What've we got?" Romano said, letting his gaze rest on Santana.

"I'm guessing a murder made to look like a heart attack."

Romano placed his hands on his wide hips. "Because Singer was involved in heroin smuggling?"

Santana shook his head. "I think his death is connected to the murders of Catalina Díaz, Tania Cruz, and a woman named Glenda McCarthy who died twenty-five years ago."

"How come I haven't heard about McCarthy?"

"You just have, Pete."

"A little late, don't you think?"

"I told John about McCarthy when he returned from Costa Rica," Hawkins said. "You want to blame someone for not telling you, blame me."

"I'm sure there's enough blame to go around, Detective Hawkins." Romano noticed the keys in Santana's hand. "Where're you going?"

"To Paul Lenoir's house. There's something I need to see again."

"Don't worry," Romano said. "I'll handle the press."

"I'm sure you will," Santana said.

Twenty minutes later, he and Hawkins pulled up in front of Lenoir's studio and parked at the curb. The crime scene was still under search warrant, and the SPPD was holding on to it indefinitely at Santana's request, till the manner of Lenoir's death had been determined.

Santana ducked under the crime scene tape and headed straight for Lenoir's bedroom, Hawkins following close behind him. On the desktop, he picked up the framed photo taken of Paul Lenoir and James Elliot. They were standing in front of a Buddhist temple in Japan. Both men wore Air Force caps and short-sleeved shirts and were smiling broadly. Elliot had his right arm draped over Lenoir's right shoulder.

Hawkins stood beside Santana. "Tell me what you see, John."

"Maybe the solution to this whole puzzle," he said. He took out his cell phone and dialed Elliot's number. The call went immediately to voice mail. He disconnected and headed for the front door.

"What's up?" Hawkins asked, hurrying after him.

"We need to find Elliot."

"Why?"

"Because he murdered Catalina Díaz, Tania Cruz, and Glenda McCarthy."

* * *

Santana used the flasher, but it still took twenty minutes before the Crown Vic skidded to a stop in the gravel driveway in front of Elliot's white clapboard two-story farmhouse just outside the city limits. Santana and Hawkins drew their Glocks as they exited the sedan.

Dusk was settling over the countryside, muting the spring colors and darkening the eerily quiet landscape. In the sun's orange afterglow, Santana could see the condensation trail from an airliner as it bore through the blackening sky, high above the distant horizon.

Fifty yards to the north stood a gambrel-roofed, galvanized steel barn. A dirt road led to a pair of garage doors that faced east. Santana recognized the red Honda Accord parked in front of the nearest door. He pointed toward the barn. "That's Sarah Malik's car, Kacie."

"What's she doing here?"

"I don't know. But check the house. I'll check the barn."

Hawkins nodded and headed toward the house.

"Kacie."

She stopped and turned toward him.

"Be careful."

She smiled. "You, too, partner."

Santana ran fast across the flat, soft ground toward the standard door on the south side of the barn, his body slightly hunched, making him a smaller target. He'd been in these situations enough to know that he had to keep his focus, had to concentrate on the task at hand, and not let fear or panic dictate his moves.

When he reached the south side of the building, he pressed his back against the wall and caught his breath. He saw no windows and no indication that the building was occupied — though Elliot could be in there. If he was, Santana hoped he was alone.

He crept along the wall and put an ear against the door. Nothing. He turned the knob. The door sagged in, away from him. He waited, listening. Then he eased the door open and stepped inside the barn.

It was at least eighty feet long and forty feet wide. The twenty-foot-high ceiling was fixed with bright, hanging flood-lights. Along the wall to Santana's left were two enclosed, windowless offices. A black Mercedes sedan was parked in front of the far garage door on his right. Santana recognized Ricky Garza's red lowrider parked in front of the second garage door. Strangely, the air smelled of astringent.

He moved forward behind his Glock, his eyes scanning the interior, searching for any movement or sign of Elliot. When he reached the first office door, he pressed his back flat against the outer wall. He waited a moment while he released a slow breath. Then he turned the knob, pushed the door open, and followed his gun into the office space.

It wasn't an office at all, but a clean, well-lit operating room with overhead surgical lights, an anesthesia machine with built-in monitors to control the mixture of gases, a crash cart containing emergency resuscitation equipment, a generator for backup electrical support, oxygen tanks, and containers for disposables—everything Elliot needed to remove the heroin-filled implants from Isabel Soto's breasts and replace them with saline implants.

She was lying on the operating table, her eyes closed, a sheet pulled up to her chin. Santana moved quickly to her. Her breathing was slow and steady, as though she were under anesthesia. He considered calling the paramedics, but immediately rejected the idea. He needed to find Elliot first and make sure the scene was secure.

He exited the room and made his way to the second door, twenty yards from the first. He followed the same procedure, keeping his body pressed against the outer wall while he turned the knob and shoved open the door. Then he crept inside and surveyed the much smaller room, corner to corner, with the barrel of his Glock. It was a typical-looking office with a metal desk, chair, laptop computer, two metal file cabinets, and bookshelves—except that Ricky Garza was slouched in the chair behind the desk, a bullet hole in the middle of his forehead. A door on the far wall was partially opened. Santana advanced cautiously, pushed the door on the far wall till it opened fully, and peered around the doorframe.

Forty-five degrees to his right and about thirty yards from his current position stood a wide red barn. It had a tall sliding door and weathered wooden boards. The doors to the second story hayloft were open. A corral on the far side of the barn held two horses. Santana hadn't seen the building from the driveway because it was hidden from view behind the larger pole barn. Instinct told him it was where he would find James Elliot and Sarah Malik. He hoped Sammy wasn't there as well, but he had a sick feeling that hung like a shroud around his heart.

Lightning flashed in jagged white spider webs in the dark clouds building above the horizon. The air was thick and close with humidity and the smell of rain as Santana ran toward the smaller barn with a growing sense of urgency. He moved quickly to the sliding barn door. It was partially opened, enough for a person to fit through. He took a position to the right of it and peered into the barn over the barrel of his Glock.

The barn smelled of hay, feed grain, and old saddle leather. Dark gray light filtered through the hayloft and fell on the four 10' x 10' box stalls flanking each side of the dirt-floored main aisle, where Sarah Malik lay flat on her stomach, facing the far end of the barn, her head turned to the left, her arms outstretched above her head. Santana saw no movement and heard no voices. He turned his shoulders and squeezed through the opening.

He knelt beside Sarah Malik. He could see external bruising on her neck. She wasn't breathing and had no pulse.

Santana's eyes swept the barn, his heart a thundering stampede in his chest. The doors on the four stalls were closed. The top half of each wooden door had a grill section with close-set steel bars. He took a deep breath and exhaled slowly. Then he stood and opened the first stall door to his right.

Empty.

He crept across the aisle and opened the first stall door on the left. It, too, was empty. He stayed on the same side of the aisle and opened the second stall door on the left.

A stab of pain knifed through his heart.

Sammy Malik lay on a bed of hay in the back corner of the stall, her eyes closed, her head at an odd angle to her body, her doll in one hand. Santana rushed forward and knelt down beside her. She had a red welt on her cheek where she'd apparently been struck. He felt her carotid artery, searching desperately for a sign of life, hoping she was still alive—but he felt no pulse. He set his Glock down, tilted her head back, and performed CPR. He'd just completed two rescue breaths and thirty chest compressions when a thick right arm with an eagle tattoo encircled his neck and yanked him to his feet. Santana felt Elliot's left hand pressing against the back of his head and the big man's right arm tightening around his throat. Santana knew if he were unable to gain release from the chokehold, he would lose consciousness in a few seconds—and his life soon afterward.

Reaching back behind his neck with his right hand, he grasped Elliot's left wrist while using his left hand to push Elliot's left elbow upward over the top of his head. He kept his grip locked on Elliot's wrist as he twisted to his right, pressing his left hand against the elbow, levering the arm straight into a come-along hold and forcing him to bend at the waist.

Santana held him in a submissive position, like a wrestler controlling an opponent. His insides felt as if he'd swallowed a pan of boiling water. He heard a roar in his ears like that of an approaching tornado. An image of Sammy Malik formed like a kaleidoscopic pattern before his eyes. He saw her holding a forefinger against her chin, her jade eyes wide and innocent as she smiled at him and pointed to the picture of Tania Cruz, before the beautiful image dissolved into a blazing red haze.

He kicked Elliot in the stomach and kicked him again. Then he grabbed him by the lapels of his jacket, straightened him up, and slammed him against the stall boards. He stepped back and drove his right fist into Elliot's face, putting everything he had behind the punch. Elliot bounced off the boards and went down.

Santana rolled him over and sat on his chest. He clamped his left hand over Elliot's throat to hold him steady and drove a second punch into Elliot's face and then a third, hitting him again and again, raining blows on him with his fist.

Then he felt hands pulling on the back of his coat and heard a distant voice. From his knees he whirled and flung his right arm back, pushing away whoever had grabbed him.

"John! That's enough!"

As if waking from a deep sleep, he heard the distant voice once more.

"Stop, John! You're going to kill him!"

The blood red haze before Santana's eyes faded. He saw Kacie Hawkins sitting on her backside, her legs stretched out in front of her, the palms of her hands flat on the floor.

She got to her knees and cupped his face in her hands. "He's not worth killing, John. Stop. Please."

With his heart pounding against his ribcage, his breath coming in short gasps, his nerve endings humming like a thin wire suddenly pulled tight, Santana looked to where Sammy still lay motionless. He struggled to his feet and shuffled to the corner of the stall, where he sat on his haunches and felt again for a pulse. The fingers of his right hand were numb. He switched quickly to his left.

Hawkins called 911 and then squatted on the opposite side of the body. "You find a pulse?"

Santana shook his head, unable to speak, unwilling to believe Sammy was dead. He placed his right ear against her lips. "Please," he heard himself whisper.

He started CPR again, silently counting thirty chest compressions, tilting her head back, covering her mouth with his own, pinching her nose shut, and giving her two rescue breaths. Then he placed an ear close to her mouth, watching for chest movement, hoping he'd feel a breath.

He performed the repetitions once again, feeling more desperate with each passing second.

Hawkins touched him gently on the arm. "It's no use."

"No, Kacie," he said, performing chest compression once more. Counting, breathing, watching.

Finally, he sat up and looked blankly at Hawkins.

"She's gone, John."

Santana stared into Hawkins' eyes, breathing as if he'd been running hard and for a very long time, hoping, despite what he'd seen in his partner's eyes and heard in her voice, that she was wrong.

Then his eyes were drawn by a sound behind him. James Elliot, his face a bloody mass, still reeling from the beating Santana had inflicted, had managed to get to his feet. He held a pitchfork in his hands, the sharp tines pointed toward Santana. He let out a high keening noise and charged forward.

As Santana reached for his gun on the ground, he saw Hawkins draw her holstered Glock and in one quick motion aim and fire.

The first bullet stopped Elliot in his tracks. The second dropped him.

Hawkins moved forward and felt for a pulse. She looked at Santana and shook her head.

With his ears ringing from the gunshots, Santana started CPR again, mentally counting the chest compressions and rescue breaths. Then he leaned over and placed his ear close to Sammy's mouth.

Like a feather, a faint breath tickled his ear.

Santana sat up with a start. "She's breathing, Kacie!"

"You sure?"

He felt for a pulse, and there it was, faint but detectable.

Santana brushed the strands of dark hair off Sammy's face, leaned over and kissed her forehead.

Her jade eyes blinked open and glimmered with life. Santana picked her up and held her gently in his arms. He squeezed his eyes shut, trying to hold back the tears that spilled from them, but he could not help himself. He lowered his head and wept.

Chapter 23

While Hawkins typed a computer affidavit and e-mailed it to the Ramsey County attorney, who forwarded it with an application for a search warrant to a judge, Santana made sure paramedics safely loaded Sammy Malik into an ambulance that would take her to Regions Hospital. A separate ambulance transported Isabel Soto while the ME's wagon took the bodies of Ricky Garza, Sarah Malik, and James Elliot to the morgue.

Thirty minutes later, the judge e-mailed a warrant authorizing a search of James Elliot's house, garage, barns, and Mercedes, and Sarah Malik's Honda.

"Let's do this before the OIS team gets here, John," Hawkins said.

Santana knew that once the Officer Involved Shooting team arrived, they'd take Hawkins' gun and then interview her at the station. She'd be placed on administrative leave till they'd completed their investigation.

"You up for this, Kacie?"

She nodded. "How did you know it was Elliot?"

"Call it a hunch," Santana said.

Hawkins nodded again and looked away, saying nothing more as they walked to the house.

They began their search in Elliot's living room, where Hawkins pointed to a Ruger LCP on the hardwood floor. It was a small, lightweight handgun popular with women. Santana saw that an ejected casing had not cleared the ejection port completely and had caught in an upright position before the slide cycled forward. Santana knew that a gun could stovepipe if it wasn't held securely when firing.

"I saw the gun when I entered," Hawkins said.

Next to the gun on the floor was the large black purse with the embossed leather Ruger pistol and chrome plated metal foliage Sarah Malik had carried the day she'd brought Sammy to the LEC. Santana noted once again the green, horizontal figure eight in the center of the silver pendant attached to the chainmail strap, and the three phrases scripted around the scalloped edge: There is No Beginning; There is No End; There is Only Change.

"You think Malik shot Garza?"

"I doubt it."

"Then it had to be Elliot," Hawkins said.

They searched Elliot's home office next, where the walls were filled with framed photos of him in his flight suit standing beside a fighter jet and with small groups of similarly dressed men. Other photos were of Mount Fuji, Buddhist temples, Shinto shrines, and judo matches.

"It's Lenoir," Hawkins said, pointing to one of the framed color photos on the wall of Lenoir and Elliot in a group of four men. "He looks younger, but it's him."

In the master bedroom closet, Hawkins discovered a pair of long silk charmeuse scarves, the same type found around Catalina Díaz's waist.

Inside a nightstand drawer in the master bedroom, Santana found a letter-sized manila envelope containing a handful of 3" x 5" faded color photos held together by a rubber band. The first photo was of a pretty redheaded woman in a tight black skirt and low cut white pullover that accentuated her ample breasts. Smiling broadly as she held a baby in her arms, she appeared to be in her late teens or early twenties.

In a second photo the woman stood with a small red-headed boy in front of a mobile home in a desert landscape reminiscent of the Southwest. The woman wore a long charmeuse scarf around her neck and had an arm around the boy's shoulder as he leaned into her. Based on their hair and eye color, Santana was certain the redheaded boy was James Elliot and the woman was his mother. A third photo was nearly identical to the second, except it was a big-boned man who stood with Elliot now. The man had black hair, scowling eyes, and a hard, cruel mouth. His arm was draped over Elliot's shoulder, but the boy was twisting away from him, as though he were trying to escape.

In another photo, Elliot's mother stood with an older woman beside an open gate in a tall black wrought iron fence. She still was very pretty, but her dusky eyes were colder and bordered by worry lines. High over her left shoulder was a sign that read WORLD FAMOUS MUSTANG RANCH.

"The Mustang Ranch is a brothel," Hawkins said, leaning close to Santana as she gazed at the photo in his hand. "Elliot's mother was a hooker in Nevada?"

"Appears to be."

"Maybe this is what the killings are all about, John. Maybe he hated her."

"Or hated what she did," Santana said.

In a cabinet below a workbench in the double garage was a large duffel bag filled with cash.

"Must be thousands," Hawkins said. "Got to be drug money." She handed Santana a 10 mL bottle of a slightly cloudy liquid labeled Ketaset. "You know what it is?"

"It's a brand name for ketamine hydrochloride. Vets use it as an animal sedative. I saw it used on horses when I was growing up in Colombia."

"It's also a date rape drug," she said.

He nodded. "It's fast acting and numbs the body. I'd guess Elliot used it to control Cruz and Díaz before he strangled them. But unless Tanabe was looking for it, she wouldn't find it in a typical tox screening."

Hawkins went quiet for a moment. Then she shook her head and looked at Santana with a questioning look in her eyes. "You think Sarah Malik came here to kill Elliot?"

Santana shook his head. "She wouldn't have brought her daughter along."

"But she tried to shoot him."

Santana nodded, but offered no reply.

* * *

Darkness had enveloped the landscape when Santana left the crime scene. Rivulets of rain ran out of the trees and bled across the road. The rain continued into the night, clattering on the shingles, sluicing out of the gutters, and running in streams along the curbs and into the grated sewers. The birch trees in his yard bent in the wind, and leaves trembled whitely when lightning arced across the black sky.

First light was still hours away, but he knew he would not sleep.

He sat at the kitchen table, soaking his sore right hand and red knuckles in ice water and drinking Cristal *aguardiente*, hoping that the strong drink would clear the ugly thoughts from his mind and calm the demon that raged inside him, the demon that had urged him to kill James Elliot. But he knew he had to get beyond the anger that flamed his chest if he hoped to answer the questions lingering in his mind. What was Sarah Malik doing at James Elliot's farm? What had apparently provoked her to try and kill Elliot, and why had she brought her daughter along?

* * *

The following morning, Santana called Regions Hospital and checked on Sammy Malik. Then he completed an interview with the OIS team before meeting with Pete Romano in the commander's office.

"How's the little girl doing?"

"She's still in intensive care, but her vital signs are stable. No apparent brain damage."

Romano nodded and looked at the incident report on his desk before casting his gaze on Santana. "Hawkins was searching Elliot's residence when your altercation with Elliot began."

Santana nodded.

"You've got the bungee cords, computer-erase software, and stored value card implicating Paul Lenoir in the murder of the escorts."

"But we found the same type of silk scarves used on the vics in Elliot's farmhouse. I think he planted the evidence implicating Lenoir when we were closing in. He had an operating suite in his pole barn. He was using escorts to smuggle heroin, Pete."

"Where's the evidence that Elliot killed Campbell, Lenoir, and Singer?"

"I don't think Elliot killed Campbell and Singer. But I'm betting forensics will match the tires on Elliot's Mercedes with the tread marks we found in the alley behind Lenoir's house. He tossed a hair dryer in the bathtub and killed Lenoir."

"But why?"

"So he could frame him for the escort murders, Pete. Plus, he could take over the heroin smuggling operation he and Lenoir were running with the SUR 13s and Mara Salvatruchas."

"Well, if Elliot didn't kill Campbell and Singer, then who did?"

"I'm working on it."

"Have you located any of Malik's family?"

"Not yet. I know she has an ex-husband who lives in India."

"Anyone told the kid about her mother?"

He shook his head.

"Someone is going to have to tell her."

"I know. I'm hoping I can speak with her father soon. He should be the one."

Romano chewed on that thought for a time. "What the hell was Sarah Malik doing at Elliot's?"

"I'll find out," Santana said.

* * *

After leaving Romano's office, Santana phoned Nina Rivera. When she didn't answer, he left a message on her voicemail.

Then he dialed Nathaniel Burdette's number and requested that the doctor come to the station. An hour later, a patrol officer escorted Burdette to an interview room where Santana was waiting.

Burdette paused momentarily at the doorway, as if he'd had second thoughts about agreeing to the interview, as if he'd seen something in Santana's eyes that frightened him. With his rumpled white shirt and jeans and his uncombed dark hair, Burdette looked like he'd just gotten out of bed.

"Have a seat, Dr. Burdette," Santana said, gesturing to the empty chair on the opposite side of the small table.

Burdette offered a thin smile and made his way to the chair. The patrol officer closed the door.

"I'm not really sure why I'm here, Detective Santana."

"Matthew Singer and James Elliot are dead."

"Yes. You told me that on the phone."

"Philip Campbell and Paul Lenoir are also dead."

Burdette nodded his head slowly.

"It doesn't concern you that your friends are dead?"

"Of course it does."

"And wouldn't you like to know why, Dr. Burdette?"

"Absolutely."

"I'd like to know why as well. I think you can help me."

"I'll help in any way I can," he said.

"Let's start with Glenda McCarthy," Santana said.

Burdette's eyelids rose suddenly, as though he'd been startled by a loud noise. "Who?"

"Glenda McCarthy. She was a student in medical school at the U of M when you and your friends were there."

Burdette shrugged his shoulders. "That was a long time ago. I don't remember all my classmates."

"Oh, you should remember Glenda. She died in the same manner as Tania Cruz and Catalina Díaz."

Burdette started to speak and then stopped. He licked his lips and reached for the water bottle on the table, drinking a third of it before setting it down. He fiddled nervously with the bottle cap in his hand.

"James Elliot killed Glenda McCarthy, didn't he, Dr. Burdette? And you and Campbell and Singer helped him cover it up."

"I don't know what you're talking about, Detective."

"You sure as hell do," Santana said in a voice filled with anger. He leaned toward Burdette, who arched his body against the back of the chair as if he thought he was about to be struck. Santana pointed an index finger at Burdette's chest. "I'm in no mood for games, Dr. Burdette. I want answers and I want them now."

"I think I should speak to an attorney."

"If you do that," Santana said in a calmer voice, "you're going to create all kinds of problems for yourself. I already know that Elliot killed three women. If you cooperate, I'm sure something can be worked out with the Ramsey County attorney. But if you want to play hardball, that's up to you."

Burdette thought about it for a long while. Then he looked at Santana again. "Okay. But we all thought Glenda's death was an accident."

"What gave you that idea?"

"She was kind of wild."

"Describe wild."

"Well, she worked as a stripper to raise money for medical school."

"Did Elliot date McCarthy?"

"No."

"What happened the night she died?"

"She had a party at her house. We all hung around after everyone had left."

"What do you mean by 'we'?"

"Matthew, Phil, James, and I."

"You all raped her."

"No! It wasn't like that."

"So what was it like?"

"Well, Glenda wanted to have sex with all of us."

"At the same time?"

Burdette lowered his head. "I'm not proud of it."

Santana rested his forearms on the table and leaned forward. "Did all of you have sex with her that night?"

Burdette raised his chin, his expression rigid and glazed. "Not Campbell. He wouldn't do it. He left."

"So you and Singer and Elliot had sex with Glenda McCarthy."

He gave a slight nod. "But then Singer and I left, too. Elliot stayed. The next day, her roommate found her body. Elliot denied having anything to do with it. He claimed McCarthy was alive when he left, that she liked autoerotic asphyxia. Knowing her history, we believed him. We all were about to graduate from medical school. Our futures were on the line."

"But Glenda McCarthy had no future," Santana said.

"Elliot convinced us that it must've been an accident."

"What about forensics?"

"We used condoms. The ME ruled her death accidental."

"And then you forgot about it."

"No," Burdette said. "None of us ever forgot. But the memory of it really weighed on Campbell. I think Glenda McCarthy's death was the source of his depression, even though he was never involved."

"Except in the cover up," Santana said.

Burdette nodded.

"You didn't see each other for years."

"No, we didn't. But we stayed distant friends. Elliot dropped out of school and joined the Air Force. That helped. Eventually, Singer met Lenoir and the fishing trips to Costa Rica started."

"But they weren't really fishing trips, were they, Dr. Burdette?"

"At first they were. Then Lenoir introduced us to the young women—and Elliot returned to town. It was all pretty tame. Campbell, Singer, Elliot, and I became close again. We formed a business partnership and opened the Genesis Clinic. Elliot started his charter business. Things were going very well."

"Until Tania Cruz was murdered," Santana said.

"We didn't know it was murder."

"Dr. Burdette," Santana said. "She died in the same manner as Glenda McCarthy. You mean to tell me that you and your colleagues never suspected James Elliot?"

He offered no response.

"So you looked the other way again."

He nodded.

"What about the heroin?"

"What?"

"The heroin that Elliot and Lenoir were smuggling from Costa Rica."

"I don't know anything about that, Detective Santana."

After a beat, Santana said, "You took the day off yesterday, Dr. Burdette."

"Yes. I had an appointment with my accountant."

"And the name?"

Burdette told him.

Santana wrote it down. "Where were you last night, Dr. Burdette?"

"I had a dinner date."

"I'll need her name as well."

Burdette let out a sigh and gave him the name.

"You ever take any other trips to Costa Rica, Dr. Burdette?" Santana asked.

"What kind of trips?"

"Maybe for a medical conference?"

"I guess I have."

"You guess?"

"Okay. I've attended some medical conferences there. All of us did."

"You mean Campbell and Singer and you."

He nodded.

"On those trips to the medical conferences, did you ever meet Dr. Luis Calderón?"

Burdette's eyes shifted sideways momentarily. "I may have."

"You're a plastic surgeon, Dr. Burdette. So is Luis Calderón."

His gaze tracked across Santana's face. "Lots of doctors attend those conferences."

"But lots of doctors in Costa Rica aren't as well-known as Calderón."

"All right," he said. "I met Calderón."

"Why the hesitation?"

"Because you probably think that he's involved in something. Otherwise, you wouldn't have asked me about him. But I barely know the man and have no connection with him outside of a medical conference."

"Let's get back to Catalina Díaz," Santana said. "When she was found dead, you didn't suspect Elliot might be responsible?"

Burdette inhaled a deep breath and released it slowly. "Matthew and I met. We talked about going to the police."

"But you didn't."

"We were confused. Campbell was the last one seen with Díaz. We thought maybe he had something to do with her murder. That maybe we'd been wrong about Elliot. And then Campbell killed himself."

"What if he didn't kill himself?" Santana said. "What if Elliot killed him to keep him quiet?"

"I never thought of that."

"Why not? Elliot had murdered three women."

Burdette rested his elbows on the table and massaged his forehead with the fingers of both hands, his gaze focused on some inner point, some distant memory.

"Did Elliot ever talk about his childhood?" Santana asked.

"Not to me."

"Did you know he'd lived in Nevada?"

"Yes. But he was always evasive when he talked about his past, even when we were in medical school."

"So he never mentioned his mother or father."

Burdette thought for a time. "I remember he got a phone call from his mother one night when we were at the U of M. He asked me to tell her he was out for the evening."

Santana could understand why Elliot would be reluctant to discuss his childhood and his mother's profession. "How did you know it was his mother?"

"Because she told me. She sounded really disappointed when I said he wasn't home. I don't think she believed me."

"James Elliot murdered a woman named Sarah Malik last night and nearly murdered her young daughter, Dr. Burdette."

He stared at Santana, his mouth open, his face twisted in anguish. "Why?"

"That's what I'm attempting to find out. Maybe if you'd have come forward sooner, Tania Cruz, Catalina Díaz, and Sarah Malik would still be alive."

Burdette shook his head slowly, but his non-verbal response was more a recognition of his complicity in the deaths of the three women rather than an admission of guilt.

* * *

Santana called Hawkins to see how she was.

"I'm doing all right," she said.

"How did the interview with the OIS team go?"

"Good. Was it okay for you?"

"Yes. Don't worry."

"I'm not," she said, though he could hear the anxiety in her voice.

She'd been placed on administrative leave till the departmental investigation was completed, which was standard procedure after an officer involved shooting.

"You need anything, Kacie, you let me know."

"Thanks, John. But I'll be fine. It was a good shooting."

"Yes," he said. "It was. You saved my life."

Santana spent the afternoon looking for information on Sarah Malik's immediate family and ex-husband but found nothing. He called Indira Kahn at the Hindu temple, thinking she might be of some help, but he got her voicemail. He left a message to call him.

That evening, over a dinner of chicken Marsala and glasses of Chardonnay at his house, Santana told Jordan what had happened at Elliot's farmhouse and what he'd learned.

"Are you okay?"

He nodded.

"You've got a slight bruise on your neck and a swollen hand."

"I'll be fine."

"How's Kacie?"

"She'll be all right."

"And Sammy Malik?"

"The doctor I spoke with this afternoon says there's no indication of brain damage. But he'll keep her in the hospital for another day or two."

Jordan gave Santana's hand a gentle squeeze. "How are you coping?"

He raised his glass of wine and drank.

"Is it working?"

"No," he said.

"Usually in these cases," she said, "the crimes are not just ones of opportunity, but an expression of male power and rage. Given Elliot's childhood and his mother's profession, he could easily have a lot of rage."

"He was divorced three times. He obviously had issues with women."

"So if Elliot killed the escorts and Lenoir, then who killed Campbell and Singer?"

"I'm not sure." He drank some wine and asked Jordan about her therapy.

"It's going well. I like Karen Wong. And I'm sleeping better."

"It'll take time," he said.

"I hope we have that, John."

"We will."

She smiled and clasped his hands in hers. "Only if you quit risking your life."

* * *

That night in Santana's dream Fila Brasileiros are chasing him through a dense forest. Raindrops prick his face, and lightning splinters across the white sky like fissures in a block of ice. He feels a sharp pain in his lungs with each breath he takes, as if a spike is being driven deep into the tissue. The growls and barks grow louder as the dogs close in on him. He's sweating hard and gasping for breath. His legs feel like stone. He knows the dogs will soon run him down.

Stopping in a small clearing, he searches for something he can use to defend himself. Finding nothing, he turns to face the animals, weaponless, his clothes soaked and sticking to his skin, his heart thudding in his chest.

As a Fila Brasileiros races into the clearing and stops five yards in front of him, Santana realizes that only one dog has been pursuing him—but it has three heads.

Santana stands his ground, his hands at his side, and makes no sudden movement. He braces himself and commands the dog to "Stay!" Saliva drips from the teeth of the three-headed animal as it crouches and suddenly leaps toward him.

Santana awoke with a start and sat up in bed.

"What is it?" Jordan said, leaning on a forearm beside him.

He flicked on the light next to his bed. "A dog was chasing me."

She touched his swollen right hand, the one with the long jagged scar. "You were upset about what happened to Sammy Malik. It could symbolize your own feelings of anger and aggression."

Santana knew the dream could also mean that he'd been acting too much on impulse, and that he needed to think more before he acted. Dreaming of a vicious dog could symbolize an enemy and misfortune as well, but he made no mention of it to Jordan, not wanting to alarm her.

"The dog had three heads, Jordan."

"Like Cerberus?"

He nodded. "The dog that guards the gates of hell." Then it hit him. "The night we attended the fundraiser at Nathaniel Burdette's, I noticed he had a statue of Cerberus near the fireplace."

"I saw it, too. Do you think your subconscious is telling you something?"

"It's happened before."

"Maybe Burdette killed Campbell and Singer?"

"If he did, I still have to prove it."

Chapter 24

The following morning, with his thoughts focused on Nathaniel Burdette and the possibility that he'd murdered Philip Campbell and Matthew Singer, Santana sat at his desk in the Homicide Unit, opened the copies of Glenda McCarthy's case file that were in the folder on his desk, and read the autopsy report. The Hennepin County ME had determined that McCarthy had accidentally suffocated herself in the act of autoerotic asphyxiation.

Santana then read the Crime Scene Report filed by an investigating officer named Al Briganti. Glenda McCarthy had been found dead in her rented house the morning after a party. The description of the scene was remarkably similar to those of the Tania Cruz and Catalina Díaz scenes, including the bungee cords and silk scarf. Santana wondered if McCarthy was Elliot's first victim or if there had been others before her.

Next in the file were the statements obtained from friends, family, and guests at the party. Campbell, Singer, Burdette, and Elliot had all attended the party. They'd stated that McCarthy had been alive when they'd left and also had provided alibis for one another during the timeframe the ME had established for her death. Fibers taken from McCarthy's clothing had matched samples provided by a number of people who'd attended the party, which implicated nearly everyone—and no one.

Santana was beginning to see why the ME had ruled McCarthy's death accidental—and why Briganti had agreed with the ME's conclusions—when he read a statement taken from a woman named Sarah Colby, identified as McCarthy's roommate and best friend. She claimed Glenda had been murdered, though she could provide no evidence to support her contention and had been out of town the night of the party.

Maybe it was just a coincidence that Sarah Colby had the same first name as Sarah Malik, but Santana had never believed much in coincidences. He phoned Dave Reynolds at the Minneapolis PD. "Thanks for faxing me copies of the McCarthy file."

"Don't know what good it'll do, Santana."

"Maybe it already has."

"How?"

"I need to speak to Al Briganti, the I/O on the case."

"Good luck. He retired a few years ago."

"You have a number where he can be reached?"

"Well, he spends his winters in Florida. But he still might own his house in Minneapolis. Hold on a second."

Santana waited.

A minute later, Reynolds said, "Write down this number. It's an old one I have in my Rolodex."

Santana thanked Reynolds, dialed the Minneapolis number, and identified himself when Briganti answered.

"What the hell does the SPPD want with me?" he said with a bemused chuckle.

"Twenty-five years ago, you worked the Glenda McCarthy case."

"Maybe I did, but that's a long time ago."

"McCarthy died of autoerotic asphyxiation. Does that jog your memory?"

Briganti didn't reply for what seemed like a long time. Finally, he said, "It does. Isn't easy to forget a death like that. So what's your interest, Santana?" His tone had turned serious.

"I'm investigating two similar cases."

"You think they're connected?"

"I do."

"What do you need?"

"You interviewed McCarthy's roommate, a woman named Sarah Colby."

"Oh, yeah. The reason I remember is she wouldn't accept the ME's conclusion. Kept calling and stopping by the station, bending my ear, wanting to know the names of any suspects. She about drove me crazy."

"Why do you think Colby was so certain that Glenda McCarthy's death was murder and not an accident?"

"I asked Colby that same question. She said they were very good friends. I suspected they might be lovers. Either way, she knew McCarthy didn't practice autoerotic asphyxia."

"You remember what Colby looked like?"

"Well, not off hand. But I do recall she was kind of an unusual looking woman."

"What do you mean by unusual?"

"Well, kind of like a boy and a girl."

"Androgynous," Santana said.

"Huh?"

"Thanks, Briganti, you've been a big help."

"Hey, Santana. Let me know what happens."

"I will," he said.

Santana disconnected and considered what he'd just heard. Then he flipped open his cell phone again and called Indira Khan at the Hindu temple. "I left a message for you yesterday, Ms. Kahn."

"Yes. I'm sorry. I was out with a cold and came in late today. How can I help you, Detective Santana?"

"Do you know a woman named Sarah Malik?"

"I don't know her, Detective. However, I know she's attended our temple on occasion, though I haven't seen her in quite a while."

"She was killed last night."

"Oh, my goodness. That's terrible."

"Did you know her ex-husband?"

"I do remember Ravi. But last I heard, he had returned to India."

"Do you know where in India?"

"I believe he was from Kerala."

"What, if anything, do you know about him, Ms. Kahn?"

"Not much. He and Sarah were married such a short time. I do remember he was a doctor."

"General practitioner?"

"I believe he's a medical toxicologist."

Santana felt his heartbeat increase. "You said a toxicologist?"

"Yes. Unfortunately, Kerala, where he's from, is known for its high death rate due to poisoning."

"From what?"

"The presence of cerbera. I'm not from that part of the country, but many Indians are familiar with the drug."

Santana thanked her and hung up. He turned to his computer and typed the word "cerbera" into the Google browser. Instantly, he got pages of information on the plant.

The seeds of the Suicide Tree contain a toxin called cerberin, a potent compound capable of disrupting calcium ion channels in heart muscle, which can lead to an irregular heartbeat that is often fatal if the toxin is ingested in high enough quantities. Some have called the plant the perfect murder weapon since serving it with spices in food can disguise its flavor. More people use cerbera odollam to commit suicide than any other plant. But toxicologists also warn that doctors, pathologists, and coroners are failing to detect how often it is used to murder people. Although the kernels of the tree have a bitter taste, this can be disguised if they are crushed and mixed with spicy food.

Santana printed two copies of the information. Then he called the ME. "Are you familiar with cerberin, Reiko?"

"It's similar to digoxin, which is used to treat a whole lot of heart problems, including atrial fibrillation," she said. "Problem is, you give too much of it, and suddenly it starts causing things like ventricular fibrillation and heart block, symptoms that can be fatal."

"What are the symptoms?"

"Within an hour there would be retching, nausea, vomiting and abdominal pain. Later, the vic would become weak and drowsy and lapse into coma."

Santana recalled the evidence of vomiting at the Singer crime scene. "I believe Matthew Singer was poisoned with it."

"A tox screen on Singer will only tell me the class of drugs, John. In order to identify a specific one, I'd have to use high-performance liquid chromatography coupled with mass spectrometry to examine autopsy tissues for traces of the plant. That's going to be costly."

"I'll run interference with Romano and Branigan."

Santana disconnected and phoned Bobby Jackson, the SPPD's computer forensic analyst. "You had a chance to look at Sarah Malik's computer yet?"

"I'm looking at it right now."

"I'll be right over, Bobby." Santana was beginning to see what he'd missed. How he could finally solve the case.

* * *

Nina Rivera had a towel wrapped around her hair and a terrycloth robe tied around her waist when she opened the door to her condo. "Come in, Detective," she said with a smile. "I've just stepped out of the shower." Her complexion had a healthy pink glow from the hot water. "Help yourself to a drink. I'll be with you in a few minutes."

"Take your time," he said.

Ten minutes later, she returned, dressed in jeans, sandals, and a baggy pullover. Her brunette hair was still damp as it hung long and loose over the top of her shoulders. Without makeup, Santana thought she looked much younger.

She poured a glass of red wine and sat down on the sofa across from him, letting her sandals slide off and tucking her feet under her. "I'll testify against Ricky Garza and James Elliot," she said.

"They're dead, Ms. Rivera."

She raised her eyebrows. "Really? How?"

"My partner shot Elliot."

"Why?"

"Because he was going to kill me."

"What about Ricky Garza?"

"Someone else shot him."

She nodded and sipped her wine. "Well, I'd still like to help. After all, I don't have much of a choice, do I?"

"Life is all about choices, Ms. Rivera."

A flicker of concern ignited her amber eyes. "What do you mean?"

"Let me spell it out for you. When Sarah Malik read about Tania Cruz's murder six years ago, she followed Arias Marchena's trial closely, learning all she could about Cruz's murder, including how she'd been killed. Malik became convinced that the same man who killed Tania Cruz had also killed her roommate, Glenda McCarthy, twenty-five years ago. She knew you testified at the trial and came to you and asked for help. But Paul Lenoir had already used you to frame Marchena for Cruz's murder. And Ricky Garza had threatened to kill you if you refused to cooperate in the frame-up."

Nina Rivera set down her wine glass and slid a Derby cigarette out of the package on the coffee table, lighting it and inhaling with the practiced efficiency of a habitual smoker. She blew out a small cloud and gazed at Santana. "Go on," she said. "It's a fascinating story, even if it is fiction."

"You and Sarah Malik became friends. After Sammy was born, you taught her Spanish. That's how she was so familiar with your condo. She'd been here many times. When Catalina Díaz was murdered, Sarah Malik came up with a plan. She'd use her daughter and her knowledge of reincarnation to convince me that Sammy was the reincarnated soul of Tania Cruz. In the process she hoped to learn the names of the primary suspects in Díaz's murder. She asked you to teach Sammy everything she needed to know about Cruz and her death. And that whole charade with Sammy talking about your father was a wonderful practiced performance."

"My father did abuse me." Hurt and shame were still evident in her voice.

"I know that, Ms. Rivera. And I'm truly sorry it happened to you. But three days ago here in your condo, when Sammy's mother asked her why you ran away from home, she said it was because of your father. That was a vague answer. Sammy could easily be coached to give that simple response while not knowing about your sexual abuse. And being abused doesn't give you a license to commit murder."

"I really don't know what you're talking about, Detective. Regardless, it seems to me that you'd never have known who'd murdered Glenda McCarthy, Tania Cruz, and Catalina Díaz without Sarah Malik's help. There's no crime in that."

"I'm afraid there is. When Campbell's name was leaked to the press, Sarah Malik did some research and discovered that he was in medical school at the same time as Glenda McCarthy."

"How do you know that?"

"Forensics found the information on her computer. Malik assumed Campbell had killed Tania Cruz and Catalina Díaz as well. She shot Campbell and made it look like a suicide. The print found on the mini-revolver was hers."

Nina Rivera smoked her cigarette and gazed at him without comment.

"When I came around with the photos of other suspects, Malik concluded that maybe it wasn't Campbell after all. She'd learned that Singer and Burdette were also in medical school at the same time as Glenda McCarthy. But it would look too suspicious if Singer committed suicide like Campbell. So she poisoned him."

"With what?"

"Cerberin."

Nina Rivera remained completely still, her face blank, her eyes distant with thoughts.

"My guess is Malik would've poisoned Burdette as well if she hadn't been killed. She knew about the poison through her husband's work as a toxicologist and her visits to India. Forensics found an online order on her computer. She didn't know James Elliot was one of the suspects because I never showed her a photo. And his picture wasn't in a U of M yearbook since he dropped out of medical school before graduation."

"My, you do have a vivid imagination, Detective. I wish we could have a chance to pursue it."

"That's never going to happen, Ms. Rivera."

She smiled. "That's too bad. But why are you telling me this?"

"Because you invited Sarah Malik and her daughter to come to Elliot's house, probably on the pretense of letting Sammy ride one of his horses. You knew that's where Elliot performed all the surgeries, and that Garza would be there picking up the smuggled heroin in exchange for cash. You saw

333

a way to get yourself out from under Garza's thumb. You shot him and took the heroin."

Nina Rivera shook her head slowly, as if she were searching her mind for an answer. "You have absolutely no proof of this, Detective."

Santana had no proof, but he had a hunch. Where would Rivera hide something she didn't want found? He stood, placed a copy of the search warrant on the coffee table, and went upstairs to Catalina Díaz's bedroom. He slid out the nightstand drawer and then the hidden drawer underneath. Inside it were the two bloodstained, heroin-filled implants Elliot had removed from Isabel Soto's breasts. As Santana turned, he saw Rivera standing at the top of the stairs, a Glock in her hand.

"Aren't you the clever one?" she said.

"I like to think so. But I was wrong about the list of apostles. You wrote it, not Catalina Díaz. I assumed the night stand belonged to Díaz because it was in her bedroom. But you own the condo and all the furniture. Sarah Malik had convinced you that at least one of the men on the list was a murderer. Díaz didn't know about the hidden drawer or the previous murders. You hid the list in case your place was ever searched."

"Or in case anything ever happened to me, Detective, and my death was investigated."

"You were hoping someone would get lucky and find it?"

"You did," she said.

Santana thought about it. Everything was coming together now. "You knew I'd found the list because it was missing from the hidden drawer. That's when you and Malik decided to play me."

"Who wrote the list wasn't all you had wrong, Detective."

"How so?"

"I did invite Sarah and Sammy to meet me at the farmhouse in the afternoon to ride horses. I didn't know that

Garza or Soto would be there or that Elliot was performing the surgery. I assumed Singer was Lenoir's partner and the surgeries were performed at the Genesis Clinic. And I certainly wouldn't have asked Sarah and Sammy to the farm if I'd known Elliot was a murderer."

"You and Sarah Malik thought Campbell, Singer, or Burdette had killed Glenda McCarthy and Tania Cruz," Santana said. "That's why Elliot's name wasn't on the list. You were even more convinced one of the three men was involved after Catalina Díaz was killed."

"I know you won't believe this, Detective, but when Sammy saw Elliot, she screamed that he was the one."

"Meaning?"

"You know what she meant. She recognized Elliot or recognized something about him."

"So you're saying Sammy really was Tania Cruz reincarnated?"

"I don't know. But Sarah believed it ever since her daughter was born. Sammy's abilities are what triggered her plan. I do know that Sammy had a proclivity for Spanish. For as long as I've known her, she was afraid of eagles and plastic bags. I didn't have to teach her that."

"Maybe her mother did?"

"Sarah always denied it. And Sammy had a birthmark on her neck that looked like a rope burn. I leave it to you to be the judge."

Santana let the silence sit there awhile before speaking again. "So what happened after Sammy screamed?"

"Sarah tried to shoot Elliot, but her gun jammed. He grabbed Sammy and threatened to choke her. He took us to the pole barn. Ricky Garza was there. Elliot told him to watch me. He left with Sarah and Sammy. I was sure Garza was going to kill me."

"But you killed him first."

She nodded. "I had my Glock in my purse. Elliot never checked."

"What about Sarah and Sammy? You had a gun. You could've gone after them."

"I was afraid Elliot had armed himself. I felt terrible about leaving Sarah."

"But not terrible enough that you tried to save her and her daughter."

Nina Rivera shook her head.

"And you took the heroin."

"Yes. And now that I have you and the heroin, I'm going to deal."

"With the Mara Salvatruchas?"

"Yes. No more recruiting escorts. No more risking my life. I'll finally have my freedom."

"You really think they'll deal with you?"

"The Maras want their heroin—and the Sinaloa cartel wants you. I asked *Santa Muerte* for my freedom and promised her you in return." She waved the Glock at him. "Let's go."

"I don't think so," Santana said.

"It would pain me greatly to have to kill you, Detective."

"But you would."

"If I have to."

"It wouldn't bother you if the Maras killed me?"

"I'm a survivor. I have been ever since I was a teenager. I'll do what I need to do."

Santana stepped toward her.

"Don't!" she said, raising the gun to chest level.

Santana kept coming.

Nina Rivera pulled the trigger. There was an empty click.

Santana grabbed the Glock by the barrel and took it away from her. "While you were changing after your shower," he said, "I emptied your gun instead of a drink."

"How did you know?"

"The first time we met, you said you kept your Glock behind the bar when it wasn't in your purse."

She let out an exasperated sigh. "That was my first mistake."

Santana slipped the handcuffs off the back of his belt. "Unfortunately," he said, "it wasn't your last."

Epilogue

A week after Nina Rivera's arrest—and the day before Santana left on a vacation— Assistant Chief Tim Branigan climbed aboard Santana's boat docked at the St. Croix Marina in Hudson, Wisconsin. Wearing a pair of sand khakis, brown deck shoes, a melon-colored polo shirt, and a white windbreaker, the AC was the kind of man, Santana thought, who looked stiff even in casual clothes.

Branigan stood on the aft deck with his hands fisted on his hips, surveying the low gray sky and still water as he might a class of young recruits at the academy. "You think we're ever going to see the sun this spring?" he said with a wide, unnatural smile.

"Why meet here, Chief?"

Branigan turned and looked at Santana. "I thought if we met informally, we could talk more freely."

Santana figured he knew what the AC wanted to discuss.

"How about a Sam Adams?" Branigan said.

"So you know I like Sam Adams."

"I know a great deal more about you than the brand of beer you prefer, Detective." It was said in a light-hearted, off-handed way, but Santana understood the implied threat behind the words. He retrieved two bottles of Sam Adams from the refrigerator in the galley and handed one to Branigan.

"I understand the boat is a recent purchase."

"First year in the water," Santana said.

338

"*Alibi*. Catchy name. You plan on doing much fishing?"

"Some."

"I find it relaxes me."

"What is it you want to discuss, Chief?"

Branigan held his gaze on Santana and smiled crookedly. "No beating around the bush with you, Detective."

"You came here for a reason."

Branigan nodded and drank some beer.

There was little activity in the marina and on the boats in the slips. Incessant rain and cool weather had lingered long after the late snow melt. The typical excitement associated with the advent of spring had given way to a grim realization that this year's boating and outdoor season would be short-lived.

Branigan took another swallow of beer, as though he were working up some courage. "I read the ME's autopsy report on Matthew Singer. Tanabe found high levels of active glycosides in his plasma samples and high serum potassium levels and digoxin in his tissues."

"He was poisoned with cerberin," Santana said. "Forensics found online orders Sarah Malik had placed for the seeds."

"You don't think Rivera was in on it?"

Santana shook his head. "But forensics will match the bullet taken from Garza with Rivera's Glock. She'll be charged with third-degree murder for killing Garza and first degree assault for pointing the gun at me."

"You know she's going to claim self-defense for killing Garza and deny she ever threatened you with a gun. It's your word against hers."

Santana shrugged. "The first degree drug possession charge will get her a thirty year prison sentence. That's long enough. And Isabel Soto will go down for importing a controlled substance across state lines. That'll be good for a thirty-five year sentence."

Branigan paused for a few beats before speaking again. "Tanabe ruled Paul Lenoir's death a homicide based on the damp hair dryer you found."

"James Elliot killed Lenoir," Santana said. "Forensics matched the tracks in the alley behind Lenoir's place to Elliot's Mercedes. Elliot killed Glenda McCarthy, Tania Cruz, and Catalina Díaz, too. Alvarado Vega wants the court to overturn Arias Marchena's conviction."

"The great Alvarado Vega," Branigan said sarcastically, swallowing more beer.

"Marchena is innocent."

"Nick Baker and I worked the Tania Cruz case. Sending an innocent man to prison is a black mark on my record, Detective."

"So we're supposed to let Marchena rot in jail for a crime he didn't commit?"

"I never said that. I just hope nothing else comes out."

"We all make mistakes."

Branigan shook his head. "That's not how the city council looks at it when they're paying out large settlements. You realize, of course, that Vega will sue the department for wrongful imprisonment. That's going to cost the city a small fortune and could impact my career choices."

"You have your eye on the chief's job when he retires?"

"Something wrong with that?"

"Not at all."

Branigan narrowed his eyes and stared at Santana as if he doubted his response. "You know, Detective, I'm a man who remembers his friends."

"Meaning?"

"If I *were* to become the next chief of police, those in the department with excellent records could be in line for a promotion."

Santana smiled. "You know that would never work for me."

"Why not? You're the best homicide detective we have. The men respect you. You're a natural leader."

"What do you want, Chief?"

Branigan studied him for a long moment. "I need assurances that you and Detective Hawkins will keep quiet about my encounter with Catalina Díaz. You heard the OIS team cleared Hawkins for the Elliot shooting."

"I heard. But I can't speak for her."

"She's your partner. She looks up to you. She'll do whatever you tell her."

"Except I won't tell her."

Branigan let out a long breath. "That's the problem with you, Detective. You're not a team player."

"Which is why I wouldn't make a good administrator. Something you already know."

"Suppose I did know that. It doesn't always have to be that way, Detective. Things change. New opportunities arise."

"Hawkins won't say anything."

"How can you be sure?"

"Because I trust her."

"Trust is a two-way street."

"I won't say anything either."

"I certainly hope not. But let me make one thing clear. You used the knowledge of my unfortunate dalliance with the escort to your advantage once. I expect you'll not attempt to use it again."

"That's a reasonable expectation." Santana had intentionally given a vague answer, hoping that the AC would accept it. He waited till the puzzlement in Branigan's eyes had faded before he said, "You leaked the information on Campbell to the paper, Chief."

"But I never leaked information to Gloria Whitaker at the *Pioneer Press*. How come she knows so much about the murders?"

"She has her sources."

"And you wouldn't have any idea who those sources are."

Santana shook his head and changed the subject. "I understand the smuggling network in Costa Rica has been shut down."

"For now. The feds arrested the perps running the money laundering firm—which reminds me. How is it that Mike Rios happened to show up at Nina Rivera's condo right after you arrested her?"

"I called him."

"Why?"

"I owed him. He should get some credit for the drug bust. It might help him with his supervisor at the DEA."

"Why not help yourself when an opportunity arises, Detective?"

"I like what I do."

"Then I hope you'll take our conversation to heart." Branigan finished his beer and handed the empty bottle to Santana. "We'll talk again, Detective. Enjoy your vacation."

* * *

The following day Santana took Jordan and Gitana cruising for a week on the upper St. Croix, the more scenic and secluded stretch of the long smooth ribbon that divided Minnesota and Wisconsin, where walleye, sauger, muskies, bluegill, crappie, catfish, and smallmouth bass were in abundant supply.

He'd purchased two inexpensive Berkley rods and Cardinal 300 reels, and in the cool mornings when the glistening green landscape came alive with the smell of earth and the false promise of unending life, he rigged live crayfish to float in the current while the boat drifted against the anchor line.

In the afternoons, he would clean and fillet the small-mouth bass they'd caught, and while the sun was high in the sky, they'd swim off the starboard ladder and tan on beach towels unfolded on the foredeck.

As dusk gathered in the trees, they'd anchor in the shallows along the riverbanks that were forested with oak, sugar maple, birch, aspen, pines, and basswood. They'd grill the bass or the Atlantic salmon, lobster tails, and steaks Jordan had purchased, and drink wine, margaritas, or ice-cold beer. Later, when the sky was sprinkled with stars and moonlight glazed the water, they'd sit on deck and talk late into the night.

"You saw Sammy?"

Santana nodded. "And her father."

"Any lingering health issues?"

"Outside of a bruise on her cheek, she appears fine."

"Kids are pretty resilient when it comes to their health."

Santana recalled the scene at the hospital and the joy he'd felt when he'd returned her doll.

"How is she taking her mother's death?" Jordan asked.

"I'm not sure she understands it."

"Do any of us, John?"

Santana took a deep breath and let it out slowly. "There's one thing that still bothers me about the case."

"What?"

"Sammy's phobia about eagles. According to Nina Rivera, Sammy started screaming 'he is the one' when she saw James Elliot at his farmhouse. I think Sammy recognized the Air Force eagle tattoo on his forearm. I made the same deduction when I saw a photo of Elliot and Lenoir in Japan. I figured Elliot had killed Cruz and Díaz."

"You know what you're suggesting, John?"

Santana nodded.

"But Sammy's mother could've taught her to be afraid of eagles."

"Why would Sarah Malik teach her daughter to be afraid of them? She had acquired lots of information about the Cruz case, but neither she nor Sammy knew that Elliot had an eagle tattoo on his forearm. Only Tania Cruz knew that."

Santana could hear the tinkle of ice in Jordan's cocktail glass and see her hazel eyes looking at him in the moonlight.

"Were you thinking about death when Rivera pointed the Glock at you?"

He drank some Sam Adams and shook his head. "I knew it wasn't loaded."

"But you've had loaded weapons pointed at you before. You have thought about dying."

"I have. And so have you," he said. "When you saved our lives, you were risking your own."

"I was just reacting and not thinking."

"There you go."

"But I mean afterward. After it's all over, and you realize you could've died."

"I don't dwell on it."

"But you know it's always a possibility."

Santana drank the last of his beer. He saw the running lights of a powerboat slide through the darkness and heard the low rumble of its engine and the sound of waves lapping against the *Alibi*'s hull.

"You ever look at your shadow, Jordan?"

"Sometimes, I suppose."

"Death is like that for me. I know it's there, but I try not to pay attention to it."

"What if you could prove that Sammy Malik was the reincarnated soul of Tania Cruz, John? It would change the whole meaning of death."

"But I can't."

"So what are we left with?"

344

Santana leaned back in his seat and looked up at the endless darkness. Tomorrow, he remembered, was the summer solstice, the longest day of the year in the northern hemisphere; a time when the seasonal movement of the sun's path stood still in declination; a time when the earth warmed, flowers bloomed, and days seemed to extend forever; a time when thoughts of the coming of winter and the eventuality of death were as distant as the stars.

He reached out and held Jordan's hand in his. "Maybe in learning how to die," he said, "we learn how to live."

Acknowledgments

My thanks to—

—University of Minnesota Professor Ned Mohan for the tour of the Hindu temple and for answering my many questions.

—my friends Abby Davis, Linda Donaldson, Lorrie Holmgren, Jenifer LeClair, Chuck Logan, and Dave Knudson for their time and suggestions regarding the manuscript.

—my editor, Jennifer Adkins.

—my beautiful wife, Martha, for her love and inspiration.

—my growing family of readers for your wonderful support and e-mails.

An Invitation to Reading Groups/Book Clubs

I would like to extend an invitation to reading groups/ book clubs across the country. Invite me to your group and I'll be happy to participate in your discussion. I'm available to join your discussion either in person or via the telephone or Skype. (Reading groups should have a speakerphone.) You can arrange a date and time by e-mailing me at cjvalen@comcast.net. I look forward to hearing from you.